CONQUER THE NIGHT

"You can make a difference," Fallon insisted. "I know you can, if only you will."

"Such faith," Draegan murmured. "Such determination. You are a difficult woman to refuse."

"Then don't refuse," she said, coming closer. "Consider what I've said. It's the least you can do." She was gazing up at him, her eyes glistening with tears beneath her damp and starry lashes.

Without a word, Draegan drew her closer, drew her soft, alluring curves up against his lean, hard length, smiling at her involuntary gasp.

"What you propose is tempting, I admit, and I'm almost convinced," he said. "Perhaps you'd care to persuade me further . . ."

Other **AVON ROMANCES**

AWAKEN, MY LOVE *by Robin Schone*
CAPTURED *by Victoria Lynne*
MAGGIE AND THE GAMBLER *by Ann Carberry*
SPLENDID *by Julia Quinn*
TAKEN BY STORM *by Danelle Harmon*
TEMPT ME NOT *by Eve Byron*
WILDFIRE *by Donna Stephens*

Coming Soon

THE HEART AND THE ROSE *by Nancy Richards-Akers*
LAKOTA PRINCESS *by Karen Kay*

And Don't Miss These
ROMANTIC TREASURES
from Avon Books

A KISS IN THE NIGHT *by Jennifer Horsman*
SHAWNEE MOON *by Judith E. French*
TIMESWEPT BRIDE *by Eugenia Riley*

CONQUER THE NIGHT

SELINA MACPHERSON

AVON BOOKS ◆ NEW YORK

CONQUER THE NIGHT is an original publication of Avon Books. This work has never before appeared in book form. This work is a novel. Any similarity to actual persons or events is purely coincidental.

AVON BOOKS
A division of
The Hearst Corporation
1350 Avenue of the Americas
New York, New York 10019

Copyright © 1995 by Susan McClafferty
Published by arrangement with the author
Library of Congress Catalog Card Number: 94-96865
ISBN: 0-380-77252-3

First Avon Books Printing: August 1995

AVON TRADEMARK REG. U.S. PAT. OFF. AND IN OTHER COUNTRIES, MARCA REGISTRADA, HECHO EN U.S.A.

Printed in the U.S.A.

RA 10 9 8 7 6 5 4 3 2 1

This book is dedicated to my mother, Elizabeth (Liz) Bonner, and my aunts, Ann (Millie) Smith, Margaret (Peggy) Toy, Catherine (Kate) Delp, and Dora Atherton, with love for all.

A special thanks to Mr. Sean Conley and the staff of the Catskill Library, in Catskill, New York, for generously giving their time and resources, and for making a tough job just a little more pleasant.

And I looked, and beheld a pale horse: and his name that sat on him was Death, and Hell followed with him.

—Revelation 6:8

CONQUER THE NIGHT

Prologue

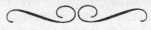

Ulster County, New York
April 1, 1777

Throughout the day the wind had been un-
ceasing. Sweeping southeast out of the Adi-
rondack Mountains, the icy blast moaned in the
treetops like a living thing, pelting the horse and
rider plodding along the narrow rutted track with
stinging shards of sleet.

Enveloped in an oft-worn woolen cloak and an
air of bone-deep weariness, Draegan Youngblood
glanced at the lowering skies, and then at the small
stone structure down the way. By straining hard,
he could just make out the steeple that served as a
bell tower, silhouetted a dim gray against the bleak
countryside.

Be damned if it wasn't a church.

His mouth twitched slightly at the corners; he
was too cold and numb to smile. He was sadly in
need of shelter, yet somehow this was not quite
what he'd had in mind.

Like some wistful old maid dreaming of a husband, he'd been hoping to happen upon a tavern.
Nothing fancy, mind you, just a simple sleepy

1

place with a roaring fire and a dram of good whiskey to banish the chill. A place where a ragged stranger could buy a night's lodging with the last of his coin without having to answer a host of questions or fend off the suspicious stares thrown his way.

As he approached, Draegan saw that the stone walls looked sturdy. Sturdy enough, certainly, to provide an adequate buffer against the icy bite of the ceaseless wind. The windows were black and empty. Not a flicker of light shone from within to dispel the encroaching darkness; not a single whiff of smoke rose from the chimneys to taint the wind.

The skeletal remains of last season's weeds, the rectory door hanging slightly askew on its hinges, spoke clearly to the weary traveler.

The place was deserted, and a damned far cry from the haven that he had envisioned throughout the bitter afternoon. There would be no dry wood, no comfortable fire, no whiskey to warm him. Then again, there would be no probing questions to answer, not a single suspicious stare.

And he'd quite had his fill of questions.

For a moment, Draegan sat his mount in the midst of the track, torn between his desire for privacy and his fondness for the pleasures of the flesh, while the sleet gathered in the folds of his sodden cloak and his matted sable-colored hair lashed his windburned face. He glanced again at the forlorn-looking chapel and decided to press on. Though he'd given up hope of finding a cheery taproom, with a bit of luck, he might yet come upon a Dutch *boerderij*. There, in exchange for news of the war, the farmer and his wife would provide him a length of sausage, a hard-cooked egg or two, and grant him leave to sleep in the barn until cock's crow.

Fate, however, saw fit to deny Draegan that bit

of good luck. Indeed, the good fortune that had seen him through a harrowing autumn in British-held New York City had seemingly run out. At that moment, the ancient sway-backed nag he'd purchased from a farmer on the outskirts of Princeton, and which had carried him all the way to this secluded hollow in the Catskill Mountains, refused to budge. No amount of cursing or coaxing could persuade the weary beast to take another step.

With a sigh of disgust and no other recourse, Draegan dismounted and, taking up the reins, limped heavily along the rutted lane, leading the triumphant animal toward the cheerless little chapel.

His progress was painfully slow, the path treacherous. He slipped on the wet, uneven ground, cursing at the pain in his left thigh. By the time he reached the small shed behind the rectory and stabled the mare, he was sweating profusely and beginning to see the abandoned church in a different light.

There was nothing like a cold dose of misery to bring one's priorities clearly into focus, Draegan thought, making his way to the chapel. At the moment, his own were abundantly clear.

The wound he'd suffered just before Christmas while en route to Washington's winter encampment had been taxed to its limits in his effort to reach Albany.

He needed rest—in a place where he could lick his wounds in peace. As he stepped into the sanctuary and closed the door on the wintry night, Draegan knew that he had found that place.

A living, throbbing, profound silence filled the air around him . . . reached out to enfold him . . . promised him the solace he sought, despite the sinful, pleasure-loving creature he was . . . despite the fact that he hadn't come to worship...hadn't come seeking forgiveness.

Nearly two years had passed since he'd seen his home in the Mohawk Valley, near Albany, and it seemed a lifetime ago that he'd set foot inside a proper church. For a long time Draegan had avoided God, knowing that He wouldn't approve of the things that he'd done for the sake of his country, for the sake of his somewhat dissipated self.

Spying was an unsavory business at best, but in wartime, a necessary one. It was also a business to which Draegan was well suited, and he had little doubt that his singular lack of conscience had played a large part in his success. But then, he was a firm believer that moral convictions had no place upon the battlefield...*or in the boudoir*, for that matter.

The bedchambers of New York City had been his battleground throughout the previous autumn months—the lonely wives and daughters of Tories serving the King were resources to be used in order to gain a victory.

General Washington, unfortunately, did not share Draegan's lack of principle, and once the general had gotten wind of Draegan's scandalous escapades in New York City involving a married woman, as well as the disastrous consequences of the affair, he had taken it upon himself to chastise Draegan for what he deemed "an unpardonable lack of ethics."

In a matter of hours, Draegan, too valuable an asset to the Army to be summarily dismissed, had been presented with a transfer to Schuyler's command at Albany. He was being sent home in disgrace.

Yet oddly enough, tonight, this instant, none of that seemed to matter. He was there to rest, not to be judged. Shrugging out of his damp cloak, he sank down onto the high-backed wooden pew and closed his eyes, willing the pain to lessen. A few moments' rest was all that he needed. A few moments and he would be nearly good as new . . .

Sometime later Draegan abruptly awakened, dragged from a deep and dreamless sleep by voices, sounding very near.

"Don't look like much, now, does he, lads, to be causin' such a stir?" one man said.

"He don't at that," another replied. "But neither did that rabid wolf that kilt old Homer Jameson five month back."

Feeling disoriented, Draegan glanced around the semicircle of faces, floating disembodied in the watery light of a tallow lamp held high. "Who the devil are you?" he demanded. "What do you mean, disturbing my sleep?"

"We're the Esopus Rangers," said the man who held the lantern, "and ye'll do well to keep yer yap shut until ye're told!"

Draegan glanced from one man to another. By now his eyes had adjusted to the light, and he could see that the six men gathered around the pew on which he sat were similarly dressed, in short buckskin coats and homespun breeches. Each man had a wide leather belt slung over his left shoulder and a jaunty hat of soft black felt perched upon his head. "Local militia," Draegan said with soft derision. "I might have known. You're too well fed for Continentals."

The comment seemed to anger the man who held the lantern, for he growled at Draegan, "Tory scum! Ye'll show a bit o' deference, or by God, I'll—" He underscored his unfinished threat with a kick and a cuff, the first of which caught Draegan on the shin of his injured leg.

With a muttered imprecation, Draegan started up, but he was instantly seized by half a dozen hard hands, shoved back against the pew, and pinned. "I'm not a Tory," he said with rising fury. "And I'll be damned if I'll be detained by a bunch of homebound vigilantes!"

Draegan threw off the restraining hands and started to rise, but a thin pockmarked man on the far left pulled a pistol from his coat and thrust it into Draegan's face. "Tory or no, you ain't goin' nowhere, till you talk to Captain Quill!"

As if on cue, those gathered about parted, allowing a burly young man to take his place in the fore. The new arrival was garbed like his companions with two exceptions: his hat was made of expensive beaver, and he wore a brace of elegant silver pistols thrust conspicuously through his wide leather belt.

Draegan glared up at the newcomer, unimpressed by his air of self-importance. "Are you the master of this pack of slavering hounds?"

"Captain Randall Quill of the Esopus Rangers," the young man said with a flash of pearly teeth. "And you, sir, would be well advised to keep a civil tongue in your head. My men are understandably short on patience. We lost a man half a mile south of here not a quarter hour ago, shot down by a certain varlet we were chasing. The assailant eluded us, but we've good reason to believe he didn't get far."

"These are troubled times," Draegan responded. "But it doesn't give you leave to burst in and lay hands on me. And I would strongly suggest that you call your men off."

The light in Quill's eyes turned brittle; his expression lost all traces of affability. "You aren't in any position to be making demands."

"And you are in no position to detain me," Drae-

shoulder. The sight of it should have calmed him; instead he felt an overwhelming sense of presentiment, as if he were teetering on the edge of a precipice, and the earth was disintegrating beneath his feet.

"My mount is old," he said, "a dappled gray I purchased from a farmer on the outskirts of Princeton, and so rheumatic she can barely manage a trot."

Quill planted his hands on his hips and leaned slightly toward Draegan. "We followed our man here to this church, where he disappeared. Upon entering we find you feigning sleep, in possession of a cloak whose folds still hold the chill of the elements; the murderer's horse is stabled in back and your own mount nowhere to be found. Yet you claim the cloak and horse don't belong to you; you have seen no one enter and no one leave, and have no knowledge of our comrade's murder! You must take me for an idiot!"

Draegan's expression darkened. "I was not feigning anything, Captain, and everything I have told you is true. I haven't been out of this church since nightfall. What earthly reason could I, a stranger passing through this valley, have to harm your friend?"

Draegan's demand was met with silence.

"You don't have to take my word for it!" Draegan said. "Search my things, dammit! You'll find my transfer papers there. Or better yet, send word to Schuyler in Albany. He'll substantiate everything I've told you."

The pockmarked man crouched to rummage through Draegan's belongings. "Papers, Cap'n."

"Let's see those." Quill took them from his hands, and as he read his face hardened. "This is a report on the strengths and weaknesses of the

American fortifications near Nevilton. . . . It's signed 'Sparrowhawk'.''

Draegan was on his feet in an instant, facing down Captain Randall Quill. ''I don't give a damn how it's signed,'' he shouted angrily. ''Those papers were planted, don't you see! As were the cloak and the horse! Someone pilfered my things and left these in exchange, to make me look guilty of a crime in which I played no part! *For the love of Christ, Captain, you have to listen to me!*''

Quill's expression was cold and unyielding. ''You surprise me, sir. Somehow I would have thought the wily Sparrowhawk would spin a livelier tale than the one you are telling. But then, your talents do seem to lie in other directions, don't they? And I don't suppose it ever occurred to you that you'd be caught . . . much less by the *local militia.*''

Draegan grabbed the breast of Quill's deerskin coat in both fists, desperate now to convince him. He'd gone cold as the grave in that instant, and could almost feel his life ebbing away. ''I swear by all that's holy, Captain, I am not the man you seek!''

Quill shoved him roughly off, nodding to his men. ''Take him.''

At that moment, something snapped inside Draegan. He drew back his fist and swung with all his might at Randall Quill. The blow connected solidly with the militia captain's outthrust chin and sent him sprawling across the back of the forward pew.

Several of the rangers grappled for a hold on Draegan while he sought to break away. Heart racing, driven by a wild desperation, he flung them off and vaulted the high back of the pew on which he'd so soundly slept moments before, only to land on his injured leg.

He fell hard, cursing as his tormentors caught him by the arms and dragged him to his feet.

Randall Quill stepped forward. Blood trickled from the corner of his ruined mouth; his eyes were filled with rage. Without preamble, he pulled back his fist and slammed it into Draegan's middle . . . once . . . twice . . . thrice. . . .

Draegan fell to his knees, unable to draw breath. His head spun crazily, and for one awful moment he was afraid he was going to be sick.

"Bind his hands," Quill ordered. Then, turning to the man nearest him, he said, "Jacob, ready the rope."

But Jacob seemed wont to argue. "Beggin' your pardon, Cap'n, whether the man's a spy or no, he deserves a hearin'. Maybe we should take him to Lucien Deane. He'll know what to do."

"I gave you an order, Private Deeter," Quill said, pressing a handkerchief to his mouth. He barely glanced at Draegan, whose hands were being forced up and tied behind his back. "What will it be, Private Deeter? Will you follow me, or swing with Sparrowhawk?"

Silence followed Quill's question, broken only by Draegan's occasional gasp. Those observing the confrontation between Quill and his subordinate exchanged uneasy glances.

Without another word, Jacob Deeter turned and went out, and Randall Quill looked pointedly at those remaining. "Well? What of the rest of you? Have you something to say concerning these proceedings?"

The rangers looked at one another, at their feet, or at the dark windowpanes . . . anywhere to avoid looking at Draegan. "That's more like it," Quill said after a moment. "Now, get him out of here."

Taking Draegan by the upper arms, the rangers

hauled him to his feet, propelling him through the church doors and into the night.

At the far corner of the graveyard stood a stately old maple with strong, spreading limbs, and from one of those limbs a hastily fashioned noose swung in the wind. A few feet away, the pockmarked ranger waited beside a tall stump.

Jacob Deeter was nowhere to be seen.

Quill seemed not to notice. He motioned for his men to aid Draegan's ascent, then stood smiling as the noose was positioned around his neck. "I will doubtless receive some sort of commendation for bringing Sparrowhawk to justice." He grinned up at Draegan. "Well, sir, is there anything you wish to say before you leave this world?"

Draegan stared down into the ranger captain's face. "You'll earn more than a commendation for this night's work, Quill. You'll earn a place in Hell."

Draegan heard Quill curse as he kicked Draegan's legs from under him, and then he heard nothing but the howl of the wind in the boughs of the maple, and the protesting creak of the rope. . . .

Crouched in the shadow of a headstone at the graveyard's farthest edge, Jacob Deeter watched with horrified fascination as the macabre scene unfolded. Moments before the deed was done, the rangers who had taken part had begun to melt away. Perhaps, like Jacob, they were ashamed in the face of such righteous defiance, yet too afraid of crossing Randall Quill to call a halt to the unjust proceedings. They had families to think of, after all, and so they slunk quietly away, leaving only Randall Quill to carry out the distasteful task and Jacob to bear a silent witness.

In less than a heartbeat it was over. And Jacob could do nothing but mutter a hasty prayer for the soul of the unfortunate stranger.

Randall Quill glanced once at his victim, then hastily made his exit.

As soon as Quill was out of sight, Jacob slipped from cover and ran to the maple. Clambering up on the stump, he severed the rope and eased the body to the frozen ground, sinking down beside it.

"Dear Lord in Heaven, what have we done?" Jacob moaned, covering his face with his hands. "Murder, that's what. We've done murder. And I'm as damned in the eyes of God as Captain Quill!"

Jacob rocked on his knees in nervous agitation. The wail of the storm wind seemed to mock him. "Oh," he said, "if only there was something I could do. Calm. Stay calm, and try to think." He reached inside his coat, his trembling fingers seeking the comfort of the familiar flask. "A drop or two will help me think, and then I'll decide what's to be done for you."

The ranger sat back on his heels and tipped the flask, just as the man beside him gave a violent shudder and sat straight up, gasping for breath, causing Jacob to drop the whiskey and scramble back in terror.

Chapter 1

❦

Albany, New York
April 10, 1778

Each time he came to Molly Harmar's bed, he came in darkness and left before the rising of the moon. The absence of light, the concealment of the shadows, suited his needs perfectly, allowing him to maintain a measure of privacy, to prevent the questions he did not wish to answer from ever being raised.

Molly's curiosity, once aroused, was a fearsome thing. Yet at present she slept—the moon was just topping the trees—and for the moment his secrets were safe.

It was time to move.

Slipping silently from the bed, Draegan Mattais Youngblood dragged on his stockings, breeches, and boots, and reached for his linen shirt, which lay on the coverlet, half under Molly's small white hand.

Frowning, he took hold of the shirt sleeve and, inch by torturous inch, eased it from under her, praying that he would not wake her, that he could

13

slip away without argument, explanations, or tearful entreaties.

In a moment, Draegan's patience was rewarded. The garment came free, and Molly slumbered on. Triumphantly, he donned the shirt, took up his uniform coat, and, turning, tramped on the tail of Molly's brindle cat, which had been curled on the rug by the foot of the bed.

The cat let loose with an unearthly howl and flew beneath the bed; Molly came awake with a start. "Draegan? What is it? What's wrong?"

Draegan bent to kiss her lips, to stroke her tumbled tresses, to placate her in whatever way he could. "Molly, love. It's late. Go back to sleep."

Instead, she sat up, reaching for the tinderbox on the bedside table.

Draegan covered her hand with his. "Save your candles. I can see well enough in the dark."

But she could not. And he knew it.

"You aren't leaving?"

"I must." He straightened up, tucking in his shirttail, wrapping and tying his stock. When the scar was concealed, he relaxed the smallest bit. "I was due at headquarters an hour ago. If I stay with you now and ignore Schuyler's summons, he'll strip me of my officer's commission. You don't want that, now, do you?"

She shook her head, and Draegan saw the faint glimmer of tears coursing slowly down her cheeks. *Curse her for crying,* Draegan thought. All the same he found his handkerchief, gently dried her tears, and pressed it into her hand. She was watching him intently now, her gray eyes huge and luminous in her pale oval face. "Will you come again tomorrow night?"

Draegan was stubbornly silent. He'd been sharing Molly Harmar's bed for nearly two months, since shortly after the death of her husband, Asa.

Mutual need had brought them together, yet in the past few weeks Molly had grown more demanding, and their relationship had become strained.

The change in Molly troubled Draegan. He'd thought at first that he had recognized in her the same deep thirst for life he himself had. Now he realized he'd been mistaken, and it was becoming increasingly clear that Molly Harmar wanted far more from him than he was willing to give.

When he failed to answer, Molly prompted, "Draegan? You will come again tomorrow eve?"

"How the devil can I make promises when I've no way of knowing what tomorrow will bring?" He took up his coat, kissed her pouting lips a final time, and made his way from the room.

He knew that Molly was far from satisfied with his noncommittal answer. But he truly didn't give a damn.

A short while later, Draegan reached Schuyler's headquarters on the outskirts of Albany. The private standing guard outside the front entrance saluted as Draegan mounted the steps. "Evenin', Major, sir."

"Private, the general is expecting me."

"Aye, sir, and ye'd best hurry on in. I believe he mentioned something about sendin' out a search party to comb the taverns if you didn't show your face within the quarter hour."

Draegan thanked the private and entered, closing the door on the cold spring evening. He found the general in the parlor, his gout-ridden foot propped on a feather pillow. Pastor Jonathan Akers, Draegan's uncle, sat in a chair opposite.

The general's expression as he regarded Draegan was marked by pain and a vast irritation. "You are late, Major!" he snapped.

"My apologies, sir, but I was unavoidably detained."

"This is the second time in as many months that you have been 'unavoidably detained,' Major. And if you value your position, you will not let it happen again. I will not be kept cooling my heels while you dally with some tavern trollop, no matter how fetching she is! Have I made myself sufficiently clear to you?"

"Aye, sir."

"Good," Schuyler said. "Let's get down to the business at hand. Since you are already well acquainted with my guest, I shall dispense with the formalities."

Pastor Jonathan Akers, the youngest brother of Elloise Youngblood, rose from his chair to grasp Draegan's hand. "Draegan, lad, it's good to see you!"

"Uncle Jon," Draegan said, "is something wrong?"

Akers shook his head and smiled, urging Draegan closer to the hearth. "The family is well, and they all send their love. Come, warm yourself by the fire while General Schuyler explains."

The pastor resumed his seat, and Draegan gave his attention to the general. He did not have long to wait.

"You recall those two gentlemen who were apprehended night before last trying to infiltrate the perimeters of our camp?" Schuyler asked.

Draegan nodded. He did indeed. The two men, pretending to be Dutch farmers delivering a wagonload of hay to camp, had turned out to be Tories. "I heard that one escaped during the night. Has he been retaken?"

Schuyler grimaced, shifting in his chair. "No, but as it so happens, his sudden leave-taking loosened his companion's tongue considerably, and some

surprising information has been brought to light—
information concerning a certain British agent,
which, if substantiated, will prove a veritable wind-
fall."

Draegan raised his dark head and he stared hard
at Schuyler. "Which agent?"

Schuyler smiled humorlessly. "Sparrowhawk.
After sixteen months of chasing my ruddy tail, I
can finally put a name to the villain's infamous
deeds."

"Are you certain?"

"As certain as I *can* be," Schuyler replied, "given
that this information comes from an unscrupulous
bastard. I've little doubt that Phelps would sell his
own mother to avoid the noose."

Draegan said nothing as Schuyler went on, "The
man in question is Lucien Deane. He lives on the
outskirts of Abundance, near Esopus Creek. Phelps
swears he's Sparrowhawk."

Draegan's aspect was grave, but his roiling emotions were barely held in check. Sparrowhawk, the
most notorious British operative of the war . . .
Sparrowhawk, who had been at the root of untold
destruction all along the border . . . Sparrowhawk,
who along with Randall Quill had caused him agony, humiliation, and pain . . . who'd nearly cost
him his life.

There was a moment of pregnant silence, in
which Draegan fought down his fury. And when
at last he spoke, his voice was strangled. "How is
it that this Phelps can do what no one else has been
able to? How can he put a name to Sparrowhawk?"

"He claims to have had dealings with Deane in
the recent past. Whether he is telling the truth or
lying to save his worthless hide remains to be
proven."

"Do you intend to bring Master Deane to Albany

for questioning?" Draegan watched as Schuyler
and Pastor Akers exchanged glances.

Jon Akers replied. "I'm afraid it isn't that simple.
Lucien Deane is from an old and revered family.
We cannot afford to approach him with these ac-
cusations until we have something more on which
to found them."

"No man is above the law," Draegan said.

"Lucien Deane *is* the law," Jon replied. "He is
the local magistrate, and has been for many years.
And if that is not enough, he is also the son and
heir to the village's founding father, an elder of the
Congregationalist Church that serves the community. He is a man of wealth and position, a man
above reproach, and proving him to be Sparrowhawk will not be easy."

Schuyler snorted. "I don't give a damn about
how revered his family happens to be, or how lofty
his position is in the community! If he's found
guilty of treasonous activities beyond a shred of
doubt, I shall hang him higher than Haman. And
that, Youngblood, is where you come in. It has
come to my attention through Jonathan that the village of Abundance is experiencing some difficulty
in attracting and maintaining a local minister. As
an elder of the church, Lucien Deane quite naturally turned to Jonathan for assistance, in the hopes
that he could recommend a suitable candidate for
the vacancy. Jonathan and I considered the matter
carefully, and have concluded that you are that
candidate.

"You have the background, if you will," Schuyler went on, "the education—with your theology
studies at Harvard—to be convincing in the role
you are to play. You also have the cunning. The
church, as you know, is the hub of the community.
The citizens of Abundance, so long deprived of ecclesiastical guidance, will doubtless welcome you

with open arms. In turn for serving their spiritual needs, you will enjoy an unlimited access to the community as a whole, and Lucien Deane in particular. And so long as you conform to the strict moral standards dictated by the Church, you will be able to conduct your investigation into Deane's activities without arousing suspicions." Schuyler paused, pinning Draegan with his probing stare. "Well, Major," he said, "what say you?"

Draegan sent both men a dark look. "The good citizens of Abundance have appealed to you for guidance, and you are sending them a wolf in cleric's clothes."

"I have known you since you were in swaddling, Major. I know your family, and know every scrap of scandal attributed to your name as intimately as I know the throb in my big toe, and if I for one moment thought you incapable of laying your personal peccadilloes aside long enough to see the task through, I would not consider you." He paused to glare at Draegan and then at Jon Akers, as if daring either to question his judgment. When he continued, his tone was less harsh. "Yes, Major, I am very much aware of *whom* and *what* I am sending the good people of Abundance. But it may well take a wolf to put an end to Sparrowhawk." He shifted in his chair. "Well, sir, what say you? Will you accept this assignment, or must I look elsewhere?"

"I will take it," Draegan said softly. "And rest assured, you shall have Lucien Deane's head served up on a silver platter."

"Good. Now, if you gentlemen will excuse me, I shall take this blasted foot of mine to bed." Schuyler rose and, with some difficulty, made his way from the room, leaving Draegan alone with his uncle.

* * *

It was nearly midnight when Draegan returned to the large brick house on Pearl Street and his rented room. Anne, his landlord's youngest daughter, had left a candle burning in the hallway to aid his passage, and he thought absently that he must remember to thank her for her thoughtfulness before he took his leave of Albany.

Draegan picked up the taper in passing, and found his way to the first-floor rented room, closing and bolting the door.

Shut away from the rest of the world where prying eyes couldn't see, he began to relax. Placing the taper on the candlestand by the bed, he removed his coat and unbuttoned his shirt. Taking up the crystal decanter, he splashed a liberal amount of brandy into a glass. Then he moved to the washstand, gazing into the mirror as he drank.

There was little resemblance between the unkempt stranger framed by Sparrowhawk and hanged by Randall Quill that fateful night a year before, and the man he was today.

Since his return to Albany, he'd regained the flesh he'd lost while serving under Washington. No longer was he gaunt and hollow-eyed. The matted beard that had covered his cheeks and chin had been meticulously shaven, and except for the livid scar that ringed his throat—and which he would carry for the rest of his days—there was nothing to link the Reverend Draegan Mattais to the unfortunate Major Youngblood, nothing to give him away.

One other man knew of his resurrection that night in the churchyard, but because of his fear of Randall Quill, he was unlikely to talk.

Draegan tossed back the remainder of the brandy and set the glass aside. Molly's perfume still clung to his skin, cloying and sweet, mingling with the fumes of the brandy, reminding him of everything he was about to forsake by accepting this assignment. Another man in his position might not have been so eager to accept Schuyler's offer, to return to a place where he'd undergone a horrendous ordeal. Yet strangely enough, Draegan found he relished the task at hand.

Opportunity awaited him in the village of Abundance. He would put time and distance between himself and Molly and also settle the score with Sparrowhawk.

Staring intently into the looking glass, Draegan traced a finger over the thick pad of livid flesh that ringed his throat. Not until Sparrowhawk was dead could he put the pain of his recent past behind him; not until he had achieved a final reckoning with a certain militia captain could he lay his ghosts to rest.

Abundance, New York
April 19, 1778

"Are you certain I can't persuate you to stay a little lonker? I baked a nice pear tart just yesterday, unt dere's a tiny bit of green tea in de kitchen pantry my Killian has not fount yet." Ona Schoonmaker glanced out the window at her husband, putting a plump finger to her lips. "If he knew he vould haf a fit! He's very set on supportink de cause, you know."

Silhouetted by the buttery sunlight flooding through the top of the Dutch door, Fallon Deane smiled and shook her head. Ona, wife to Killian Schoonmaker—a tenant of Lucien Deane's—was well known for her genial nature. There was nothing the Dutch *vrouw* loved more than a good gossip, and on several occasions over the past few weeks when Fallon had come bearing coltsfoot tea for Ona's persistent cough, she'd bowed to the older woman's wishes and lingered an hour or two. Despite the difference in their ages, Fallon had found that she enjoyed the older woman's company. That day, however, she knew she could not spare the time to sit and talk. She had already stayed longer than she'd intended. "I really must be going. Willie will wonder what's become of me. I was supposed to meet her at the bridge an hour ago."

Vrouw Schoonmaker clucked her tongue at Fallon. "Dat Vilhemina Rhys! She's off vid some younk man by now, I bet, unt has forgot all about de britch! You might do vell to stay unt haf a nice cup of tea." The older woman smiled, and a mischievous light shone in her blue button eyes. "Maybe you shoult take a leaf from Vilhemina's book, unt fint yourself a nice younk man."

"All of the nice young men have gone off to war," Fallon said. "Now, don't forget. One cup of coltsfoot tea with honey twice a day to soothe your cough." Fallon opened the bottom half of the door and went into the yard.

"I'll remember," *Vrouw* Schoonmaker called after her. "Unt gif my best to your *oom* Lucien!"

Fallon waved a hand in answer and hastened down the crushed shell walkway, past the small patch of ground where *Vrouw* Schoonmaker's husband labored. Killian was the local miller, employed by Lucien Deane, but at that moment he was busily turning the earth in preparation for a kitchen garden. "Good afternoon, *Mijnheer*," Fallon said.

Killian paused in his labors and leaned on the handle of his spade, touching the broad brim of his hat with his free hand. "Mistress Deane. De missus says your uncle has fount a new minister for the church."

Fallon nodded. "It appears so, yes. We are expecting him to arrive in a fortnight."

Fallon was reluctant to say more until she'd had the opportunity to meet the Reverend Mattais and take his measure. Since Pastor McCrea's death three years previous, the village had employed several ministers, none of whom had remained for more than a few months.

There had been Timothy Breton, whose patriotic zeal had carried him off to minister to the New England troops soon after the fighting began; lay preacher James Holden, whom Fallon suspected had moved on in the hopes of finding a richer parish and a more lucrative position; and lastly the Reverend George Antwhistle, a disagreeable little man with a fondness for strong spirits, which had only served to alienate him from the community.

Reverend Antwhistle had complained vociferously of strange goings-on at the church and rectory, of lights in the black heart of the haunted wood that lay very near the rectory; of voices and unexplained bumps in the night. But because of his drinking no one had listened. Then one day he'd simply drifted away.

"Vell," Killian said. "It vill be goot to have a shepherd to guide the flock once more. De town needs a man of Got in its midst. It has been too lonk vithout." Always a man of few words, Killian returned to his task, filling the warm spring air with the smell of freshly turned earth as Fallon hurried on, past the millpond and through the village streets.

Situated some thirty miles southwest of Albany and tucked up in a mountain hollow, the village of Abundance remained untouched by time and the ravages of the war that continued to rage in the East.

There were but twenty-four houses in the village

proper, no more, no less, some built of the native
stone so abundant in the Catskills, others of good
Dutch brick. All were huddled close upon the
banks of Esopus Creek. Some villagers were Dutch
and others English in origin, yet all lived amiably
side by side. There were Scotch-Irish too, but they
hunted and farmed in the outlying districts, and as
a rule, kept to themselves.

Before long Fallon reached the old stone bridge
that arched over the swift waters of Esopus Creek,
and found Willie Rhys there waiting.

"Ye certainly took long enough," Willie said,
pushing away from the low stone wall against
which she'd been leaning. "The old biddy must
have chewed yer ear off."

"You mustn't be so impertinent, Willie," Fallon
chided, starting off down South Road, which led
past the church and on to Gilead Manor. "*Vrouw*
Schoonmaker is a good-hearted soul. Besides, if
you were anxious to leave, you could have returned home without me."

"And walked past the churchyard all by myself!" Willie looked at Fallon as if she'd taken leave
of her senses. "I'd sooner beg the use of *Vrouw*
Schoonmaker's broomstick and fly home!"

"Wilhemina Rhys!"

Far from chastened, Willie turned a sulky face to
Fallon. "Tout her as good-hearted all ye like! I still
haven't forgiven her for telling Mother that she saw
me kissing Thomas Smith by the millpond last
week!"

Fallon smiled, glancing at the other girl, who was
making cheerful small talk as they walked along.
Willie was the daughter of Zepporah Rhys, the
housekeeper at Gilead Manor, and of an age with
Fallon. Indeed, she and Willie had often played together as children. Indulgent by nature, at least
where his niece was concerned, Lucien had made

no attempt to discourage the budding friendship, and it had never occurred to the democratic Fallon that her friendship with the daughter of a servant was in any way improper. As the years passed, they had become the best of friends, yet they remained as different as day from night.

Willie was impetuous, flirtatious, and eager to wed. Fallon had never been impulsive like Willie, was given to pragmatic thinking, considered flirtatious behavior a waste of time and effort, and, at present, had little if any desire to wed.

That wasn't to say that she didn't like men. One or two of her half-dozen suitors had captured her interest—until she had opened her mouth, betraying the presence of a keen and questioning mind behind her topaz-colored eyes and thick black lashes. Then each in turn had beaten a tactful retreat, failing to darken her door again . . . with a single exception.

Randall Quill, the son of a prosperous farmer and the ranking officer of the local mounted militia, had proven more persistent than most. Fallon was not particularly fond of Randall, but he had managed to garner her uncle's approval and so was welcome to call at the manor whenever he chose to do so.

"Fallon. Fallon! Are you listening to me?" Willie's demand jolted Fallon back to the present.

The rutted road they followed was flanked on the right by patches of forest and fields lying fallow. On the left lay Vanderbloon's Wood, a dense stand of virgin forest and tangled vine. Set against that eerie backdrop, at a little distance off the beaten path, was the small stone chapel and rectory built by Fallon's grandfather, which soon would be occupied once again.

"Yes, of course," Fallon replied. "You were lamenting the fact that your mother found out you were trysting with Thomas. Perhaps you should try and be more discreet."

"Nay! It isn't that!" Willie insisted, plucking nervously at Fallon's sleeve. "Look there! Don't ye see it?" She pointed at the small stone chapel down the way, and the thread of gray rising from the rectory chimney.

"It's smoke." Fallon frowned. "But that can't be. The workers I hired aren't to start until next week."

Determined to investigate, Fallon started forward, Willie still dragging at her sleeve. "Ye aren't goin' in there!"

Fallon gave Willie a determined look. "I most certainly am. And *you* are coming with me."

"What? Oh, no!" Willie dug in her heels, begging and pleading. "Fallon. Fallon, please! Ye've heard the tales they tell about this place. Ye know a man was hanged in that big tree yonder, and there are those that say he still walks!"

"That's ridiculous," Fallon said, pulling a reluctant Willie along. "There is no such thing as ghosts, and no earthly reason for you to be frightened. Now, come."

"It ain't the earthly things that worry me," Willie replied. "What about Reverend Antwhistle? He told my mother about the odd happenings here, and he claimed he was goin' to look into it. Then one day he simply disappears. Mother thinks the ghost of the hanged man got him, and so do I."

"Don't be childish." Fallon strode through the weed-choked dooryard with Willie in tow, and rounded the corner of the building, pushing the rectory door inward.

The room was indeed occupied, but not by the Reverend Antwhistle, her uncle's workmen, or the ghost of Willie's hanged man.

A man was seated in a large wing chair drawn

comfortably close to the blaze that crackled in the fireplace grate. His long legs were stretched out, the parish records resting open across his lap. Still holding on to Willie, Fallon craned her neck to one side, trying to peer around the wing of the chair in which he sat. She could see little more than two long booted legs and a hand that casually flipped through the pages of the book lying open in his lap. "I know it must be mentioned somewhere," he said to himself, "but I'll be damned if I can find it."

His voice was deep and resonant, the voice of a young man, strangely pleasing to the ear. It was a moment before Fallon recovered enough to speak. "Precisely what are you looking for, sir?" she asked.

For the space of a heartbeat he was very still; then, with care, he closed the old tome and laid it aside, slowly coming out of the chair and turning to face her.

Fallon caught her breath. Standing before her was the most arrestingly handsome man she had ever seen.

He was tall and lean and had the look of a fallen angel, dark and alluring, almost shockingly sensual. His long sable hair was tied at his nape with a wide black ribbon; his features were cleanly molded, decidedly aristocratic, with just a subtle hint of arrogance. The straight nose and slightly rounded chin, the shallow indentation below his full lower lip, had been sculpted with an artist's precision and were worthy of a master, but it was his eyes that captured Fallon's attention. They were unsettling eyes of pale green, set like bright peridots in his tawny face—unusual eyes, eyes that seemed to shine with an unnatural light.

He must have noticed her staring, for he smiled, and the momentary spell he'd cast over Fallon was

most anxious to begin my work here, I saw no reason to delay." He furrowed his brow and pinned her with his best implacable stare. "Is something amiss of which I'm unaware? The parish has not found another to fill the vacant position?"

"No," the chestnut-haired beauty hastened to say. "No, it isn't that. It's just that—well, I didn't expect to find you here. I rather expected that you would present yourself at the manor *before* you settled in."

"It seems I have offended you by my impetuosity." He bowed deeply. "I'll gather my things and go."

"You have not offended," Fallon hastened to reassure him, "but there is still a great deal of work to be done to make the rectory habitable. I'm afraid the roof leaks when it rains, and then there's the cleaning. We wanted everything to meet with your approval, and as you weren't expected so soon, I assumed there would be ample time."

"Your concern for my welfare is heartwarming, but I'm a man of God. And as such my needs are few."

She shook her shining head and sighed. "I suppose it is useless to argue now that you are here. And I would be remiss in my duties if I did not take this opportunity to bid you welcome." She came forward and put out her hand. "My name is Fallon Deane. Lucien Deane is my uncle and this is my friend Willie."

Draegan enfolded her small white hand in his large tan one, and marveled at her cool, soft skin. "Fallon," he said softly, "an uncommon name for an uncommonly attractive young lady. Irish, is it?"

The compliment warmed Fallon's cheeks, a fact that she strove very hard to ignore. "I was named for my mother's grandmother. She was a Calloway and lived all her life in Dublin."

He smiled his knowing smile, and his green eyes glinted. "That would explain a great deal."

"Oh?" Fallon said with an unconscious lift of her chin.

"The flame in your hair . . . the fire in your eyes." Fallon's discomfiture increased, a fact that seemingly did not escape his notice, for he deftly changed his tact. "Tell me, Mistress Deane, does your family live near your uncle's estate?"

"I reside at Gilead Manor with Uncle Lucien," Fallon replied. "He *is* my family. My mother died when I was quite young, and my father six years ago."

"I am sorry," Draegan said.

"There is nothing to be sorry for, Reverend Mattais. It happened a long time ago. Now," she continued, "to the business at hand. I'll arrange for a room in the village where you can stay until the reparations and the cleaning can be completed." She tapped one index finger against her creamy cheek and narrowed her golden eyes at him. "I think the widow Hadley's house will do nicely, and she had been hoping for a boarder—"

"Oh, no, I couldn't," Draegan said. He had to be free to come and go at will, without arousing the interest of the town gossips. Besides, he had work to do here at the rectory, work that her unannounced arrival had already delayed.

"Reverend Mattais, please listen to reason. You cannot possibly stay here."

Crossing his arms before his chest, Draegan stared down at her. "My dear Mistress Deane, I can and I shall. Now, please, let us speak no more of this."

She sighed in defeat. "Very well, then. But I shall send someone by this afternoon to help make the place habitable."

Draegan took her by the arm, gently steering her

toward the door, where her friend waited. "There is no need to trouble yourself on my account. I have already found a man who has graciously agreed to help me. His name is Jacob Deeter. And though I thank you for the thought, I think we should be able to manage quite nicely on our own."

She furrowed her lovely brow. "But Jacob Deeter has been gone for nearly a year."

"That was my understanding, yes. Yet as luck would have it, he recently returned," Draegan said. "Now, if you will just tell me when it will be convenient for me to meet with your uncle. I am most anxious to get started."

"Tomorrow at two," Fallon said. "We can take care of your initial interview then."

"I shall look forward to it," Draegan said, leaning against the door to watch as Fallon Deane and her companion crossed the dooryard. When they were nearly out of sight, Jacob Deeter joined him there.

"You find anything?" Jacob asked.

Draegan shook his head. "No mention of a passage anywhere in the volume I examined. And the young lady, Lucien Deane's niece. Do you know her well?"

Jacob dragged off his hat and mopped his brow with his shirt sleeve. "Since she was just a wee thing."

Draegan clapped the older man's shoulder. "Come in, then, won't you? We'll have a tot of brandy and you can enlighten me."

Chapter 2

At precisely two o'clock the following afternoon, Draegan arrived at Gilead Manor, the sprawling estate of Lucien Deane, Esq. At the front of the manse he was greeted by a young Negro servant. "Suh, Mistress Fallon's 'round the back. If you'll allow me, I'll take your mount and show you the way."

Draegan fell into step beside the servant, his glance lingering momentarily on the structure that was home to Lucien Deane and his niece.

The central portion of the house rose a full three stories above the spring-green lawn and was built of salmon-colored brick in time-honored Dutch fashion—spacious, square, and crowned with a gently sloping hip roof. To the original central portion, two identical wings had been added. These last were two stories high, with steep gabled roofs and dormer windows, decidedly English in influence and made of the gray sandstone so abundant in the Catskills.

The overall effect should have been jarring, Draegan thought, yet somehow it was not. Instead, the great house exuded a permanence and quiet grace from having weathered countless tumultuous

32

years. Age sat well upon its weathered walls, and the influence of two very different cultures, while each was clearly evident, failed to clash. In fact, they blended well.

At the far corner of the edifice, the servant paused. "The young mistress is in the garden yonder, suh," he said, indicating with a nod of his head a low stone enclosure joined to the rear of the house. "You just go on ovah, whilst I put up your mount."

Draegan gave the stallion's pale withers an affectionate pat before turning toward the garden where Mistress Deane waited. She must have heard his approach, for she rose from her seat and met him at the gate. "Good afternoon, Reverend Mattais. Won't you come in?"

"Mistress Deane," Draegan replied. "You're looking exceptionally well today. Have you done something different with your hair?"

She put a hand to her gleaming auburn tresses, somewhat self-consciously. "My hair is just as I always wear it."

"It must be your dress, then," Draegan said. "The color provides the perfect foil for those tigress eyes of yours. What shade is it?"

She pursed her lips, and her glance was filled with mild annoyance. "It's green. Now, if you've no other questions, I would like very much to get down to business." She swung the gate open and waited for Draegan to enter.

"My, what a charming place," Draegan said, ignoring her prickly replies. After Molly's tearful entreaties and not-so-subtle attempts at manipulation, he found her frank nature oddly refreshing. "Has your family resided here long?"

"For nearly half a century. The lands were originally part of a five-hundred-thousand-acre patroonship granted to Peter Van Ust. Van Ust's son Brom built the main section of the house in 1694, using ballast bricks brought from Holland in the bellies of Dutch East India Company ships. The patroonship failed in 1723. After emigrating from England my grandfather bought a portion of the original grant, some fifty thousand acres, improved upon the house, and founded the village. It has been home to the family ever since."

They came to two stone benches that sat facing each other, with a small carved table between them. "I hope you don't mind if we conduct the interview here in the garden. The weather is exceptional, and I do so hate to be cooped up in the house on a day like today." She gathered her skirts and sank down on one bench, watching as Draegan took the other. "What of you, Reverend Mattais? Are you from the Hudson Valley?"

"Connecticut," Draegan said, amazed at how easily the half-truth slipped off his tongue. "But I've worked in New York for the past ten years."

"Oh? Doing what?" she asked without looking up.

He smiled tightly. "This and that. Nothing that merits a mention."

She pursed her lips in displeasure and raised her gaze to his. "Had it not merited a mention, sir, I wouldn't have asked. Please continue."

"Very well, then, since you insist. My grandsire, like yours, was English. At the age of twenty, he settled in New York City, married Gertrude Van Ryker, a shopkeeper's widow. They prospered, and when he passed on a few years ago, he left the shop to me."

She glanced up sharply. "Trade makes for a lucrative living. If you don't mind my asking, why did you not pursue it?"

Because the columns of figures, the ledgers, the ink, and the endless inventory had bored him nearly to death, Draegan thought. After a few months, he'd turned the controlling interest over to his brother Christian, who was far more suited to the business than he, and had gone off in search of something more intriguing. Aloud, he said, "Suffice to say, it didn't suit. And so I tried my hand at surveying."

"But it did not suit either?"

He shrugged. "I confess, I'm somewhat hedonistic by nature, and that sort of existence is Spartan at best. Weeks in the wilderness, with no rooftree over my head. And the mosquitoes . . ." He shuddered. "It was nearly as intolerable as my brief stint aboard the *Ida Lee*."

She paused, her quill poised above the page, and stared at him. "You were a seaman, as well?"

Her tone was incredulous, but no longer clipped and cool. Draegan smiled. "An appallingly poor one, I'm afraid. I spent so much time at the rail that the captain threatened to cast me adrift in a dinghy."

He was rewarded with a soft dulcet laugh. "Fie, sir! You are making that up!"

Draegan donned his most solemn face and raised his right hand. " 'Tis the unvarnished truth, I swear."

"Perhaps it would better serve to ask if there is anything you haven't done."

"Politics and the military," he readily replied. "The former is for godless individuals, the latter—well, you know what they say about men who make their living by the sword—and I myself hope to die in bed."

"I see," she murmured. "Why don't you tell me about your religious instruction."

"I studied theology at Harvard College some years ago, but it wasn't until recently that I felt the calling. I suppose I am rather remiss in choosing a profession."

The worthy Mistress Deane feigned a cool detachment, though Draegan thought he detected a glimmer of interest in those remarkable tawny eyes of hers. "You do have references?" she asked. "I am certain my uncle will wish to review them."

"Yes, of course." Draegan produced the requested papers. "They are from Pastor Akers in Albany. Are you familiar with him?"

"I do believe I have heard the name, yes." She studied the pages carefully, while Draegan lazily studied her. "I see from this letter that you have been associated with Pastor Akers and with his parish for a number of years."

"Indeed, we are very close," Draegan said evasively. "By the by, will Master Deane be joining us soon?"

Scratch, scratch, scratch—her pen never faltered as she replied, and she didn't look up from her work. "I'm afraid that won't be possible."

"Not possible?" Draegan repeated. "I'm afraid I don't understand."

Fallon took a deep breath and met the enigmatic young minister's questioning gaze, wishing he did not possess the power to unsettle her. Since meeting her at the garden gate, he'd barely taken his eyes off her, and she found it difficult to maintain her calm, with him watching her so intently. His eyes were so startlingly clear, so bright in his tanned face, so penetrating, that she felt as if his slightest glance bared her secrets, plumbed the depths of her very soul.

It was a ridiculous notion, of course, yet no matter how Fallon tried, she could not seem to dismiss it. Nervously, she wet her lips, annoyed that her highly prized level-headedness had chosen this inopportune time to desert her—annoyed at him for making her feel this way.

"A few years ago, Uncle Lucien suffered a terrible accident, and for a time lost the use of his legs. His convalescence was slow, and he never completely regained his mobility. Since his recovery, he has become something of a recluse."

"Perhaps he will make an exception just this once," Draegan said. "A bit of Christian fellowship might do him a world of good."

"I have no doubt it would," Fallon replied, "but it simply isn't possible. Uncle Lucien is involved in a very important project at this time, and has become quite self-absorbed. Therefore, he is unable to help you during your period of adjustment."

"And what is your uncle's important project?"

"My uncle is a student of natural philosophy," she told him matter-of-factly, "and, to quote Dr. Franklin, 'one of the most brilliant minds of our enlightened modern age'." She stopped, deciding she'd told him enough.

"I see."

His dark brows came together above his patrician nose, and he pinned Fallon with his unwavering stare. "But the position is available?"

"Nothing has changed in that respect," Fallon hastened to reassure him. "The village is in desperate need of a minister. We have been without spiritual guidance since the latter months of 1776. Most of the families in Abundance have sons, husbands, or brothers who have gone off to war, some of whom will never come home. Having the solace of the church to turn to in time of need would greatly comfort them."

At that moment, a stout woman of middle years appeared, bearing a silver tea tray. "I brought ye both some tea, if ye wish to call it that," the servant said, pulling a face. "Raspberry leaves and peppermint. Herbal brews are all we have in these parts since the war has cut off supplies."

Fallon smiled at the older woman. "Zepporah,

this is Reverend Draegan Mattais. Reverend Mattais, Zepporah Rhys."

"Madam Rhys," Draegan said. "It's a pleasure. Shall I see you Sunday morning at the worship service?"

"Indeed, sir. So long as the Lord is willing." She bobbed a curtsy and returned to the house.

"Zepporah is Willie's mother, and has been our housekeeper for a number of years. I daresay she doesn't approve of the blockade--or the war, for that matter."

"But you do."

"Without reservation. I would take up the sword myself if they would let me." He was conspicuously silent. Fallon felt his censure, yet she would not apologize for her patriotism. "You disapprove," she said.

He spread his hands. They were elegant hands, broad at the base, with long, tapering fingers. "As a servant of the Lord, I would far prefer a peaceful resolution to our differences with the Mother Country. Yet, I know in my heart that it has gone too far for that. A great deal of blood has been shed, and there is seemingly no end to the killing. I fear that if certain forces have their way, the earth shall run red with blood before it is ended."

"Doubtless you are right," Fallon admitted. "Once set in motion, the rebellion cannot be stopped. And I can only pray that the lives being sacrificed will not be lost in vain."

He was silent for a long moment, broodingly so. In the interim, Fallon poured the herbal brew that served as tea. There was honey for sweetening, but Draegan declined. He continued to watch her as he sipped his tea, and when he spoke again, he did so over the rim of his cup. "What of your uncle? Does he share your passion for liberty?"

Fallon smiled slightly. "My uncle, like you, is a

pacifist, and has chosen a neutral stance. The search
for knowledge and enlightenment is his passion."

"But he is aware of your differing views?"

"We have no secrets here at Gilead Manor."

Draegan's pale eyes glittered beneath the sooty
fringe of his lashes. "Everyone has secrets."

There was that touch of wry humor again in his
voice, a subtle twist of his firm mouth—that certain
undefinable something that told her there was
more to the Reverend Draegan Mattais than met
the casual eye.

Fallon was intrigued. She tilted her head and
considered him, her cup poised halfway to her lips.
"If that is so, then one is given to wonder what
manner of secrets you yourself are keeping."

He laughed low. "If I told you, they wouldn't be
secrets, now, would they?"

Fallon finished her tea and placed the cup in its
saucer. Among other things the man was a terrible
tease. "If I didn't know better, I would think you
were trying to charm your way into this position."

"If I thought it would work, I would make a valiant effort," he said jokingly. In the next instant he
was serious, all traces of humor having fled his
handsome visage. "I *need* this position, Mistress
Deane. Perhaps as much as you need to find a reliable clergyman to serve your village."

"I do not doubt your sincerity," Fallon replied.
"And I expect you shall have my uncle's final decision very soon." She gathered her papers together and put them back in the portable desk,
along with the quill. "I believe I can finish my notations from memory, so unless you have something to add, the interview is concluded."

Draegan rose from the bench and took her hand,
bringing her knuckles briefly to his smiling lips. "I
shall be waiting to hear from you," he said. "Good
day to you, Mistress Deane."

Fallon watched as he made his way through the garden gate to where his mount was waiting. But it was not until she'd gathered her things and gone into the house to finish her notations that she realized she'd completely forgotten to question him about his activities at the rectory the previous day . . . or to ask precisely what it was he'd been searching for.

With a shake of her head, she entered the library and settled down to her work. If Lucien confirmed the man's appointment, as Fallon suspected he would, there would be ample time to satisfy her curiosity. In the meantime, Draegan Mattais had certainly given her a great deal to think about.

Later that evening, Fallon tapped on the door of her uncle's study. At his soft, distracted murmur, she entered the room. Stacks of books and untidy mounds of paper littered every available surface in the spacious room—the only room in the house the housekeeper was forbidden to set foot in.

In the midst of the clutter, Lucien Deane sat hunched over a sheaf of papers spread across his massive walnut desk. Beside the desk was a tall standing candelabrum with seven branched holders, yet only one taper had been lit. Its feeble wavering light did little to dispel the encroaching darkness.

Fallon crossed the room and carefully lifted the candle from its holder, using it to light the other six. As light blossomed in the room, Lucien Deane looked up from his work. "You really should take better care with your eyes, Uncle. It isn't healthy to read in the dark."

"Fallon, dear, you are far too young and pretty to fuss about my eyesight. You ought to worry more about finding a suitable husband. Besides, I was going to light the candles in a moment or two.

I wanted to finish reading Trumbolt's treatise on toxins first. Fascinating stuff! Trumbolt claims that belladonna poisoning can be detected by the infusion of a single drop of the victim's urine in a cat's eye. If within an hour the pupil fully dilates, *atropa belladonna* is clearly indicated. If not, then one must look to other toxins for the cause of the complaint."

"I should think the cat would have the greatest cause to complain," Fallon replied. Then, "The Reverend Mattais was here today."

Lucien propped his elbows on his desk. "Oh? How did you find him?"

Intriguing, Fallon thought, *mysterious, disturbingly sensual . . . possessed of a dry wit . . . not at all what she had imagined him to be.* Aloud, she said, "I think he is competent, intelligent, personable . . . and he needs the position."

"Ah," Lucien said with a crooked smile, "he is impoverished. That's in his favor, then. A bit of deprivation is good for the soul, so they say. *And* if the man is dependent upon his parishioners for his bread, he's less likely to become a religious tyrant."

"Uncle!" Fallon chided.

"Yes, I know. I shouldn't say such things." Lucien rose and slowly moved around the desk, pausing before Fallon. "It's just that you so resemble your mother when you admonish me that I cannot seem to help myself. 'Tis a pity that she and your father cannot see the woman you've become. They'd be quite proud of you, you know."

"I thank you for the compliment," Fallon said, answering his smile with one of her own. She didn't remember her mother. Sabina Woods Deane had died of diphtheria when Fallon was very young, yet Lucien, out of sheer kindness, had striven to keep some small part of her alive for Fallon—as he had with her father, Osgood, Lucien's younger brother. For that, Fallon was grateful.

"Zepporah has the stew warming on the hearth," she went on. "If you like, we can go over the notations I took this afternoon while you sup."

"I shall of course review your notes," Lucien said. "But a little later. Just now I want to get back to Trumbolt's treatise. I really must send him a note complimenting him on his ingenuity. The eye of a cat—now, who would have thought?"

Fallon sighed. Lucien Deane's mind was given to wandering at will, and unless he was gently reminded, the problem of installing the new minister could have gone unresolved for weeks. "About the Reverend Mr. Mattais, Uncle. I promised him that he could expect a decision soon on whether he will be awarded the position."

"Oh, of course, yes. And so he shall." He considered her a moment, thoughtfully stroking his chin. "You said that you deem him competent."

Fallon nodded. "He is Harvard-educated."

"Well spoken?"

"Exceedingly so."

"Do you think him as qualified for the position as his predecessors?"

"He did not seem to be under the influence of spirits, and given his neutrality, he isn't very likely to go off to war—"

"Then the matter is settled," Lucien said emphatically. "Hire the man."

"Simply on my word? Are you certain you would not like to meet with him first, to gauge his attributes for yourself?"

"There will be time for that later," Lucien replied. "Indeed, we can have him to the manor for dinner very soon. In the meantime I shall trust to your wisdom. You've always been a good judge of character. You have your mother's spirit and your father's shrewdness, and I like to think that I have taught you to look beyond the exterior to that which lies within. So, unless there is something that concerns you about the Reverend Mattais that you aren't telling me, I shall consider the thing done."

Fallon had no objections to Lucien's hiring Draegan Mattais, besides the fact that he unsettled her. And *that* she could not admit without sounding silly and childish, so she held her tongue. "Are you certain you won't come down to dinner?"

"Not just yet," Lucien said. "There's Trumbolt to see to, and in any case, I don't have much of an appetite this evening." He linked his arm with Fallon's and walked her to the door. "You will keep me informed as to how the good reverend is faring in his new environs, won't you, my dear?"

"Yes, of course." Fallon leaned down to kiss Lucien's cheek. "Good night, Uncle."

"Good night, my dear." Fallon stepped into the hallway but paused as Lucien called her back. "Oh, and Fallon?"

"Yes, Uncle?"

"Be certain to convey a hearty welcome to our Reverend Mattais on my behalf."

After a brief nod of acknowledgment to Lucien's wishes, Fallon left him, making her way down the stairs to sup alone.

Chapter 3

Later that same evening, Jacob Deeter rapped hesitantly at the rectory door. Hearing an answer from within, he entered the parson's modest dwelling. "Ye said ye wanted to see me before I retired, Reverend, sir."

Draegan was seated at the small table, with several large and crumbling tomes spread out before him. The vellum pages were brittle with age and smelled of must. "Come in, Jacob. And close the door. There's rain on the wind this evening, and I'd like to keep the damp at bay." With one hand, he unconsciously massaged his thigh, where a deep-seated ache had begun to blossom.

Jacob stepped in and, without turning, closed the heavy panel. "Bothers ye much, does it?"

"When the weather changes," Draegan replied, "but that's not why I asked you to stop by. I want you to tell me again what happened that night, and this time don't omit the smallest detail."

Jacob turned his hat nervously in his gnarled hands. "But, Reverend, sir—we've been through this all before. I fail to see how it can help ye to hear it again."

Draegan drew a deep breath and let it go slowly.

44

"Humor me, Jacob. Tell me again. Everything you can recall."

"Well, sir, as I mentioned before, we met that night at Samuel Sike's Tavern just after supper. The boys and me had a couple drinks whist we was waitin' for Cap'n Quill to come. He'd been over to the magistrate's house that evenin' and come straightaway to the tavern from there."

Draegan's dark head came up, and he stared hard at the older man. "Quill had business with Lucien Deane?"

Jacob snorted. "Monkey business, most like. But not with the lord of Gilead Manor. Ye see, the cap'n had been sweet on Miss Deane for a while, and was tryin' his level best to get her to notice him."

"And did she?" Draegan asked pointedly. For the life of him, he could not picture the staid Mistress Fallon Deane keeping company with that pompous bastard Quill.

Jacob scratched his bristled chin, squinting into the lengthening shadows. "Can't rightly say as I would know what goes on at the manor. But from what I seen of Miss Deane, I'd say she's got more sense than to have truck with the likes of Cap'n Quill."

"My thoughts exactly," Draegan said, concurring with the slightest of smiles. "Quill joined you at the tavern. What happened then?"

"We stayed at the tavern awhile, till the cap'n got restless and suggested we ride patrol along South Road. No one was itchin' to go—as you may recall, the weather was foul that night. But Quill insisted. And so we went south a ways, past the church and Gilead Manor, before we decided to call it a night and started back. A mile south o' here we seen a rider settin' his horse in the middle o' the road."

The hand that had been absently massaging the

aching wound went still. "You did not recognize this rider?"

Jacob shook his head. "He was too far afield for these old eyes to see—"

"And the others? Was there anything said that might have provided a clue as to the rider's identity?"

"Only mutters and oaths at the weather and the cap'n's restlessness, and that soughing wind in the trees."

The mournful wail echoed unbidden in the dark recesses of Draegan's mind, faint now, but just as mournful, just as dispirited—a ghost of a memory that would continue to haunt him if he lived a thousand years . . .

The hand resting on Draegan's thigh closed in upon itself, the knuckles showing white against the tan of his skin. "No one recognized the mounted man. What happened then?"

"The cap'n hailed him, and that's when he wheeled the horse and took flight. Never seen no man ride like that, not before, and not since," Jacob said with a doubtful shake of his head. "Pure madness, 'twas, over the slickery ground. Pure madness."

"Is that when Quill gave chase?" Draegan asked.

Jacob nodded. "Jim Sike, Samuel's brother, was in the lead. Jim always was a might loose in the head, if ye take my meanin', a trifle too loud and boastful, reckless for recklessness's sake alone. He liked to take chances. 'Laughin' in the devil's face,' he called it." Jacob's voice had softened; he raised a gnarled hand to swipe at his brow. "He laughed in Old Nick's face that night, for certain. Only, Satan was in an evil humor. Jim tore on ahead lickety split on that sure-footed little nag o' his. She was a fast un. Too fast, I s'pose, cause when the rest of us rounded the bend, poor Jim was lying in the road with a bullet hole in the middle of his fore-head."

"And you followed Sparrowhawk to the church?"

"He was hardly out o' sight for more than a min-ute," Jacob said, "and his trail led straightaway here. There weren't no mistakin' it."

Draegan frowned, leaning back in his chair. "If Sparrowhawk came into the church with the rang-ers hot on his heels, his route of escape must have been clear—one well known to him, one he'd used before."

"It does seem likely," Jacob agreed. "But where can it be? We've searched this place twice over."

"Some passageway, some hidden access route we cannot see, something planned out at the buil-ding's initial construction."

"If there is such," Jacob said, "then it's a well-kept secret, for I've never heard tell of anything like, and I've lived here all my life."

Draegan flicked one hand at the volumes spread out before him. "The earliest entry in the parish records is August of 1730, and aside from the fact that Lucien Deane's sire built this church, no details about the construction of the building are men-tioned. There's no indication that such a passage-way exists."

Jacob Deeter was silent as Draegan pushed out of his chair and ambled to the hearthside, where he leaned against the mantel, staring down into the flames. The heat was a balm to his aching bones, but it did nothing to lessen his restlessness.

He knew he would need to dig a great deal deeper to unearth whatever secrets Lucien Deane was keeping, and it was becoming more apparent with each passing moment that the answers to his questions lay not in the chapel but at Gilead

Manor, with the great man himself—and with his lovely niece.

Still standing just inside the door, Jacob coughed discreetly, drawing Draegan's attention. The older man seemed suddenly nervous in his presence, and shifted from foot to foot. "I was wonderin', Reverend, sir—I mean, since ye aren't really a reverend—would ye mayhap have a bit o' liquor lyin' about? Beggin' yer pardon, sir, but these past two days has been a bit of a shock to my poor old system, and I sure could use a wee nip."

"I can well understand that my return came as something of a surprise," Draegan allowed.

"Truth to tell, I didn't expect I'd see ye ever again, after what happened here that night. In fact, after I helped nurse ye back last year and took ye up to Albany, I couldn't stand this cursed place no longer. I went to stay with m' sister in Pennsylvania, and only just got back last month. Ye got grit, I'll give ye that, comin' back to the scene o' yer almost demise. It ain't nothin' I myself would have done willingly, Sparrowhawk or no Sparrowhawk."

Draegan regarded Jacob for a long moment before making a reply, and when at last he spoke, his voice was quiet. "Not grit, Jacob," he said. "Just an overwhelming need to see things set to rights. What happened here that night was the worst sort of injustice, and I mean to exact my pound of flesh tenfold." He reached into his coat pocket and tossed the caretaker a coin. "Why don't you go on into the village and have a glass or two at Sike's Tavern? Catch up on all the town gossip, and I'll see you tomorrow. Just be careful what you say."

"Aye, sir. Thank you, sir. Rest assured that I'll take care."

Draegan turned back to the fire as Jacob went

out, seeing in its golden glow the frank amber gaze of Fallon Deane.

Unless the young lady was a consummate actress, she knew nothing of her uncle's perfidy, yet Draegan believed that fact could very well work in his favor. The most interesting things ofttimes tumbled from the lips of unsuspecting innocents. Fallon Deane's lips seemed luscious indeed, and he thought with a smile that he was greatly looking forward to seeing her again.

The next day dawned gray and wet. Fallon rose at her accustomed early hour, and after she'd performed her morning ablutions and arranged her hair, she dressed in a gown of russet silk and went downstairs to breakfast.

Zepporah was kneading bread dough at the scarred plank table when Fallon entered the kitchen, while Willie sat on a high wooden stool, unenthusiastically scraping last season's carrots. "Good morning, Miss Fallon," Zepporah said, never pausing as she vigorously worked the dough. "I trust you slept well."

Fallon smiled. "Quite well, thank you, Zepporah."

"There's samp and fresh cream for breakfast, and the kettle's steamin' on the hob. Willie!" Zepporah scolded her daughter. "Quit gatherin' wool and fetch Fallon a bowl!"

The sound of her name spoken so sharply made Wilhemina jump, but the dreamy light never left her wide blue eyes, and Fallon knew that her friend had been thinking of Thomas. "A cup of tea will be fine for now, Zepporah, thank you. And I can manage myself. There's no need to disrupt Willie's task on my account."

"Oh, please!" Willie hissed softly. "Do disrupt me!"

Fallon sent a smiling glance Willie's way, placing a handful of dried lemon-verbena and mint leaves in the small china teapot. She poured boiling water into the pot, and fragrant steam filled the air, all but obscuring Willie, who pulled a face and nudged Fallon's slippered foot with her toe.

Once Willie had gained Fallon's attention, she frowned at Zepporah and glanced meaningfully at the kitchen door. Fallon placed the lid on the teapot and crossed to the tall standing cupboard to find the velvet cozy, two cups, and two saucers.

"Has Uncle come down yet?" Fallon asked the housekeeper, knowing full well that he hadn't. Lucien Deane never stirred before the "civilized" hour of ten.

Zepporah shook her head. "Nay, not as yet."

"Then you haven't heard. Uncle Lucien confirmed Reverend Mattais's appointment," she told Zepporah.

"Why, that's wonderful news, my dear," Zepporah replied, turning the dough and giving it a hearty slap. "I can't say I'm surprised, though. He seems like such a nice young man."

"And handsome, too," Willie added.

Zepporah gave her daughter a dark look. "The carrots, please, Wilhemina."

Fallon smiled. "I intend to send word to the rectory this morning, imparting the good news and suggesting that we begin work at his earliest convenience."

"Oh, dear." Zepporah glanced up. "Do you think he'll come soon?"

"He *was* rather eager to begin," Fallon said, remembering the hungry gleam that had entered his eyes when he'd told her that he needed the position.

Zepporah covered the dough and went to take the knife from Willie's hand. "I'll finish the carrots,

Willie, and put the venison roast that Mr. Mac-Cullough sent by on the spit. You hurry along and polish the furnishings in the library—" She turned a hawkish eye on Fallon. "You will be working in the library, won't you?"

At Fallon's nod, Zepporah thrust the beeswax and cleaning rag into her daughter's hand and gave her a gentle nudge toward the kitchen door. "Do your job well, Willie. We want to be certain to make a good impression!"

The conspirators entered the library; Fallon set aside the tea tray and closed the door, turning to her friend. "Well? Are you going to tell me what that was all about?"

Willie laid the wax and the rag aside, heaving a ponderous sigh. "Mother is drivin' me mad, that's what. She won't let me out of her sight for a moment, except when ye're around."

"I thought perhaps the furor over your tryst by the millpond would have died down by now." Fallon placed the cups and saucers on a table and poured the tea, then sat back in her chair to enjoy it.

"And well it might have, if not for Miss Cordelia Plum!" Willie replied, her blue eyes fairly snapping with ire.

Fallon blew on the steaming liquid, a tiny frown appearing between her finely arched brows. "What has Cordelia to do with this?"

Willie paced to and fro before the great bank of windows, clearly agitated. "She's set her sights on my Thomas!"

"Now, Willie, how do you know that?"

Willie snuffled loudly and swiped at a tear on her cheek. "Sulee, the laundress, said that Cordelia called at the Smiths' twice this month, and that on both occasions Thomas walked her to her pony. Oh, Fallon, what am I to do? Mother watches me too closely for me to slip away and meet with Thomas! What if it's true? What if he's tired of waiting for me and is courting Cordelia?"

"I daresay you've little to worry about on that score," Fallon reassured her. "Cordelia is pretty, I'll grant you, but she has none of your attributes, and I am certain that Thomas will see right through her. Besides, you know that Sulee is a notorious gossip. I would not be so swift to put stock in anything she says. Now, come sit down and have a cup of tea. It will help to calm you."

Willie sank into the chair opposite Fallon. "Attributes?" she said. "Cordelia has several new gowns. What do I have that could possibly compare?"

Fallon hid a smile behind her cup. "It takes more than a comely new gown to interest a man like Thomas! And while Cordelia does not want for muslin and lace, she lacks your loyalty, your vivacity, your spirit. Why, if you ask me, she pales by comparison, and Thomas Smith would be the worst sort of fool to let her turn his head for even a moment!"

Willie was quiet while she stirred sweetening into her tea. "Ye're a dear for tryin' to cheer me, Fallon, the best friend a girl could ask for, but I still don't know what to do about Mother. She won't allow me to see Thomas, though I've begged and I've pleaded. She says that I'm willful, and too young to think of marriage, though she herself was wed when she was just sixteen! I'm worried that Thomas will think I don't love him, that I'm not true—and that he'll turn his thoughts elsewhere. Oh, Fallon. What should I do?"

"If you will try to be patient, I will have Enoch carry a message to Thomas, explaining the situation," Fallon suggested. "I must pen a note to Reverend Mattais in any case. We can send them both at once."

"But patience comes terrible hard when ye're this much in love," Willie countered.

"If you think of your ultimate goal, you can do it," Fallon said emphatically. "You want Zepporah's blessing, don't you?"

Willie nodded. "More than anything."

"Then you must show her how wrong she is—be patient and biddable, sensible, mature enough to accept responsibility, and sweet. Show her that you are a young woman ready to wed, instead of the willful miss she thinks you are, and I am certain she will change her mind about Thomas."

Willie pulled a face. "It won't be easy, but I'll try, for Thomas's sake."

An hour later Draegan took the note from Enoch and quickly scanned the perfect slanting hand. The message was clipped and to the point, but then, he would have expected no less from the cool and reserved Mistress Deane.

Enoch waited patiently, hat in hand, while Draegan folded the foolscap and placed it in the inner breast pocket of his coat. "There's no need for a reply," Draegan said. "Just give me a moment, and I'll accompany you."

At the stroke of ten, a flushed and gimlet-eyed Wilhemina Rhys ushered Draegan into the library at Gilead Manor, where the worthy Mistress Deane was already hard at work.

"Do come in, Reverend Mattais," she said without looking up. She was seated at a heavy oaken table that was ornately carved and highly polished, scratching persistently away with her ever-present quill.

Draegan moved closer, tilting his head to study the document she was transcribing. "You missed crossing a *t* on the third line from the top."

The comment clearly annoyed her. A frown appeared between her brows, and she pursed her lovely lips. When she spoke, her voice was tight. "Thank you, sir, for your kind assistance. Now, if you please, take a chair. I shall be with you in a moment."

Draegan ignored her suggestion that he sit, choosing instead to wander the room, lifting a book from the shelves here, examining a strategically placed curiosity there. "Are you certain you wish to begin work this morning? It's apparent you are otherwise occupied, and I would so hate to impose."

"It's no imposition," she assured him. "All I require is a moment or two."

"Fascinating," Draegan murmured to himself, scanning the titles that lined the tall shelves. There were books of every manner and description; the cerebral vying for space alongside the French romances. He recognized a particular volume, a scandalous tale of a randy French *comtesse* with a bevy of lovers, and impulsively plucked it off the shelves, while a host of bittersweet memories came flooding back.

Lettice Beauchamp had been many years, many women, gone from his life. Indeed, he had all but forgotten her. How strange that she should be brought to mind here in the library of Gilead Manor, in the presence of Miss Prim-and-Proper Fallon Deane.

How wicked of him to think of Lettice while looking at Fallon and holding the lusty French novel in his hands. How typically, irresistibly immoral.

He'd been sixteen and staying with his grandfather in New York City when he'd first met Lettice, a dark-haired young widow whose seductive smile had mesmerized him, whose whispered promise of untold physical delights had lured him to her silken bed and kept him there for months. To this day the thought of her made Draegan smile.

Lettice had loved chocolates—had loved to read torrid French romances aloud in bed, simply to inflame him. Returning the book to the shelves, he glanced covertly at Fallon, who still scratched diligently away with her quill. For a moment, just a moment, he saw her in his mind's eye, her red hair fanned against the pillow, her small face tinged with gentle pink embarrassment, and as he read to her from the scandalously sexual, sweet forbidden prose she hung on every word . . .

For a long moment Draegan stared at Fallon, a contemplative look on his darkly handsome visage. Then, with a will, he forced his gaze away.

His wayward thoughts would only bring him trouble. After all, the young lady around whom his lustful musings centered was kith and kin to Lucien Deane and, if his suspicions were borne out, to Sparrowhawk. To become involved with her romantically would only cloud his thinking, obscure his purpose, something that in his current precarious position he could ill afford.

Thrusting his hands deep into the pockets of his waistcoat, Draegan wandered the room, still scanning the shelves. Before he realized it, he'd come to stand behind Fallon Deane, who had ceased her scratch-scratching, and was carefully sanding the neatly scribed sheets, setting each aside to dry as she finished with it. From where Draegan stood, he could just make out the heading. It was addressed to the Most Honorable Richard Lee Pratt. He did not recognize the name. But perhaps Fallon would give him a clue to the man's identity and what sort of connection he had to her uncle.

"Penning political essays, my dear Mistress Deane?" Draegan softly drawled.

Fallon had been so absorbed in her task that she hadn't heard him slip around behind her. Now she slowly turned in her chair to face him. "What would make you say that?"

He shrugged; and the barest of smiles touched his sensuous mouth. "I must admit, your impassioned statement yesterday about taking up the sword has yet to leave me. I was quite impressed."

Fallon's throat and face grew warmer by slow degrees. *Was he making sport of her political fervency?* For the life of her, she couldn't tell. His face did not betray his thoughts. "It was a statement, sir," she replied coolly. "A simple truth, which I assure you, was not uttered for the effect it might have on the listener."

He lifted a hand to smooth the stock at his throat. He was garbed in unrelieved black, his white linen shirt a vivid contrast to his somber dress, but the gravity of his clothing suited him, Fallon thought. The bright, gay satins and silks worn by the gentry would have made him a strutting peacock; as it was, he appeared more a raven—sleek, darkly elegant, infinitely mysterious.

"It was merely a statement, perhaps," he said, "but nonetheless thought-provoking. Tell me, is"— he reached out and turned the paper and squinted at the heading for effect—"Mr. Pratt a fellow patriot? A member of the Congress, perhaps, or the New York Assembly? I must say, the name sounds deuced familiar."

"Mr. Pratt is Uncle's acquaintance, not mine," Fallon said primly. "And this is a letter which I am transcribing for Uncle Lucien. Though I am not at all sure why it should interest you."

"Call me curious," he answered with a smile. "Do you transcribe all of his correspondence, or are you just helping him during his ongoing project?"

"Correspondence, notes, accounts ... Uncle's hand is nearly illegible."

"That's a great deal of responsibility for—"

Fallon bristled. "A woman?" She had heard those same words a hundred times, from a hundred different men, but somehow, coming from him, she found them even more infuriating.

"For someone so young." His smile deepened slightly, and tiny lines appeared at the outer corners of his odd, unsettling eyes. It made him look less mysterious, more human, somehow vulnerable.

Fallon replied softly, "I am twenty years old this past January. Old enough to assume a measure of responsibility, to take some of the burden of the estate from Uncle's shoulders."

"How very admirable. I wonder if Master Deane realizes what a treasure he has in his niece."

"I would hardly term myself a treasure, Reverend. Mine is a small contribution in the greater scheme of things, but I like to think that I am in part repaying Uncle Lucien for all the kindness he has shown me."

He merely continued to watch her, saying nothing, his expression unreadable. Fallon cleared her throat. "Now, sir, shall we begin? We have a great deal to accomplish before the Sabbath." She rifled through the papers littering the desk top. "I compiled a list of your parishioners, which I seem to have misplaced."

"I have a better idea," Draegan said, sinking down in the chair opposite Fallon. "Why don't we begin with a brief history of the village itself, and leave the particulars of my flock until later?"

"Well, I suppose—" Fallon began, but in his eagerness to pursue his chosen topic, he cut her off.

"Jacob tells me that your grandfather built the existing chapel."

"That's correct. Grandfather designed the church and even helped to lay the stone for the outer walls. He insisted on stone for the walls and slate for the roof because he feared marauding Indians. When he came here, this country was wilderness; I like to think he had a hand in taming it, making it prosper."

Reverend Mattais considered her, his pale, translucent eyes glinting in his dark face. "I can see that you take pride in his accomplishment."

Fallon's chin went up a notch. "Though some might think ill of me for it, yes, I suppose I do."

"Think ill of *you?*" He seemed perplexed.

"Pride is a sin, is it not?" She waited for his soft chastisement, but none was forthcoming. There was only that infinitesimal curve of his sensuous lips, which she found so very intriguing—which always caused her to consider him more closely-- as she did now.

He grimaced. "So I have been told, countless times."

Fallon smiled at that. *"You?"*

"My dear Mistress Deane, you seem surprised."

"Somehow I cannot imagine your being chided for being proud," Fallon admitted.

"Yes, well, you have never met my lady mother," he answered dryly.

She tilted her head to consider him. "That seems an odd thing to say. I would think that your mother would applaud your devotion to good works, to God."

Draegan chuckled softly. "I daresay she doesn't know."

"You have not told her?" Fallon was incredulous. "But how can that be?"

"Mother and I don't get on very well, I'm afraid.

She speaks her mind with remarkable frequency and appalling bluntness, and as a result, I keep my distance. It's safer that way." He shifted in his chair, seemingly discomfited by their topic of discussion. "I can see that I have shocked you with my candor. I offer my humble apologies, and promise that it will not happen again—if you promise in turn not to betray my dark secret to your uncle. I would not wish him to think ill of me because of it."

"Well, I suppose that he need not know every detail of this discourse. And since it is unrelated to your current duties . . ."

"My dear Mistress Deane, you are most kind. A gracious young lady. I wonder," he continued, and a speculative gleam entered his translucent eyes. "Does your graciousness extend to granting me the privilege of addressing you by your Christian name?"

Fallon was disconcerted by the way his slight smile deepened, by the deep indentations that flashed in his lean cheeks. There was something decidedly devilish about his smile, she decided, something that called an unaccustomed, hot rush of blood into her cheeks. "Why, yes—I suppose that you may—if it pleases you to do so."

He reached across the desk and closed his hand over hers, lifting it, pressing an unholy, lingering kiss into her sensitive palm. "It pleases me very much, Fallon."

His voice, as smooth as the surface of the mill pond on a windless day, made Fallon feel hot and cold at once. She shivered, tearing her gaze from his, paying sudden close attention to the papers that littered the desk top. But that didn't help her predicament. She remained terribly conscious of his presence, his every movement, his every breath, of every pulsing beat of his heart, and she feared that if she didn't escape his presence, she would do or say something that she would come to regret.

If only she could have a breath of fresh air, a moment away from Draegan Mattais, she thought, then she would be fine.

She mumbled some excuse about Lucien needing the papers she'd finished earlier, and she hastily gathered the sheets of foolscap. Fallon's hands were trembling, her movements embarrassingly awkward. Several pages eluded her grasp, fluttering to the carpet.

Draegan and Fallon bent simultaneously to retrieve the errant sheets, and his hand brushed hers.

Fallon caught her breath—she could not help it. The contact was strangely electrifying. A shock of pure pleasure ran through her; she snatched back her hand and lifted her startled gaze to his.

"There's really no need—I can manage quite well on my own, Reverend—"

"Draegan," he said softly.

Fallon moistened her lips with her tongue. "What?"

"Draegan," he repeated, his dark head coming slowly down. "My name is Draegan. I'd like very much to hear you say it."

Fallon licked her lips and spoke his name, unable to do otherwise. "Draegan."

He was close, so close that she could detect the faint scent of his cologne mingled with the sweet smell of tobacco and the pungent odor of horse that clung to his clothing, close enough for her to drown in the fathomless depths of his eyes.

Raising his hand, he touched his fingertips to her blushing cheek, then brushed his thumb in a light, teasing fashion across her lips. "What a treasure you are, Fallon Deane," he said again. "A charming, if prickly, feminine delight."

"I really should go," Fallon said breathlessly.

"The papers—Uncle Lucien—this isn't at all part of your orientation—"

"No," he murmured so softly that she had to strain to hear. "But it could be part of yours." The hand that had stroked her cheek now glided along the curve of her jaw. He had wondrous hands, did the Reverend Draegan Mattais, so warm and gentle, so experienced. "Have you had many suitors, Fallon?" he asked, then quickly amended his question. "I mean, is there a special young man in your life just now?"

"I don't know what you mean," she said, trying to avoid his probing stare, anxious that he could read her thoughts.

"A man who leaves you breathless," Draegan continued, staring down into her upturned face. "Who makes your heart beat twice its normal rhythm?" As his seemed to be doing, he thought.

Draegan watched her nervously lick her lips again, and he felt an answering catch in his loins. Her tongue was small and pink and deliciously pointed. Seeing it dart across the lush expanse of her lower lip made him think again of the steamy French romances on the shelves behind her, of decadent chocolates and musk-scented sheets, of all the wondrously wicked things that he could teach her—the things that a worldly Lettice had taught him so long ago.

"You should not say such things—a man in your position. It isn't right." This was a proper protest, he thought, yet she didn't move away.

"Why not?" Draegan asked softly. "I'm wed to no one, not even the Church. The Congregationalist doctrine has made no outrageous demands on me. Therefore, I can be faithful in spirit, and still enjoy the company of a beautiful woman. And I find you quite beautiful, Fallon." He trailed his fingers along her delicate curving jaw and down the long column of her neck. "Would you prefer that I pretend your nearness has no effect upon me? Would you have me tell you falsehoods that would stain my soul and in the process deprive myself of the pleasure of seeing your becoming maidenly blush? Would you have me play the eunuch, when in truth, I am just as any other man?"

When his hand reached the hollow at the base of her throat, she set it from her forcefully. "I would have you *act* the part of my minster, and I ask that you strictly adhere to the subject at hand. I would also remind you that the sole purpose of our meeting today is not for you to ply me with your pretty compliments, or to court my 'maidenly blush': it is to lay the foundation for what I hope will be a long and fulfilling tenure as our minister. Do you take my meaning, sir? Or must I elaborate?"

Draegan stood up and walked to the chair he had occupied earlier, sighing as he sank down. "Mistress, you are a difficult woman, who would doubtless try the patience of Job."

She stood by her own chair, holding the sheaf of papers before her breasts as if they alone would shield her from him, and her stubborn chin lifted a notch. "I can see that *I* will need the patience of Job if I am to continue working with you." When he said nothing, she perched on the edge of her chair, ready to take flight at the first sign of an inappropriate remark. "Now, where were we?"

"I believe we were discussing the church," Draegan said, "and how your grandfather helped to build it. Would you happen to know if the original plans still exist?"

Later that afternoon, Draegan returned to the rectory, and for the better part of an hour he made a halfhearted attempt to scan the old parish records again, hoping to find something he'd missed. But he came up empty-handed once again. Finally, he closed the books and wandered to the hearth. The meeting with Fallon Deane that morning had left him feeling restless and dissatisfied. In the three days since his return to the church, he had learned very little about Lucien Deane, and nothing at all that would link him to Sparrowhawk. His impatience to finish what had begun in that very church a year earlier was beginning to eat away at him; if that was not enough, there was the added problem of Fallon Deane.

Draegan tipped back his head and closed his eyes, seeing her bright auburn head in his mind's eye. General Schuyler had been so certain that Fallon's uncle was Sparrowhawk that he had come up with the perfect plan to put an end to him.

But Schuyler hadn't planned on Fallon Deane. Working so closely with Mistress Prim and Proper was posing more problems for Draegan than the most obvious one: being denied access to Lucien Deane. The meetings wore on him.

And more to the point, *she* wore on him. Her frankly questioning gaze, her hesitant smile, her coolness, all wore away at his resistance.

Draegan leaned against the mantel, easing his weight onto his right leg and bending the left at the knee. The persistent ache in his thigh eased somewhat.

His task would have been so much easier had the young lady in question been lacking in looks and wit. Instead she was candid and bright, her manner honest and natural, an innocent who was easily given to blush. He reacted to her without thinking, and given his current position it would have been far safer for him simply to avoid her.

Yet he could not.

The irritating truth was that he needed Fallon

Deane, needed to stay in close contact with her in order to gain access to her uncle, needed her implicit trust. As her confessor he might gain a small portion of that trust; as a friend perhaps a measure more. The devil in him slyly suggested that as her lover he could have her trust, her sweet supple body, and whatever secrets her heart might hold. . . .

Pushing away from the mantel, he took up his coat and slowly walked to the door. A liaison was too dangerous to consider—wholly out of the question . . . yet the erotic fantasies his thoughts had conjured stayed with him as he prowled the moonlit grounds of Gilead Manor.

Chapter 4

On the moon-dappled grounds of Lucien Deane's estate, Draegan watched and waited, unaware that his quarry was at that moment emerging from the deep shade of the woods halfway between the church and the estate.

In the midst of South Road another mounted figure waited, albeit impatiently. "You took your good time in getting here. I was beginning to think you'd changed your plans."

Lucien walked his mount closer to where his partner waited. His voice was distinctive, and he would not risk its carrying. "You need to cultivate patience, my friend. Your haste has brought you trouble once and will again, if you don't learn to temper it."

"I didn't come here in the dead of night to hear a lecture, sir. Have you the dispatches for Stone, or shall I go to him empty-handed?"

"Lower your voice, you arrogant fool," Lucien sharply warned. "Someone may be listening, and while a good neck-stretching would be a sort of poetic justice where you and I are concerned, I have no desire to see the deed carried out."

The man being chided for his arrogance shifted

on his mount, tugging at the short deerskin jacket he wore and glancing nervously around. His obvious agitation prompted Lucien's soft, scornful laughter. "Lost your taste for espionage so soon? I must say, I'm surprised. You were eager enough at the onset to have a piece of this plump pigeon pie."

"After that unfortunate incident at the church, I was left with no other recourse," Randall replied bitterly. "I hanged an innocent man, Lucien, without benefit of trial! A Continental officer, for Christ's sake! What else was I to do?"

"Yes, well," Lucien said in a voice dripping sarcasm, "I suppose I do see your point. It makes more sense for you to abandon your loyalty to the American cause and to join forces with the British than to admit your error and risk being reprimanded."

"Reprimanded!" Randall seethed. "They would have hanged me!"

"Perhaps not."

"I could not risk it," Randall insisted. "I would not take the chance, when I'd been as much a victim of your schemes as the major! *You* sent his horse off into the night and put yours in its place; *you* planted those papers in his belongings, stole his wrap, and disappeared, *knowing* what the outcome would be!"

"I set him up, 'tis true enough," Lucien admitted. "But how the devil was I supposed to know you'd hang him?"

Randall fairly trembled with fury. "I *believed* him to be Sparrowhawk! How could you think I would not!"

Lucien sighed ponderously. "Little minds," he muttered. And then, louder, "You may cast blame for your troubles if you wish, but it does not change your actions after the fact. You had a clear choice, Randall, my boy. Turning me in would have gone a long way in righting the wrong done that night—but you chose instead to keep silent about my involvement so that you could blackmail me."

Randall's face was swollen. He seemed about to burst. "You owed me something for dragging me into this! You owed me, dammit! Enough! Enough, I say. Have you the papers for Stone, or shall I report that the great Lucien Deane has failed him once again?"

"Is that a threat, dear boy?" Lucien asked, reaching inside the voluminous cloak he wore and coming away with a small sealed packet. "Are you perchance suggesting that you would attempt to gain through my destruction what you have been unable to gain through extortion?"

"The papers, sir."

"Lud, what a disappointment you have turned out to be. But then, I learned early on that life is full of little disappointments." He gave the packet into the hands of the liaison. "Just so you'll know, Randall, lad. The target is a settlement just twenty-five miles northwest of here, called Peterskill. I believe you have heard of it. Stone will like this assignment. He can be in and out in an hour or two. It's easy pickings, as the saying goes."

Randall Quill secreted the packet inside his short deerskin coat before breaking the uneasy silence that settled between them. "Rumor has it the new minister has arrived."

"Yes, well, good news travels fast in a town like Abundance."

"Yes, but *is* it good news?"

Lucien shrugged. "I can only report that he is young and exceedingly well favored, and that Fallon seemed quite flustered in his presence. I watched them from the windows of my study while they talked in the garden, and I must admit, they make a striking pair."

Randall stiffened, and Lucien thought he heard him gnash his teeth. "I don't give a damn about the man's looks! Will he cause us any trouble?"

Lucien smiled into the dark. "Time will tell," he answered. "In the meantime we proceed as before, and we'll hope that our Reverend Mattais does not prove as inquisitive as his predecessor."

The Settlement of Peterskill, New York
April 22, 1778

The twenty-second day of April dawned chill and misty, but the kitchen of the Kriegers' spacious *boerenwoning* on the outskirts of Peterskill was always toasty warm. Greetje Krieger rose each day before the dawn to stoke the fire and prepare a hearty breakfast for her family, and each day she watched with silent pride as one by one her husband, Freidryck, daughter, Alida, and son, Jan, were enticed from the cozy warmth of their beds by the smell of her good Dutch cooking.

As a rule, fourteen-year-old Jan was the slowest to respond. His attic room was tucked up high under the farmhouse eaves, and the beckoning aroma of sausage and supawn took longer to reach him there. This particular morning proved an exception, however, for this was the day that Jan, his mother, and sister were to depart for a long-awaited visit to Jan's Aunt Ona and Uncle Killian Schoonmaker's house, and Jan's excitement at the prospect of the twenty-five mile journey had kept him from sleep.

For a long while that morning he'd lain in the warm darkness of his attic room, fidgeting with nervous excitement as he tried to picture the town of Abundance from his mother's description, imagining his jolly Aunt Ona and her tall, spare husband, whom his mother claimed rarely spoke. Jan had never been far from his father's *boerderij*. He had never met his aunt and uncle. In fact, he had never been to a village that lay a mere five miles west of the Hudson, the great river his ancestors had called the Tappan Zee.

The gray light of dawn filtered in through the small window in Jan's attic room. Impatient for his adventure to begin, the boy crept from his bed to quietly draw on his best woolen stockings, his breeches, and the scratchy new tow-cloth shirt his mother had sewn for him the previous week. Then, with shoes in hand, he crept to the stair to listen.

Jan heard the soft pad of feet on the stair, and he knew that his mother had wakened. In less than a moment, he entered the kitchen, and after donning his shoes, he took up the pail that hung from a peg by the door. Humming softly under his breath, he made his way to the cow shed.

Hiltje, his father's Guernsey cow, was dozing in the warm shed. Jan settled onto the low stool beside her, taking her long soft teats into his hands. Hiltje, always biddable, was strangely obstinate that morning. She would not release her milk, and she bumped against Jan and the bucket, lowing and blowing as if she had caught the scent of wolves on the wind.

The thought raised the fine hairs on Jan's forearms. To combat his prickling fear, he hummed a bit louder and shot a surreptitious glance over one coated shoulder.

Abruptly his humming ceased.

Something moved in the shadows outside the cow shed—it was too big to be a slinking wolf! Jan slid off the stool and crouched behind Hiltje's warm, concealing flank. Then he remembered his mother, who was hard at work in the kitchen, preparing his breakfast, and his father and sister, who by now must have risen. Jan eased away from Hiltje, away from the dubious protection of the shed.

A half-dozen figures crouched at various positions around the dooryard. Five were dusky-skinned Mohawk warriors, armed and painted for war; the sixth was a white man garbed in a scarlet coat and snowy breeches, a black cocked hat trimmed with the gold braid of a British officer perched on his white-wigged head.

As a wide-eyed Jan watched, the door of the house opened and his ten-year-old sister Alida appeared on the stoop. In her hands was a bowl of vegetable peelings for the chickens.

One of the warriors crept forward toward Alida.

"Don't scream, Alida," Jan barely breathed. "Don't scream. Stay quiet and still."

Alida looked up, catching sight of the Mohawk, and a piercing squeal of pure terror tore from her throat. The warrior raced forward and grabbed the girl, covering her mouth with his hand to stifle her cries.

Jan's mother's voice, raised in alarm, issued from inside the house, followed by the deep-throated rumble of his father's reply. There was not a moment to lose.

Jan darted from the shadowed doorway of the cow shed into the yard, running as fast as his legs would carry him, straight toward the warrior who held a struggling Alida.

The door of the house opened again, only this time the great bearlike figure of Freidryck Krieger filled the doorway. Freidryck held an ancient blunderbuss in his huge hands, but before he could lift the weapon, the warrior nearest Jan raised his rifle and squeezed off a shot.

The bullet took Freidryck through the chest, but it didn't stop him. Face alight with fury, he launched himself bodily at the man who held Alida captive. Freidryck caught the warrior easily and wrapped his massive hands around his neck. The two went down in a tangle of limbs.

Alida, thrust aside in the struggle, was still screeching wildly as she ran for the house.

Jan continued his desperate sprint, but before he could reach his father, a second man stepped up behind Freidryck and raised his steel war hatchet high. Jan opened his mouth to cry out, but his scream seemed frozen in his chest, and he could only watch in terror as the lethal blade came arcing down.

It was Sunday morning. Word of Draegan Mattais's arrival had quickly spread throughout Abundance, and the villagers, long deprived of a worthy man to lead them in worship, turned out in full to welcome him.

The Schoonmakers were present, as were Samuel Sike, the tavern keeper, his wife, Cicely, and their brood of eight youngsters, all freshly scrubbed and fidgeting in their Sunday best. The cooper, James McCord, recently widowed, occupied a pew with Thomas Smith and his father, Evan, who sat snoring softly between them.

Positioned strategically across the aisle were Willie and Zepporah; the former cast longing looks at Thomas as frequently as she dared without risking a punishing pinch from the latter's deft fingers.

Cordelia Plum, daughter of a prosperous wheelwright, and her three sisters, June, July, and Augusta, had squeezed into the pew directly behind Fallon, along with their stepmother, Nancy Mae. July and Augusta were busily whispering behind their hands, while Nancy Mae did her level best to shush them. June made faces at Cordelia, who, with glowing cheeks and fat yellow curls, hung on Draegan's every word.

Fallon had never cared much for Cordelia Plum, but she could hardly have faulted the girl for her fascination with the Reverend Dreagan Mattais.

There was no denying that the man was a presence at the pulpit, and even Fallon was impressed.

The Reverend Mattais seemed an endless well of hidden talents. He had questioned her about the most intimate details of her life in such a way that she would answer him—almost before she knew it. His manner was teasing, almost flirtatious, and at times irritating. If that was not enough, he'd already proven himself quite adept at straddling the political fence. It was this last, so far as Fallon was concerned, that was his greatest and most unpardonable sin.

Mattais closed the service with a prayer, then descended the steps from the pulpit and limped from the sanctuary to the vestibule, where he stopped and waited. Fallon followed, breathing a prayer of thanks that her obligation to Lucien was nearly fulfilled. Soon she would no longer need to concern herself with Draegan Mattais—and shiver beneath the weight of his unsettling stare.

The thought was a slim comfort, however, as she stood by his side, introducing each of the parishioners as they filed from the church, listening as they spoke to him in glowing terms, hearing his smooth but humble replies.

"Wonderful sermon, Reverend," said James McCord. "My Emma would have loved to hear it."

Draegan grasped the widower's hand, noticing the lines of sorrow etched into his face. He regretted that he could offer him nothing but tired old platitudes. "Take comfort in the Lord, sir, and in the knowledge that your dear wife resides with Him in heaven."

"It does help to hear it. Thank you, Reverend, sir." McCord hesitated. "Perhaps you'd stop by of an evening to pray?"

Draegan grimaced inwardly. His evenings were well occupied. Yet in his mind, he heard the admonishing voice of Pastor Akers, warning him of the gravity of his undertaking, his responsibility to the God-fearing citizens of Abundance, whom he served. "Aye, sir. I'll stop by of an evening to pray, if you wish."

Mr. McCord took Fallon's small hand in his. "Thank your uncle on our behalf, won't you, Mistress Deane? He's done the town a wonderful service in finding us a clergyman to serve our needs."

Mr. McCord stepped through the open door, and *Vrouw* Schoonmaker and her husband took his place in line. "Velcome, Pastor Mattais," Ona said. "Our dear Fallon has tolt me so much about you, but it is goot to meet you at lonk last."

Draegan bowed. "*Goeden dag, mevrouw; mijnheer*," he said. "I am honored that you have come to worship with us, and hope you will come again soon."

"All denominations are equal in de eyes of de Lord," Ona Schoonmaker told him. "Unt since de British burned Kingston, dere's no proper Dutch Reformed Church close by, isn't dat so, Killian?"

Killian Schoonmaker stepped forth to grasp Draegan's hand. "Sadly, what Ona says is true. We lost our own church last year, but I don't expect Got will mind if Ona and I gather here among our friends and neighbors until it can be rebuilt." With a nod and a parting smile, Killian went out into the bright spring sunshine, where he lit his pipe and waited for his wife to join him.

Ona paused to speak to Fallon. "Vat a nice man de reverent is!" Draegan heard her say. "Unt so younk and handsome! I hope you vill be helping him for a lonk time to come."

Fallon was about to reply when Draegan stepped in. "Mistress Deane's help has been invaluable," he replied in Low Dutch, "and I wouldn't dream of giving her up so easily."

Vrouw Schoonmaker patted Fallon's hand, her eyes twinkling. "Oh, Fallon, I do belief I like dis younk man!"

As she joined her husband for the walk home, Fallon turned toward Draegan. "What did you say to her just now?"

"Only that you'd been a great help to me, and that I hoped to continue working with you." There was no time for more, for in that moment four fresh-faced young ladies and their dour-faced chaperon entered the small vestibule, fairly filling it to overflowing with their voluminous skirts. It was obvious that the four were siblings; they all had coy little mouths, fat saffron curls, and light blue eyes.

"This is Mrs. Nancy Mae Plum and her step-daughters, Cordelia, June, July, and Augusta," Fallon announced with a tight little smile.

Cordelia Plum came forward and then suddenly appeared to stumble. Draegan instinctively reached out to steady her, and for a moment she clung to his forearms, her touch almost caressing. "My dear Miss Plum, are you quite all right?" he asked.

"How clumsy of me," Cordelia said, turning the full force of her bright blue eyes upon Draegan as she leaned in against him—eyes that held a decidedly predatory gleam. "I don't know what's come over me."

"The same thing that comes over a she-cat when she sees a likely tom," Willie put in, yelping as her mother yanked her arm forward.

Still gazing up at Draegan, Cordelia ignored Willie's remark. "I really would like to thank you properly, Reverend Mattais—for saving me just now, I mean."

Draegan hastened to set the young lady aside. "Think nothing of it, Miss Plum."

"Oh, but I do," Cordelia insisted. "And just to show you how your sermon touched my heart, I would like to be the first to invite you home to dinner. I'm a wonderful cook, and I would love nothing more than to serve you."

"There is nothing that would please me more," Draegan said, "but I'm afraid it's quite impossible. Fallon—ahem, Mistress Deane—was kind enough to invite me to dine at the manor. Indeed, she was most insistent. And since she has been so cooperative—so unfailingly generous thus far—I simply could not refuse."

Miss Plum nodded and reluctantly trailed out the door, leaving Draegan, Fallon, Zepporah, and Willie inside. "Come along, Willie," Zepporah said. "We'll wait for Fallon outside." The two went quietly out, and Draegan and Fallon were left alone.

"Indulging in white lies, Reverend?" Fallon's tone was scathing.

Draegan observed her coolly. "I thought we'd agreed you were to call me Draegan."

"Draegan—Reverend Mattais—teller of untruths. What else should I call you, I wonder? What other names suit?"

He placed one hand on the breast of his shirt, looking as innocent as he dared. "I'm not at all sure what you mean."

"You lied to Cordelia Plum just now."

"That is one way to look at it."

She pursed her lips as she stared at him. "I daresay it is the only way, from a righteous standpoint."

He made a noise of disgust and thrust his hands in his coat pockets. "Since it seems this must come down to a discussion of what is morally right, I must ask you: was it more Christian for me to tell the truth and risk the anger of Miss Plum's entire family, or to take the small sin of telling a half-truth upon myself in the interest of sparing her feelings? Because the truth is that I recognized the gleam in the wide blue eyes of Cordelia Plum, and it is not salvation she is seeking!"

There was no time for Fallon to reply, for in that instant hooves sounded along South Road, coming from the direction of the village.

Draegan went out and Fallon followed, their brief but provocative discourse forgotten as the rider galloped up the rutted lane. At a little distance, he sawed on the reins, bringing his animal to a shivering stop.

Willie broke away from her mother's side and ran to the flush-faced young horseman. "Thomas, what is it? What's happened?"

"There's trouble in town," Thomas told them breathlessly. "They've hit Peterskill, Reverend—a band of damnable Tories and Indians. It happened early yesterday, and the folks who survived are starting to trickle in—Ona Schoonmaker's sister and niece among them. They need you. Will you come?"

Draegan shouted for Jacob. In a moment the caretaker appeared, leading the white stallion.

Fallon caught at Draegan's coat sleeve. "Wait! I'm coming with you."

"I'd rather you didn't," he said.

"Please," Fallon said, gazing earnestly up into his dark countenance. "They are my friends and their families. I must do whatever I can to help."

Draegan hesitated. "Things like this have a way of becoming dangerous."

"I'll be just fine," she insisted. "Now, will you

take me with you, or must I find my own way there?"

"Very well." He stepped into the saddle; then, leaning down, he pulled her up before him, turning his attention to the housekeeper. "Zepporah," he said to the housekeeper, "please inform Master Deane that Fallon is needed at the Schoonmakers', and assure him that I will see to it personally that she gets home safely."

Without giving the housekeeper time to reply, Draegan booted the white horse. With a leap the animal took off, thundering down South Road.

Chapter 5

A score of people had survived the carnage at Peterskill, a score left alive from a once-thriving settlement of forty-odd souls. The survivors had been fortunate, for except for the shock of their ordeal and the sorrow that inevitably came with the loss they had suffered, most of those present at the Schoonmakers' had arrived unscathed.

The children among the refugees were tired and hungry. Fallon worked with Ona to feed them, while Zepporah and Willie carried fresh linens and warm woolen blankets to the Schoonmakers' garret to make up their beds. Not until the last one had dropped off to sleep did Fallon join the others.

Most of the adults had gathered in *Vrouw* Schoonmaker's spacious parlor, except for Ona and Killian Schoonmaker, Greetje Krieger, and a black-clad Draegan Mattais, who stood in the kitchen listening to Greetje as she spoke in hushed tones.

"Dey must haf been watchink de house dat mornink when my Jan vent outside. I don't know if he saw dem. He never said a peep. I only know dat when liddle Alida vent out to feed de chickens, she saw de red men and started to scream. Dat's when

Freidryck took down de gun and went to de door-way."

Greetje paused to draw a deep breath and dab her tear-filled eyes with her handkerchief. "One of dem had Alida. Freidryck gave his life for her. Dey shot him, but he got Alida free, and she ran into de house. Ve hid in de cellar, but dey fount us, and made us to go back out into de yard. Dat's ven I saw my poor Freidryck. He vas just lyink dere in the dirt; Jan vas—Jan vas dere too. He looked vhite, like a ghost. De Mohawk captain tied his hands and put a rope around his neck to lead him; den dey marched us to Peterskill."

She sniffed and continued her tale, seeming to need the telling as much as those listening needed to hear. "Valkink into dat town vas like valkink to Hell. Many of our neighbors had been kilt, and de sight vas terrible to look upon. De Mohawks vere in a frenzy; dey looted de houses and took every-tink dey could carry, lightink de houses afire as dey left dem. Five men of de town barricaded dem-selves in a barn, and de Indians set it afire. Not one escaped."

"What happened to Jan, *Vrouw* Krieger?" Drae-gan asked quietly.

"Dey took him avay. I saw dem, and I cried out his name—he looked so frightened. How vill I fint him, Reverent? How vill I ever see my Jan again?"

Watching and listening quietly from the shelter of the stair, Fallon felt tears well hot in her eyes. Greetje Krieger's quiet grief tore at Fallon's heart. She wanted desperately to help, yet there was little she could do, and mere words were useless.

"Can you tell us what happened next?" It was Draegan again who broke the silence, Draegan alone who dared to coolly question Greetje in the face of her grief.

She wiped her eyes and sniffed. "After a vhile one of de officers gathered everyone togeder and tolt us dat Kink George vas displeased vit us. He said dat many powerful men vere helping dem to vin de var—dat soon it vould be over, and only dose loyal to de British vould be rewarded, only dose who, like Sparrowhawk, had helped dem."

The mention of the British agent was like a black pall descending over the room; the mood changed immediately from pathos to impotent rage. Fallon went cold, and her hands began to tremble; Killian Schoonmaker, usually so silent, ground out an angry curse; Greetje's tears flowed unchecked over her plump cheeks, while Ona tried in vain to comfort her.

Draegan Mattais alone seemed unmoved. Motionless, he stood by the hearth, his arms crossed before his chest. His dark, handsome face was devoid of expression, his clear, pale eyes chill, his manner detached.

Watching him from her vantage point on the stair, Fallon felt her fury mount. If his heart did not bleed for poor Greetje, then he had no heart at all beneath his cleric's clothes, nothing but a lot of grand ideals about conciliation and neutrality, about turning the other cheek.

His cold indifference was too much to bear. Fallon couldn't look at him. Indeed, she couldn't abide the close confines of the kitchen where his presence loomed so large, and so she turned, and as quietly as she could, she exited the room.

Her leave-taking did not go unremarked.

Draegan saw Fallon slip away and, after murmuring an acceptable excuse, discreetly followed. He found her standing on the bank of the millpond, gazing at the glassy surface of the water.

"It's a fair day, Fallon, but too early in the season to venture out without a wrap. There's a brisk northern wind. You court a grievous chill." Draegan shrugged out of his coat and draped it over her shoulders.

"I can't forget about poor Jan Krieger," she said. "Witnessing his own father's murder. Being forcefully dragged from his home. He must be terrified. And Greetje—not knowing if her son lives—"

"She's a brave woman," Draegan said, "and that bravery will see her through her time of trial. I only hope the lad has half his mother's pluck."

"What will become of him?"

"That will depend largely on his conduct. If he shows spirit, there is a good chance he'll come through just fine."

"And if he does not?"

"Then it may not go so well for him."

She drew a trembling breath, and when she spoke again her voice was taut with unshed tears. "Suppose that he does survive. What will become of him?"

"If one of the Mohawks or their allies takes a liking to him, they may take him to one of the villages to live. If they decide to sell him instead, they will probably take him to Fort Niagara and turn him over to the British, who offer a bounty for prisoners. Once there, his name will appear on the lists of those captured, and eventually word will filter down."

"Eventually. But what happens in the meantime? Greetje Krieger's husband has earned a shallow grave, her home lies in ashes . . . and she is not alone. There are hundreds of Greetje Kriegers out there, Draegan—how many will there be before it ends? Before English eyes are opened to the cruelty being inflicted on innocents in the name of their sovereign? How many more must die before English hearts soften and Britain awakens to the fact that she is wantonly killing her own?"

Draegan Mattais Youngblood, Continental soldier and dissolute gentleman, skirt-chaser and spy, sought something to say, some fitting reply for the Reverend Draegan Mattais. He searched for something, *anything* to soothe her, to stem the tears streaming over her lower lashes and down her peach-bloom cheeks, to lessen her impotent anger—the same impotent anger that had filled him as he listened to and questioned Greetje Krieger. He sought but failed, miserably.

Somehow, in the face of Fallon Deane's tears, he could not find the words, could not force himself to play the role he was assigned to play. And so he kept his silence, reaching out to her instead, gathering her in against him, holding her close against his heart as she wept.

She was soft and warm and smelled of fresh-cut lavender. Draegan pressed his cheek to her soft copper tresses and sighed deeply. "Go on and cry if it makes you feel better. There's precious little else to be done for any of this."

She pushed back, away from him, out of his arms. "I will not accept that!" she said, clearly agitated. "There must be something, some way to help Greetje and the others. Some way to prevent this from happening again."

"I can think of nothing—" Draegan said, but Fallon cut him off.

"*Can't?*" she questioned scathingly. "Or won't?"

Draegan braced his hands on his hips and fixed her with a steely stare. "Perhaps you would care to explain that remark."

"I watched you questioning Greetje," she said. "I could read the indifference in your face."

"I am not indifferent, Fallon. Greetje is Ona's sister, and Ona is a member of my flock—"

"Your 'flock' could go to the devil tomorrow and

you wouldn't bat an eye, so long as it failed to shake your precious neutrality!"

Draegan frowned down at her. "You mistake me, mistress."

"I see perfectly what and who you are!" she fairly spat.

"Do you indeed?" Draegan asked coolly. "Then, pray enlighten me as to what and who I am. I can hardly wait to hear."

"A coward. A man afraid to commit himself wholly to cause, or to community!"

"What would you have me do? March off to battle with a Bible in one hand and sword in the other? Would you have me abandon my position here, and leave bereft the people I promised to serve in order to smite the enemies of the cause of liberty?"

"I would have you step down from the political fence you are straddling! The country is coming apart all around you! What will it take to move you, Reverend? To make you see that maintaining your chosen position is impossible!"

Draegan opened his mouth to defend himself, then abruptly closed it again. What could he possibly say to her that would not add to his troubles? Not the truth, certainly. She was the niece of his enemy, and as such she could not be trusted with the truth of his situation, or with his life. It was far safer for her to think him a coward than for her to tell her uncle who and what he truly was, however inadvertently.

"What a trial you are," he said.

"You can make a difference," Fallon insisted. Her tone was softer now, devoid of stridency and anger. "I know you can, if only you will."

"Such faith," Draegan murmured. "Such determination. You are a difficult woman to refuse."

"Then don't refuse," she said, coming closer,

placing her hand on his arm. "Consider what I've said. It is the least that you can do."

She was gazing up at him, her eyes glistening with tears beneath her damp and starry lashes. Without a word, Draegan drew her closer, into his embrace, drew her soft, alluring curves up against his lean, hard length, smiling at her soft, involuntary gasp.

She was so soft and so alluring, at that moment so accessible, that he simply could not resist. "What you propose is tempting, I admit, and I'm almost convinced. . . ." he said. "Perhaps you'd care to persuade me further."

Her eyes widened slightly and her lips parted, as if in silent protest. Yet not a word did she utter, nor did she attempt to push away as he closed the little distance left between them and bent to savor her tempting red lips.

Fallon was shaken by Draegan's sudden, sweet assault. She'd been kissed before, by a boy when she was sixteen and then again by Randall Quill, but never, never had she experienced anything to compare with this. The boy's kiss had been little more than an embarrassed peck on the cheek; Randall had proved overeager, rough, almost fumbling.

But this . . . *this* was beguiling . . . a slow and smoldering seduction that frightened yet compelled her, coaxing her arms up and around his neck before she even knew what was happening.

For a short time, Fallon forgot herself, forgot the difficulties that had driven her into his steely embrace, forgot everything except for the dark, enigmatic young minister who held her, who seduced away her once-strong will with such careless expertise. . . .

She felt the teasing caress of his tongue against her lips and uttered a shocked little gasp, which provided him the access he seemed to crave. He urged her closer, bending her ever so slightly over the arm he held at her waist, his free hand gliding along the curve of her cheek, his long and elegant fingers slowly threading into her hair.

How warm and wondrous was his kiss! How shockingly intimate! He tasted faintly of brandy and hinted at a vast experience, of mysteries that, sadly, she had no time, no opportunity to explore before a noise in the distance brought her world rushing back upon her.

With painful clarity, she recalled the scene in the Schoonmakers' kitchen, his cool indifference. She was grateful, for the memory made it easier to push away, out of his arms.

The moment she was free, Fallon turned and fled, back to the safety and warmth of *Vrouw* Schoonmaker's kitchen.

This time Draegan didn't follow, choosing instead to linger on the banks of the millpond, where his tall, black-clothed form and the thoughtful expression on his dark, sardonic face were reflected on the mirrorlike surface of the water.

Late that same evening, long after the rest of the house had retired, Fallon stood by her bedchamber window, staring out at the moonlit grounds. The night was crisp and cool, a typical evening in spring, all silver light and midnight shadow. Breathtakingly beautiful, yet somehow disturbing . . .

Like Draegan Mattais.

Sighing, Fallon glanced at the moon, so high and white and aloof as it rode the night sky.

From the moment she'd broken away and returned to *Vrouw* Schoonmaker's kitchen, she'd been trying to put him from her thoughts. She had been wholly unsuccessful.

Unlike Randall Quill, Draegan Mattais would not be easily dismissed. His heady nearness, the warmth and strength of his arms, his masterful kiss, haunted her thoughts and caused her body to quake beneath the soft folds of her voluminous night rail.

Draegan affected her in ways she couldn't begin to comprehend and seemingly couldn't control. He was so different from Randall--different from any man she had ever known.

Randall was all bluff and bluster; Draegan was polished and impeccably smooth. His dark good looks, his dress, his demeanor—all proclaimed his refinement. Yet Fallon sensed another side to that polished exterior, a dark and dangerous undercurrent that lurked just beneath his thin veneer of gentility.

She sensed that there was a great deal more to Draegan Mattais than met the casual eye. The notion was not only intriguing but more than a little frightening.

Who was he, really?

He'd told her precious little about his past, and that which he had revealed, Fallon was beginning to doubt. In their initial interview, he'd claimed to have lived in Connecticut, yet he didn't sound like a Yankee. In fact, the inflections in his voice were very much like her own.

And then there was the fact that he'd lied to Cordelia. Oh, he had attempted to explain his untruth, but knowing he could bend the truth to suit his whim had given Fallon more cause to wonder.

Had he lied about his origins as well? And if so, to what end?

God's Commandments did not allow for fabrications, great or small, for the sake of avoiding unpleasantness. The telling of untruths was a breach of those commandments, a sin.

As God's representative on earth, Draegan was to guide by example, to strive as best he could to be the embodiment of wholesomeness and purity, and the one thing about which Fallon was convinced was that there was nothing pure or wholesome about Draegan Mattais.

Fallon frowned into the night, uneasy with her thoughts. Lucien had taught her that it was imperative to make a thorough examination before drawing conclusions, yet when it came to Draegan, she reacted instinctively. And her instincts told her that something was not quite right at the rectory. Although there was nothing that she could lay a finger on, nothing obvious, she could not help but worry over the growing list of little inconsistencies she noticed concerning their new minister.

Female intuition and unfounded suspicions, however, were not sufficient cause for her to speak out against him. The position was his, he was more than adept at his job, and the villagers had warmed very quickly to him. And so, whether she liked it or not, Draegan Mattais was there to stay.

With a final lingering glance at the night sky, Fallon left the window and climbed into bed, pulling the quilts about her. And though she was determined to put the enigmatic young minister from her thoughts as she drifted off to sleep, she was powerless to prevent him from invading her dreams.

Draegan came twice that week to Gilead Manor, but Fallon managed to avoid him. There was no avoiding him at Sunday worship service, however. The turnout that day was even more impressive than the last one had been. Several families had come from the outlying farms, traveling a considerable distance through a fine spring mist to bask in the eloquence of Reverend Draegan Mattais's weekly sermon.

The service ended, and the congregation filed out of the sanctuary. Fallon stayed close to Zepporah and Willie, hoping that she could pass by him unnoticed. A foolish hope indeed, for as she approached him, he caught her hand in both of his and smiled down at her. "Stay a moment, will you?" he said. "I'd very much like to have a word with you."

Fallon felt her heartbeat quicken, felt the heat of a telling blush creep up her throat into her cheeks. "I'm afraid that won't be possible," she replied. "Uncle Lucien was stricken last night with a violent headache. I really must get home."

"Your uncle seems to suffer greatly from these headaches of his. Perhaps he should consult a physician."

She studied him through narrowed eyes, trying to fathom his mood. But his expression was as unreadable as his motives for asking her to remain. "He has," she said, "countless times. All of the powders and potions have proved useless. The only thing that helps him when he falls ill is rest and quiet. You will therefore understand why I do not wish to upset him with my absence."

James McCord followed Fallon. "Reverend," the cooper said. "I just wished to thank you again for coming by this week. I took great comfort in our fellowship."

Draegan shook McCord's calloused hand, and the cooper went out, still smiling. "My dear Mistress Deane," Draegan said quietly to her, "if I didn't know better, I'd think you were trying to avoid me."

"Don't be ridiculous," she said, steadfastly refusing to meet his gaze. "I have already explained;

if you find you cannot take my word, you may ask Zepporah."

"If Lucien Deane is ill abed and cannot be disturbed, then a moment or two of your time will make no matter."

"You are impossible," she muttered beneath her breath.

He heard her and smiled. "Impossible, yes, among other things. Now, will you agree to stay, or shall I make a scene by insisting?" Without waiting for Fallon's reply, he turned to Miss Nancy Mae Plum and flashed the matron a smile that called color into her thin cheeks. "Good day to you, Madam Plum," he said, then turned his attention to each of the girls in turn. "Miss June and Miss July, you both look lovely this morning. Miss Augusta, is that a new gown I see? My, how pretty you look."

The girls were tittering behind gloved hands as Nancy Mae herded them out the door, leaving only Cordelia, whose lavender muslin skirts swayed enticingly as she approached.

"Miss Cordelia," Draegan said. "I trust you enjoyed the service."

"W-why, yes. In fact, I fear I—I'm a bit overcome, sir, I—" She looked up at Draegan, a look of adulation in her wide blue eyes. "You speak with such mastery and power, I—can't begin to tell you how it—how it affects me. . . . "

Cordelia's lashes fluttered down, and she wilted against Draegan in a carefully executed swoon.

Fallon smiled tightly as Draegan lifted the unconscious girl in his arms. They made a charming picture, Fallon admitted to herself—Cordelia's lavender form fairly filling Draegan's arms, her fair head nestled against his black-coated breast. Yet for some reason, unknown even to Fallon, the idea of his holding the other girl in his arms vexed her sorely. "I suppose one must assume that your 'mastery and power' proved too much for poor, frail Cordelia."

Draegan frowned at Fallon. "In any other circumstances, I would applaud such biting sarcasm. However, at the moment I would far prefer that you save your scathing wit for a time when I'm at liberty to enjoy it, and come with me. Our dear Miss Plum is much heavier than she appears, and I should like to take her inside, where I might lay her down."

"I have little doubt that is precisely what Cordelia had in mind," Fallon said.

At Fallon's words, Cordelia offered up a smothered gasp, her lashes fluttered, and she swooned again.

Muttering beneath his breath, Draegan turned and strode through the church door with his burden, brushing by Ona and Killian Schoonmaker, who were just about to emerge from the sanctuary.

Vrouw Schoonmaker caught at Fallon's sleeve, her eyes bright with interest. "Fallon, dear! Vat happent here?"

"Mistress Plum has fainted," Fallon said. "Reverend Mattais is going to try and revive her, and has asked me to act as a chaperon."

"Two younk unt innocent girls in de company of a hantsome younk man like de reverent? Och! It isn't fittink! Vhy, people vill talk."

"They will talk a great deal more if he is left alone with Cordelia." Fallon had little doubt that that was precisely what the wheelwright's eldest daughter had intended.

Draegan reached the door leading to his quarters and turned to look for Fallon. "Mistress Deane, if you will?" he said crisply. "My burden grows no lighter."

Fallon smiled. "I suppose I'd better hurry."

"Go. Go," Ona said, having made up her mind. "I'm comink vid you. Killian!" she cried as she followed after Fallon. "Go unt fint Mrs. Plum. Tell her vhat has happent, unt brink her back here to collect Cordelia!"

Fallon passed through the door that separated Draegan's quarters from the church proper, Ona Schoonmaker following close upon her heels. As she watched, Draegan deposited the unconscious girl on the faded blue divan. "There's brandy in the armoire in the bedchamber," he said, glancing up at Fallon. "Would you mind bringing it?"

With little more than a terse nod, Fallon turned and exited the room.

The rectory was much tidier than it had been the last time Fallon had glimpsed it. The dust and the cobwebs had been swept meticulously out; the state of the furnishings, items garnered through the years by Dreagan's predecessors, had been improved with a profound cleaning and a light coat of beeswax, whose sweet, unmistakable odor still hung in the air.

In the center of the adjoining bedchamber was a narrow cot, neatly spread with a patchwork quilt, the only splash of color in the sparsely furnished room. In one corner sat a camel-backed trunk, its hardware gleaming dully in the soft morning light that filtered through the uncurtained window. In the opposite corner, nearest the hearth, was the great cherry armoire to which Draegan had referred.

Fallon grasped the small metal latch on the armoire and swung the double doors open wide, scanning the contents: shaving brush and straight razor; soap and several towels; cologne and a half dozen immaculate linen shirts, all neatly folded and sharing shelf space with several pairs of black breeches; and a rumpled black coat that had been cast carelessly inside.

There was a spot of mud showing on the sleeve of the latter that had yet to be brushed away. Impulsively, Fallon reached out to run her fingertips over the soft superfine, certain it was the coat he'd worn that day at the millpond, when he'd drawn her close and held her so tightly, casting his dark, seductive spell over her senses.

Knowing that she should not, yet unable to resist, she lifted the coat from its resting place. Her breath caught in her throat, for lying on the bed of spotless linen was a pair of pistols.

This was not a brace of ornate dueling pistols, the kind of keepsake that was sometimes passed down in wealthy families from father to son. No, these were heavy, lethal-looking weapons with well-worn walnut grips—*strange possessions indeed for a self-proclaimed man of peace.*

Chapter 6

The soft spring rains and warming weather had brought about a change in the countryside in the fortnight since Draegan's arrival. The harsh grays and lifeless browns of winter and early spring were softened now by the pink haze of the budding maple, the dappled white of the dogwood, and by a host of new green leaves.

Fat white ducks waddled by row upon row of nodding daffodils, which bordered the village yard and the nearby lush green pasture. They searched for insects to feed their trailing ducklings before heading off to the swollen waters of Esopus Creek.

At dawn each day, Wilmer Pritt, the cowherd, collected the cows from sheds behind each village house and drove them through the streets to graze on land owned by Lucien Deane. At day's end he drove them home again, their brass bells clanking softly in the purple dusk.

Industry and prosperity were apparent everywhere in this bucolic mountain setting, and unless one looked into the careworn faces of the Peterskill refugees, it would have been difficult indeed to discern that there was a war being waged not many miles away.

Draegan Mattais Youngblood, however, found it impossible to forget. In fact, the war made the coming of spring something of an irritant for him. The greening of the countryside, the ever-increasing warmth of the sun, proclaimed loudly the passing of the days, and as each day settled into dusk and Draegan returned to Gilead Manor to keep his nightly vigil, he was reminded that he was no closer to putting an end to Sparrowhawk's reign of terror than he had been the first day of his arrival at the rectory.

His lack of progress in his ongoing investigation was frustrating, and Draegan was not by nature a patient man. He had not anticipated such difficulty in gaining the evidence that he needed in order to take down Lucien Deane. Indeed, he thought, watching as the waning moon rose high above the black line of the trees that bordered the grounds of Gilead Manor, he had never imagined that the great man would have proven so damnably elusive.

After more than a fortnight of diligent waiting and watching, Draegan had yet to lay eyes on his enemy. More than once he had wondered if Schuyler's informant had lied about Lucien.

Fallon claimed that her uncle was physically incapacitated, that he suffered from debilitating headaches, and rarely ventured from the grounds of the estate.

The two claims did not support each other; Lucien Deane could not have been both a studious cripple and an infamous spy.

Or could he?

Was Deane in fact Sparrowhawk, as Schuyler and Jon Akers suspected? Or was he simply a scapegoat, a cover for another's treachery?

Draegan had no ready answers. And each tiny morsel of information Jacob Deeter did manage to bring him, each conclusion at which he himself arrived, raised even more questions, more doubts, more suspicions, until he was certain only of his seeming inability to sort it all out.

Draegan frowned at the mansion. The moonlight glinted ghostly white off the dark upstairs windows, but the long bank of mullioned windows in the library were softly luminous.

His frown deepened. Was Fallon Deane at this moment in the library, her pert nose buried in ledgers and letters and India ink for her will-o'-the-wisp uncle? Or was she in fact plotting the downfall of yet another American settlement, secure in the knowledge that the world thought Sparrowhawk a man?

Draegan forced his gaze away from the library windows. He didn't like to consider that the fiery beauty he had kissed a week earlier by the millpond might be a dangerous fraud, that all her talk about liberty and the tears she had shed over the Peterskill tragedy could actually be false.

Yet in order to ferret out the truth, he must look to every possible angle, and like it or not, Fallon Deane must be among his considerations. A gently reared young lady of impeccable background, bookish and prim almost to a fault, she was, as Schuyler had said, "beyond reproach."

Yet was she the innocent that she seemed? Or had she led Randall Quill and his rangers a merry chase that night a year ago? Had she planted the papers in a stranger's belongings and left him to face a cruel and undeserved death, uncaring of the agony he suffered?

Squeezing his eyes shut, Draegan ran a hand over his face, trembling ever so slightly. For an instant, he felt the sleet sting his face . . . felt the cold caress of the wet hemp against his throat . . . felt the noose tighten. . . .

His breath rasped in his throat; he forced his eyes open and stared hard at the stars shining brightly in the ebony skies. With every fiber of his being he hoped that he was wrong about Fallon Deane. He remained unsure of just what he would do if he was not.

The thought that he might be forced to kill a woman to have his reckoning with the one who'd come so close to destroying his life had never occurred to him. It was not a thought he savored.

Moments ticked by, and Draegan calmed down. The moon rose high overhead, and he pushed the idea of Fallon as a suspect into the dark recesses of his mind, fighting hard to summon up his near-exhausted patience.

If Sparrowhawk was indeed using Gilead Manor as a base of operations, then it only followed that at some point the spy would have to emerge from hiding to meet with his contacts to plan his next strike.

The war was not going well for the American forces. Washington was still in his winter encampment at Valley Forge, in Pennsylvania, Schuyler was still scrambling to hold the tribes in check, and stores to feed the Continentals were becoming harder and harder to come by as the fighting dragged on.

England was a world power, industrialized, established in trade. Sir Henry Clinton had all of the supplies that he needed to feed and clothe and care for his troops at his disposal, which gave the British a decided advantage over the fledgling United States of America, an infant nation still struggling to rise off its knees and toddle toward freedom and self-sufficiency.

Sparrowhawk was very well aware of the vulnerability of his homeland, and it would prove too tempting an opportunity to pass by. He would strike soon; of that Draegan was certain. And when he did, Draegan would be waiting.

Yet seemingly not tonight.

For hours he'd been keeping watch. The moon had set, the darkness was complete, and not the faintest flicker of light or life could be detected within the manor. The inhabitants had long ago sought their beds, and perhaps it was time he sought his too.

Three-quarters of a mile to the north, two men sat upon their horses on the lightless road.

"Show them the way, and make sure they maintain their silence. It would bode ill for all of you if they were seen. The furor over Peterskill has yet to die down, and I daresay that nothing would rally the good citizens of Abundance right now like a good British bloodletting."

"You are taking a hellish chance, bringing them here so soon after the raid on Peterskill. What in God's name possessed you?"

"Oh, fie, Randall," Lucien said, clucking his tongue. "Such whining from one so young! Where is your sense of adventure?"

"This is not adventure," Randall said through his teeth. "It's sheer madness. You think this business some bizarre jest, some game in which you match wits with the militia! It is not a game, Lucien, not when our lives hang in the balance!"

"That's where you err, my dear boy." Lucien reached inside his cloak and brought forth a pistol. "It is indeed a game. The ultimate game of cat and mouse. A game that I am winning. And if you speak my name again with such vigor, I assure you, I shall pluck you from the playing field and leave your lifeless form lying in the road—bait for the ravens. I have not come this far to have you muck up my progress with your tantrums."

"You would not kill me," Randall said with his usual bravado. "Without me, there would be no one left to do your bidding."

"Wouldn't I? I might remind you that I managed this entire operation myself before you came into it, and I can again, if need be. It might be wise to humor me." Lucien smiled, but there was ice in the expression. "I have killed twice, albeit that poor ragged beggar in the church was more a sacrifice to your temper and greed than to my ambitions, for I had no burning desire to see him dead. As for you—well, that's different, now, isn't it?" He laughed, and the sound was harsh and abrasive, like steel grating on stone. "One more body would not trouble me greatly."

"What keeps you from it?" Randall sneered. "Not honor, not goodness. Not conscience, surely!"

"Honor brings cold comfort," Lucien replied matter-of-factly, "and goodness gets you nothing. But conscience? Now, there is something to ponder at length. What is conscience, I wonder? That intangible something that keeps the soul on an unerring track toward goodness. Yet it can't be seen or proven, so how does one know if it truly exists?" He gave another low chuckle, as if at some secret joke. "I really must invite the good reverend to dine, of an evening. It would seem that he and I have a great deal to discuss."

"Take care not to encourage him where Fallon is concerned," Randall warned. "It would not do to have the man sticking his ecclesiastical nose into places it does not belong."

Lucien replaced the pistol and waved the young man away. "Just you take care of the business at hand, Master Quill, and leave my niece to me."

Turning a stiff back on Lucien, Randall clucked to his horse, guiding it off the rutted road onto the rocky forest ground. At a little distance, thirteen

men, silent black silhouettes, waited for Randall
Quill to lead them to a safe haven.

Lucien lingered in the dark road long after the
contingent of men led by the American militia captain had melted into the night, long after it was
prudent for him to do so.

His alliance with young Quill was an uneasy one
at best. Conceived by force and bound by the silken
thread of a shared treachery, the partnership had
begun to sour almost from the moment of its con-
ception.

Randall Quill was full of pomposity and self-
importance, and Lucien loathed him. Yet the
younger man had proven the perfect pawn in Lucien's game.

The militia captain had a greater mobility than
the limited one Lucien himself enjoyed, and his position as commander of a company of rangers allowed him to come and go without attracting
undue notice.

At present he was useful, and it was that very
usefulness that kept him safe from harm.

Lucien breathed deeply, reveling in the cool
freshness of the night air, in the headiness of an
unaccustomed freedom, yet aware that he should
have been getting back.

To return to the manse while Fallon and the servants slept would have been the wise thing to do.
Yet he continued to linger, reluctant to return to a
prison that, though of his own design, had proven
nonetheless loathsome.

Sighing wistfully, he glanced at the heavens,
barely visible through the heavy canopy of leaves
overhead. The stars still glimmered brightly. There
were several hours remaining until cock's crow.

What matter would a few stolen moments make?

Perhaps he would ride north, past the church,

into the sleeping village. It had been a long while since he had dared to venture that far from the estate, an eternity since he had glimpsed the town his father had founded—a town that, once his plans came to fruition, he would never lay eyes on again.

Intent upon following his whim, Lucien started to turn his horse toward the village when a sound like the rumble of distant thunder somewhere to the rear caught his attention.

Curious, he turned toward the south, back toward the sound, and saw a pale horse emerge from the shadows. When the rider caught sight of Lucien sitting on his horse in the road, he reined in his mount, allowing Lucien a clear view of horse and rider.

The animal itself was huge, with eyes that glowed like dark red coals against a milky coat. Plumes of vapor streamed from its nostrils. Had Lucien not known better, he'd have sworn he'd caught a whiff of brimstone on the chill night wind.

The horseman was no less impressive than his mount. Raven hair, tossed by the wind and his wild ride, framed features that were as classically molded as Michelangelo's David's, and appeared every bit as hard and pale and pitiless.

As Lucien watched, the rider nudged the white and walked it forward, the stallion sidling anxiously under the stranger's restraining hand.

Lucien cast an anxious glance to the rear. They were alone on the darkened road; the phantom rider was approaching with cold deliberation. Was he friend or foe? Or was he merely curious at finding another rider abroad so late? Lucien did not know and could not afford to wait long enough to satisfy his curiosity. He could not risk being recognized, and so he wheeled the hunter he rode, digging his heels into its sides. The horse lunged forward as the phantom rider called out for him to halt, breaking into a hard run, reacting to each nudge of Lucien's heels with a renewed burst of speed.

Down the lightless road they pounded, past the gravestones gleaming white in the churchyard, past the darkened church—the phantom white several lengths behind, and gaining fast.

Lucien risked a glance at his pursuer, and a chill snaked up his spine. The crazy bastard was standing in his stirrups, a fiendish grin on his marble-white face. Lucien spurred his hunter to a breakneck speed. He had no idea who or what was chasing him, but one thing was becoming infinitely clear: the rider was absolute Hell on horseback, and he had every intention of running his quarry to ground.

Escape seemed improbable. His hunter was aging, his chances of outrunning the phantom white incredibly slim. Lucien Deane, however, did not despair. He had played a good game thus far; if he forfeited now, it would all be over. He would be stripped of the fame, the glory, the satisfaction he'd known as Sparrowhawk, and he would be given in its place a traitor's grave.

Into his dismal thoughts crept the light and heart that were Fallon. Fallon, Sabina's child. Fallon, who embraced the American cause with so much fervor. Fallon, who cherished truth and honor, who gave her heart unstintingly. His truth would crush her, Lucien knew, and he simply could not allow that to happen.

Bending low over the hunter's neck, he dug his heels into its heaving sides and felt it give another forward lurch. Several yards to the rear and coming up fast, the rider shouted for him to yield. Lucien ignored the warning cry. There was too much at stake for him to think of yielding, and one chance left of escape....

Two lengths to the rear, Draegan spoke to the stallion, urging the animal into a dead run. He hadn't expected to come upon another rider so late upon the road, and he had been quite curious to ascertain the rider's identity and the manner of business that kept him out at such an hour. The fact that the fellow had chosen to cut and run rather than face him aroused Draegan's innate suspicions. He could not let the fellow escape without answering for his actions.

Draegan shouted again for the rider to halt. Twisting in the saddle, the rider snatched a pistol from the concealing folds of his cloak. Draegan tried to swerve as the rider took hasty aim and squeezed off a shot. The weapon's muzzle belched orange fire, but the shot went wild. Draegan came recklessly on.

Just ahead, Draegan's quarry was hunched forward over the neck of the bay, the voluminous cloak billowing out behind the slight form like the outspread wings of a great black bird. The cloak, combined with a dark tricorn hat pulled low to shadow the rider's face, made it impossible to discern if the rider he was chasing was male or female, old or young.

Urging Banshee on, Draegan raced along the flat, the night wind stinging his face. He fairly flew around a sharp bend in the road, hot upon the hunter's churning hooves. The dark horse followed the outside curve, leaving the way clear for Draegan to cut him off. A hoarsely barked command and the pale stallion lunged to the left, neck to flank with the smaller bay, carrying Draegan closer, ever closer to his goal. Suddenly, as they rounded the blind curve, they charged directly into the path of a farmer's wagon laden with a loose mound of last year's hay.

Mouthing an oath, Draegan hauled on the reins, bringing his stallion back upon his haunches. The stallion's gleaming hooves struck the air precariously close to the heads of the farmer's team; the animals reared and pulled against their traces. It took a full moment for the farmer to right his team and set his wagon into motion again, and as he moved off into the distance, Draegan heard the old man curse him roundly in guttural Dutch.

But Draegan paid little heed to what was said. He was too concerned with what lay ahead. The road leading into the village was empty, and except for the fading creak of wagon wheels the night had gone suddenly still.

He glanced around, listening intently for the sound of hoofbeats. He heard nothing.

Sparrowhawk had escaped.

Chapter 7

⧖⧗

May arrived with a welcome warmth and a profusion of flowers. The village wives, both Dutch and English, took great pride in their gardens. Yet no matter how abundant the blooms or how lovingly tended, not a single garden could come close to comparing with that of Ona Schoonmaker.

Ona's Holland tulips grew larger and brighter than anyone's, nodding noble scarlet heads in rows that flanked the broad shell walkway leading to the house, the advance guard for an army of yellow daffodils and white trillium lilies bringing up the rear.

Few visitors could resist lingering a moment or two to drink in the bright blaze of color, to savor the sweet fragrance that filled the air, before making their way to the door. Fallon was no exception. At last she tore herself away, hurrying up the walk to ply the iron knocker that graced the top half of the heavy Dutch door.

A few seconds later the door opened, and *Vrouw* Schoonmaker's round face appeared. "Fallon! How nice it is to see you. Come in, come in! I vas just about to put de kettle on."

"I hope I'm not intruding."

"Vhat? Intrudink? Never!" The Dutchwoman raised her brows and peered intently at the basket slung over Fallon's arm. "Vhat's dis you haf here?"

"I found some clothing in a trunk in the attic and thought the children might like to have a look. The clothes are a trifle old-fashioned, but sturdily sewn." She handed the basket to Ona and asked, "How *are* the children, Ona? And Greetje? I remember them all in my prayers each night, but it feels so inadequate a gesture. I wish there were more that I could do."

"Talkink vid Got is never inadequate, child. And vheder you know it or not, your prayers haf been answered."

Fallon glanced sharply up at her friend. "Has there been news of Jan?"

Ona shook her head, but her lips were smiling.

"I'm afraid I don't understand," Fallon said.

"You vill; now, come." Ona Schoonmaker led Fallon into the large, warm kitchen, whose interior was dark, compared to the brilliant day outside. At the table by the window sat Killian, pipe in hand, and Greetje. Alida hovered near her mother, darting surreptitious glances at the tall man who lingered in the shadows near the hearth. "Behold," Ona said with a flash of her dimples and a flourish of a plump hand in the man's direction, "our own minsterink angel."

A dark angel, Fallon thought, *standing silent sentinel over the Schoonmakers' humble kitchen.* Conscious of the others watching, Fallon inclined her head deferentially. "Reverend Mattais, I didn't see you standing there."

His gaze, like pale green fire, flickered over Fallon. It was oddly caressing, from the crown of her bright head to the toes of her leather slippers peeping from beneath the hem of her skirt.

There was heat in that penetrating gaze, and heat bred heat. Fallon felt it rise from her toes into her trim ankles, creeping slowly, languidly, up her shapely legs and beyond. It curled and coiled in her belly until she unconsciously touched a hand to her waist and he slowly smiled.

"Mistress Deane," he murmured in reply. "What a pleasant surprise."

Pleasant for him, perhaps, Fallon thought. His presence, as always, was potent, and she felt it more keenly than she liked to admit, even to herself. It was difficult for her to look at him and fail to notice the air of menace that seemed so much a part of him, hard to banish the memory of a brace of lethal weapons lying on a stack of pristine linens in the rectory armoire, impossible to stem the flow of questions that his little inconsistencies raised—and that doubtless were destined to go unanswered. . . .

Fallon tore her gaze from him and turned abruptly to Ona, who watched the exchange with ill-disguised interest.

"De reverent stopped by to talk vid Greetje about Jan," Ona said. "He has graciously offert to help, and Greetje has accepted, most gratefully."

Draegan inclined his dark head. "*Mevrouw* is exceedingly kind to make so much of the humble assistance I can offer."

Vrouw Schoonmaker clucked her tongue at his reply. "Och! De man brinks us hope, unt calls it humble!"

"Hope?" Fallon's gaze slid from the Dutch dame to the enigmatic young minister, who looked slightly discomfitted.

"Vell, it seems our Reverent Mattais has friends in prestigious places," *Vrouw* Schoonmaker said, "unt is goink to enlist dere aid in findink Jan."

"Indeed," Fallon murmured, watching him

through narrowed eyes. "How intriguing."

Her words prompted Draegan's smile. "One is given to wonder which intrigues you more: the fact that I have offered my humble assistance or that I actually have friends."

Fallon was swift to reply. "It is the caliber of those friends that intrigues me, sir. Your neutrality is widely touted; yet, unless I'm mistaken, the lists of Americans held prisoner are available only through military channels. Tell me, if you will, how a 'man of peace' comes to move in military circles?"

Draegan's smile deepened, and something flickered behind his pale, translucent eyes, something dark and dangerous, something that sent a chill up Fallon's spine. "What matters more to you, Fallon? The deed itself, or the method by which it's accomplished?"

Fallon lifted her chin. His reply had been smoothly uttered, but it was no less the verbal thrust. It had brought his point home quite clearly: he was doing Greetje a service, and inquiries as to his resources were unwelcome.

Ona served the raspberry-and-mint tisane that served as tea, and the conversation turned to other things.

Fallon did not take part, nor did she listen to what was being said. She finished her tea, and when Ona came again with the kettle, she placed a restraining hand over her cup. "Thank you, no. I really must be going. Zepporah came down with the grippe late last night, and I really must be getting back."

"Vilhemina did not come vid you?" *Vrouw* Schoonmaker looked shocked.

"Zepporah needed her more than I did," Fallon explained.

"But a pretty younk girl all alone . . . vhy, somethink might happen." She turned to Draegan, who had emerged from the shadows, the better to observe. "Reverent, tell her she must not go off alone, dat it is not fittink!"

"I can tell her, Ona, but I doubt that she will listen. Mistress Deane has a will of her own, and if she has made up her mind to go, then nothing I say can stop her—"

"You needn't discuss me as if I'm not present," Fallon hissed at him, incensed.

Her protest had no effect; he blithely continued: "—and there is but one solution I can think of, *if* the young lady agrees." He paused, and in the interim Fallon uttered an exasperated sigh. "I'll take it upon myself to escort her home."

"There really is no need for this," Fallon said. "It's only a mile to the manor, a pleasant stroll this time of year. There is ample daylight left, and I found my way here unescorted. I can certainly find my way home!"

"Ah," Draegan said, taking her arm in his firm grasp. "I insist."

"De perfect solution!" Ona clasped her plump hands together, beaming. "Fallon, be certain to tell Zepporah ve vill be thinkink about her. Reverent, do take especial care vith our dear Fallon, unt get her home before de *schemerlicht!*"

"Rest assured, dear lady, she will be safe with me, and I shall have her home long before twilight." He bowed low over the Dutch *vrouw's* hand as Ona smiled and Fallon seethed, then he guided her through the door and into the slanting, late-afternoon sunlight.

When they stepped onto the walkway, Draegan gave a low whistle. In a moment Fallon heard the plodding of hooves on soft earth, and the stallion ambled across the millpond yard like a huge white hound.

"Come," Draegan said, "I'll help you up."

But Fallon hung back. "Ride if you like; I'd rather walk."

He frowned at her. "Fallon Deane, you aren't afraid of horses, are you?"

"I am not afraid, specifically," Fallon said, gazing into the distance. The sun's rays were still bright, yet the great bulk of Blue Mountain looming in the near distance seemed hazy, shrouded in mystery. "It's just that I've never been terribly fond of horses. I suppose their size and power intimidate me."

"And then there was your uncle's accident."

"After that I had no wish to ride."

"What became of your uncle's stable?"

"We still have several animals. My mother had a passion for horses, as did Uncle, once. . . . " Her voice trailed away as the stallion shook his head, pressing his nose into Fallon's hand.

"Touch him if you like," Draegan said softly. "He's large, it's true, but relatively harmless."

She tentatively stroked the stallion's muzzle, marveling at its velvety softness. "He's a fine animal. How did you come by him?"

By unspoken agreement he took up the reins and they began walking down South Road. "He's called Banshee, and he was a gift from my father, Edmund."

"Your father is still living?"

"Indeed he is."

"Since you never mentioned him, I just assumed—"

"I don't see my parents often," Draegan interrupted.

"It must be difficult for you, being so far removed from family. Connecticut is far away."

"Not so difficult as you may imagine," he said with a grimace, "and not so far removed. Mother lives in Connecticut with her family, it's true, but Father resides in Albany. He's in the New York Assembly."

Fallon frowned up into his face, shocked by his admission. "They are parted?"

"For several years now," he explained. "Their marriage was always tumultuous, but in the early years they argued violently. Mother was strong-willed, bent on having her own way with everyone, and the moment Father left home on business, she would pack up the children and cart us all off to Connecticut, where we would stay until he came to bring us back again."

"Did he always follow?"

Draegan nodded. "And she always came back to New York once they'd reconciled."

Fallon frowned at him. "But you said you were from Connecticut."

"I was born in New London, on one of Mother's many sojourns," he admitted. "I haven't been back since the war began, but it's probably just as well. Mother has a shrewish bent, and I'm afraid we don't get on well."

"Why, Draegan Mattais! What a harsh thing to say of your mother!"

He smiled slightly. "If it's harsh, then I suppose I must be a harsh man. It's the truth."

Fallon stole a glance at him from under the curve of her lashes. He was a man who seemed to dwell in shadow, infinitely mysterious, closely guarded, and the secrets that he had were well kept. Yet for the moment he seemed almost open, and she was swift to press her advantage. "What else are you?"

His smile deepened into a grin, and his voice, when he replied, was beguiling. "Intrigued, my dear Mistress Deane?"

Fallon's pulse quickened. She remembered the

way in which he'd assessed her in the Schoonmakers' kitchen, recalled his burning glance, and she felt the heat return to her cheeks.

Yet she kept on. "Call it what you will; there is much about you that I find—"

"Titillating?" Draegan supplied roguishly. "Stirring . . . irresistible?"

"*Disturbing*," Fallon said, correcting him.

Draegan placed a hand upon his spotless linen breast and feigned a look of innocence, yet it was apparent from the unwavering light of suspicion in the golden eyes of Fallon Deane that he hadn't quite pulled it off. "I, a simple country cleric, disturbing? Fallon, I am crushed."

"You are not even fazed," she said. "And neither are you a simple country cleric! You play the rogue all too well, sir, for the other role to be convincing!"

"You wish me to don my most sanctimonious Sunday face for your benefit," he said. "How very dull."

"I wish you to be truthful."

"When have I been less than truthful, my lady?"

Fallon cast him a sidelong glance from beneath her lashes. "The untruth you told Cordelia leaps to mind," she said.

Draegan sighed. "You are a difficult woman, Fallon Deane."

"I am curious."

Draegan groaned inwardly. As far as he could tell, "difficult" and "curious" were one and the same. Doubtless she was filled with questions—troublesome, niggling, insignificant questions—questions he must answer with care and discretion if he were to lay her doubts, her innate curiosity, to rest.

He smiled wryly, and steeled himself to withstand the coming inquisition. "I swear, the words *woman* and *curiosity* are synonymous. It began in the Garden with Eve, and man has been in a veritable stew ever since."

She lifted her pert nose and slanted a look at him that was not quite approving. "Had someone bothered to explain matters to Eve, that whole unpleasant incident could have been avoided." She paused, and a tense silence stretched between them. When she spoke again, her tone was level, and it was almost as if they'd never argued. "I believe you mentioned siblings," she said. "How many brothers and sisters do you have?"

"When Mother and Father were together, they were nothing less than prolific. There are nine of us living—there were twelve altogether. Three of my sisters died in infancy. My sister Claire is the firstborn, then came Clayton and Anna, the twins. I'm fourth in order of birth and the second son, followed by Lysander, Christian, Nathan, and Payne. My sister Ardis is the youngest. She just turned sixteen."

Fallon glanced at him and then away, and there was something wistful in her expression. "What is it like, I wonder—to come from such a large family?"

"Noisy," Draegan said. "Chaotic. But never uneventful."

"I used to imagine that Papa would remarry and I would have brothers and sisters."

"But he didn't."

Fallon shook her head. "I don't think he ever quite recovered from losing Mother. She died when I was small. I don't remember her, and Papa rarely mentioned her name in my presence. Uncle Lucien says it was too painful for him. I was thirteen when Papa died. He took a chill, developed a fever in his lungs, and simply slipped away...." She sighed and brushed back a gleaming strand of auburn hair that had escaped her neat chignon and fallen onto her brow. "I don't know what I would have done if not for Uncle Lucien. He has been a constant in my life, and I owe him more than I could ever hope to repay."

They had arrived at the manor, and paused by the garden gate to watch the sun set. The mountains to the west were a hazy lavender, and the sky above was awash with red and gold and soft violet-blue. . . .

Fallon watched the colors deepen, and Draegan watched Fallon. He could not dispute the fact that she owed Lucien Deane a debt. Lucien had taken her in, given her a home and a family of sorts, and in return he received her gratitude, her love, her loyalty. Yet Draegan couldn't help but wonder, as he watched her, just how far that loyalty extended. Was Fallon a party to Lucien's treachery, or was she completely ignorant of it?

She claimed that she didn't like horses and preferred not to ride. But was her reticence genuine, or a clever feint by a wily little vixen specifically designed to throw any pursuing hound off the scent?

Draegan didn't know. He knew only that the figure on the road last night had known the countryside more intimately than he, that he or she had been slight and quick and agile. Concealed beneath tricorn and cloak and abetted by the inky darkness, it could have been a woman—could have been Fallon Deane.

"You are very quiet." Her soft, dulcet voice dragged Draegan from his dark musings into the pastel beauty of the Catskill sunset.

Leaning on the garden gate, he gazed down into her upturned face, and his doubts and suspicions began a slow retreat, leaving him standing in the twilight, a captivating young woman close by his side.

And she was captivating.

He leaned closer, catching the fragrance of lavender that clung to her skin, her hair, drinking it in as he murmured, "Inane chatter in the face of such exquisite beauty seems nothing short of blasphemous."

"It really is a lovely evening, isn't it?"

Draegan took her hand and drew her close. "It wasn't the evening to which I was referring, Fallon. 'Twas you."

She met his gaze, but briefly, before her glance again shied away. "You should not say such things," she said.

"Why not?" he wished to know. "Are you promised to another? You did not answer me before."

"No, I—"

"There is nothing, then, to prevent us." He brought the hand he held to his lips, kissing her fingertips. Turning it over, he pressed his mouth against her palm, and Fallon caught her breath.

His touch was fire—a blessed heat, radiant with life, seething with excitement, everything Fallon remembered and more. She watched his lids lower slightly, masking the hard, bright gleam of his eyes, and she wondered for the thousandth time what it was that drew her to him, why she could not seem to resist the temptation and the imminent peril that were Draegan Mattais.

There was danger in him, of that Fallon was certain. Yet she could not spurn him. She could not snatch back her hand, denying him this liberty, as propriety dictated she should have.

Something kept her from it, kept her standing close to him long after she should have stepped away—so close that she could feel the heat of his body bathing hers in subtle warmth, even through the many layers of their clothing.

What would it be like, Fallon wondered recklessly, to peel away the layers of superfine and linen, of cotton and lawn, and lie pressed against his lean, hard length . . . to feel his arms so strong about her . . . to wake in his embrace?

The direction of her thoughts was new and wondrously exciting.

Titillating . . .

He'd been teasing when he'd said that, but he'd also been correct. He did titillate her senses, her imagination, awakening within her a thirst for adventure she had not realized until this moment that she even possessed. Being with Draegan made her feel vibrantly alive, stirred her to an acute awareness, aroused within her soul a restlessness, a need she couldn't begin to comprehend and that she strongly suspected only he could satisfy.

Wordlessly, he closed what little distance remained between them. His dark head dipped, and Fallon knew that he would kiss her. Her lips parted slightly, and she waited for the searing warmth of his sweet possession, the intimate invasion of his tongue. . . . She waited, but the kiss never came, and when she chanced to look at him again she saw that he had straightened. He was watching a familiar twisted figure emerge from the shadows inside the walled enclosure of the garden.

Garbed in a suit of deep brown worsted, which was ever-so-slightly out of fashion, Lucien Deane came slowly forward. His gait was awkward—sidling, almost—due to the deformity in his spine, which, combined with his emaciated state, lent his figure an air of frailty. "Ah, there you are," he said in his peculiar, creaking voice. "Zepporah has been working herself into a froth this past half-hour for fear that you'd come to grief on your way home. I tried to reassure her that such was not the case, but you know how the woman can be."

"I didn't mean to worry her," Fallon said. "But

the evening was so lovely—I'm afraid I didn't think to hurry home."

" 'Tis no matter, child," Lucien said. "It's easy to see that you were in good hands."

Fallon felt her color rise and was infinitely grateful for the encroaching darkness. "Uncle, this is Reverend Draegan Mattais, our new pastor. Draegan, my uncle, Lucien Deane."

"Master Deane." Draegan inclined his dark head in a shallow bow. "Sir, it is a pleasure to meet you at long last."

Lucien smiled his crooked smile. "I assure you, Reverend Mattais, the pleasure is entirely mine. Fallon has told me a great deal about you, but I am afraid she neglected to mention that you were a connoisseur of horseflesh. An Irish hunter—lud, what a magnificent animal. Long of leg and deep of chest." Lucien sighed appreciatively. "Not planning any excursions to New York City, are you, Reverend? If you are, then take my advice, and leave the lad in the country. I hear that Sir Henry has as avid an eye for a handsome steed as he does for the ladies, and it would be a ruddy shame for you to lose him."

"There is little worry on that score, Master Deane," Draegan replied. "I've no interest in New York City; my present business is here, in Abundance."

"And what business is that, Reverend?"

Draegan smiled as he replied, but there was an underlying chill in his words that Fallon found confusing. "Why, salvation, of course."

Lucien's amber eyes glinted with some secret humor. "Tell me, Reverend Mattais, what think you of conscience? Does it truly exist? Or is it yet another fallacy invented by the early Church to keep the unwashed masses in line?"

"Uncle, please!" Fallon said. "It grows late, and

I'm certain Reverend Mattais would very much like to return home to the rectory."

"Oh, fie, Fallon!" Lucien said. "You spoil all my fun!"

Fallon took her uncle's elbow and bent near his ear. "We have tried these past three years to find a pastor worthy of the name, and now that we have, you wish to hold him at the garden gate to catch his death from chill, discussing conscience!"

Lucien sighed in defeat. "All right, then, miss. You shall have your head." He turned to Draegan. "My niece is appalled that I would keep you from your cozy bed to learn your views on conscience, and to please her I suppose I must relent, but not until I extract a promise that you'll join us for dinner some evening next week. By that time, Zepporah should be sufficiently recovered, and I shall have had ample time to consider which tack I wish to take for our discussion."

"I accept your invitation, sir," Draegan said. "And I greatly anticipate our discussion." Bowing again, he took up the stallion's reins and swung easily astride. "Mistress Deane, Master Deane. Good night to you both." He walked the pale stallion away from the garden gate and was soon gone from sight.

"I suppose I had better go in," Fallon said. "I really should look in on Zepporah before I retire. Are you coming, Uncle?"

"Do go on, my dear, and I'll be along in a little while. I thought perhaps I'd linger in the garden. The moon is on the wane, and it promises to be a fine night for star gazing."

"Good night, then." Fallon bent to kiss her uncle's weathered cheek, then hurried toward the house.

Lucien watched her go, a thoughtful expression on his lined countenance. How very strange that he hadn't truly realized what an exquisite young woman Fallon had become until he'd spied her standing with the handsome young cleric at the garden gate. She was all grown up, the very image of her mother.

At the thought of Sabina, Lucien felt the sluggish stir of emotions long suppressed. Sabina had been exactly Fallon's age when he'd first laid eyes upon her, Lucien thought with a sigh. More than twenty-one years had passed since that day, and the image of her standing with her sister Edith on the village green was still vivid in his mind. They'd been watching old Colonel Henry Brown put the young and untried lads of the newly formed militia company through their paces, and their attention had made Lucien unaccountably nervous. At each misstep he'd made, Sabina had burst into gales of girlish laughter. From that first moment, he'd thought her the most enchanting creature he'd ever seen.

Dear God, he had been so young, and so smitten! So eager to impress her. And for a time he had naively believed that she returned his feelings and would accept his suit.

Saying nothing of his plans to his father or to his younger brother, Osgood, Lucien had traveled to New York City, where he'd purchased a pigeon's-blood ruby ring, a ring he had planned to give to Sabina upon their betrothal. He'd carried it in his breast pocket, close to his heart, all the many miles upriver to Kingston, dreaming of the day when he would bring Sabina to Gilead Manor as his bride.

Smitten, yes, Lucien thought, *he'd been smitten.* Too smitten to see that it was not he whom Sabina loved, but Osgood. Very soon after his return, however, the sad truth of his situation became apparent. Osgood had spoken to Samuel Woods, Sabina's father, who had given his approval to the match, and the preparations had begun in earnest for their wedding the following spring.

Lucien had been devastated; yet there was a small, bitter part of him deep down inside that had not been surprised that the fair Sabina preferred his brother to him.

Osgood, after all, was taller and straighter and more handsome than he. Osgood had a winning personality, a jovial wit, an easiness that was lacking in Lucien. Osgood, Lucien had thought, collected friends, while he himself collected specimens for his studies.

It had seemed only natural that Sabina should love Osgood, who had been given everything in life for which a man could ask. Because he was the younger son, he had wealth without the ever-increasing burden of the estate, he had prestigious friends in Philadelphia, New York, and London, and he had their father's unconditional love.

Lucien had gone on with his life, though he had never quite recovered from Sabina's rejection. Within the year, he had given the pigeon's-blood ruby to Sabina's sister Edith, and they were wed in the library at Gilead Manor.

Edith, like Lucien, was the eldest child, and every bit as plain as Sabina was lovely. She was twenty and five when Lucien took her to wife, and twenty and six when he buried her in the family plot, alongside their stillborn son.

Lucien had not mourned Edith's passing. There had been no time to grow to love her; and the little contentment they had shared, seemed, in the light of her absence, somehow unreal. In their brief time together she had moved through the manor, quiet, shy, and reserved, a shadowy presence that had come into his life without altering it. She had departed it shortly thereafter in the same timorous fashion, leaving only two stone markers in the family plot, one large, one small, as tangible evidence that she had ever touched his life at all.

One month to the day after Edith's passing, Osgood had brought his bride to live beneath his brother's rooftree. At first, it had been painful for Lucien to dwell with Osgood's good fortune when his one chance at happiness had turned to dust, yet as time passed, the pain had eased somewhat, and Lucien had derived a certain pleasure in just being near the vibrant Sabina.

In the second year of Osgood's marriage, Sabina had presented him with a daughter, and Lucien with a niece. At the time of Fallon's birth, Osgood was away in Kingston, and so it was Lucien who paced the floor and prayed to the God he doubted existed, Lucien who received the swaddled infant from Zepporah's hands, Lucien who gazed with wonder into that tiny wrinkled visage and saw the beauty the child would someday achieve.

Four years later, Lucien had stood in the doorway of his brother's bedchamber as Sabina faded, as silent an observer of her death as he had been of her life. Osgood's grief had been terrible, while Lucien had mourned Sabina as he had loved her, unbeknownst to anyone.

The days had passed, the months, the years. Osgood had thrown himself into his political pursuits and traveled extensively. Because of Fallon's tender years, she was often left behind. In her father's absence, she spent her days in Zepporah's care and Lucien's company. Having given his heart to the mother, it was only natural that he adore the child.

As time passed, he thought less and less of Fallon as being Osgood's flesh and blood. In his mind, she was Sabina's, and he indulged her childish whims shamelessly.

Fallon alone had free access to his study, and quite often she interrupted his work to bombard him with endless questions. Her curiosity had always been boundless, her mind quick for a female, and since it pleased him to make of her a pet, Lucien had personally attended her studies.

He had taught her to read and write at an early age, then introduced her to Latin, Greek, and mathematics. By the age of twelve she'd exhausted the classics on Lucien's library shelves, having read Homer's *Iliad* several times through.

In the next year, the year of Osgood's death, she'd moved on to Voltaire, Jean-Jacques Rousseau, and John Locke, and begun displaying a fascination for radical political theory that Lucien found disturbing.

His ties to England had always been strong, and as he began gaining recognition in influential circles for his work in the field of natural philosophy, they quite naturally grew stronger still. In 1773 he met Lord Lovewell Artemis Stone while Stone was visiting the Catskills.

Stone was an English nobleman who, like Lucien, had a passion for learning and a keen interest in botany. In August of 1773 Stone returned to England, but that wasn't the end of his association with Lucien. During the autumn and the early winter months he and Lucien kept up a steady correspondence; by the time spring's gentle hand touched the countryside, Lucien had sought and won Stone's patronage for an ambitious project he had long been planning, in which he would venture into the mountains to collect seedlings and cuttings of plants indigenous to the Catskill Mountains. In turn, the cuttings would be shipped to England for use in the decorative gardens that were currently in vogue with the English peerage.

Lucien sighed, remembering how elated, how certain, he had been that the dark cloud which had cast an ominous shadow over his life for so long was about to dissipate.

But he could not have been more wrong.

On his first day out, his mount was startled by a rattlesnake and plunged into a rocky stream bed, where it lost its footing and fell, rolling onto its rider.

It took the servants two days to devise a litter and carry him back to the manor, and months for his broken body to heal. His dreams of success, of at long last achieving the recognition he deserved in his chosen field, seemed broken beyond repair, and Lucien greatly feared that he would pass from this life leaving nothing behind to prove that he had ever existed.

He began to walk again just as the hostilities, which for years had been simmering between Britain and her colonies, reached a full rolling boil. Lord Stone was among the first to offer his sword to the King, and as a result, the funding that had allowed Lucien to continue his studies without depending upon the estate for an annual income was suddenly withdrawn.

Yet as luck would have it, this was not the end of Lucien's association with the Englishman. Stone was assigned to a post at Fort Niagara in the northwestern wilderness, and after a few months, he contacted Lucien, assuring him that his interest in their joint venture had not died away completely; it had merely been supplanted by the unlawful insurrection being perpetrated against His Majesty the King by his American subjects.

When the hostilities were concluded in England's favor, Stone assured Lucien, they could return to business as usual. Stone's offer, however, was not without cost to Lucien. The Englishman implied that it would be to Lucien's credit if he disassociated himself from the Americans in some noticeable way and proclaimed his unswerving loyalty to the King. . . .

As it happened, Stone's thinly veiled suggestion had spawned Sparrowhawk.

Oh, it had begun innocently enough, Lucien thought, gazing into the star-filled night—a regular correspondence between himself and a Tory named Trumbolt, who resided in the Mohawk Valley, to the north. Trumbolt had connections with Chief Joseph Brant, England's Mohawk ally, and Brant in turn passed the information on to Stone at Niagara, who, with Major John Butler, planned the strikes against the American settlements.

It had all come off so easily, and even Lucien's physical limitations had worked in his favor, for who would have suspected Lucien Deane, studious cripple, of being the infamous spy Sparrowhawk? He quickly learned to utilize his infirmity, and as he grew stronger physically, he was careful to keep his progress hidden behind a mask of pain.

With a sigh, Lucien turned back toward the welcoming lights of the house. As he reached it, his thoughts turned toward Fallon.

If the tender scene he'd interrupted a while earlier at the garden gate was any indication, then the girl was quite fond of the Reverend Mr. Draegan Mattais, and that fondness gave Lucien good cause for concern.

He knew now that Mattais had been the hell rider on the road the night before, but why had the fool been chasing him? What kept him abroad so late? And why had he come from the south, when the rectory lay to the north, between the manor and the village? Was it possible that Fallon was stealing from the manor to meet Mattais secretly? Or was there some other purpose behind the man's seemingly lunatic bent that sent him thundering after phantoms in the black hours of the night?

Lucien did not know, but as he ambled through the shadowy garden, he was exceedingly glad that he'd had the foresight to invite the young rector to dinner. They did indeed have a great many things to discuss.

Chapter 8

The grave was situated at the far corner of the churchyard. Sheltered by the spreading limbs of the sentinel maple, the mound measured six feet by three, and still had the raw look of freshly turned earth. Time was said to heal all wounds, and time alone would serve to soften the harshness of the scene. In years to come, the green grasses would crowd close, and tender shoots would find a firm purchase in the rocky ground. The violets Jacob had just finished planting at the foot of the crude wooden cross would take root and flower, lending a touch of beauty to the dismal scene, but nothing, nothing, could dispel the anger and the bitterness that filled Draegan each time he saw the wooden cross with the name *Youngblood* scratched into its rough surface.

As he drew near, his shadow crept across the grave, across the caretaker, who shaded a furrowed brow with a grimy hand in order to stare up at Draegan. "Reverend," Jacob said. "Headed out to hunt for Sparrowhawk, are ye?"

Draegan's mouth curved slightly. "In a manner of speaking," he said. "Lucien Deane has invited me to dine with him and his lovely niece, and I have accepted."

"The magistrate? Beggin' yer pardon, sir, but do ye think that's wise? Master Deane never was one to socialize. If he's asked ye to sup, then he must want somethin' from ye."

"What Master Deane wants is to take my measure, in order to ascertain if I am fitting to keep company with his niece."

"Mistress Fallon?" Jacob said with a look of sudden concern.

Draegan adjusted his cuffs inside his coat sleeves and his smile tightened. "Indeed, Mistress Fallon, the auburn-haired bookworm. I had the pleasure of seeing her home one evening last week, and while I was bidding her a good night, her reclusive uncle appeared from the depths of the garden. His timing, I must say, was very fortuitous, for the exchange he witnessed piqued his interest and won me an invitation to dine."

"Ye're moving into dangerous waters, Reverend. Lucien Deane's a wily one, and strong willed, for all that he's a cripple. If he thinks for a minute that ye've got a mind to harm Miss Fallon, he'll likely be having ye for dinner."

"I thank you for the warning, Jacob. And I shall be sure to keep it in mind." He paused, and when he spoke again the amusement in his voice had been replaced by a thread of melancholy. "Why do you insist on tending that cursed plot? Surely it has served its purpose. Those involved that night believe that Major Youngblood is dead. So what matter does it make if it grows rife with weeds?"

Jacob clambered to his feet, but he had difficulty meeting Draegan's gaze. "It matters to me, sir. I ain't been able to forget for a single minute the reason behind this here plot. Call it a sort of penance, if ye will, or just an old man's foolishness, but this here's hallowed ground, a monument to a grievous wrong that ought never to be forgotten!''

Draegan sighed but said nothing as he absently massaged his throbbing thigh.

Jacob noticed, and he seemed abashed at his vehemence of a moment ago. "Are ye certain ye're feeling up to this? Ye could always send a message, and sup with the Deanes some other time."

"Lucien Deane might think the better of it and withdraw his invitation. I cannot risk it, Jacob. Besides, I'm fine."

It was an outright lie, meant to pacify Jacob, who still wore that look of concern. He was not fine. The wound troubled him. Fallon troubled him. Everything about this accursed assignment troubled him. And he could seemingly do little more than continue on as he had been doing, watching the manor, haunting the darkened road that led into the village in the hope that he would come upon someone or something that would lead him to Sparrowhawk.

Yet tonight all his efforts seemed futile, and he was having a great deal of difficulty dragging the sainted facade of the Reverend Draegan Mattais about him. "We all must do penance of a sort at one time or another, mustn't we, Jacob? Yours is to tend an empty grave; mine is seemingly to dwell in an endless state of frustration, to smile benevolently down upon my flock each Sabbath morning, to seek to charm the lovely Fallon Deane, and all the while plotting her uncle's downfall . . . his death."

"Are ye certain ye're all right, Reverend?"

"It is this place," Draegan said, gesturing toward the grave, "this situation. Everything is so much more complex than I ever imagined it would be. Lucien Deane is not at all what I expected. Somehow, I did not imagine him as being so frail, despite his niece's references to his limitations, and then there is the congregation—" He broke off, shaking his head. "God help them all, they have come to depend upon me."

He made a noise of disgust, at himself, mostly, and deliberately turned the conversation away from his own moral dilemmas. "That isn't why I sought you out. Before I go, I wished to know the news from Sike's Tavern. What do you know of Quill and his bully boys?"

At the mention of the militia captain, Jacob spat. "He come by the other evening with a belly full o' whiskey and spoilin' for a fight. Tom Neelly was with 'im, and Jack Mills, but most of the boys have drifted away. It ain't no militia these days, and from what I've heard, Quill's out of town more'n he's in. I asked what for, and was told that it was 'business.' "

"Yes, but what manner of business?" Draegan wondered aloud. "Our friend Quill did not strike me as being intelligent enough to strike out on his own."

"You 'spose the cap'n's found a partner?" Jacob asked.

"A partner—that does seem a likelihood. Yet I'm given to wonder what sort of man would link his fortune with that of Randall Quill, and to what end they are striving. Interesting," Draegan murmured, pulling out his timepiece. It was half-past six, time to go. "You've given me a great deal to think about, Jacob. Keep me informed, will you?"

"Aye, sir. I'll do that, and may God be with you this evenin', Reverend."

Draegan turned, and without a word he walked slowly toward the small barn where Banshee waited. Jacob's God was consistent, an ever-present source of light and hope. Draegan's God was a doubtful deity with a macabre sense of humor who had left him to the wolves in the chapel sanctuary on a stormy night one year before—not a great, benevolent power to whom he could turn in times of trouble. Indeed, there were times when he doubted His existence at all, times when he stood at the pulpit, looking down at the faces of the believers, Fallon Deane among them, and felt that he would choke on his own hypocrisy. . . .

Draegan arrived at Gilead Manor in a timely fashion and was greeted by the saucy Miss Wilhemina Rhys. "Ye're lookin' fit this evenin', Reverend, sir, if ye don't mind my sayin' so."

"Why, thank you, Willie," Draegan said. "Has Mistress Deane come down yet?"

"Half an hour ago," Willie whispered. "She sent me out to watch for you, and said to show you in the moment you arrived."

"Nothing's amiss, I hope," Draegan said. "Master Deane hasn't taken ill?"

Willie shook her mobcapped head. "Miss Fallon's beau has come unexpectedly to call, and when Mr. Deane learned of it, he invited him to stay."

"How very fortunate," Draegan said with more enthusiasm than he felt. "I shall take great pleasure in making her young man's acquaintance."

Willie pulled a face. "I wouldn't count on that if I were ye. The pleasure part, that is." She bobbed a quick curtsy and turned back down the hallway, leaving Draegan standing in the open parlor doorway.

Full dark was an hour hence, yet the beeswax tapers had been lit, bathing the parlor and its occupants in a warm golden light, which set off to perfection Fallon's peach-bloom complexion.

She was seated on a divan of rose damask, her spreading skirts arranged elegantly around her, and it was obvious that she had dressed with great care that evening. Draegan's gaze warmed as it traveled slowly over her, and an appreciative smile tilted the corners of his mouth.

The gown she wore was fashioned of gold-and-green-striped Mantua silk, a fitting foil for her flaming autumnal beauty. The tight-fitting bodice and elbow-length sleeves set off her willowy form to perfection; the décolleté neckline was fashionably low—*daring*, almost—yet her sense of propriety had seemingly prevailed over fashion's dictates, for she'd drawn a fine lawn fichu about her shoulders and knotted it with care in front, concealing the ripe curves of her bosom. The effect was endearingly feminine and typically, enchantingly, Fallon.

Smiling softly, a rosy bloom high upon her lovely cheeks, she appeared more radiant, more strikingly beautiful, than any woman of Draegan's vast acquaintance, and he couldn't help but feel a pang as he wondered if the young man seated next to her, his back to the door, was the cause of her radiance.

This thought should not have troubled Draegan greatly. Yet for some unfathomable reason it did trouble him. Indeed, it made him angry—angry at her young man for his impossibly poor timing, angry at Fallon for looking so lovely. But most of all it made him angry at himself for his inability to remain unaffected by her. The very sight of her set his blood to pounding in his temples; her slightest smile cast doubt upon his doubts.

How could he trust her?

How could he not?

For a moment he stood in the doorway, torn between his desires and his instinctive wariness. In that moment, Fallon raised her eyes to meet his, and something kindled in their dark golden depths.

"Draegan," she said, "I did not see you there. Won't you come in?"

Draegan started forward, and at the same time Fallon's young man came to his feet, turning.

The flat blue eyes and florid face, the curly fair hair and the air of self-importance—all were shockingly familiar. Draegan felt the cold, dark fury, conceived in cruelty and injustice on a bitter storm-swept night a year before, rear its ugly head and stir to life inside him. It screamed for retribution, swift and sure, and it took every ounce of self-control that he possessed to keep his bland expression firmly in place, to feign a polite disinterest as his hostess introduced him to his would-be executioner.

"Randall," Fallon said, "this is the Right Reverend Draegan Mattais. Draegan, Randall Quill."

Quill extended his hand, and Draegan reluctantly took it. To refuse would only have aroused suspicion, though he couldn't help thinking that he'd have far rather wrapped his hands around the pompous bastard's throat than to participate in this gentlemanly show of civility. "Sir," Randall said. "Fallon has told me a great deal about you."

Draegan shifted his gaze to Fallon, and he allowed a slight and very satisfied smile to curve his lips. "Really? How very gratifying. I must confess, though, that it puts me at somewhat of a loss, for in all of our considerable dealings she has not mentioned *you*."

Quill reddened. "Yes, well, I've been out of town for several days on business, and I only just returned this afternoon. Quite naturally, I came to pay my respects to Fallon." He bestowed on Fallon a look that spoke of utter confidence in his claim upon her affections.

Draegan clenched his teeth. "Military business," he inquired softly, "or something more self-serving?"

Randall stiffened, sensing the barb couched in the smoothly uttered words, yet seemingly unable to pinpoint its source. "I am not sure I know what you mean."

Draegan was about to reply, when Fallon hastened to intervene. "I'm certain Draegan meant no offense, Randall. He was only expressing a polite interest in your remark. *Isn't that so, Reverend?*"

She glared at Draegan and saw his smile deepen, growing slightly wicked, and the demons that drove him so mercilessly sprang forth to dance in his eyes. "Our dear Mistress Deane is correct, of course. I meant no offense. It's just that I can't help but wonder what manner of trade you are conducting. It's my understanding that since the war began nearly every legitimate aspect of commerce has been curtailed."

Quill drew down his brows and looked hard and long at Draegan. " 'Tis odd," he said, uncharacteristically allowing the slight against him to pass unchallenged, "but you look somehow familiar. And I have had the impression since you entered the room that we have met before."

"I can't recall ever laying eyes on you before this evening, and I daresay I'd recall such a face as yours." He pretended deep concentration. "Harvard College, perhaps?"

Randall glowered. "I've never been to Harvard College—or to any other, for that matter. It must have been elsewhere."

"*Indeed?*" Draegan muttered wryly to himself. "*I never would have guessed it.* You seem such a bright young man." And then, aloud, "If not Harvard, then it must have been Connecticut. I've family in New London. They used to be in shipping, yet since the war most have turned to privateering."

Randall grew red in the face. "Impossible. I'm a New York man, born and bred, and I have as little truck as possible with Connecticut Yankees!"

Draegan's lids lowered over eyes that burned fever-bright, but his tone was decidedly lazy. "That leaves the church, Captain, but since you've been sinfully remiss in attending Sunday service . . ."

Quill's sandy brows lowered over eyes gone suddenly suspicious. "How is it that you know my rank, when Fallon made no mention of it just now?"

"Did she not? Well, I suppose I must have heard it elsewhere."

"Elsewhere."

Draegan's smile faded. He was the hunted no longer, wounded, outnumbered and weak, and in his present black humor he didn't give a damn if Quill connected him with the ill-fed scarecrow Major Youngblood. The truth of his situation was too fantastic, and the militia captain doubtless would not have believed the facts if confronted with them. In any case, Draegan had grown bored with baiting him, when he had larger, more clever fish to fry.

As if on cue, the odd, distinctive voice of Lucien Deane issued from the doorway. "Fallon, my dear. You are looking exceptionally lovely this evening. Gentlemen."

Quill came to his feet as Draegan bowed to his host; Fallon rose to kiss the elder man's weathered cheek. "Uncle, I was just about to come and find you. I feared you'd become immersed in your studies and completely forgotten our guests."

"I was making notes on Joshua's cat's-eye theory. I've a mind to test it myself, if I can just find a willing participant. I'm afraid my preoccupation has made me fashionably late," Lucien said with a rusty laugh, "but I am certain our guests will forgive an old man's temporary lapse. Alas, there are times when passion overcomes all else, a point with which I am sure our guests both agree. But then, I rattle on. Best not to discuss my studies in company." He nodded to Randall and Draegan in turn. "Randall, you are looking well. Reverend Mattais, how good of you to join us. I hope you are feeling up to a rousing discussion."

"Indeed, sir," Draegan replied, "I cannot tell you how I have anticipated this evening."

"Very good," Lucien said. "Then let's get down to it, shall we? If you will be so kind as to escort my niece to table, Reverend?"

Draegan crossed to Fallon and offered his arm, and for the space of a heartbeat Fallon hesitated, searching instead his darkly angelic countenance, trying to grasp the unsettling undercurrents that swirled all around her.

Something was happening here tonight that she couldn't comprehend—a drama in which the enigmatic young gentleman who offered his arm played a significant part. She'd closely observed him with Randall. Every word he'd uttered to the militia captain had been shot through with a soft-voiced scorn, and Fallon had the distinct impression that his disdain for Quill stemmed from more than a mild dislike. In fact, it was clear that Draegan Mattais loathed Randall Quill.

Yet why should he have had such a strong reaction to a man whom he claimed he had never met?

"Your uncle is waiting," Draegan said to her softly. Then, more softly still, "Perhaps you would rather Captain Quill escorted you to dinner."

She flushed slightly, and dutifully laid her hand on the curve of his elbow, feeling the wondrous heat of him through his coat sleeve.

"What were you thinking just now?"

Fallon glanced first at Randall, who had fallen into step beside Lucien several paces ahead, then up at Draegan. "I was wondering . . . about you and Randall."

He pulled a face. "The dashing and wildly courageous Captain Quill."

"You hate him, don't you?" Fallon said bluntly.

"Hate is such an ugly word, and I daresay the teachings of Christ do not allow for hatred of one's fellow man in one of His disciples."

"But the teachings of Christ do allow for one of His disciples to own and use a brace of large-bore pistols."

He looked at her then, a half-amused, half-searching look, and sighed. "You are far too observant for your own good, *or for mine,* as it would seem."

"Fie, sir! Do not make it sound as if I had intentionally rifled through your personal effects! You sent me to your chamber to find the brandy for poor dear Cordelia, which I did. It isn't my fault that you left them lying there in the open!"

"I almost wish that you had," he said, his pale eyes glinting in his tawny face. "Rifled through my belongings, that is. It would indicate an interest in me, in my life."

"I am quite naturally interested in your well-being," Fallon countered. "I am also interested in the weapons we were discussing. They seem quite serviceable, and I can't help wondering why a man in your position would feel the need to be armed with one pistol, let alone two."

"Questions," she heard him mutter to himself, "always questions." Then, "Faith, Fallon, that isn't the sort of interest to which I was referring, and you know it."

He covered her hand with his free one, his elegant fingers sliding around hers, squeezing gently.

"Have I told you how lovely a home you have here?"

"You always seem to tell me what I don't wish to know, and neatly manage to sidestep what I do. Why is that, I wonder?"

"Fallon," he said. "You fairly wear me out with your questions. If you don't relent, I shall be forced to say good night to your uncle and leave you to badger Captain Quill."

"But that would be terribly rude," Fallon replied. "Besides, you cannot go until you have satisfied my curiosity."

"Dear God in Heaven," he said, casting a pleading glance at the ceiling. "I feel yet another barrage of queries coming on."

"Regrettably, there is time for only one. Answer it, and I shall relent. You have my word on it."

"Pray God it is something simple. Well, then, go on. Ask me."

"What was going on in the parlor between you and Randall?"

"I'm not sure I know what you mean," he said, looking too innocent for Fallon to believe him.

It was a look she'd seen before, one that he hoped would help allay her suspicions. This time, it did not serve him as well as it had in the past. "You know precisely what I mean, sir. Randall felt that you had met before."

"And there is a simple explanation for it."

"Which is?"

"Captain Quill is an idiot."

Fallon smiled at his soft-voiced assessment of Randall, and for the moment, she let the subject drop.

Willie and Zepporah brought heaping platters of roast venison to the table, thinly sliced and accompanied by a rich gravy. Baked squash, onions in

cream, and fresh bread with sweet butter rounded
out the fare.

Good food had a way of lightening the gloomiest
outlook, and Fallon hoped the delicious fare would
help mellow the mood at table. That hope was
short-lived, however, for just as the plates were being cleared away and the Indian pudding served,
Lucien fixed Draegan with his bright amber gaze.
"Was the meal to your liking, Reverend?"

Draegan's reply was smooth. "It was indeed, sir.
In fact, it's the finest fare I've had in quite some
time. My compliments to Mrs. Rhys."

Lucien looked pleased. "Excellent. Are you comfortable, sir? More wine, perhaps?"

Draegan smiled. "Thank you, no. My glass is
nearly full."

"Well, then," Lucien said. "If you are quite certain there's nothing else you require, you won't
mind if we begin our discussion. There are several
issues I wish to take up with you, concepts that I
have pondered at length in the past." He pressed
his fingertips together, forming a tent with his
hands. With his chin lightly touching his fingertips,
he surveyed Draegan carefully. "What think you,
Reverend? Is there truly life after death?"

Lucien's question was punctuated by Fallon's
impatient sigh. "Now, miss," Lucien said. "None
of that! Reverend Mattais is not only my honored
guest, he is a willing captive. And I intend to take
shameful advantage of that fact. God knows when
I'll have another such opportunity to match wits
with one so willing."

"But, Uncle, you promised!" Fallon chided.

"I promised to be on my best behavior, and I
have kept my word implicitly. Why, I've yet to
goad the man—not even the smallest bit! I merely
put to him a legitimate question, and one I myself
as a scholar have pondered at length." He turned

his impish gaze on Draegan. "Never mind my niece, sir. The question."

"Well, sir, the Scripture says—" Draegan began, but Lucien interrupted.

"Scripture, pah! Put aside your Bible for the duration of the evening, Reverend. I wish to know what *you* think!"

Draegan smiled, but there was no warmth in the expression. "Since I have not passed on recently, I cannot say with any certainty."

Lucien pulled a face. "You forfeit too easily. However, I'd like to propose another topic, one we broached last week at the garden gate and might have pursued, had Fallon not insisted that I not keep you. . . . "

Fallon glanced at Lucien, whose amber eyes fairly gleamed with mischief. He was enjoying himself immensely, Fallon thought. Like a child with a new toy, he had found someone with whom he might match wits, an adversary worthy of the name.

Seated on Lucien's left, Randall looked bored, and for the most part he sat quietly, swirling the dregs of his wine in his glass. Yet every now and again, he raised his gaze to the impassive face of Draegan Mattais and frowned, as though the puzzle of where he had glimpsed the other man continued to plague him.

It plagued Fallon as well. The soft musical chink of silver on fine china plate, the polite discourse to which she was an interested observer, all were strangely at odds with the tension in the room—a tension that seemed to eddy and swirl around the dark-haired young cleric.

Fallon watched Draegan intently. Was Randall right in his assumption that he and Draegan Mattais had met before? Was the animosity between them more than an instinctive and immediate dislike? Would she ever understand Draegan Mattais? Or would he always be a mystery?

"I wish to know about conscience," Lucien was saying. "Can you define it for me?"

"Child's play," Draegan replied. "Conscience is that inner voice, a guiding beacon toward the light, which alone separates man from the lowly beasts."

Lucien stroked his chin while musing aloud. "Proper, cautious, noncommittal. Anything less and I would have been disappointed in you; however, your answer raises yet another question."

Draegan's pale gaze came to rest on Fallon, and he smiled his enigmatic smile. The smile was slight and never touched his eyes, yet it warmed Fallon considerably. "It seems that you and your lovely niece have much in common. You are both articulate, keenly intelligent, and brimming over with questions."

Lucien cackled softly. "How astute of you to notice. Fallon and I are as companionable as two peas in a pod. We both enjoy a rousing discussion, believe that learning comes through curiosity, and know an attempt at evasion when we see one. So, sir, since you can see that you are neatly caught, I shall ask of you this: if indeed conscience is what separates man from beasts, and we all possess conscience in equal measure, how do you account for men like that nefarious fellow Sparrowhawk?"

At the mention of the spy's name Fallon gasped and Randall choked on his wine. Draegan alone gave no indication he was upset, and he turned a bland face to his host. "There is no accounting for inherent evil."

Lucien threw Draegan a superior look. "Ah, here it is! The perfect opportunity to drag out that oft-used cliché about Lucifer's being at the root of all evil."

"Hardly. Lucifer, like Sparrowhawk, had good

beginnings. He began his career as an angel, you know, not the terrible fellow they make him out to be. Indeed, his biggest crime was that of ambition. He wanted more than he had."

Lucien slowly nodded. "And so he changed allegiances, from God to himself."

"That is the way I see it."

"Refreshing," Lucien said. "But how can you possibly link the poor, much-maligned Lucifer with Sparrowhawk?"

Draegan chuckled low. "I would think it would be obvious. Ambition and reason. When combined, the two can often drown out the distressed cries of the conscience, permitting certain individuals to turn a deaf ear to the inner voice that discerns good from evil, to rationalize larceny, immorality, even murder, so long as they suit his will." He turned from Lucien, fixing the militia captain with his burning gaze, and the air around them fairly crackled. "Would you not agree, Captain Quill?"

Randall glowered at Draegan. "I'll not be dragged into your nonsensical discussion, sir. Sparrowhawk, conscience! What has it to do with any of us?"

"I am deeply sorry if our discussion upsets you," Draegan said with that same chilly smile and burning look. "And I sincerely hope that there is nothing weighing heavily on your own conscience, Captain—no dark deed that keeps you sleepless in your bed at night. Yet if by chance there *is* something that troubles your soul, I should mention that I would be glad to council you. 'Tis often said that 'confession is good for the soul.' "

Randall's red face grew redder still. "I haven't the slightest idea what you are babbling about, sir."

"Haven't you?" Draegan asked. His face was still carefully bland, yet Fallon detected a thread of malice in his voice, an underlying threat. She frowned.

"Then more's the pity that you are to die unredeemed, for no man is without sin."

Randall seemed about to burst a vein. Fallon looked to Lucien for aid. If anyone could have diffused the volatile situation, it was he. "Uncle," she said pointedly, "perhaps you should tell us about your current project. I am certain both Draegan and Randall are most eager to hear the details."

"And spoil the evening's entertainment?" Lucien's expression was one of incredulity. "My dear, this is the most fun I've had in years. We really must have guests more often. Randall, lad, the reverend and I are waiting."

Randall shot from his chair. "And you may wait until bloody hell freezes over, the both of you! I've had my fill of death and sin and conscience, and will not play games to appease your madness." He turned to Fallon. "Might I have a private word with you before I go?"

But Fallon was in no mood to accommodate him. "I think it best if I remain," she said, reaching for the small silver bell near her right hand. She rang it once, and in a moment, Willie appeared.

"Yes, miss?"

"Captain Quill is leaving us," Fallon said. "Would you be so good as to bring his coat?"

"My pleasure, miss." Willie bobbed a quick curtsy and hurried off. In a moment she returned, coat in hand. "Would ye like me to help ye on with it, Cap'n?"

"Thank you, no," Randall snapped. "I can manage quite nicely on my own." He shrugged into his coat, snatching the tricorn from Willie's hands and jamming it onto his head. "I vow I'll not rest until I remember just who the devil you are," he told Draegan. Then he spun on his booted heel and stalked from the room.

Draegan smiled as he watched him go, and his

smile was chilly and secretive. "I vow that you won't rest once you do," he murmured to himself.

Fallon released the breath she'd been holding. "If you gentlemen will excuse me, I think I'll say good night."

Lucien leaned forward in his chair. "Feeling peevish, my dear?"

Fallon forced a weary smile. "A slight headache, nothing more. With a good night's rest, I shall be fine." But it was not the subtle ache that had blossomed in her temples that prompted her to withdraw from company; it was the maelstrom of emotion churning inside her. Never before had she been so angry, so concerned, so confused, and the handsome young minister who watched her with his unwavering stare, who gallantly rose when she rose, was at the root of it all.

Randall had gone; the danger had passed. Yet Fallon desperately needed the peace and the quiet calm of her chamber in order to think. She could not seem to think clearly in the minister's presence. "Good night, Uncle. Reverend Mattais."

"Mistress Deane," Draegan said. "I hope you recover quickly." Fallon nodded, then walked out of the room. Draegan heard the sound of her footfalls slowly fade, and he turned back to his host. "Well, it seems the evening has ended, and I really should be going."

"So soon?" Lucien asked. "I was rather hoping that you would linger awhile, say, over an excellent glass of port or two?"

"Your offering is tempting—"

"It isn't often I get the opportunity to tempt an emissary of God," Lucien said thoughtfully. "I find I rather like the notion. Do you smoke, Reverend?"

"On occasion."

"Good. I have some very fine Virginia leaf tucked away as well, and you know how impossible it is to come by since the war began."

"You, sir, are an excellent hand at temptation. You have made it quite hard for me to resist," Draegan said.

"Then you will stay and chat?"

In silent reply, Draegan sank into his chair.

Lucien rose and sidled to the far side of the board to ring the bell. In a moment Wilhemina Rhys appeared. "Bring the port, Willie, and the tobacco."

The girl bobbed her mobcapped head. "Will there be anything else, sir?"

"That will be all. And do close the doors behind you."

Willie returned in a moment with the requested items, then discreetly took her leave. Lucien poured the wine, and raised his glass to Draegan. "To your health, sir."

"And yours." Draegan sipped the wine and waited. He had met men like Lucien Deane before and had little doubt that as a lad he'd occupied himself by pulling the wings from helpless flies. So Draegan could only wonder if, since Quill had gone, he himself was now to provide the entertainment. Or was there some other, hidden motive behind the invitation to stay?

He did not have long to wait. Lucien offered Draegan a long-stemmed clay pipe; then, taking a leaf from a box fashioned from teak and inlaid ivory, he crushed it into his own bowl. A tiny silver box, which held two small live coals, had been placed between them, along with a pair of tongs. Lucien plied the implements to ignite the leaf and settled back to smoke while he considered his guest. "How is it, sir, that a man of your physical attributes and advanced age is still unwed?"

The question was not what Draegan had expected. Yet he was coming to believe that with Lucien Deane, one could accurately predict precious little and should, as a rule, expect the unexpected. Taking up the tongs, Draegan puffed the pipe alight before answering. "What an odd question. Why do you wish to know?"

"Simple curiosity," Lucien replied, a shade too innocently. "I knew a cleric once with a proclivity for pretty young lads, but I am assuming from what I witnessed last week at the garden gate that your tastes are more acceptable, and somewhat less exotic than that."

"A man would need be blind to overlook your niece's charms," Draegan said, unwilling to rise to Lucien's bait.

"There is very little that you fail to observe, isn't that so, Reverend?"

"God hath given me five senses, Master Deane. Six, if one counts intuition. To fail to employ them would be shameful."

"You like high living, despite your holy trappings," Lucien said. "You like taking risks. That's why you ride that devil white."

"You believe I am ungenuine?" Draegan feigned a wounded look.

"I have yet to decide precisely *what* you are. But I give you fair warning where Fallon is concerned. I'm more than passing fond of the child, and I would not be at all pleased to see her brought to grief."

"Begging your pardon, sir," Draegan said, "but she is hardly a child. At twenty she's a woman, with a mind of her own." He laid down his pipe and rose to go. "It might be wise to allow her to make her own decisions—and her own mistakes."

"Just heed my advice, Reverend. I would so hate to see you leave this position in disgrace. And then there's the fact that the villagers need you. Clerics are hard to come by these days. Oh, and Reverend?"

Draegan turned back at the door.

"Do try to avoid the chill night air in the future. You truly are liable to catch your death."

The air was still and oddly silent when Draegan returned to the rectory that same night, devoid of the chorus of tree frogs and cicadas that normally commenced with the sunset and went on ceaselessly until the dawn. Nothing moved. Nothing stirred. The world seemed to be waiting, holding its breath. . . .

The low rumble of distant thunder sounded beyond the Blue Mountain as Draegan dismounted, causing the very earth to tremble underfoot. Banshee sidled uneasily and tossed his sleek head, dragging the reins from his master's grasp and ambling toward Jacob Deeter, who hurried across the churchyard to take the white in hand.

Jacob tugged at the brim of his hat, and there was no misreading the look of relief in his eyes. "I was beginnin' to worry that ye wouldn't make it back—before the storm, I mean to say. Looks like a bad one brewin'. Why don't ye go on in. I'll see the lad, here, bedded down."

Draegan didn't reply, and Jacob didn't press him.

Theirs was an odd alliance. They had begun as adversaries that night in the church. Jacob had been sent to find the rope meant to end Draegan's life, but in a moment of remorse he had become his salvation. Jacob had hidden him in the caretaker's shack those first few desperate days, when he'd hovered somewhere between life and perdition. Jacob had dug the grave, keeping the truth from Quill, and nursed Draegan back to health. Jacob had helped him make his way to Albany. Jacob alone knew all of Draegan's demons by name, and when the black moods came over him and he struggled to stay afloat in his dark sea of fury, Jacob dutifully left him alone.

That night, of all nights, Draegan was grateful to the caretaker for respecting his privacy.

Without a word, he turned and went into the rectory. Like the night without, his quarters were silent . . . broodingly so. His footfalls echoed as he made his way to the hearth and took down the lantern, lighting it with a sliver of kindling that had recently been added to the fire burning low in the grate.

When he straightened, Draegan stared at the chair where he usually took his ease. Tonight he shunned it. The ache in his thigh was nearly intolerable, yet he felt too edgy, too restless, to sit.

And so he wandered, slowly, from room to room, not pausing his restless roaming until he found himself standing before the altar in the chapel sanctuary.

"Thou preparest a table in the presence of mine enemies; thou anointest my head with oil; my cup runneth over," he said with a dark, humorless laugh, his gaze drawn to the cross that hung behind the altar. "I have indeed supped with my enemies this evening, and my cup was filled to the brim with bitter gall."

He spoke more to himself than to any deity, but the sound of his voice did little to ease the tension that hung in the air. Nothing could lessen his searing frustration.

The evening had taken a heavier toll on him than even he had realized. Sharing a table with Randall Quill, seeing him speak familiarly with Fallon, looking into the face that he saw in his nightmares and striving to hold his hatred in check had proven a Herculean effort—more, almost, than he had been able to bear.

And then there was Lucien, who liked to toy, cat and mouse, with everyone around him. Lucien, who seemed to feel himself omnipotent, superior in intellect to all other beings. Lucien, who relished his charade as much as Draegan detested his. And Draegan was beginning to suspect that Lucien's frailty was a charade.

Was Draegan the only one to see through it, the only one to recognize the malignancy of the magistrate's spirit?

Had Lucien been the one on the road that night? The one Draegan had tried to run to ground? The one who'd framed him that night in the church a year before?

Was Lucien Deane Sparrowhawk?

All of Draegan's instincts told him that he was. Yet he could not prove it, and he still hadn't a clue as to how Lucien Deane had managed to slip past him in the church the night of the hanging and disappear without being heard, without being seen.

For months he had lived with the phantom image of Sparrowhawk, had tried to solve the mysteries surrounding the man's disappearance that night. For months he had felt the frustration of trying to reason it all through, until he was sick to death of thinking of it. Sick and consumed by a feeling of impotence, because he could not let it go.

That night his frustration climbed to perilous levels, welling up from the depths of Draegan's soul to fill him while images flashed unbidden in his mind's eye. *Lucien presiding over the table, watching with undisguised glee as Draegan goaded Randall and Randall's anger flared.* Images of Fallon that filled his days and haunted his nights. *Fallon standing at the garden gate, her small face tipped up as she awaited his kiss. Fallon, with her sweet, tempting innocence, her ti-*

gress eyes, her ruby lips. Fallon, who had smiled so graciously upon Quill, the man Draegan hated above all others. Quill looming over the high-backed wooden pew in this very chapel, his round face swollen with power, while the cross gleamed dully behind his left shoulder . . .

In that instant, the burden of Draegan's masquerade, his impotence and rage, his unquenched thirst for vengeance, the tension that coiled so tightly inside him, clamored for an instant, violent release.

Outside, there was a loud sizzle and a deafening crack. Blinding blue-white light and pulsing energy filled the sanctuary, surging over Draegan, unleashing the demons that earlier that evening had driven him to bait Randall Quill.

The heavy walnut Bible stand was close at hand. Before he could stop himself, he picked it up and hurled it with all of his strength at the cross.

The rest happened slowly, as if in a dream. The Bible stand struck the cross with the sound of splintering wood . . . the cross tumbled to the floor, revealing a small lever affixed to the wall . . . and with a soft, almost imperceptible groan, the left portion of the paneled wall swung slowly inward.

Chapter 9

Seated in the middle of the bed, pillows at her back and quilts drawn close beneath her chin, Fallon listened to the howl of the rising wind. More than an hour had passed since she'd fled the dining hall for the comparative peace and solitude of her bedchamber, and in that time her mind had trudged around and around the same worn track.

Draegan, Draegan, Draegan. Try as she might, she could not get him out of her head. *Draegan, man of God, champion of the weak, comforter to the sick, confessor and spiritual guide. Draegan the rogue. Dangerous, beguiling, mysterious Draegan . . .*

Oh, how he plagued her! Invading her dreams, sleeping and waking, slipping wraithlike into her thoughts at the most inopportune moments—distracting her, robbing her of her ability to concentrate, driving her mad!

There were times when she was convinced that he possessed some strange power to control her thoughts, to manipulate her desires, to bend her effortlessly to his will. There were times when she felt that he was more the Devil's emissary than God's. And then, unexpectedly, she would catch a fleeting glimpse of yet another side of this multifaceted man, and all of her previous conclusions about his motives, about Draegan himself, would instantly be blown to bits.

Time and again it had happened. That day weeks earlier at *Vrouw* Schoonmaker's when he'd kissed her by the millpond, when he'd lied to Cordelia, when she'd searched for the salts in the rectory cupboard and found the brace of pistols—and that very evening at dinner.

Randall had vowed that he would not rest until he remembered who Draegan was and how he knew him. But it had been Draegan's cryptic reply that had chilled her blood, staying with her long after she'd left him alone with Lucien.

I vow that you won't rest once you do.

The comment seemed a clear indication that Randall had indeed crossed paths with Draegan before, despite Draegan's reluctance to admit it either to her or to Randall. Yet where? And why the cryptic reply? Why the seething hatred she'd seen in the fathomless depths of his pale green eyes?

Outside, the storm battered the house. Lightning blasted the earth not far away, punctuated by a deafening crack, and the first wind-borne gust lashed the dark glass of the windows.

Fallon shifted restlessly. The bed was warm and cozy, yet it held little appeal. The direction of her thoughts had made her edgy and, when combined with the ferocious storm, seemed destined to keep her from sleep.

What she needed was something to occupy her thoughts, something other than Draegan Mattais! Something to keep all of her unanswered questions at bay. Throwing back the covers, she slipped into her flannel wrapper, then padded barefoot from the room.

There were documents in the library that wanted transcribing, a letter from Lucien to his friend Master Trumbolt and several other pieces of correspondence, enough to keep her occupied until she was too weary to think.

With a determined lift of her chin, she made her way down the stairs and along the hallway, through a house that was dark and silent and sleeping—*except for the narrow ribbon of light that showed beneath the library door.*

Fallon frowned.

A light in the library? But how was that possible, when Zepporah and Willie had retired to the servants' quarters long since, and Lucien had taken himself off to his study some time before the storm had broken over the hollow. As he'd passed her chamber door, he'd called a soft good night to her, just as he always had done. Fallon had heard him and answered.

So how had a light come to be left burning in the library?

Fallon hadn't an inkling, but there seemed only one way to find out. Raising a hand, she rapped softly on the panel. "Uncle? Is that you?"

Silence . . . broken only by the low rumble of thunder, and in the next instant the ribbon of light disappeared. The child lurking inside Fallon urged her to turn and creep back up the stairway to the safety and security of her bedchamber, to postpone the investigation until morning, when all would appear safe and sound. Frightening things lurked in the darkness—bats and rats and the restless spirit of the hanged man said to haunt the hollow, childhood terrors she'd somehow never outgrown.

Ridiculous things, Fallon thought, deliberately grasping the doorknob, for a thinking young woman to fear.

With a turn of her wrist, the door eased slowly open. The room was dark—silent and still. But Fallon wasn't fooled, for the unmistakable odors of melted beeswax, of something dank and undefinable, lingered in the air. Someone had been there recently—perhaps was there still. Blocking the doorway, she felt her spine prickle, and she nervously moistened her lips with her tongue. "Who's there?" she demanded in a shaky voice. "Show yourself this instant, or I'll have no choice but to wake the house!"

No reply or entreaty was forthcoming, just the soft sound of movement, more felt than heard, and a black mass broke from the shadows and rushed to engulf her.

Fallon opened her mouth to scream at the same instant that he grabbed her, pulling her back up against him, his hand clamped tightly over her mouth.

She struggled violently, jamming an elbow into her captor's ribs, kicking his shin, and was rewarded with a virulent curse. But he didn't release her. To combat her struggles, he merely strengthened his hold, bringing her up so tightly against him that she could feel the flexing of steely muscles against her shoulders and back.

"Be still, now. You can see there's nothing to fear." His voice sounded close at her ear, so cultured and smooth, so shockingly familiar, that Fallon relaxed in his arms. "There's a good girl. You won't cry out, now, will you, if I take my hand away?"

She shook her head, and he eased his hand from her mouth. But he made no move to release her. "Have you lost your mind? Let go of me!" she said too loudly, for the hand was again placed over her mouth.

"Ah, ah! If you want me to release you, you first must promise me you'll speak in a voice lower than a shout. As you so astutely warned a moment ago, a word from you could wake the house, and I'd rather not have to explain to your uncle how I came to be in the house uninvited, in the company of his lovely and somewhat scantily clad niece."

Fallon sighed, capitulating, and he eased the hand from her mouth by slow degrees. Then he released her. Fallon turned to confront him, only this time she was careful to soften her tone. "You have a choice, sir. You can either explain to my uncle or explain to me precisely what you are doing here."

"You are perfectly justified in demanding an explanation," he said, "and you shall have one, first thing in the morning—"

"I shall have one now, tonight!" Fallon swiftly countered. "Unless you wish me to scream this house down around your ears." It was a harsh tack to take, but Fallon had had her fill of his evasive answers, his secretiveness. She wanted to know who he was and what he was about, prowling the darkened house, and she wanted to know immediately.

"Fallon, be reasonable. The hour is late, and surely you'll agree that this is neither the time nor the place for a lengthy discussion. Why don't you go back to bed, forget that you saw me, and I'll simply make my way out the way I came in."

Fallon planted her fists on her hips and glared at him. "Since you are the one prowling around my home in the dead of night, you are hardly in any position to make suggestions."

Draegan clenched his teeth. She had a valid point. He was caught, and there was but one way out that he could see. "I need a bit more time," he said.

"Time for what?" Fallon demanded. "To think up some plausible-sounding lie as to why you broke into my house? To ply your silken tongue and worm your way into my good graces?"

"Fallon, this is not what you think."

"Then tell me what it is," she said. "Why and how is it that you come to be in this house when everyone is asleep? You didn't come in by way of either entrance, for both are barred and someone would have heard you."

"That's true enough."

"Well?"

"Suffice to say there is another way—" Draegan began, hoping to placate her without giving himself away—"a way that I was not aware of until tonight."

"That will not suffice," she returned angrily. "I want specifics. Just who the devil are you? And pray, sir, if you hand me some rot about being a simple country cleric, I shall scream in earnest, and you can explain straightaway to my uncle."

"Christ, how I hate explanations," he said softly; then, seeing the bright golden fire that flared in her eyes, he continued. "All right. All right. But first I must be certain that I can trust you. There are many issues involved here, the least of which are my continued good health and longevity."

"Not to mention your position as pastor. A word to my uncle, and you, sir, are out on your ear!" She crossed her arms beneath her firm young breasts and waited, tapping one slender foot impatiently beneath the hem of her soft flannel gown as Draegan considered his options.

He could have subdued her and carried her off at that moment, with no one the wiser. It would have been one way to still her questions, since she was looking soft and delectable in her flannel gown and wrapper. It was terribly tempting, but far too risky to consider for long.

Had she disappeared without a trace, a hue and cry would have been raised that would have been heard all the way to Albany. Lucien was already

suspicious of Draegan's intentions toward her--
with good reason—and in his present position,
Draegan knew he could ill afford the close scrutiny
an intense search would have aroused. What he
needed was a little more time for Lucien's suspicions to be set aside, time for Lucien to grow secure
once again, and careless, time in which to watch
and wait, now that he'd found the passageway.
Fallon alone had it within her power to provide or
withhold that time.

Her cooperation was paramount to his success in
catching Sparrowhawk, and he hadn't the slightest
notion how he was going to obtain it.

While he pondered just how best to control her,
Fallon lost all patience, and without a word of
warning, she spun on her heel and dashed for the
door.

Draegan caught at her wrist, but she whirled
back and took a wild swing at him with her left
fist, hitting a porcelain vase filled with spring
blooms. He ducked, and the vase crashed to the
floor, sending water in a cold rush over the puncheon floor.

Fallon bounded forward again in her bid for the
door and freedom, and instead she landed in the
midst of the slippery mess. Before she knew what
was happening, her bare feet flew from under her,
and with a startled squeal she landed on her rump
at Draegan's booted feet. "If you so much as smile,
I shall—" she huffed.

"My dear Mistress Deane," he said with the utmost gravity, "I would not dream of making light
of your misfortune—at least not until after we've
reached an understanding of sorts. Will you allow
me to help you up?"

Fallon scorned the hand held out to her, pre-
senting him with her haughtiest stare. "What sort
of understanding?"

Reaching down, he grasped her arms, setting her on her feet a safe distance from the puddle. Fallon's flesh tingled long after he had released her. "You shall have all that you ask, but I must warn you, it comes with a price."

"I am listening."

"Before I reveal myself to you, I must have your sworn oath that all I say will remain the strictest secret. *You cannot tell anyone;* not Zepporah, or Willie, or even your uncle. Do you understand what I am saying?"

Fallon frowned at him. "Indeed I do. You are asking that I set myself apart from my loved ones and pledge an oath of loyalty to you, a stranger."

He smiled darkly. "It is the only way."

Fallon shook her head. "I don't like this."

He took a step closer. The shadows masked his features, masked his intent. "Your silence is all I am asking. *Your word.* If you speak of this to anyone, it could cost me my life." Taking another step forward, he closed the distance remaining between them.

Fallon tried to back away, but the desk and chair prevented her escape. "You would say anything, do anything, to have it go your way," she softly accused.

"Yes." He latched the door, then grasped her hand, bringing her close. Fallon stared up into his shadowed visage and saw the light of desperation in his eyes. This was her undoing—his final bid for trust. "Yes, I would say anything, do anything . . . and if you care at all for me, you will do as I ask without question."

Fallon didn't reply immediately, and in the ensuing silence a soft, insistent rapping sounded at the door, followed by Zepporah's voice. "Miss Fallon, are you in there? Miss Fallon, is everything all right?"

Draegan brought her hand to his lips, kissing her fingertips, the sensitive heart of her palm . . . her wrist . . . and all the while he watched her.

"Fallon?"

"Yes," Fallon said. "Yes, I'm here."

"Is everything all right, child? I thought I heard a noise."

Undaunted by the danger of discovery he moved onward, pushing up her sleeve to nibble along her inner arm. He gave her a gentle nip, and Fallon felt the rough heat of his tongue test the soft flesh at the inner bend of her elbow. She gasped aloud. "*Oh.* Oh, it was nothing. I was startled by the lightning and knocked over Mother's vase."

"Well, if that's the case, I'd best come in and clean it up." The housekeeper turned the knob. At the same time Draegan quickly advanced, nuzzling the slight hollow beneath Fallon's collarbone, the indentation at the base of her throat, and on down. . . .

"No!" Fallon said, making a halfhearted effort to push him away. "No. Truly, Zepporah. There's no need. I've already taken care of everything. Go back to bed. You need your rest, and there are a few insignificant matters needing my attention before I sleep."

Draegan halted his sensuous exploration and raised his dark head to peer down at her as Zepporah's query came clearly through the door. "Are you certain?"

Fallon looked at Draegan and then away. She was not at all certain. Indeed, at that moment she had very good cause to question not only her judgment, but her sanity as well. "Yes," she said. "Quite certain. Good night, Zepporah."

The housekeeper turned away from the door, the soft creak of the floorboards marking her progress through the manse.

Draegan lifted one dark arched brow. "I've been called a great many things, but never insignificant."

He would have bent to his task again, but Fallon placed her hand over his mouth and broke away, hurrying to put some distance between them. He took a step forward; she held up her hand. "Pray, sir, do not touch me! We have a great deal to discuss, and I will not be swayed from my purpose by your underhanded tactics."

"Then you will not betray me?" he asked. "To anyone?"

Fallon shivered, sinking down onto the edge of the chair. His choice of words chilled her far more than the cloying caress of her damp wrapper. "That depends."

"On what?" he wished to know.

"On how truthful you are with me," Fallon said flatly. "I warn you, I am no Cordelia Plum, to be wheedled into complacency with lies and half-truths. My cooperation, like your revelations, comes with a price."

He smiled ever so slightly, and some of the tension drained from him. "I cannot say that I like your terms, and it remains to be seen if I can live with them." With a negligent flick of his wrist, he gestured toward the desk. "You'd best light a taper or two to allay suspicion. Unless, of course, it's your habit to work in the dark."

Fallon fumbled through the desk drawer while the lightning flickered beyond the great bank of windows. It took her a moment to locate the tinderbox, and when she finally found it, she was trembling so hard that she couldn't manage the flint and steel. After several failed attempts, Draegan took the implements from her hands and struck a live spark into the bit of cotton provided, lighting the taper on the desk from the resulting flame.

A warm light blossomed in the room, dispelling the shadows; the golden flame was reflected in the translucent depths of his eyes. "There's no reason for you to fear me, Fallon," he said. "I am not here to harm you."

"Then why are you here?"

"I have come to Abundance on a mission of some importance."

Still more evasions. He did not give way easily. And neither was Fallon easily satisfied. "What mission? Sent by whom?"

"By my superiors. Men of import concerned with the Tory activities being carried out within our borders and along the frontier."

"That is not good enough."

Draegan's expression clouded, but he said nothing. He was too busy weighing his options, which were frustratingly few.

Meanwhile, the young lady was growing impatient. "Time grows short," she said. "So unless you wish to stay to breakfast and explain to uncle as well just how you came to be here, I would suggest you stop delaying—"

"Very well, then, mistress. You shall have your answers—at least as many as I am at liberty to give—but first I would know one thing."

She awaited his query, silent and seemingly calm.

"Are you in love with Randall Quill?"

"What on earth would make you ask such a thing?"

"He seems uncommonly possessive of you," Draegan said.

"Possessive! Don't be ridiculous!"

"Ridiculous, perhaps. But do you love him?"

"Of all the impertinence," she grumbled softly.

"I do not see what bearing this can have on anything, but no, I *do not* love Randall Quill. He is an acquaintance, nothing more."

"Wilhemina said he was your beau."

"Willie speaks her mind too freely." She frowned at him. "Randall was correct, wasn't he? You do know each other."

"We met but briefly a year ago," Draegan admitted. "It was not a pleasant encounter, to put it mildly, and I owe Master Quill a heavy debt, which I hope to satisfy very soon."

She seemed to read his thoughts. "Precisely what are your intentions? "Her frown had been replaced by a look of concern, but concern for whom? Himself or Randall Quill?

He merely smiled. "No matter. Young master Quill is in no immediate danger. At the moment I have concerns that are far more pressing."

His reticence was making her agitated, and she drummed her fingertips on the top of the desk. "Such as?"

"Finding and destroying Sparrowhawk." The drumming ceased. Planting his palms on the desk, Draegan leaned forward, his voice low and concentrated. "I am here in the Catskills to take down the most notorious, most successful, most dangerous spy to tread American soil. You know firsthand the havoc he's wreaked; you've seen the faces of Greetje and Alida Krieger and the others. That's why it is so crucial for you keep silent. As the Reverend Mattais, I stand a good chance of success—of preventing incidents such as Peterskill from being repeated. If I am unmasked, the mission is lost, and Sparrowhawk wins."

He paused. The storm had ceased without Draegan's even having noticed, and there was no sound but the soft, repetitive plop, plop of rain dropping off the eaves of the manse to the sodden ground below. He plied his final gambit. "You told me once, not long ago, that you'd take up a sword if you were permitted. Well, this, my rebel lady, is the opportunity for which you have been waiting, and you have only to agree to keep silent about what you've learned here this evening to earn the eternal thanks of your fellow patriots."

Fallon lifted her chin and gave him a level look. His seeming patience as he awaited her reply was intentionally misleading, but she wasn't fooled for an instant. She could sense the tension that gripped him, and she knew that the difference between his success and his failure, his life or his death, hinged upon her willingness to cooperate with him. He was an accomplished fraud, was Draegan Mattais ... or whoever the devil he happened to be! And if she acquiesced without a whimper of protest, he would be able to go blithely on conducting his mysterious business, leaving her alone and uninformed to wait and wonder and worry.

But Fallon wanted more than that.

When she replied her voice was surprisingly calm; on the inside she was quaking. "I would very much like to help you, but I'm afraid your terms aren't acceptable to me."

His cool, aloof facade slipped a notch. He gaped at her. "I beg your pardon? I'm afraid I didn't hear you correctly."

"You want me to sit passively by while you continue your investigation and capture Sparrowhawk. That simply is not good enough. I want to play an active role in your investigation."

He stared at her as though she'd lost her mind. "You can't be serious!"

"Oh, but I assure you I am. Quite serious."

He shook his head and softly cursed. "You don't know what it is you are asking."

"On the contrary, sir. I know precisely what I am about."

"There are hazards involved. And you're a woman! I would not see you hurt."

"You needn't concern yourself about my welfare. I'm a grown woman, not a child. And I can look after myself. Besides, you need me."

He considered her for a long moment, while Fallon held her breath. "This is sheer madness, a bargain forged in Hell—one that I fear you will come to regret."

Fallon breathed a little more easily. His iron will was crumbling. She had only to hold fast to her determination and he would give way completely. "If you are trying to frighten me, then you must try again. I do not frighten easily."

"Don't you?" he asked softly, reaching across the desk to lift a silken curl from her breast and twine it around his finger. "Then you are an even greater fool than I imagined." With a deft motion of his hand, he freed the errant curl and arranged it precisely as it had been. He didn't touch her woman's flesh. He didn't need to. The sensitive bud capping the soft mound of her breast hardened instinctively, standing erect and aroused beneath the soft layers of flannel. . . .

His implication was clear. By insisting upon a close alliance with him, she was quite possibly courting damnation. A more weak-willed woman would have flown from the room and his dangerous company rather than risk it.

But Fallon felt stronger than that. She possessed the power to reason, and the will to resist, despite the traitorous but temporary lapse of her senses. And she had only to keep her wits about her, keep firmly in mind her ultimate goal, to render herself immune to his seductive presence.

It was a simple strategy, but simple strategies

were often the best ones, and when weighed against the end result—the eventual destruction of an enemy to the ongoing struggle for independence from Britain—it was surely worth the risk.

"Will you agree to my terms?" Fallon asked, eager to seal the bargain before she changed her mind.

He smiled his slight smile, as full of mystery and hidden meaning as ever it had been, a smile that never reached the icy depths of his eyes. "Since it appears to be the only end to the means I seek at the present, yes, I will agree."

"You will not regret it. I promise you." Fallon offered her hand to seal their newly made agreement, and Draegan took it, lifting it to his lips.

"My dear Mistress Deane," he corrected, "I regret it already."

Fallon ignored his sarcasm. She had won out against his obstinacy—just as together they would win out over Sparrowhawk—and she was not about to let him spoil her victory. "When shall we meet again?"

"Tomorrow night, after the house is asleep. Come to the garden."

Step, pause . . . step, pause . . . The sound of an uneven, shuffling gait came clearly through the panel, and then the sound of Lucien's voice. "Fallon, dear, I'd like a word with you."

Fallon frowned at Draegan, putting a finger to her lips. "One moment, Uncle." She opened and closed the desk drawer, shuffled through some papers lying on the desk, then, snuffing the candle's flame, crossed to the door and opened it a crack as Draegan shrank back in the shadows. "Uncle, I thought you'd gone to bed."

Lucien gave her a sidelong smile that only served to accentuate his look of weariness. The lines around his eyes and mouth seemed more deeply etched than they had at dinner. That night he looked every bit his fifty-seven years. "And so I had, but the lure of the storm proved too great for me to resist. I stood observing by the study windows until Zepporah sought me out. Fool woman. She was muttering something about your acting strangely. Sometimes I think she's growing dotty on us. That blasted Dutch cooking is what does it! It's far too rich for anyone's blood, and it muddles the thinking. What she needs is something boiled."

"She shouldn't have disturbed you, Uncle," Fallon replied. "Like you, the storm kept me from sleep. I couldn't see the logic in lying idle, so I came down to finish transcribing your letter to Master Trumbolt." It was just enough truth to be wholly convincing, Fallon thought.

Yet Lucien did not accept it without question. "It was the storm, and nothing more, that kept you from your rest?"

"Yes, of course. What else could it possibly be?"

"Well, I must admit, a certain dark-haired young minister comes to mind."

Fallon's hand tightened on the doorknob as she fought down the urge to glance back at the shadows. "Uncle, I—"

Lucien stilled her protest with an impatient wave of his hand. "No need to deny it, child. I've seen the way you look at him, and worse, the way he looks at you." He sighed heavily and shook his head. "I am no cursed good at this business of being a parent! Rousseau was right, you know. It is not the parent's, or in my case, the guardian's place to meddle in the child's life—to dictate. Yet—yet, for your mother's memory, I feel strangely compelled to ask after your feelings for this man."

Fallon searched her mind for some plausible reply, something evasive yet acceptable, something Draegan himself might have employed, but found nothing. She was forced to settle for the truth. "In all honesty, Uncle, I am unsure just how I feel about him." She was terribly aware that he was there in the shadows, listening to every word she said. "He's an asset to the community, learned and compassionate. But there are times, such as tonight, for instance, when I find his presence greatly vexing."

"Vexing, eh?" Lucien peered at her intently. "Not in love with the fellow, are you?"

Fallon's cheeks flushed scarlet. "Good heavens, no! Why, I barely know him!"

"Nor do I," Lucien replied. "Indeed, that's why I asked. Well," he went on, seemingly satisfied for the time being, "that's enough foolishness for one evening. I'm going to take myself off to bed, and suggest you don't tarry. Zepporah will be stirring near cock's crow, and her banging around in the kitchen always sends sleep to the devil for me."

"Good night, Uncle." Fallon listened to Lucien's footfalls fade as he moved down the hall toward the stair. When she could no longer hear him, she took a deep breath, slowly turned to search the shadows . . . and found that she was alone in the room.

Draegan had vanished as mysteriously as he had appeared, leaving Fallon to wonder if he'd ever been there at all, or if indeed she'd only imagined it.

Chapter 10

⟡

Fallon rose at the usual time the following morning. She bathed and dressed and went down to breakfast with Willie and Zepporah. The kitchen was warm and cozy as always, and as always the kettle was steaming on the hob. Fallon helped herself to a cup of Oswego tea, wild bergamot gathered from the shaded wood near the manor, and she sat down at table, watching as Zepporah filled her plate. "A bit of supawn will do, Zepporah," Fallon said. "I'm not very hungry this morning."

The older woman planted one fist on an ample hip; she held the empty delftware plate in her other hand. "There's bacon and headcheese and yesterday's rye bread, and ye want to pick like a bird! Ye'd best be careful, miss, lest ye become as neglectful of yer well-being as yer hardheaded uncle!"

"Very well, then," Fallon said, giving way with a sigh. She hoped to get through the day without arousing suspicions, a feat she suspected would prove unbelievably hard, since the merest thought of her upcoming assignation with Draegan Mattais awakened a host of butterflies in her stomach. "A

166

slice of rye bread and a rasher of bacon, but nothing more. I've correspondence to finish this morning, and I would like to begin very soon."

The stare Zepporah fixed upon Fallon was decidedly hawkish. "More letters? I thought ye finished those last night."

Caught up in her fabrications, Fallon was momentarily taken aback. She'd never excelled at evasions and intrigue, and thus had left them to Willie. Quite suddenly, she found herself wishing she'd paid closer attention to Willie's tactics. "I finished most of the transcribing. But I fear several pages will need to be completely rewritten—ink blots," she said, praying Zepporah was convinced. "It happened when I knocked Mother's vase from the desk."

Willie perched on a stool near the table, peeling potatoes for dinner. "Letters and sums and endless quill and ink," she said. "It makes my poor head spin just to think of it."

Zepporah's critical gaze slid to her daughter. "Ye might do well, young lady, to turn yer own thoughts to something constructive, and away from yon Master Smith!"

Willie sighed and rolled her eyes. "Oh, Mother!"

"*Wilhemina Blessing Rhys!* Don't ye 'oh, Mother' me!"

Zepporah's sharp reply was the beginning of a long and lengthy discourse on the virtues of minding one's elders, and one that at that moment, Fallon—who had hurried through breakfast—could have done without. So she took her tea and, feeling slightly disloyal for abandoning Willie in her hour of need, tiptoed noiselessly from the room.

In the library, she settled down to review the letter she had finished transcribing the previous day, then worked to complete the remaining unfinished sheets. But concentration came hard, and the day dragged interminably on.

Each time Fallon thought of her planned rendezvous with Draegan Mattais, that irreverent reverend-turned-spy-catcher, the butterflies she had noticed earlier came to life, flitting maddeningly about inside her stomach. At each creak, each shift, of the stately old mansion, Fallon glanced up, half-expecting to find that he had somehow materialized—so tall and lean, so menacingly handsome in his dark cleric's clothes—from the dim recesses of the hearthside shadows. The mental image so unnerved her that she was forced to recopy the final page of Lucien's letter to Trumbolt three separate times.

By the time she finished, the day had dwindled and the sun was slipping behind the western hills, leaving a red-gold glow in its fiery wake.

Lucien did not come down to dinner that evening. He'd taken to his bed with another of his notorious headaches, and had left word with Brewster, his manservant, that he was not to be disturbed for any reason.

Fallon supped alone. Then, terribly aware that night was closing in, she bade Zepporah and Willie good night and made her way upstairs to wait.

The moments passed, and as the purple twilight slowly deepened into night a light scratch sounded at the door. "Fallon? Fallon, are ye awake?"

Fallon eased the door open and peered at her friend through the crack. "Willie. What is it?"

"Can I come in? I need desperately to speak with ye."

"Can't it wait until morning?" She yawned widely for effect. "I'm exhausted, and I need to sleep."

Willie's look was long-suffering. "Go on, then.

I'll bother ye no more this night, and wish ye wonderful dreams, since my own are all but lost."

"Oh, for pity's sake," Fallon said, casting an imploring glance at the ceiling. Willie's strangled sob decided the matter. With a muttered imprecation, Fallon caved in. "All right. All right." She opened the door, waiting impatiently for Willie to pass through, then closed it again. "I surmise there's trouble with Thomas."

Willie plopped down on the bed, looking thoroughly miserable. "And Mother. I've been biddable as a newborn lamb these past three weeks, thoughtful and sweet, just as you suggested, and where has it gotten me? I'm no closer to gaining Mother's approval on this match! Why, she bristles and glowers at the very mention of Thomas's name! Fallon—oh, Fallon! What shall I do?"

"Did you reason with her calmly, as I suggested?" Fallon asked as patiently as she could manage.

"I told her how much I loved him," Willie replied with an audible sniff, "that I can't live without him. And she flatly refused to listen! She says I'm too young to know my own mind, and she won't have me actin' the light-skirt for no farmer's trash!"

Fallon sighed. "That's awfully harsh." It was also a weighty problem, not easily solved in the space of an evening, let alone a moment or two. She glanced at the window, feeling the press of the passing moments and her steadily mounting impatience. The waning moon was rising. She could see the cool white sliver hanging just above the black silhouette of the trees. "What does Thomas have to say about this?"

"I haven't had the heart to tell him. He sent me a message last eve by way of Sulee, the laundress, whose husband, Joe, works at the Smiths'. I had to make an excuse that I couldn't meet him." She sniffed again, and a single tear slipped over her pale lashes and down her plump cheek. Fallon feared a veritable deluge. "I'll die without Thomas! I can't give him up!"

Fallon sank down on the bed next to Willie and slipped a comforting arm about her friend's shaking shoulders, thrusting aside for the moment her own mounting impatience. "Come, now, don't cry. It can't be as bad as all that! Given a little time to grow accustomed to the idea, Zepporah will come around. You'll see! You must try to be patient."

"By the time she gives her approval, I'll be old and gray, and Thomas will have taken another to wife!"

"If he loves you, he'll wait," Fallon reasoned.

The face Willie turned to Fallon was mottled with red and ravaged with tears. "Ye don't understand. When ye're this desperate in love, each minute ye're apart seems ten thousand years!"

"No," Fallon said softly. "I don't suppose that I do." Never having been in love, she didn't understand the excess of emotion that seemed to accompany that much-touted, rather-tortured state—nor could she imagine allowing her heart to rule her head.

She tried very hard to empathize with Willie's plight, but she had no similar experience with which to compare it, no lapse of willpower—unless one could count the momentary lapses she'd experienced when in the company of a certain counterfeit cleric.

But that was hardly the same thing, she reasoned with a frown. Her association with Draegan was purely political, purely business, and had been from the start. There was no pleasure involved, no softhearted, softheaded sentiment.

Yet even now, she recalled the warmth of his

mouth at her throat . . . the delicious feel of his experienced hands on her skin. . . . and shuddered.

After a long and arduous battle, she managed to banish the images, though try as she might she could not wipe away the residue of uncertainty they left behind. She was not falling in love with Draegan Mattais, she told herself emphatically. A thinking, reasoning, intelligent woman like herself did not make such fatal mistakes.

Willie dried her eyes on her apron, then took the handkerchief Fallon offered and blew her nose noisily. "If only someone could speak to Mother on Thomas's behalf, convince her that he would make a good husband. Someone she looks up to. Someone she'd be likely to listen to." When she turned her bright gaze on Fallon again there was a calculating gleam in her eyes. "Someone like Reverend Mattais."

Fallon shifted uncomfortably on the mattress. "I'm not certain that's a good idea—" she began, but Willie cut her off.

"Are ye daft? It's the perfect idea! All you have to do is convince him to help us, and Thomas and me are as good as wed!" She sprang from the bed, snatching up Fallon's dress as her friend removed it and put it in the large wardrobe. "You'll speak with him, won't ye, Fallon? For my sake?"

Fallon sighed, reluctant yet resigned. It was the end to a means. It was what Willie truly wanted, and it would bring to a close the siege she was under, so that she could slip out to her rendezvous without further delay. In addition, it would make her friend happy—and after all, what harm could it do? It wasn't as if he were going to marry them. "I will speak with him about your difficulties, but I must warn you. There is always the chance that he will agree with Zepporah."

Her caution didn't dampen Willie's enthusiasm

one whit. "He'll help us, Fallon. Just you wait and see!" Willie finished tidying the chamber, and then, hugging Fallon, she bade her a cheerful good night.

An hour later, when the sickle moon was high above the trees, Fallon dressed in a soft woolen gown of deep hunter green, donned her dainty black boots, and crept from the house.

In sunlight the garden was tranquil, serene; it held no secrets. At night it was shrouded in mystery. The obsidian shadows, where the feeble light of a waning moon failed to reach, offered perfect concealment. Fallon moved along the garden path, steeling herself for Draegan's sudden emergence from the lightless depths of the garden. Nevertheless, when she passed a honeysuckle bush and he fell in beside her, her heart skipped a beat.

"What kept you?" he softly inquired. "The rest of the house has been dark for nearly an hour."

"Willie," Fallon replied. "She needed to talk, and though I tried, I couldn't put her off."

"Romantic troubles with young Master Smith?" His voice was silky, tinged with amusement.

Fallon frowned up at his shadowed countenance. "How on earth did you know?"

"You might be surprised at what I hear," Draegan replied with the slightest, most secretive of smiles. "I'm a man of the cloth—trustworthy, somewhat benign, safe to confide in. That perception, however false, tends to loosen tongues about town."

"And you take shameless advantage, I'm sure," Fallon retorted.

A casual shrug. "Remorse is a luxury I can ill afford, my dear Mistress Deane. I do what I must to succeed and get out with my skin intact. To develop a conscience at this point would be worse than counter-productive; it would be silly indeed."

Silence settled between them. They walked to the gate, but instead of going through it, Draegan seized Fallon's waist, lifting her over the low stone wall and attempting himself to vault it. He landed awkwardly, however, going down on one knee, and Fallon heard him curse. He recovered quickly, but his voice, when he spoke again, betrayed his irritation. "Will you tell me about Wilhemina?"

"Why do you wish to know?" Surely he could not suspect Willie!

"I rather like the girl. She's spirited and saucy. A pert little piece."

"A bit too saucy, perhaps, for her own good," Fallon muttered. "She's set on wedding Thomas, but Zepporah is proving difficult. Willie is terribly upset by the whole situation. She came to me tonight to ask if I would speak to you on her behalf."

"And you agreed."

"I could hardly tell her that the esteemed Reverend Draegan Mattais is a base fraud, now, could I? A man lacking in honor and undeserving of trust—"

"You needn't elaborate, Fallon. I believe I understand the point you are striving so diligently to make."

Secure in the fact that she'd nettled him quite thoroughly, Fallon softened her tone. "What do you intend to do about Willie?"

"The decent thing, of course. I shall speak to Mrs. Rhys, and try to persuade her against standing in the way of young love."

"You would do that for Willie?"

"I will speak for Wilhemina," he said firmly. "Christ knows if it will do any good. Careful. The ground here is uneven." He took hold of Fallon's elbow and steered her toward the orchard, where the ghostly white stallion stood cropping grass.

Fallon saw the horse and hesitated. "Surely we've

gone far enough. There's no one about to hear."

"Your reluctance, quite frankly, surprises me. Just last night you were passing eager to sink your teeth into this intrigue, eager enough to use less-than-ladylike means to pressure me into this unholy alliance of ours. Can it possibly be that the gloss has worn thin on our partnership so soon?"

Fallon narrowed her eyes at him. "You'd like that, wouldn't you?"

He took up the reins. "My lady rebel can do as she pleases. I'm for the rectory. It's much safer than standing out here in the night, where anyone can eavesdrop. If you are still hell-bent on this partnership, then I suggest you hie yourself over here. If not, then I shall take great pleasure in bidding you good night."

Draegan made as if to mount, stealing a glance at her from the corner of one eye. She stood with her hands braced on her curvaceous hips, a troublesome, inquisitive little wretch with a will to match his own and a body that was pure temptation. He wanted desperately for her to turn on her dainty heel and flounce back to the manor, back to safety. Yet he wanted her help, her acquiescence. . . . He wanted to know that he could trust her implicitly, and that she could come to trust him.

But trust must be won. And none of it would come easily.

"You may think the rectory a wise alternative to standing out here in the open; I do not happen to view your living quarters as a safe haven."

Draegan's look was arch. "Which do you fear more, Fallon? Ravishment at the hands of an unprincipled rake, or your own lack of self-control?"

Was it a trick of the shifting moon shadows, or did he detect an incriminating blush blooming high upon her petal-soft cheek? Draegan was intrigued. She held tight to her anger and continued to balk.

"A lady does not visit a gentleman's living quarters," she said flatly. "It isn't proper. It isn't acceptable behavior. And in my case, it simply isn't done."

"She does if she intends to further this partnership and catch Sparrowhawk." He shifted his weight onto his good leg and eased the other by bending it at the knee. "If you are worrying that your reputation will suffer, then lay your fears to rest. I'm too damnably preoccupied at the moment to entertain thoughts of sexual fulfillment, and I shall have you back safe in your bed long before the dawn, with no one the wiser. The choice is yours, lady. You may indulge your fears and thereby waste my entire evening or come with me and help me in my quest to catch Sparrowhawk. What will it be?"

She looked at him, a long and measuring look filled with trepidation. "Doubtless I will come to regret this," she said. But she came to him nonetheless, wordlessly accepting his assistance in mounting the great white beast.

A short time later, they entered the rectory. It was as immaculately kept as Fallon remembered, with everything neatly in its place. A fire burned in the grate, adding warmth and cheer to the simply furnished room.

She watched as Draegan removed his coat and draped it over the back of a chair. "Would you care for some refreshment? There's coffee and brandy. I won't offend your patriotic sensibilities by offering you tea."

"Coffee?" Fallon raised a speculative brow. "I should be interested to know how you came by such a rare commodity in these days of scarcity. It was my understanding that only the British had coffee and tea."

He smiled. "I believe I mentioned once before my hedonistic nature. I like my little luxuries, and as you pointed out, the British want for very little."

Fallon's eyes widened. "Are you saying you stole it?"

His smile remained fixed in place, revealing nothing. " 'Steal' is such a harsh word. Why don't you sit down and make yourself comfortable? We've a long night ahead of us, and a very great deal to discuss."

"We do indeed," she said. "And you can begin by telling me just who you really are."

He walked to the hearth and stood, holding his hands out to warm them. "I thought we'd gotten past all of that. We are partners, pledged to work together toward a common goal. Why must you complicate our relationship by dwelling on inconsequential matters?"

Fallon raised her chin a notch and met his stare unflinchingly. "Because it is not inconsequential to me."

He turned slightly, and the firelight was caught and reflected in those unearthly eyes of his. "It will not ease your mind to know, and there are more important things that want addressing."

Fallon opened her mouth to object, but he silenced her with a look. "Leave it for another time. Perhaps when we know each other better, when I am certain you merit my trust."

To that, Fallon said nothing. He didn't trust her; she didn't trust him. They were on an equal, if unfamiliar and tenuous, footing. "Perhaps, after all, I will have that coffee you mentioned. It has been a very long time since I enjoyed such a luxury."

"And knowing it's been pilfered from the enemy will no doubt render it all the more enjoyable."

For the first time that evening, Fallon smiled. "It cannot hurt, I suppose." She couldn't help noticing as she watched him move about the room that his limp was far more evident than it had been to date. When he was distracted, he kneaded the flesh of his left thigh, the same way she'd seen *Vrouw* Schoonmaker cup a sore tooth with a plump palm, protectively. "How did you come to be injured?"

Putting the beans in the grinder, he vigorously cranked the handle, but Fallon saw his face flush dark and knew that he had heard. "I'm sorry," she said, struggling beneath the sudden discomfort of her own embarrassment. "It was rude and unthinking of me to ask so personal a question. I promise you, it won't happen again. I—"

Draegan crossed the room and, with a sigh, sank into the chair opposite Fallon's. "I was wounded at Princeton," he said matter-of-factly. "It's something I've tried since to forget."

Her head came sharply up, and she stared at him. "You were with Washington?"

"Most of my work was conducted behind the lines. It was my task to cultivate certain individuals and funnel the information I managed to obtain to my superiors at the front."

"A spy," she said, her amber eyes glinting.

"Call it what you will; it's dirty, thankless work, devoid of honor or decency—work that men with loftier morals wouldn't deign to turn a hand to."

Fallon tilted her head and looked at him. "If you find it so objectionable, then why do you continue to do it?"

"Because I am good at it," he said simply.

"Good at convincing others that you are something you're not. An accomplished fraud. Were you thoroughly disappointed that I saw through your masquerade?"

"Surprised, disgruntled. You mystify me, Fallon. You are different from any woman I have ever known."

A becoming blush pinkened her cheeks. "You must have known legions of beautiful women, and all of them half in love with you, I've little doubt. I cannot imagine that *I* would impress you."

He'd certainly had more than his share of illicit affairs, Draegan thought darkly, from comely experienced widows, to a serving wench who worked in Sir Henry Clinton's own household, to the Tory wives and daughters of British-held New York City, all of whom he'd led astray for a scrap of pertinent information. Of course, none of that he could ever admit to the wide-eyed young woman who watched him so intently.

Filled with a sudden impatience with the direction of their conversation, he raked a hand through his hair. "Enough of this. I brought you here so that we might begin sorting through the pieces of my present puzzle, not to sort through my tangled past!"

"You are right, of course. My pardon." She bowed her bright auburn head, while he scowled at her.

Fragrant steam started to rise from the spout of the coffeepot. Draegan poured and served the hot black brew. He went to the great cupboard and brought out the last of his precious cone sugar, already cut into small, manageable squares. "The cream is in the springhouse. If you like, I can send Jacob."

"Thank you, no, this is fine." She added the sweetening and stirred, then swirled the tip of her forefinger in her coffee and placed it in her mouth. The gesture was childlike, but Draegan's reaction to her innocent play was not. Seeing her lush red lips close around the slim digit brought other more erotic images to mind, which triggered an answering pull in his groin. It was by supreme dint of will alone that he stifled his instinctive groan and tore his gaze away. "We've delayed long enough. It's time we got down to business. Tell me all you know about this church's design and construction, and do not omit the smallest detail."

Her lovely brow furrowed. "The church was constructed forty-eight years ago. What possible relation could it have to your investigation?"

"More than you know," Draegan replied. "Go on."

She was still frowning at him. "Well, let's see. The cornerstone was placed in August of 1730, if I remember correctly. Uncle Lucien was nine years old, Papa little more than a toddler. Grandfather helped to lay—"

"Yes," Draegan interjected, "he helped to lay the foundation. You told me as much the first time I questioned you. But what of the building itself? Think hard, Fallon. Did you ever hear mention— even in passing—of any unique features that would have set the building itself apart?"

She shook her head. "Nothing that comes to mind."

"Forty-eight years," Draegan mused aloud. "Most of your grandfather's peers would be deceased by now, so it only stands to reason that few people would know of its existence."

"Know of what's existence?" When he failed to respond to her query, her amber eyes turned stormy. "It will save you considerable time and irritation if you give it over willingly. You should know by now just how dogged I can be."

"Indeed," he muttered into his cup. "There are times when you are a very persistent pain in the—

"And you, sir, cannot be trusted to deal fairly with me, unless forced to do so. Out with it. Precisely what have you uncovered?"

He rose from his chair and limped to the hearth. "More coffee?"

"Draegan Mattais. We have an agreement, a pact!"

"Fallon, for Christ's sake. Be reasonable." He glanced at her, a grievous error. She sat, her spine ramrod straight, shoulders squared, firm round breasts straining against the soft woolen fabric of her gown.

She was his weakness, his Achilles heel. And he couldn't help staring, any more than she could help her reaction to the tension throbbing between them. As he watched, he saw the slow transformation, the gradual awakening of her woman's flesh through the protective layers of her clothing. Beneath the soft, sheer lawn and thin lamb's wool, her nipples slowly emerged from sleep, growing taut, aching to be kissed. And God, how he wanted to kiss them, how he ached to worship her sainted white flesh with his hands and his lips and his—

Draegan gave an inward groan and turned away, back to the fire, to the coffeepot steaming on the hob. "Perhaps after all," he said softly, "I'd better see you safely home."

"But we aren't finished here."

He turned his head to look at her, a look he knew clearly conveyed his deep, abiding hunger. "Yes. We are."

She came out of her chair and crossed the room, forcing him to face her. "Draegan, please. Don't force me to go. I *want* to stay."

"Fallon, I made a mistake in bringing you here. It's more dangerous than you know, and you would be safer tucked up in your bed at the manor. An upstanding, moral young lady like you has no business being with a man like me, cavorting about at night, unwittingly placing yourself in jeopardy."

Fallon reached out instinctively and touched

him. She wanted his attention, his understanding, she wanted openness between them, and she couldn't quite comprehend the shudder she felt run through his lean, hard body. "We share a common goal. We are allies! And we shall face whatever comes together."

He raised his dark head and looked at her, his eyes filled with the harsh light of longing. "You don't know what you're saying." He sighed impatiently and raked her with his burning gaze. "Before, when you named me a man lacking in honor, undeserving of trust—"

"You had vexed me, and I was but getting even," Fallon said, but he went on as if he hadn't heard.

"—you were right about me," he uttered in a low, emotionless tone, a tone that belied the light of desperation in his eyes. "I have never been over-burdened by honor. Indeed, I am an accomplished libertine, a despoiler, and you might as well toy with a rattlesnake as allow yourself to become involved with me. I am poison, Fallon, and I am going to escort you home."

Fallon knew instinctively that he was telling the truth. Yet the irony lay in the fact that she didn't want to hear him.

It was far easier to imagine that he was once again trying to evade and discourage her, to believe that perhaps, just perhaps, she possessed honor enough for the two of them, that some inherent spark of goodness would shine through the dark morass of his soul and keep him from bringing her to grief.

"Why are you telling me this?" she asked. "If you are truly bent upon evil, then why warn me away?"

He brought his hand up slowly, brushing his fingertips in a feather-light caress along the curve of her cheek. "My motives are simple. Your nearness distracts me. The scent of blood on the wind will draw the ravenous wolf, and in that same way your innocence calls to my baser instincts. That wolf lives to kill and feed; I live to corrupt."

His caressing hand glided along her jawline, his elegant fingers sliding into her hair, plucking out the pins. Free of constraints, it fell, tumbling about her shoulders, and Fallon heard the soft, satisfied sigh that caught in his throat. "Since that first day, I have wondered how you would look with your hair unbound, and now at last I know. 'Tis glorious," he murmured, bending slightly to nuzzle the shining strands, capturing Fallon's hands as she frantically tried to repair the damage he had done. "A veritable river of flame."

"The church—the investigation—there's so much to discuss. Oh, Draegan, no. No, we cannot— we shouldn't—oh . . ." He gathered her into his arms, pulling her tightly to his lean, hard body. Fallon's hands were braced against the hard-muscled wall of his chest, but as he bent to kiss her throat they slipped upward to his broad shoulders and stole around his neck.

With a slight tug, she undid the ribbon that kept his shining sable locks neatly clubbed at his nape. A nearly inaudible whisper of sound, and the heavy mane fell forward to frame his face . . . to rasp softly against her throat.

Threading her fingers into the thick, shining strands, Fallon pressed her lips to his, lightly at first, tentatively, and then with the full wanton force of her awakening ardor.

In her mind, there was no longer any doubt. This deliciously wicked man, whoever he happened to be, brought out the worst in her, and though she knew it was wrong, she reveled in her feelings. The sensations his hands and lips evoked were wondrously new and unbearably sweet, so heady that they managed to wipe away every conscious thought, allowing her to concentrate fully on the languid warmth stealing over her, the iron-hard strength of Draegan's arms as he lifted and carried her to the divan.

Kisses . . . endless hot, unbridled kisses. Draegan teased and taunted, kissing her deeply, slowly drawing her small pointed tongue into his mouth, coaxing Fallon to new acts of boldness, to brave explorations she otherwise would not have dared.

She found that she liked the press of his weight as he slowly bore her down onto the cushions of the divan . . . liked the warm brush of his fingers as they loosened the laces of her gown and glided along the bare skin of her back—laces that she herself had struggled to tighten and tie not so long before.

His were powerful hands, adept at soothing, seducing, putting her totally at ease, the warm and wonderful hands of a sorcerer . . . hands that worked magic as they slid past the curve of her spine, lifting her skirts. She loved his touch, craved his warmth, wanted more than anything to touch him as he was touching her.

Caught up in the heat of the moment, Fallon slid her fingers up, over the linen breast of his shirt to the knotted neckcloth. The knot was secure, but she managed to loosen it, and in an instant the ends of the wrapping came free.

Draegan felt the linen binding that concealed the scar slacken, and he grew still. The fire still burned brightly, as did the taper on the table. The room was filled with warm golden light.

He eased upright, away from her, retying the ends of his stock with a jerk, watching in angry, frustrated silence as the warmth went out of her eyes.

She tried to manage the laces that closed the back

of her gown, but he could see that her fingers were shaking. He brushed them aside. "Here, let me help you."

"No, please." She shrugged away, careful, so careful, to avoid his slightest touch. "I can manage."

He stood by, watching her struggles, his guilt melding with his scorching desire. "It's for the best that this happened now," he said, "before you became too involved with me. Surely you can see that it's better if we simply forget everything that's occurred these past two days. We'll dissolve this partnership. It was ill-fated from the beginning in any case—insane. I must have been insane to agree to it."

"Dissolve our alliance?"

"Aye, dammit. It's the best thing—the only thing."

"No."

"Fallon."

"No." She was adamant. "The partnership stands. You agreed, and I intend to hold you to it! I will not allow you to go back on your word."

"You aren't thinking clearly," Draegan said. How could she want to continue, with the memory of what had nearly happened there that night lying between them? How could she simply ignore the passion, the burning lust, the longing that he felt so keenly?

"I won't go back to the way it was before. Thanks to you I have the chance to contribute something to a cause I believe in. I won't give that up!"

Her eyes shone with a feverish light, but it wasn't the light of longing Draegan saw in the darkly golden depths. It was the incandescent glow of zealotry, a desire that went far beyond the physical. It was something he just couldn't fight.

"Baptism by fire . . ." he murmured, smoothing the knuckles of one hand against her soft cheek. "Are you certain that's what you want?"

She nodded solemnly. "Will you share your discoveries with me, your suspicions and unanswered questions?"

Draegan sighed, and his shoulders slumped ever so slightly in defeat. "Come," he said quietly. "There is something you should see."

Chapter 11

Fallon watched as Draegan lifted a lantern down from the kitchen mantel. It was ancient, cylindrical in shape, with a pierced tin shield that, as he put a straw to the fire and again to the wick, gave off an evil, tallow smell that teased Fallon's memory. "You had the lantern last night in the library, did you not?"

He glanced at her but did not deign to answer, going instead through the door that opened into the rectory parlor. Fallon followed along behind him.

In the church sanctuary, they were greeted by an eerie silence, a silence so profound that their every movement, every footfall, seemed magnified tenfold. Fallon's heart picked up its pace as Draegan mounted the steps to the altar and stood, waiting for her to join him. Raising her skirts with one hand, she ascended the steps and took her place by his side. He raised the lantern high.

"Beneath the cross is a small lever. Reach under and pull it down."

Fallon slipped her hand beneath it, found the lever, just as he had indicated, and pulled it down. A low, rumbling groan issued from deep within the building and a section of the wall gave way. "How on earth did you find this?" she asked.

"My method hardly matters now. Suffice it to say that after weeks of searching through musty parish records, of endlessly combing over the structure itself, I found it. Will you go first, or shall I?"

Fallon frowned at him. "This is the reason behind your questions about Grandfather and the church's construction? How did you know it even existed? I've lived here all my life, and I hadn't the smallest inkling! And more important still—where does it lead?"

"It leads to the manor."

"My home? But that can't be!"

"Oh, but it can. You asked last night how I came to be in the library so late. Here lies your answer."

Fallon shook her head. "I don't understand. How can it have been here all these years, with no one the wiser?"

He lifted his broad shoulders in an elegant shrug. "The elders who knew of it have gradually died away, and the passageway's usefulness decreased as the land grew tame and the danger of Indian attack lessened."

"Thus it was forgotten," Fallon said.

He smiled, but the expression was devoid of humor and totally lacking in warmth. "Not completely. Someone remembered. The lever concealed by the cross and the panel hinges have been kept well oiled, and the passageway itself shows signs of a recent use."

"What use?"

Draegan raised the lantern high. Sparks of light danced over his darkly handsome visage, catching in his sable hair, kindling in the translucent depths of his eyes. "Its intended purpose—concealment, escape."

"Dear God," Fallon whispered as realization

dawned. "You think that Sparrowhawk—"

"I know it." He took her arm and drew her closer to the gaping black maw. The chill damp reached out to caress her like an unseen hand, carrying the smell of dank, moldering earth to her nostrils. Inwardly, Fallon shrank back. She'd never liked closed-in spaces, and standing on the precipice of the lightless hole was like standing at the crumbling edge of an empty grave.

For a long moment, Fallon's fear waged war with her innate curiosity, and there was silence between her and Draegan. The struggle was mercifully brief; her thirst for enlightenment, the driving force in her life until now, won the contest. Squaring her shoulders, she said in a level voice, "I should like to see it for myself."

"I would rather you didn't insist," Draegan said, "but by now I know better than to argue against it—however, you must swear to me by all that is holy that you'll speak of its existence to no one, and that you will never set foot inside it alone."

"I hardly think that's necessary," Fallon said, wincing as his grip tightened and his fingers bit into the soft flesh of her arm.

His dark face hovered above hers, as hard and unyielding as stone. "*Fallon.*"

Fallon readily agreed, fearing that if she delayed, her courage would surely desert her and she would shrink back from the gaping black unknown. And then Draegan's hand, the same hand that had hurt her a moment before, was urging her forward, propelling her into the void.

The staircase spiraled downward, turning ever in upon itself. Thirteen steps, a narrow landing, then thirteen more. Fallon had the surreal impression that they were burrowing into the earth, that at any moment it would close in around them and swallow them up, just as it swallowed the feeble light of the pierced-tin lantern. Then they would never see the light of day or feel the warm kiss of the sun's rays on their faces again. . . .

It was a ridiculous, childish notion, she knew, born of her aversion to small, lightless spaces. Yet the realization did little to dispel the irrational fear that crept up from her vitals to close chilly fingers around her heart . . . to strum a mirthless dirge along her nerves—nerves that became increasingly more taut with each passing moment.

They descended the final step and moved along the narrow passageway. Flickers of light danced off the heavy support beams that crossed overhead and lined the walls at regular intervals, the spine and ribs of the serpentine tunnel through which they made their way.

As they rounded a bend in the lightless track, the earth creaked and groaned overhead, and a trickle of shale filtered to the floor, liberally dusting the crates that lined the left wall with crumbling stone and dust.

Another tortured moan . . . a creak of the timbers . . . another trickle of debris . . . and then ominous, portentous quiet. Draegan seemed impervious to the danger that Fallon felt was all around them. He handed her the lantern and, crouching down, pried the lid from the topmost crate.

The instant the contents of the crate were revealed, Fallon forgot her fear. Holding the lantern aloft, she edged nearer and stared open-mouthed at the muskets that filled the crate. "Brown Bess muskets. British issue!"

"Aye," Draegan said. "And hellish hard to come by."

Fallon put a hand to her temple. "This makes no sense. There is an entrance here at the church, and another at the manor, but neither place is deserted—neither is free from discovery. How was Sparrowhawk able to move these rifles without being detected—without someone's seeing or growing suspicious?"

Draegan replaced the lid and stood, dusting off his hands. "There are a number of possibilities. The rectory has been abandoned until recently, though I seriously doubt the weapons have been down here an entire month. The dampness would very quickly corrode the metal, and as you doubtless noticed, they glint like new."

"They could not possibly have been taken in through the manor. Someone would have noticed—Willie, Zepporah, Uncle, or I."

"My thoughts exactly," he said. "Sparrowhawk is daring, but he's no fool. The chances he takes are carefully calculated beforehand. And in this instance, the risk of exposure would overshadow every other consideration."

"But if not the manor, and not the church . . ." Fallon let the thought trail away, convinced that he had already considered it and arrived at some likely solution.

She was not to be disappointed. "There is a third exit to the passageway," he said, taking the lantern in one hand, her hand in the other, and urging her onward.

The supports gradually grew fewer and farther between, then disappeared altogether, and soon they had left the man-made hell behind and entered a natural underground passage, the walls, floor, and ceiling of which were solid, comforting stone.

Fallon relaxed a little.

Just ahead, a huge stone wedge jutted into the center of the passageway, forming a Y that was somewhat lopsided and leaned to the right. Water seeped down the vertical face of the wedge, pooling on the floor near its base. Draegan guided Fallon along the left branch while inclining his head toward the right. "The other passageway leads to a huge cavern, large enough to house a score of men and several horses. It opens into the heart of Vanderbloon's Wood, and shows signs of a recent occupation."

"By whom? Sparrowhawk? If so, then he must be a townsman, someone with intimate knowledge of the countryside and this place. But who could it possibly be?"

He avoided her gaze, a fact that troubled Fallon. "Step carefully here. The third tread is crumbling."

He guided her up a second set of winding stairs at the forward end of the tunnel, opposite the rectory. When they reached the landing, he put a finger to his lips in warning, and pressed his ear to the wall. Evidently satisfied that no one was stirring, he pulled down on the lever to the right of the doorframe. As the door swung open slowly, noiselessly, Draegan indicated that she should precede him.

Fallon entered the familiar surroundings. Her desk, inkstand, and quills were just as she'd left them. The same well-loved volumes lined the shelves in a room that smelled pleasantly of vellum and leather. "This is too incredible to countenance," she said, turning slowly back to Draegan.

He hung back in the open doorway, seemingly reluctant to enter.

Fallon was oddly disappointed. She didn't want him to leave. They still had a great deal to discuss, to reason through, and somehow she'd assumed they would do so together. "You aren't leaving so soon?"

"I see no reason to tempt fate," he said softly, "or to tempt myself unduly."

Fallon thought of what had nearly occurred that

evening and shivered. The memory, however, did not prevent her from asking, "Will you come again tomorrow eve?"

He shook his head. "There are other matters to which I must attend."

"What matters?"

"Fallon." His voice was softly chiding as he lifted her hand, bringing it to his lips. "I shall see you Sabbath morning. We'll talk then." With a brush of his warm, carnal mouth on the palm of her hand, he released her, stepping back into the darkness.

A whisper of sound and the panel slid back into place. It was difficult for Fallon to discern just where it had been. For several minutes, she studied the hearth wall, searching for the mechanism that would open the hidden door, pushing against the carved mantel, testing the painted ornamental tile that framed the brick firebox itself, lifting the iron poker from its hook—all to no avail.

The house, like Draegan Mattais, seemed reluctant to share its secrets.

Draegan's thoughts, as he cautiously retraced his steps through the catacombs, revolved around the flame-haired temptress he'd left in the darkened library at Gilead Manor—the ungovernable passions she kindled in his blood. It had been hellishly hard to leave her after she'd asked him to stay, to step back into the foul atmosphere of the passageway and firmly close the door, while thoughts of their lovemaking lingered in his head. Seductive thoughts of creamy flesh and tumbled auburn tresses, of Fallon's exploring touch, remained.

God, how he wanted to possess her. She was such an enchanting young woman, so painfully honest, frank, and forthright. A flaming rebel firebrand in a soft woolen bodice and voluminous skirts, as different from manipulative Molly as nighttime from noon. She was different from Lettice, the young widow, different from all of the bored Tory wives, the kitchen wenches, and the long string of tavern maids he'd known.

She bewildered him, maddened him, bewitched him. Slowly, skillfully, through persistence and stubbornness, she had wheedled the truth from him, and he'd given it, albeit grudgingly, like a miser seduced into parting with his precious coin.

She had accepted his piddling admissions, but he knew she wasn't satisfied. Her questions were bound to continue; she was bound to persist until at last he surrendered the contest of wills and gave her what she wanted most.

Truth—God help him. She wanted the truth. He could see it in her eyes every time he looked at her, and he knew in his heart she wouldn't be satisfied until she'd extracted every painful, ugly scrap. She clearly wouldn't rest until she lay bare all of his festering wounds—his desire for vengeance, his suspicions about Lucien, his bitterness—until at last, with truth, he drove her from him.

The painful moan that sounded low in the earth echoed deep in Draegan's own soul, like the damnable soughing wind in the boughs of the sentinel maple.

Once she had dragged all the rest from him, she would want the details of that accursed night, and in the telling he would be forced to relive it. At the very thought he went cold all over.

Damn her.

He would not do it. Not even if she offered up her innocence to tempt him.

The scar was a hideous reminder of events in his life he would rather have forgotten yet could not forget. The torments of that night had been visited upon *his* flesh, *his* mind, *his* soul alone. They belonged to him, and were his alone to horde or to share, as he saw fit. And Draegan was not ready to share them—with anyone.

Not even Fallon Deane.

As he mounted the steps that led to the door behind the sanctuary altar, he shuddered to think of how close he had come. She had wanted to touch him, perhaps as badly as he'd wanted to feel the sensuous slide of her hands on his skin. Unwittingly, she had unknotted the neckcloth . . . and he had recoiled—instinctively, immediately, without a word of excuse or explanation. And all for the sake of his pride.

He reached the last tread, slipping into the sanctuary. Then, like the wraith he was, he haunted the rectory rooms, thinking dark thoughts as he rested a hand on the back of the faded divan—wandering aimlessly into the kitchen, where the rich aroma of coffee still lingered in the air. . . .

His struggle was long and arduous. Yet try as he might, he could not rid his mind of Fallon. And so he took up his coat and went out, hoping against hope that a night of hunting might grant him a peaceful sleep, for once devoid of dreams.

At the same moment that Draegan was closing the door of the rectory and preparing to ride, a flicker of light appeared in the catacombs far below.

Shadows, one small and misshapen, one large and hulking, crept through the wavering torchlight cast on the western wall, halting by the crates that held the British-issue muskets.

Randall put his nose to the air and sniffed as a terrier sniffs down a rat hole. "What is that smell?" He sniffed again. "It smells—like oil, or tallow."

"Or pitch," Lucien said with a shake of his head.

"Tell me, young Master Quill. What is it that you have there in your hand?"

Randall's eyes flashed in the glow of the flaming pine knot that he held. "Do not patronize me, sir. I tell you, I smell the taint of oil in the air! Someone has been here before us—perhaps is here still." Reaching into his deerskin coat, he came away with a pistol.

"Stop acting the ninny," Lucien said, "and I shall cease patronizing you." He looked pointedly at the pistol Randall was clutching. "Put the weapon away. We've much to discuss."

Randall hesitated.

"Very well, then, young sir," Lucien said in a silken voice, lacking his usual acid. "Persist, if it makes you feel more secure. But you might as well put the gun to your own temple as to fire a shot in this subterranean maze. If the shot doesn't find its way back to you, you risk being buried alive." As if on cue the earth shifted overhead, the timbers creaked and moaned, and a trickle of shale glanced off the toe of Randall's boot.

Randall hastened to secure the weapon inside his coat, moving away from the path of the falling stone. "Let's do what we came here to do and get out."

"In due time," Lucien said. "First I would have a closer look at the muskets." He reached down and lifted the lid of the topmost one.

Randall frowned over his shoulder. "I thought the lids were pegged shut."

"You *think* too much."

"I am certain of it," Randall insisted. "I secured them myself. Someone has tampered with them since last I was here."

Lucien sighed and shook his head. "You would try the patience of Job," he said beneath his breath, then aloud, "You are allowing your fears to run off with you once again." He gestured to the muskets, glinting lethally in the torchlight. "See for yourself. They are all here, untouched—our secret, Randall, lad. Just as the cavern is our secret, unless of course you have been careless in your carousing at Sike's Tavern and wagged your tongue too freely."

The veins swelled on Randall's face and neck; he seemed about to explode. "I am not the one to freely wag my tongue, as you so blithely put it! Nor did I invite Satan's spawn home to sup!"

Lucien's smile was knowing. "Ah, so that's what this is about. You are still seething over the Reverend Mattais's being invited to the manor to dine with Fallon and me."

"There is something about him that bedevils me," Randall muttered. "Something I can't lay a finger to."

"Come, now, admit it, Quill," Lucien sneered. "You're afraid of him. That's the real truth, isn't it? The good reverend has managed, without even trying, to instill the fear of God in you."

"But you, the great Lucien Deane, fear nothing! Not God, not man. Certainly not the Reverend Mattais!" Randall laughed harshly. "Your arrogance has consumed you, Lucien—blinded you to the danger Mattais represents! Have you stopped to consider what will occur if he stumbles onto the truth? Have you given a moment's thought to Fallon?"

"He will not stumble onto anything!" Lucien said icily. "And I will thank you to leave Fallon out of this!"

"If he discovers the truth, you may not be able to keep it from her. That bastard has designs on her. If he discovers the truth, he'll tell her, rest assured."

"He will not discover anything!"

"Antwhistle did!"

Lucien smiled tightly. "And Antwhistle troubles us no more, is that not so? *If* Draegan Mattais should prove as foolish as his predecessor, then I shall have no other recourse except to silence him. Until that moment comes, you would be well advised to forget him and concentrate all of your energies on carrying out our plans. The fighting is nearing an end, Randall. Very soon, this accursed insurrection will be squashed. Very soon, we will receive our just due. . . . "

"I pray you are right," Randall said. "I am sick unto death of sneaking about at night, of the meetings, and—"

"That's understandable. You have had a great deal of responsibility, a great deal of pressure. Perhaps you need a rest."

Randall's hand hovered near the open front of his deerskin coat. His fear was evident.

Lucien smiled. "Come, come, now. There's no need for that. I was merely about to suggest that a change of scene might do you good."

"Precisely what *are* you suggesting, Lucien?"

"Only that you take a week or two and venture down Cobleskill way for a visit. You have a friend there, don't you? Let's see, what was his name again? Green, wasn't it?"

"Captain Christian Brown," Randall corrected, "commander of the local militia."

"A militia commander, you say," Lucien said, stroking his chin. "How very convenient for you. Yes, do go there, Randall, and while you are there be certain to note any improvements upon the existing fortifications. If we are to end this conflict soon here in New York, we will need every scrap of intelligence we can muster on Cobleskill, Schoharie, and the Cherry Valley. Indeed, we'll need information on every American settlement from here to the Pennsylvania border, no matter how piddling it happens to be."

The Sabbath morning found Fallon seated in the family pew, eyes demurely downcast as she listened to Reverend Mattais sermonize in a ringing voice about the wages of sin and the necessity of adhering strictly to the Ten Commandments, the guide by which all good men must live. He was so convincing, so humble and sincere, so inherently shameless, that Fallon could not look at him.

He was an accomplished fraud, adept at keeping secrets, while she was but a novice, painfully aware of her limitations, far more comfortable with the truth than with deception. She was afraid to raise her eyes to his dark, angelic face, afraid someone might see something telling in her expression. No one must guess that he was the cause of the gentle heat that had risen to her cheeks as he entered the chapel sanctuary and mounted the pulpit steps—heat that now stubbornly refused to cool.

Not even Draegan.

He must never know how interminably the past four days had dragged for her, how many nights she had wandered down to the library long after the others had gone to bed, foolishly hoping to find him there.

Above all, he must never guess that she'd relived that last night in the rectory in her dreams, awaking each night confused and frightened, her flesh burning for something she instinctively knew she could find only through surrender to his sultry kisses, by succumbing wholly to the wonder of his touch.

Never, *never*, must he discover the pleasurable shock that shot through her vitals each time he looked her way and their gazes chanced to meet. Never must he know how his voice could cause her heart to pick up its pace. For he was a seductive, conscienceless devil who would use the knowledge against her and leave her to deal with her shame alone.

In the pew directly behind Fallon, Willie heaved a wistful sigh. Fallon knew without looking back that her friend was gazing at Thomas, who sat across the aisle looking every bit as forlorn and heartsick as she.

In an odd sense, Fallon found that she envied Willie, who seemed to know her heart, her desires, so implicitly. Willie felt none of the confusion that kept Fallon tossing and turning in her bed at night, that plagued her during her waking hours—that, these days, never seemed to leave her.

Willie knew precisely what she wanted, but aside from her desire to aid Draegan in the capture of Sparrowhawk, Fallon wasn't sure what she herself wanted. She knew only that she was not the same young woman who had stopped by the rectory the previous month to investigate the plume of smoke rising from the chimney and discovered a dark, handsome stranger seated by the fire.

She was changing, and though the changes she was undergoing were subtle, she was frightened to think of where they might lead.

While Fallon sat gathering wool, Draegan's sermon came to a rousing close. The congregation rose and stood with heads bowed piously as he led them in a final prayer. Fallon prayed for strength and enlightenment, which she hoped would not elude her.

Draegan descended the steps from the pulpit after the prayer was finished, offering his arm to Fallon. "My dear Mistress Deane," he murmured. "I hope you'll consent to uphold our tradition and stand by my side in the vestibule to bid our friends good day."

Acutely aware that all eyes were on her, Fallon smiled and nodded, slipping her hand through the curve of his arm. Together, they walked to the vestibule to take their usual places, for all the world as if they were nothing more to each other than the village pastor and his benefactor's niece.

The villagers filed out of the church, pausing long enough to exchange a friendly word or two with Draegan or to ask after Lucien's health. Fallon remained calm and unruffled throughout, despite her earlier fears, until Cordelia Plum came gliding up.

Cordelia was dressed in a cotton sateen gown of bright delft blue that matched her eyes, and her plump cheeks had been rouged to perfection. With a coy little smile and a bat of her pale lashes, she presented her hand to be kissed. "Father sends his heartfelt regrets that he could not attend this morning, Reverend. But he has been under the weather for three days running."

Draegan dutifully kissed Cordelia's plump white hand, holding it a fraction too long, Fallon thought. "I'm sorry to hear it, Miss Plum. I pray it's nothing serious."

"Miss Nancy Mae fears that it's a lingering case of the ague."

"Indeed, how unfortunate."

Cordelia hastened to elaborate, now that she had his undivided attention. "Poor Papa. He was called out in last week's rainstorm to fix the wheel of a coach belonging to some gentry who hailed from Kingston, and he got soaked clean through to his johns in the downpour."

"I'm exceedingly sorry to hear it," Draegan said. "Tell him, won't you, that we'll remember him in our prayers."

Cordelia bestowed a honeyed smile upon Draegan and pressed closer. "You might tell him yourself if you accompany my sisters and me home to dinner. Miss Nancy Mae will be so relieved to see you, and Papa will recover all the more quickly, knowing that you have interceded with the Almighty on his behalf."

"Dinner," Draegan said. "Well, I don't know—"

"If you refuse, Papa's sure to be dejected," Cordelia insisted. She licked her full pink lips as she continued to watch him, Fallon noted with rising ire, like a cat licking cream from its whiskers. "You won't disappoint a man in his sick-bed, will you?"

"My dear Mistress Plum, I assure you there is nothing I would rather do than to offer comfort to your father in his time of need, yet I do have prior commitments."

"Commitments?"

He nodded gravely. "Commitments. A young couple about to be wed have requested my private counsel. Isn't that right, Mistress Deane?"

"Hm?" Fallon feigned disinterest. She had extracted him from his last encounter with the husband-hunting Cordelia; this time she was content to let him manage on his own. "Oh, yes, of course."

"But sickness always takes precedence over wedlock," Cordelia reasoned. "Why, if Papa perished unshriven, it would be a terrible tragedy. Surely the counseling can be postponed an hour or two."

"Very well, then," he said. "If you will be so good as to wait for me outside, I'll be along in a moment or two."

Cordelia shot Fallon a triumphant glance and sailed through the church door into the bright spring sunlight.

"I hope you are satisfied," he said softly to Fallon.

"Satisfied?" Fallon replied. "I'm sure I don't know how you mean."

"I thought we'd struck a bargain night before last, a sacred pact."

"You must strive to make your terms more clear, sir. I wasn't aware that our pact included my shielding you from the avid attentions of the wheelwright's daughter."

"Well, perhaps it should have. She looks at me in the same fashion a hungry hound eyes a meaty bone, and it's damned unnerving, I don't mind telling you."

Fallon hid her smile behind a gloved hand as he turned to those emerging from the sanctuary. "Good day to you, young Master Smith," Draegan said. "Ah, Wilhemina . . . Madam Rhys. I wonder if I might have a word with you later today."

With a nod, Zepporah passed from the vestibule, and Fallon and Draegan were left alone. "If you had a heart in that pearly breast of yours, you'd consent to accompany me."

Fallon pulled a face. "She made it quite clear that your prayers alone were required. Far be it from me to interfere."

Draegan smiled and, reaching out, smoothed the knuckles of one elegant hand along the curve of her cheek. "You are such a perverse little thing. Ready to throw me to that ravening young she-wolf rather than admit that you care in the least bit what becomes of me."

"Don't be ridiculous," Fallon chided. "Of course I care. I care very deeply—about our joint venture, about Sparrowhawk's capture and your mission's success."

He tipped up her chin with gentle fingers, ignoring a call from Cordelia. "Is that all, Fallon?"

Fallon's heart skipped a beat, and she had to fight to maintain control, to meet his penetrating gaze and not let her true feelings show. "What else could there possibly be?"

Cordelia's voice came, more strident now. "Mr. Mattais? We shouldn't keep Papa waiting! Mr. Mattais!"

He sighed. "Now that my self-worth has been properly deflated, I suppose there is nothing left but to bid you good day."

Fallon caught at his sleeve. "What of tonight? Will you come again?"

"Come to the garden at twilight. If I survive my ordeal at Cordelia's plump hands, I shall be there waiting."

He went out, but Fallon didn't follow. In his absence there was no need to keep up the pretense, and the truth of the matter was that she could not bear to see him in the company of the lush Cordelia.

She'd feigned disinterest in his life, his affairs, in him, but it had all been a lie. As she stood listening to the quiet, Fallon wondered if God could forgive her blatant fabrication put forth in His house, for the truth was that she was terribly, inexplicably jealous. She was jealous not simply of Cordelia, but of all the women Draegan had known and cared for—the women who had shared his bed and his secrets, his private self, the women who had placed the smallest, briefest, most insignificant claim on his body and soul. . . .

Chapter 12

"**H**ow was your meeting with Zepporah? Were you able to convince her to allow Thomas and Willie to marry?"

"Straight to the point, as always," Draegan answered dryly.

Seated primly at the rectory table, the candlelight casting burnished highlights on her wealth of auburn hair, Fallon raised her brow. "Pray, sir, what were you expecting?"

"That for once you might beat about the blasted bush," he said, "and ask me how my day was. That you might show the slightest concern for my well-being."

She replied with a patience Draegan found maddening. "Very well, then. How was your day?"

"Harrowing," he said flatly. "I barely managed to escape the wheelwright's home with my virtue still intact."

Her full red lips curved upward. "Draegan the Despoiler, the bane of all womankind? I was not aware that you had a scrap of virtue remaining after living your oh, so dissipated life."

Draegan frowned at her. "It's apparent that I spoke hastily the last time you were here, unwittingly providing you with ammunition to use against me. In the future I shall be more wary of what I tell you."

Her amber stare was disapproving. "You are far too wary as it is, sir. Now, do tell, was your visit to the Plums successful?"

He looked sharply at her. "I beg your pardon?"

Her lips, so luscious, so kissable, twitched with secret amusement. "Master Plum. Did your visit bring him solace in his sick-bed, as Cordelia had suggested?"

Draegan snorted. "Master Plum did indeed catch cold last week, but he was not abed at all. In fact, I found him seated at the dining table, surrounded by his family, and quite relieved that I had arrived in a timely fashion. It seems he has a strong aversion to cold potatoes, and was waiting dinner on me only at Cordelia's insistence."

Fallon grinned, which further annoyed her host. "Not only did she foist my presence upon her family with little notice in advance," Draegan continued, "but she lured me there under false pretenses, completely wasting my afternoon." He dragged an impatient hand through his hair, raking Fallon with his heated gaze. "Dammit, Fallon, this isn't the least bit amusing!"

"No," she conceded, hastening to hide her smile behind her upraised coffee cup. "I don't suppose it is, since you're the one who's been outmaneuvered. But I really don't understand your upset. You did say that you left the wheelwright's house with your virtue intact. Cordelia, therefore, did not succeed in bagging a prospective husband. At least not today."

"It is the fact that I allowed myself to be maneuvered by that young she-wolf that rankles the most," he admitted. "I do not like feeling trapped."

Trapped and helpless . . . like the night of the hanging, only to a far lesser extent. Draegan's smile was decidedly grim. The incident with Miss Plum was lesser, perhaps, yet it triggered the same rage, the same feeling of impotence, that he had hoped never to feel again.

None of this could he explain to Fallon. Fortunately, she did not press the matter, but seemed content to let it pass in lieu of other things. "What news have you for Willie?" she asked over the rim of her chipped porcelain coffee cup.

Draegan wandered restlessly to the hearth and stood, one fist thrust deep into his coat pocket. In the other, he clutched his near-empty cup. "Willie, it seems, is destined to be disappointed. Madam Rhys thinks her too young and too tender to wed. There is also the matter of young Master Thomas. For some reason known only to her, she doesn't approve of the lad, and so insists that they wait."

"I feared as much," Fallon said with a sigh and a doubtful shake of her head, "but I detest the thought of breaking the news to Willie. She wants this marriage so badly. She's bound to be heartbroken."

"She does not have to be," Draegan said darkly. "They can wed if they wish."

"Why, Draegan Mattais, what are you suggesting?"

"Elopement. It's perfectly legal and an end to their means. They should have no difficulty finding a reputable minister to unite them in the eyes of God."

"But Zepporah!"

He shrugged, swirling the dregs of his coffee before tossing them on the fire. The liquid sizzled and steamed, and was quickly consumed by the greedy flames. "Zepporah thinks they should wait. But there is always the chance that they will wait for a tomorrow that never comes. Life comes with no guarantees, and neither Zepporah nor you nor I, nor even the great Lucien Deane, can say with absolute certainty that the sun will rise tomorrow. If Willie and Thomas abide by their parents' wishes, they may be squandering their one chance at happiness."

She was frowning at him, heavily, as if seeing him for the first time. "Has the search for Sparrowhawk made you so pessimistic?" she asked. Her voice was so quiet, so sincerely concerned, that Draegan winced inwardly.

"*Life*," he replied, staring fixedly into the flames, "has made me realistic, and before I say something to prompt a veritable flood of questions, perhaps we should change the subject."

"How very consistent," Fallon said, tapping one shapely finger against her creamy cheek. "The moment our discourse becomes personal, you hasten to turn the topic to something more to your liking, something *safer*."

"Fallon—" he began, but she handily cut him off.

"Pray, sir. Do not 'Fallon' me. This time it will not work. What deep, dark secret are you keeping? Have you a wife somewhere, whom you have cruelly deserted? A host of wives, perhaps?"

"I have never wed, and doubtless never will."

"Are you a thief, then? A wanton murderer?"

"Fallon, for the love of Christ. I did not bring you here so that you might badger me."

"If you would but cease closing yourself off from me each time I get the least bit close, there would be no reason for me to badger you!" She rose from her chair and stood, glaring at him, her palms braced on the surface of the table.

Draegan went to her and seized her wrists, lifting first one hand, pressing a kiss into the palm, and then the other. "Why must you bedevil me so about something that truly doesn't matter, when we have other, more important things to discuss?"

"This *is* important—to me. I have given you my trust, and in return you have given me nothing. Not even your name."

He released her and, sighing, turned away. "The less you know of me, the better it will be."

Fallon followed him to the hearth, persistent as always. "Better for whom? For me, or for you?"

"For both of us! Now, leave be! I have enough to do, trying to pacify the villagers while playing the Right Reverend Mattais, watch the road and the passageway, and keep watch on your friend Captain Quill while I fend off Cordelia's unwelcome advances! Do not add to my already considerable aggravations."

She went still. "You are watching Randall?"

"As closely as I dare."

"Whatever for?"

"I have a good idea that he may be in league with Sparrowhawk."

"Randall." She laughed disbelievingly. "But he is the ranking officer of our local militia."

"And a traitor, it would seem. Apart from the militia, he is away a great deal, 'on business,' isn't that so?"

"Yes, I suppose that he is, now that you mention it."

"Has he ever indicated to you what manner of business venture he is involved in, or with whom?"

Fallon frowned. "Other than the dispatches he carries for Uncle Lucien, I really could not say."

"Dispatches?"

"Letters. To Master Trumbolt."

"Trumbolt," Draegan said.

"Joshua Trumbolt. He owns an estate some miles west of Albany, and is an old friend and colleague of Uncle's. For a number of years, they have enjoyed a vigorous correspondence."

"And you say that Randall carries these letters for Master Deane?" Draegan probed carefully. He was terribly aware of the need to keep his suspicions about Lucien's activities from Fallon. There was no telling how she would react if she were to discover that his investigation—the investigation in which she was now playing an active part—centered around her uncle.

Quite likely, she would refuse to believe him, refuse to listen, do her utmost to convince him that he was wrong. In addition, the possibility always existed that she would turn against him, betray him, in order to save her loved one.

The bonds of blood were stronger than the tenuous threads of their own newly forged alliance, and although he had long since given up the notion that she was somehow involved in the treasonous activities of Sparrowhawk, he still could not afford to trust her.

"Randall," she said. "It seems so ludicrous!"

Draegan's chest grew tight. "Why is it ludicrous, Fallon? Because in your heart you don't want to believe that Randall Quill is guilty of the wanton cruelty for which Sparrowhawk is noted, because you care for him more deeply than you are willing to admit?"

She bristled visibly at what he was implying. "I have known Randall half my life, much longer than I have known you! Of course I care about him, but not in the fashion you are implying. And though he is at times pompous and arrogant, I do not believe him the monster you seem eager to paint him."

The sidelong glance Draegan cast Fallon's way was dark and unreadable. "Perhaps you don't know him as well as you think."

"And you *do* know him," she said.

He looked away, toward the fire, and a muscle leaped convulsively in his lean cheek. "Well enough to know that he is not worthy of your concern or your friendship. He is a man without honor, lacking in compassion, capable of unspeakable acts—the worst sort of cruelty and injustice."

His voice was terrible in its softness. It chilled Fallon, and though she stood but a short distance from the blaze Jacob had kindled earlier, she shivered. "Cruelty and injustice that you have witnessed firsthand—is that what you are saying?"

"I am saying that he is suspect, and for safety's sake, I would suggest that you endeavor to keep your distance from him."

She faced him squarely, her small chin thrust slightly forward. "That is an evasion, and not good enough. If you have cause to doubt Randall Quill, then I wish to hear what it is." Draegan looked at Fallon and then away, a fleeting glance filled with the bright light of a hatred so intense that it shocked and frightened Fallon. In less than an instant the light faded, the mask of impassivity slipped back into place, and once again he appeared cool and aloof.

Fallon was incensed. He was retreating from her again—closing himself away behind the impenetrable wall of secrecy that shielded him from the outside world, from her, from anyone who happened to venture too near.

Fallon reached out swiftly, grasping his arm, bringing him back to face her. "Draegan, no. Don't close yourself off from me. Don't turn away again."

"What do you want from me?"

"Only to understand you. To understand about Randall, about your suspicions."

"Liar," he said softly. "You want it all. My failings and my weaknesses, my past, my soul."

"I want the truth from you, and nothing more," Fallon countered. "Just an ounce of honesty. The smallest bit of trust."

" 'Just,' you say. 'The smallest bit.' You make it sound so easy, so trifling a matter." He shook his head and laughed low, a humorless sound. "You don't know what you are asking."

"Then explain it to me, and I will listen. We are partners, are we not? Dedicated and sworn to help each other. Partners share things, good and bad. And there is nothing so terrible that you cannot share it with me, if only you trust me." The hand that rested on his sleeve tightened slightly, to emphasize her point. "You *can* trust me, Draegan. I swear to you, I would never betray you to anyone."

He did not move. Indeed, he did not seem to breathe, yet Fallon had the strange impression that he had moved closer. He stared first at the hand that rested on his sleeve; then he slowly raised his gaze to her face, her lips. "Can I?" he asked, so softly, so achingly.

"With your life, if need be."

He lifted his free hand to toy with the short tendrils that had escaped her neat chignon and curled at her cheek. "You want my trust, my truth. You want to know why I detest Captain Quill. But what will you offer to me in return for all that I give you?"

"My unflinching loyalty. My all." She answered without thinking, without sensing the subtle changes in his voice during the course of their conversation. Yet when he covered her hand with his and closed the distance remaining between them, she realized her mistake.

His dark head dipped. He touched his carnal mouth to hers, briefly, teasingly. "All, Fallon," he breathed against her. "Your generosity of spirit is heartening."

"I only meant—" she began, breaking off when he stole yet another kiss. "I did not mean to—Draegan."

"Fallon," he replied, drawing her into his arms, holding her tightly to his lean, hard length. "How soft you are, how sweet. So delectably pure . . . Fallon."

He kissed her then, long and languorously, pressing her gradually, relentlessly back, over the arm that tightly encircled her waist, giving her no choice but to cling to him or fall.

Ruthless. He could be ruthless when it came to getting what he wanted.

Impossible. An impossible man to resist.

Fallon struggled hard to break free of the spell his nearness cast over her, but her efforts were slow and sluggish, halfhearted. She gripped the superfine of his coat in both fists for an instant while warring within herself, and then with an audible sigh her hands relaxed their grip, opening, sliding up and over his shoulders to tangle in the thick, dark silk of his hair.

"We're partners," he breathed against her parted lips. "There is nothing you cannot ask of me. Nothing I would not do to pleasure you. I promise you, my love, to give you my all."

His words, rich with hidden meaning, and his voice, so low and warm and hoarse with wanting, made Fallon quiver. "All," she said, echoing his former ploy. "You wish to pleasure me."

He was tracing the curve of Fallon's jaw with his tongue, doing the most delicious things to the lobe of her ear, but at her words he straightened. "Mmmm, yes . . . to unbearable heights of rapturous pleasure." He toyed with the lace that edged the neckline of her gown, tracing his fingers slowly down the bodice front. He flicked open the hooks as he went, smiling darkly down at her.

"You would do anything," Fallon said.

"*Anything,*" he vowed passionately, bending to nuzzle the hollow beneath her ear, trailing his lips along the sensitive tendon running down the side of her throat.

Fallon gasped and arched her neck, instinctively giving him greater access. "Anything at all," she breathed. She heard him murmur an unintelligible reply, intent upon nibbling his way across her collarbone and down. His hold had slackened. Fallon quickly stepped back, watching as a questioning look crossed his patrician features. "Then pleasure me thoroughly, sir," she said, "with truth."

He took a determined step toward her; she held up both hands and stepped back, still out of reach. "I want you, Fallon," he murmured, "more than I can possibly convey to you with words, and that is the blatant truth."

"That's not the truth I'm talking about," she insisted.

He looked at her narrowly. "This is no time for games, my lady."

"You're the one playing games, Draegan. I have never been more serious." Or more frightened, Fallon thought—not of Draegan, but of herself. Something in him drew her, and though she knew the dangers of her situation, his dark, seductive power was far too strong to resist. At that moment she was out of his arms and feeling stronger, more in control.

But that sense of control was misleading. One touch and she would weaken; a kiss and she was lost.

"You are seeking to strike yet another bargain," he said with a slight smile. "One more to my liking than the last. Perhaps, after all, we can parley."

Fallon moved back, placing the table between them. On the tabletop, a candle guttered in a pool of melted wax. "No bargains, sir. If I deal with you on the terms you are seeking, I might as well deal with the Devil."

"That's a trifle harsh, don't you think?" he said, coming slowly forward.

"In truth, I don't know what to think. Or what to believe. When you touch me, my will dissolves, and my inherent weakness makes me ill. I think of you when we're apart; I pray for your safety each night. I worry and I watch and I wait, until I'm convinced I must be going mad! When I try to work, I find that I can't concentrate. And all for a man I don't know, a shadowy figure without a name, devoid of truth or honesty! I cannot care for you! Letting you into my life would lead to my destruction. I will not allow myself to care!"

He looked at her for a long moment, a measuring look, and then, without a word, he wet his finger and thumb and reached out, snuffing the candle's flame, throwing the room into deep, concealing shadow.

It took a moment for her eyes to adjust to the darkness, and in that moment Fallon held her breath, certain that he would reach for her. But he only sighed wearily and slipped off his black superfine coat, draping it over the back of a chair. "I was baptized Draegan Mattais in the Congregationalist Church at Albany thirty years ago, not far from my boyhood home in the Mohawk Valley. It is the same church over which my uncle Jonathan Akers now presides."

"The Mohawk Valley," Fallon said. "Not Connecticut?"

He raised one hand to his throat and tugged at the knotted ends of his stock. "Born in New London, reared in New York."

"Your education, the shop, and the surveying. . . . the *Ida Lee*."

"At the age of eighteen I became involved with a young woman of good family. The lady in question mentioned rather belatedly that she had a husband who happened to be away on business a great deal."

"Belatedly?" Fallon said.

"She informed me as he was striding up the front walk. Escape with dignity was impossible, and so I stood my ground, much to the dismay of the lady in question. The husband was understandably outraged. He named me a young rascal and called me out. But he proved a terrible hand with pistols."

"What happened to him?"

"My shot was true; nonetheless the story has a happy ending. I wounded the man in the shoulder, much to the outrage of his lady wife, who, suddenly stricken with overriding wifely concern for her husband, nursed him back to health. The old gent gave her several little ones shortly thereafter, and I daresay the lady in question hasn't strayed since." He unwound the neck cloth and, allowing the ends to trail, began to unbutton the fine linen shirt he wore. "Father was understandably displeased with my behavior when he learned of it, but Mother was livid. She packed me off to Harvard College with an earful of admonishments, and since New York City had become a rather warm environ for me, I went willingly enough. When I arrived, I discovered that she had arranged for me to study theology, in hopes that it would provide me with 'the solid moral foundation Father's neglect had failed to provide.'"

"A background in theology," Fallon said. "That would explain your convincing performance at the pulpit."

"Performance," he murmured. "Ever astute, ever forthright. I'm not sure why I am surprised at your ability to see through me. You always have, it seems." He took a deep breath and expelled it slowly, unfastening his cuffs. "I remained at Harvard for a time, as Mother intended. Looking back now, I am not sure just why. Perhaps it was my way of trying to mend the rift between us."

"And did you? Mend the rift?" He had captured Fallon's interest and, in some odd way, her empathy.

She watched with a rapt expression as he eased the tail of the linen shirt from his tight dark trousers, her appreciative gaze taking in the loose, flowing lines of the pale garment, the dark silhouette of his muscular body barely showing beneath.

"I was expelled from Harvard in my second year for scandalous behavior, and I wandered once again to New York City. My grandfather had passed on a few months before, leaving his shop to me, as I believe I have already mentioned."

"But the life of a shopkeeper did not suit," Fallon prompted, eager to know more of him, wanting, strangely, to know all.

"It was too dull to suit my tastes. I like excitement, danger, the thrill of living on the edge." He braced one hand on the tabletop, bringing the other one up to cup and caress her cheek. His touch was gentle and soothing, and Fallon had to struggle not to turn her face into his hand. "What about you, Fallon? Do you have a taste for adventure, excitement, and danger?"

A month earlier she could have answered truthfully that she felt no thirst for anything more than she already possessed: a comfortable life, a few good friends, a purpose. And then Draegan had entered her life, and everything had changed. Her reply, however, was more cautious. "I admit, I enjoy a bit of intrigue, but in small doses, and not without a certain amount of restraint. To immerse oneself in the 'thrill of living on the edge' is foolhardy, and could very well lead to ruin."

He smiled his devil's smile. "Some of life's greatest rewards are reaped by throwing caution to the wind."

"Spoken like a man," Fallon said. "Abandoning caution is a luxury a woman cannot afford, and should not consider unless she is prepared to rue her lapse on the morrow."

"But what if tomorrow never comes? What if you let the moment slip by you for caution's sake, and find yourself robbed of your one chance at happiness? Would you not rue that loss for the rest of your days, and wish that once, just once, you'd laid aside your logic and given your heart free reign?"

His reasoning was self-serving, Fallon thought, yet in some terrifying way it also made perfect sense. "We have strayed far afield from our original course. I believe we were discussing your jaded past."

"There is little left to tell. I surveyed along the shores of Lake Oneida until the mosquitoes had sucked me dry, then signed on board my brother Clayton's ship, the *Ida Lee.*"

"What happened after?"

"Fallon." He was impatient now. "Why dwell on the past, when the present provides so many intriguing possibilities?"

Fallon opened her mouth to speak, and he hastened to place his fingertips over her lips, effectively stilling her protests.

"You know me better than anyone, more intimately, I think at times, than I know myself." Lifting her hand, he kissed her fingertips, then slowly drew her hand toward him, pressing it to his naked breast. Fallon felt a sudden shocking surge of warmth wash over her, felt the heavy thud of his heart against her palm. "Do not look to my wasted youth, Fallon, but to what's here." Holding her hand tightly to his breast, he moved around the table, halting when he came to stand before her. "The past is done, finished. I cannot change what I have been."

Fallon leaned toward him, then caught herself and tried to pull away, seizing the first thought that leaped to mind. "I much prefer the light," she said, reaching for the taper with the hand he did not hold.

"And I prefer the darkness," he said softly, drawing her to him once again. "The time for talk is past. Come to me, Fallon. Give yourself fully to our union, partake of my experience, permit me to pay homage to your beauty—your purity and innocence. It is what I want above all things, and you cannot in truth deny that the time is right."

Fallon would have sought to deny it, with her last breath if need be, had the sensuous slide of his mouth on her throat not stolen the breath from her body, driving her will so far from her that it could not be summoned back.

Her heart fluttering wildly in her breast, she watched him part the bodice of her gown and tug it off her shoulders, until only her chemise remained. The thin lawn proved a fragile barrier at best against his scorching gaze.

"So lovely," he said, "so perfect, soft, and sweet." He peeled away the sheer chemise, baring her breasts. In the next instant his dark head dipped, and he kissed the tawny coral bud that capped her breast, caught it gently in his teeth to worry it with love.

Fallon gasped and slid her hands into his hair, wordlessly urging him closer, urging him on. Sensation, as old as time and as new as each moment, instinctive and amazing, shot through her vitals, sang along her nerves to pool, white hot and molten, deep in her belly.

He suckled her breast, gentle and insistent. The flames that scorched her flesh leaped higher.

Fallon closed her eyes against the brilliant warmth as he drew her slowly, relentlessly down. The memory of that night at the garden gate weeks before and the scandalous thoughts Draegan's kiss had conjured up drifted through Fallon's mind— forbidden thoughts of lying in his arms unclothed, of basking in his animal heat. . . .

Skin on silken skin. Beguiling blessed heat. She ached to touch him, hungered to feel the sensuous slide of his skin beneath her questing fingers.

Her surrender to impulse was swift and unbelievably sweet. She uttered a soft groan low in her throat, then restlessly shifted beneath him. Casting aside her inhibitions, she slid her hands beneath the open front of his shirt and pushed the garment down.

His skin was smooth and flawless, like heavy satin beneath her fingertips, his shoulders broad, his torso lean but well muscled. Straining upward, Fallon briefly pressed her parted lips to his. Then she teased the slight indentation below his sensuous lower lip with the tip of her tongue, nibbling delicately at his chin. He would need to shave, come morning, she thought, and she wished with a pang that she could have been there to observe him in that simple, human act.

Down her playful kisses crept, slanting across his cheek to his jaw, to the hollow beneath, and down again, across the column of his throat.

Draegan closed his eyes, waiting for her to grow still, to awaken from her impassioned state, to recoil. He wondered how he would bear the loss if she left him then, like that, so abject in his longing, so desperately in need of the one thing only she could give.

Never in his life had he known such sweet, unspoiled innocence, such truthfulness, such innate goodness as Fallon's. Fallon, who was the antithesis of everything for which he had always stood. Ironically, she was the one woman who had made him wish that he could change his hedonistic, self-serving ways and settle into a life of dignity, honor, and forthrightness.

And perhaps he could have.

If it were not for Randall Quill, Lucien Deane, and the empty grave in the churchyard that lay between them . . .

His moment of truth came quickly. He held his breath. If she noticed the scar, she would question him, force him from the shadows, badger him into telling the truth, and he would lose his one chance at redemption. He could not explain about Randall without telling her of that night, of Sparrowhawk and a noose swaying in the storm wind from the sturdy limb of the sentinel maple.

If she pressed him that far, the fact that he had come to the Catskills to ruin and kill Lucien Deane might come out as well, and he would lose his precious, bookish, virginal Fallon. Fallon, who had been sheltered from the sordidness and debauchery of his world, the callousness and cruelty. Fallon, who had come to mean so much to him.

Draegan waited and feared her reaction, praying that the darkness would not fail him, that the shadows would keep his secrets a little while longer, until he could think of a way to have his reckoning with Sparrowhawk and Captain Quill—and to have Fallon too.

She kissed the thick pad of scarred flesh that ringed his throat and after an instant's thoughtful hesitation moved on to his chest, where she toyed with his nipples in exactly the fashion he had toyed with and teased hers to life.

The immediate danger had passed. Relief surged through him. He drew a ragged breath and bent closer to her, slipping a questing hand under her skirts to explore the length of her stockinged calf, the silken skin of her inner thigh, moving cautiously, steadily upward, to the downy curls that crowned her womanhood.

Fallon felt the heat of his hand as he claimed her most secret self and was filled with a mild alarm. She knew she should have stopped him. She should have stayed his shocking advances, prevented him from progressing further, before irreparable harm was done.

And she would, she assured herself, *very soon*.

A moment or two was all she required, a small space of time to define the delicious tingling sensation that centered at the point of Draegan's magic touch, radiating outward, a moment to gather her flagging will and push away from his warm embrace. A moment, she thought, or perhaps two, and she would feel stronger, more able to resist him.

Yet somehow that moment never came.

The wondrous sensations Draegan evoked with practiced hands and carnal kisses grew ever stronger; her will to leave his arms grew weak. The struggle between what she knew was right and what she wanted was mercifully brief. With a softly uttered sigh, she surrendered to him, to the sea of passion threatening to engulf her, and slowly sank beneath the scarlet waves of physical bliss.

Draegan watched as her expression grew taut and sensed her time was near. He pushed back slightly, just enough to loosen his belt and breeches.

He would take her at that moment, claim her as his own, right there on the comfortless floor of the rectory kitchen, and there was no one and nothing to stand in his way, not even Fallon, his tumbled virgin—the virtuous miss he had longed for since his return to the valley and who now lay pliant beneath him, ready and eager to please.

With his hand at his belt, Draegan hesitated, suddenly aware of their surroundings, of Fallon, laid out like a sacrifice to the fiery lust that raged in his loins. He closed his eyes and groaned as his conscience reared its ugly head and smote him hard.

God help him. This was no simple tavern wench to be tumbled at his leisure, no bored but beautiful matron seeking a temporary diversion from her mundane existence.

This was Fallon Margaret Deane, a virtuous, honest, forthright young woman of good family, who stood to lose a great deal at his hands in the coming weeks. And she deserved more than to have her virgin's stain adorning the rectory floor, more, unquestionably, than he could ever give her.

Cursing softly, Draegan closed his eyes, burying his face in the soft, fragrant mounds of her breasts. He would hate himself come the morrow, he knew, when he awoke sweating and stiff as a pikestaff after another dream of her.

He gave a dark chuckle, aimed at himself. Who the hell was he trying to kid? He hated himself already.

"Draegan," Fallon murmured softly, sweetly. "Oh, Draegan, please."

"Ssshhh," he said, pressing a kiss to her trembling breasts and moving downward. He kissed the curve of her ribs, the wonderful womanly dip of her waist, her soft belly . . . and when at last he reached the downy curls that capped her womanhood, he raised her shapely legs and draped them over his shoulders. Then, with practiced ease, he cupped her lovely rounded derriere in the palms of his hands and brought her to his mouth, worshiping her woman's flesh, not pausing until her rapturous cries rang sweetly in his ears, echoing in his lightless soul. . . .

Chapter 13

Draegan pressed his face to the cool softness of Fallon's belly and fought back a violent shudder. It had taken his last ounce of will to give to her sexually while denying himself, and now there was nothing left to sustain him.

No strength. No resistance. God help him, no shame.

He felt like a raw nerve, exposed and throbbing, incapable of the meanest civility.

If she had touched him then, murmured his name, encouraged him the smallest bit, he would have cast aside his misgivings and taken her right there on the puncheon floor, like the rakehell he was in truth.

It was what he wanted, what he ached to do. But not here, not tonight, not in this callous fashion.

He drew a deep breath. Another. And he raised his head from its soft, womanly pillow, pushed himself to his knees, and reached out to help her up. "Come," he said more gruffly than he intended, "right your clothing. It's time you were getting back home."

She stared at him for a long moment, saying nothing, and Draegan could have sworn he saw the tiny images of their lovemaking mirrored in the ebony pupils of her large and luminous eyes.

He hesitated, searching his mind for something to say, some way to make her understand why she must leave so abruptly, without making himself appear an even greater fool than he was. But he found nothing.

For a moment he stood, clenching his fist as he watched her struggle to refasten the long row of tiny hooks that secured the front of her gown. And then, with a soft, ground-out curse he turned away, stalking to the door, where he bellowed for Jacob.

But Jacob did not answer, and the night beyond the rectory walls was silent and still. "I suppose I must go in search of him," Draegan said, shrugging into his shirt. "Stay where you are. I'll be back directly."

Fallon fastened the last of the hooks with trembling fingers: then, once the door had closed firmly at his back, she squeezed her eyes shut and pressed her hands to her flaming cheeks.

Dear God, what had she done, allowing him to have his wicked way with her, here in that hallowed place?

She had acted the wanton, listening to his talk of living for the moment, of throwing caution to the wind. And like a wanton whose services were no longer required, she was now being summarily dismissed, sent home alone to deal with her shame, her growing mound of regrets, her hurt and deep disappointment, because she had expected so much more.

A single tear stole from the corner of her eye, tracing a scalding path down her cheek. She'd had no prior experience in the secret ways of man and woman, but she had somehow assumed that this intimate episode would end differently. She imagined soft words of love spoken between them, kisses in parting—so unbearably bittersweet, a lingering, meaningful touch.

Angry at herself for having had such high expectations, angry at Draegan for his callous disregard of her feelings, Fallon dashed the moisture from her cheek. Her expectations had clearly been unrealistic, for there had been no tender endearments to salve her wounded heart.

Outside in the night, Draegan shouted for Jacob again, angrily. Fallon sniffed back her tears. As if things weren't bad enough, Draegan was about to heap more indignities upon her by placing her in the care of Jacob Deeter, instead of discreetly seeing her home himself. Jacob would be certain to notice her upset; he might even rightly guess its cause.

This last was simply too much to be borne. To live with the knowledge of what they had done here tonight was one thing, a shame she would have to bear the rest of her life; having others privy to her fall from grace was quite another.

Outside, all was quiet. Fallon lifted her gaze to the mantel and the ancient lantern that sat in its usual place and saw a way to escape.

In other, more desirable circumstances, she never would have considered entering the passageway alone. Yet at this moment her pride spoke louder and more eloquently than her fear, and so she went to the mantel and took down the lantern.

A few moments later Draegan reentered the darkened rectory. "I couldn't find Jacob," he said, closing the door. "He must have gone to Sike's Tavern, in the village, so I'll see you home personally."

His words were met by an eerie silence.

Draegan swept the dim room with a glance. There was no sign of Fallon. Ignoring the creeping sensation at the nape of his neck, he stalked to the parlor door. Perhaps she was feeling worn, had decided to rest. Yet as he paused in the parlor door, he saw that the divan was unoccupied, the parlor as silent and empty as the kitchen.

"Fallon!" He stalked across the parlor to the small alcove where he slept, then limped to the sanctuary. "Fallon!" His voice echoed in the large, empty space, hollow and tense. There was no need to question where she'd gone; with dread certainty he knew.

She'd broken her promise and entered the passageway alone, and the blame was solely his. Had he ignored the ugly rumblings of his conscience and claimed her, as he'd wanted so badly to do, then she'd have been safe in his arms that instant, instead of in grave danger.

Fallon held the lantern aloft, counting each step she descended. *Ten, eleven, twelve . . .* She came off the last tread and breathed a small sigh, though not of relief.

The worst was yet to come.

At the foot of the stairs, she paused, raising the lantern high. If only it were bright enough to penetrate the malevolent darkness that lay ahead, to dispel the threatening shadows lurking all around. Quite suddenly, she thought of turning back. Her determination, her anger and hurt, had deserted her the instant the door had swung to behind her, leaving only her pride to sustain her through the long and lonely walk home.

Now her pride seemed insufficient protection against whatever evil lurked in the stygian dark, too paltry a weapon to combat her fear. And only the prospect of facing Draegan again so soon after the humiliating scene in the rectory, of admitting that she—sensible, logical, pragmatic Fallon—was afraid of the dark, kept her from turning back to the relative safety of the church.

That same bitter pride forced her to place one foot ahead of the other, to keep moving steadily forward, deeper and deeper into the bowels of the earth. She would have walked to Hell and begged Satan's largess before facing Draegan Mattais again at that moment.

For the life of her, she could not fathom him! He was too dark, too moody, a complex puzzle on which she'd spent far too much time, and she was better off without him.

Her anger leaped to life inside her, a burning torch to keep her worries, her fears, at bay. She would put him from her mind the moment she entered the library; She'd forget that he had ever existed! It was the only course left to her, in light of the evening's disastrous outcome, and Fallon felt better, just having reached a decision. She now had a purpose, and Draegan be damned.

Her first order of business on the morrow would be a curtly worded missive informing him that their recently formed alliance was to be dissolved at once.

There was little chance that he would argue the point. He had fought against including her in his investigation since the very beginning, and he would doubtless be relieved that their association had come to an end.

He would no longer have to trust her, Fallon thought with a frown, and she could go back to her world of foolscap and ledgers and books, which suddenly seemed mundane and somehow—constricting.

The realization that she would not be a party to Sparrowhawk's capture was the greatest disappointment of all, and more than anything, it served to chip away at her newfound resolve.

Who was the spy? Was it someone she knew? Was he really in league with Randall Quill, as Draegan had intimated? So many questions remained unanswered that she found it difficult indeed to resign herself to the fact that she would not know the truth until it was over. And perhaps, not even then.

Her thoughts were suddenly brought full circle. What about Draegan? When he had completed his mission, and Sparrowhawk was no longer a threat, what would become of the patriot spy-catcher? There was no reason for him to remain here in Abundance. He had no family here, no true friends except Jacob, and it would be keeping with his character to depart in the same mysterious fashion in which he'd arrived, never to be heard from again.

The thought made Fallon inexplicably sad, driving the last vestige of the anger from her, bringing her world back into stark focus.

She had entered the part of the shaft that seemed the most perilous. Pinpoints of light flickered and danced on the heavy timbers shoring up ribs and roof. Fallon saw the dim outline of the rectangular crates just ahead, and she knew that a considerable distance lay between her and safety.

She tightened her grip on the lantern. Beyond the dim halo of light, something scurried and squeaked.

Fallon cringed inwardly, but she did not stop. Turning back was no longer an option. She'd come too far for that. She had to press on, despite her trepidation. She had to conquer her irrational fears, though at that moment it seemed the most difficult thing she'd ever done. She could not allow every groan of the earth and creak of the timbers to rob the strength from her limbs.

They were noises, nothing more, caused by the

subtle, constant shift of the earth. And like the squeal of the rodent before her and the soft footfall behind, the noises were easily explained away. There was nothing worthy of her fear.

Footfall?

The hair on the nape of Fallon's neck prickled alarmingly. She had heard the sound without even realizing it. Holding her breath, she strained to hear above the sickening roar of her blood in her ears.

It came again—a whisper of sound to the rear. She heard the barely audible rustle of linen, a soft rush of breath, and then nothing but the continuous trickle of water, the occasional creak of the timbers as the barometric pressure changed, and the pregnant silence that followed.

Fallon breathed again and started forward, trying hard to ignore the hammerlike thud of her heart against her ribs, the faint quiver that had suddenly infected her limbs.

She really must get hold of herself, she thought. She was being silly, when she needed to be brave.

Late-night assignations, desperate men, and secret passageways . . . Fallon shook her head. Was it any wonder she was starting at shadows?

More confidently now, she continued on, past the crates that held the British muskets, past the last of the timbers. She kept on walking forward, toward the manor, keeping courage high until she rounded the slight bend in the passageway and saw the faint flicker of light advancing slowly along the moisture-laden walls.

Voices, muffled and indistinct, echoed along the passageway, accompanied by the hollow ring of hobnailed boots upon the stone floor of the catacombs.

She squeezed her eyes shut, counted to three, and opened them again. But the bobbing advance of the shimmering light was no trick of her imagination. Someone was approaching from the portion of the tunnel closest to the manor.

She thought of the British brown Bess muskets stored in the crates to her rear, muskets that could only have been brought there by someone with loyalist sympathies—someone like Sparrowhawk, whose callous disregard for human life was infamous.

If she were caught, she could expect to receive no quarter. She knew she could not turn back without being seen and overtaken. Her only hope was to hide, and pray that she wasn't discovered. With her heart hammering wildly in her breast, Fallon blew out the lantern she carried and set it aside, gathering the tattered remains of her courage around her as she groped for the wall to her right and began to feel her way along as quickly as she could.

Chilly wet slime clung to her palms, oozing between her questing fingers. Something wriggled beneath her fingertips; she shuddered and cringed but kept moving, feeling her way in the dark, edging forward as quickly as she dared until the huge triangular stone loomed up out of the gloom of the catacombs.

Fallon felt an almost overwhelming surge of relief.

She had come to the fork in the passageway. The shaft to the left led to the manor, to Sparrowhawk or his man; the right led to the great cavern Draegan had described and to Vanderbloon's Wood beyond—her only hope of escape.

Outside, under cover of darkness, she could wait out the danger of discovery and, once that danger had passed, return safely home to Gilead Manor.

Hope surged through her. She quickened her steps, moving deeper and deeper into the darkness.

The wall curved sharply to the right, then jutted
left again, creating a deep crevice in the rib that
seemed even more lightless than the cavernous
room that lay beyond.

In the doorway, Fallon paused to look back. The
light reflected off the wet stone walls of the main
passage was growing brighter. She heard the ring
of bootheels more clearly now, and something else
from the opposite direction, a soft, undefinable
sound, like the rush of air as an unseen object hur-
tles through it.

She glanced around, growing desperate. The cavern was huge—too large to traverse in the moment
remaining. If she tried for the mouth of the cave
she'd be seen, caught, perhaps even killed, with no
one the wiser. She *had* to hide, now, this instant!

But where?

Along the ribs of the cave, to Fallon's right, were
several scattered broken crates. Beyond that lay a
soft, misshapen pile of what appeared to be her
salvation.

Canvas. A large, rumpled length of it, carelessly
discarded and covered with dust. Enough to cover
the crates, or conceal a desperate young woman.

A large rat crept to the edge of the canvas and
sat on its haunches to survey her, its bright, feral
eyes glinting red in the darkness. Aware that she
had but a moment to spare, Fallon picked up a
sliver of the broken crate and nudged the rodent,
sending it scurrying into the darkness. Then, grasping the edge of the canvas, she tossed it back. Instantly, she started back in mindless terror, a
scream frozen on her lips.

Half-covered by the canvas shroud, bagwig
askew and a grotesque death's-head grin forever
fixed upon his sunken face, was the Reverend
George Antwhistle, former pastor of Abundance
and Draegan's predecessor. Reverend Antwhistle,

who had had a fondness for strong spirits and who had rambled on incessantly to anyone willing to listen, and to others who were not, about the strange goings-on at the church and rectory. Reverend Antwhistle, whom everyone had assumed had just disappeared . . .

Horrified, yet unable to tear her gaze away from the pitiful remains, Fallon stumbled back, mindless of anything except her need to flee from the danger and death that seemed so much a part of this place, to draw cool, fresh air into her lungs. Stepping back farther and farther, she collided with a hard, male form, and fell trembling into the safe, solid comfort of Draegan's arms.

His voice sounded in the barest of whispers, next to her ear. "Quickly, now. Not a sound, not a breath." He flicked the canvas back into place, then drew her to the deep cleft in the wall. Pressing her into the crevice, he dragged the heavy bore pistol from his belt and pointed it aloft while shielding her body with his black-coated form.

In that moment, with the voices coming closer and peril lurking all around, the last stubborn shreds of Fallon's pride loosened their tenacious hold and fell away. Slipping her arms beneath the ever-present somber parson's coat, she clung to him, pressing her cheek to his shirtfront, losing herself in the heavy, reassuring thud of his heart.

The voices paused near the entrance to the cavern, a mere dozen paces away; Draegan's heartbeat quickened. One man spoke, his voice more sensed than heard, a mere crackle of sound, like the toneless rattle of dead leaves in a brisk winter wind.

There was a brief pause, and the air around them sizzled with tension. "What do you mean, it is not enough? I spent two hellish days and nights in the heat and the rain, and two more trying to ingratiate my way into Captain Brown's good graces—which was no easy task, I can tell you. The man is no fool, sir. He sensed something odd about my impromptu visit."

The toneless rattle sounded briefly, and then Randall Quill spoke again.

"I gave him the only excuse that I could think of: that I was visiting a cousin in a neighboring county and stopped by on a whim. But I don't think he believed it for a moment. He seemed unaccountably wary." A pause, a sigh, and then Randall went on, "Indeed, every man among them is wary, from Cobleskill to the Cherry Valley. I could see it in their faces. Not that I blame them. The fortifications are the worst of jest. I've seen privies built more soundly. One solid push is all that's required, and they will fall into British hands like toppled dominoes."

Fallon caught her breath, but Draegan's hand came up to still the sound.

"What was that?" Randall asked abruptly. "I could have sworn I heard something." He approached the entrance to the cavern, his boots sounding loud against the stone floor. Just inside the narrow entrance, a dozen feet away from the cleft in the wall where Fallon and Draegan stood motionless, he stopped.

For what seemed an eternity he stood there, listening intently, while Draegan maintained his tense and deadly silence and Fallon ceased to breathe. Then, abruptly, he turned and rejoined his companion. "It must have been the night wind sighing in the rocks," he said. "I cannot fathom why you insist on meeting here! This cursed place unnerves me."

Muted laughter, more sensed than heard, and gradually the footfalls faded. Fallon, still holding tightly to Draegan, felt the tension drain out of his body. "Dear God," she whispered shakily. "You were right about him—about Randall. He's in league with the British—a turncoat."

Draegan drew Fallon out from the crevice and, with an arm about her shoulders, guided her across the uneven floor of the huge cavern. "We'll speak of it later. Just now, it's imperative that I get you safely home."

They took a circuitous route on their way back to Gilead Manor, through the black heart of Vanderbloon's Wood. Local legend had it that the wood was haunted, that here, among the rocks and deep shade of the age-old wood, Satan and his disciples lay in wait, eager to practice all sorts of deviltry against the hapless, God-fearing folk who chanced to wander too near.

Fallon had never put much stock in local folklore, yet she found she was inexplicably glad to leave the deep, eerie gloom of the wood behind and move into the apple orchard.

The gnarled limbs beneath which they made their way were rife with blossoms. Pale and delicate in the darkness, they emitted a perfume that drifted on the night wind, a perfume so beguiling and sweet that on any other night Fallon would have been unable to resist the urge to linger, to drink in the enchanted beauty of the night.

But tonight she didn't linger. The events of the evening had left her shaken, unsettled, and no matter how hard she tried, she couldn't seem to put the chill, dank catacombs from her mind, or the cavern, with its canvas shroud.

Still battling the image, she cast a sidelong glance at Draegan. His features were dark, shadowed, his expression unfathomable. Since leaving the cavern there had been silence between them, the only sounds the sharp yip of a fox calling to its mate in the depths of the wood and the soft rasp of the meadow grass as it brushed against the hem of Fallon's skirt. When they reached the garden gate—with the great black bulk of Gilead Manor just beyond—Fallon broke the silence. "How long have you known about Reverend Antwhistle?"

"Since I first discovered the tunnel," he admitted. "It was a night of revelations, it would seem."

"Is that why you exacted my promise to stay away from the catacombs?" Fallon asked.

He snorted. "That was part of it, certainly—though for all the good exacting that promise from you did me, I might as well have saved my breath." He paused by the garden gate and glanced around, watchful, cautious. "Of course, until this evening, when you yourself confirmed it, I had no idea he had been my predecessor."

Fallon shook her head. "I was so certain that he had deserted us; addled, perhaps, from drink. But we misjudged him terribly. I wish to God someone had listened to what he was saying—*I wish I had listened.*"

"You could not have prevented his death, Fallon."

"You can't know that."

"I *do* know it. Our friend back there became inordinately curious about the nocturnal goings-on at the church, and that curiosity is precisely what got him killed. More interference would only have meant more corpses stowed away in that infernal cave, and I doubt the men we are dealing with here would care if the one caught nosing about was a man or a woman. A grand show of heroics, in this instance, is tantamount to a death sentence."

"Words you yourself should remember while you are sneaking about at night," she countered.

"Mine is a different situation entirely."

"Different, yes, but no less dangerous." She sniffed. "Do you think Randall killed him?"

"Randall or Sparrowhawk."

"Is it not possible that they are one and the same?"

Draegan smiled ruefully. "I have weighed that possibility for some time, now, but I can't seem to reckon the two. He isn't cool or deliberate enough—"

"Or intelligent enough?" Fallon supplied.

"You begin to see my reasoning," he said.

She understood about Randall; it was all suddenly clear. Yet there were other, more personal aspects of Draegan and Randall's relationship that she couldn't grasp, and Draegan seemed reluctant to enlighten her. It was a subject that urgently needed discussion, yet she did not know how to broach it.

"You had better go in," he said without a trace of emotion, with no thread of regret in his voice.

"Yes." It was the wisest course for both of them, yet it was not at all what Fallon wanted. The softer words she'd longed to hear earlier had never been spoken; he remained distant, somehow unreachable, and the chasm that had suddenly opened between them was too deep and too wide for her to bridge alone.

A moment later, Fallon reentered the house and carefully closed the door. Slipping off her low-heeled black boots, she crept to the foot of the stairs and had just started to climb them, when the library door creaked slowly open.

With one hand gripping the balustrade and her skirt and boots held aloft in the other, Fallon froze, and for the space of a heartbeat she gaped at Lucien while he gaped back at her. "Uncle," she finally managed to say, painfully aware of how guilty she must look.

"Sabina?" Lucien said shakily; then, running a hand over his face, he seemed to collect himself.

"Oh, Fallon, my dear. 'Tis you. You gave me quite a start—and for a moment I thought—well," he said with a rusty-sounding laugh, "never mind an old man's fancy. What in heaven's name are you doing out of bed?"

"I couldn't sleep, and the thought of work just didn't appeal to me, so I thought I'd go out for a breath of fresh air. It's a lovely night for a stroll in the garden."

It was not precisely a lie, Fallon thought, yet the telling of half-truths still made her nervous.

Lucien, perhaps sensing her unease, searched her face. "Are you quite all right, child?"

"But of course, Uncle. Why do you ask?"

"You seem somehow . . . different. Not quite yourself."

She *was* different, Fallon thought. She was not as innocent as she had been prior to Draegan's arrival in Abundance. But she had been hoping the changes that Draegan had brought about in her life would not be so blatantly obvious. Aloud, she said, "I'm just tired. I suppose that the lateness of the hour must be catching up with me. I really should go to bed."

Lucien had ambled forward, and stood now at the foot of the stair. Bending down, Fallon bussed his cheek. "Good night, Uncle. You won't stay out too long, or tax your strength too greatly."

"Your pardon?"

"Your cloak and walking stick," Fallon said, inclining her head to indicate the fine cloth wrap folded over his arm.

"Oh, yes," he said quickly, glancing down at the garment. "It just so happens that I was about to follow your lead and indulge in a late stroll about the grounds, but I've changed my mind. I think I will warm a bit of brandy instead and leave the stargazing for another night."

With a murmured wish for his good night's rest, Fallon mounted the stairs, suddenly anxious for the solitude of her chamber, and for the first time in her life, ill at ease in her uncle's presence.

Precisely one hour after Fallon had closed her bedchamber door, shutting herself off from the world, another door was opened and closed with a resounding slam—this one at the rectory.

"Jacob!" Even as he shouted the caretaker's name, Draegan knew he was not there. The rooms—his rooms—were black as pitch. Not the smallest ember from which to light a taper glowed in the grate.

Not that it mattered, he thought, shrugging out of his coat and letting it slide from his fingertips to the floor. He had become a habitual creature of darkness, secure in the shadows, wary in the light.

Disgusted with himself, with his whole situation, Draegan limped to the great cupboard and carelessly rifled through his belongings until he found the bottle of brandy. Until now, he had abstained from the use of strong spirits, settling for a bit of wine with his dinner. His abstinence had been just one small part of the holy facade he'd been forced into donning when he'd accepted this damnable assignment—an assignment that grew more tangled, more twisted, more complicated with each passing day. More detestable.

Scowling, Draegan worked the cork from the bottle and flung it aside, then tipped up the bottle and drank, wondering how in hell he'd gotten into such a mess.

The brandy slid down his throat like liquid fire, exploding in his empty belly. A moment of intense warmth followed, and then blessed numbness threaded through his veins. He gave a long sigh, then drank again deeply, musing on how he had come to his present circumstances.

Washington—it had begun with Washington, that paragon of piety and exemplary behavior on and off the battlefield. Sinking into a chair at the table, Draegan brought the bottle to his lips for another swallow.

The general had seemed to feel that a war could be fought and won without compromising one's honor, a concept that Draegan had never quite managed to grasp.

He had always considered such lofty ideals to be specifically designed for times of peace. War, after all, was not a gentleman's game. It was best waged by scoundrels such as himself, unscrupulous individuals willing to lay aside the few principles they possessed in order to accomplish an objective.

Draegan considered that the general's edicts did not apply to men like him, men who dirtied their hands and stained their souls so that the higher-ups could maintain their integrity.

Yet, as it happened, the general had disagreed.

By the middle of March of the previous year, rumors concerning Lucy Greenhill and the circumstances surrounding Draegan's wound had begun to ripple through the ranks of Washington's army. They were unpleasant rumors of a heartless seduction and a jealous woman's rage, which, however unsavory, were uncomfortably close to the truth.

Lucy Greenhill, wife of Major General Sir Percy Greenhill of His Majesty's Army, had succumbed to Draegan's charm, as he had intended, and up to a point, everything had progressed according to his plan.

Eager to please, Lucy had passed on the news and gossip from her husband's letters to Draegan, who in turn had reported directly to Washington. Then, in December, Sir Percy had had the misfor-

tune to contract the measles from which he never
recovered.

Lucy had rushed to the tavern where Draegan
was staying in Princeton to give him the terrible
news, fully expecting that he would comfort her,
and found him in bed with the serving maid.

Crying hysterically, Lucy had run out, but before
Draegan had had time to do more than slide into
his breeches, she was back. If he lived to be ninety,
he knew he'd never forget how it felt to stare down
the barrel of that blasted horse pistol Sir Percy had
insisted she carry—or the look in her eyes when
she'd squeezed off the shot that had nearly cost
him his leg.

The fact that Madam Greenhill had meant to
geld him had struck his fellow officers as rather
droll—all but Washington, who had seen no humor in the situation. As Washington wrote out
Draegan's transfer, he had expressed his regret in
superior tones that Madam Greenhill's marksman-
ship hadn't been better.

The incident with Lucy Greenhill had set off a
disastrous chain of events that, once set in motion,
Draegan had been powerless to stop. The rumors
that had invoked Washington's displeasure and
gained Draegan an unwanted transfer had also set
him en route to Albany when the inclement
weather had struck. If it had not been for the storm,
he wouldn't have been forced to seek shelter in the
church. Undoubtedly he would have pressed on
that night and found a cozy wayside tavern instead
of a length of hemp, and he wouldn't currently
have been lying awake at night in a darkened rectory, trying like bloody hell to devise a way that
he could have his pound of flesh and his heart's
desire too.

There was no viable solution to his dilemma, no
end to his anger, his frustration, his hopelessness;

no end, it seemed, to the nightmare he was living—
and sharing—with Fallon.

Draegan tipped the bottle, then set it down again
with a dissatisfied sigh. The liquor had lost its appeal, as well as its potency, and he was destined to
remain appallingly sober while he contemplated
his failings, his follies, his sins, the greatest of
which concerned Fallon Deane.

He had no business meddling in her life, dammit, he thought. She needed and deserved some
stable young man who would make a home for her
and give her children—someone with whom she
could build a life that was safe, secure, and properly dull.

She did not need a somewhat jaded adventurer
whose luck in the past had run rather thin. She did
not need, nor did she deserve, his lusting attentions, his faithlessness. Yet realization and acceptance were two very different things, and he
suspected that it would be a long time before he
could accept the inevitable and move on.

A light tapping, a persistent bid for entrance,
broke the brooding stillness. Draegan pushed out
of his chair and made his way to the door. Half-
hoping that Fallon had found her way back to him,
he jerked the panel open, an apology lodged high
in the back of his throat. But as he saw Jacob's
homely face through the opening, his spirits were
dashed upon the doorstep.

"I'm sorry to bother ye so late, Reverend, sir, but
I thought ye ought to know there's trouble brewin'
in town."

Draegan did not invite the caretaker in. In his
mood, he was not fit for company. "What sort of
trouble?"

"It's James McCord, the cooper. He's deep into
his cups at Sike's Tavern—"

"Well, wish him a high, fine time of it, and tell

him I'd join him, but nothing seems destined to work in my favor this evening." At Jacob's look he flung himself away from the door, angry. "Hell, don't look at me that way! I may have to pretend to be the man's minister, but I'll be damned if I'll be his frigging conscience."

"Reverend, sir," Jacob said, wringing the hat in his gnarled hands, "ye don't understand. McCord can't hold his liquor the least bit. He showed up a couple o' hours ago, and started to tipple when the cap'n an' a couple o' the militia boys walked in."

Draegan came back to the door, an intent look on his face. "Quill, you say?"

Jacob nodded. "Aye, sir. There's three o' them, and McCord's alone to face 'em. I think there's a good chance it's gonna turn ugly."

"Three to one," Draegan said. "Somehow that doesn't surprise me."

"Will ye come?" Jacob asked again.

After the evening's disappointing outcome, after the buildup of all his frustration and deep-seated anger, perhaps a confrontation with Quill was just what he needed. "Aye, dammit. I'll come," Draegan said impetuously. "Fetch the white, and I'll see if I can't shave down those odds just a bit."

Chapter 14

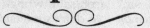

Peals of drunken laughter drifted through the open windows of Sike's Tavern into the street, followed by a reedy voice. "What'd yer Emma think if she could see ye now, eh, McCord?"

"Ye leave my Emma out of this. Ye got no right to so much as speak her sainted name. No right at all, sinful lot of toady jackasses—" McCord's tone was strident; his speech was cut off with an audible thump and gurgling gasp.

"No right to speak her name, ye say, when half the county had bedded the Tory bitch before ye wedded with her? She weren't no saint, cooper. Hell," McCord's tormentor said with a laugh. "She weren't even good."

There was general laughter then, some of it slightly uneasy, and riding beneath it like the sour strain of an amateur's violin was the cooper's low, whining protest. " 'Tain't so, damn yer lyin' eyes. My Emma was London-born, it's true, but she never was no Tory. Evil talk is all it is, evil talk from evil men, an' ye'll roast in Hades for it, every one."

"What was that ye said, cooper? Come again now, and don't be shy. My fellows didn't hear ye."

"I believe you heard him quite clearly," Draegan said from the doorway. "He said he's had enough of your doubtful company for one evening, and he's quite anxious to take himself on home. Isn't that so, Master McCord?"

The cooper nodded briefly and made to rise from his chair, but the rangers who flanked him lay brawny hands on his shoulders and pushed him back down.

At a table nearby, Randall Quill took his ease, a look of amusement on his blunt-featured face, a face that was clearly flushed from drink. "Well, well, if it isn't his saintly self," he said, sneering at Draegan. "Your arrival is timely, Reverend, but the reason for it seems unclear. Have ye come to hoist a few with the lads and me, or is it business that brings you here? Ah, yes, now I think I see. You've come to cast the demons out of the cooper, which is all well and good, I suppose, since he seems rather bedeviled this evening."

Sniggering laughter rippled through the crowd. Quill sat back in his chair, his chest expanded, obviously pleased with himself.

Draegan smiled thinly. His reply was silken. "As a matter of fact, I've come to cast the swine out of Sike's Tavern."

Randall slowly straightened, and his ears grew fiery red. The rangers who had flanked the cooper left him and moved threateningly forward as one.

"I wouldn't, were I you." Draegan slipped a hand inside his coat, his fingers closing over the smooth walnut grip of one of his pistols.

"You ain't me, parson," the larger of the rangers snarled, "and unless you got something mightier than the Word of God under that coat of yours, you'd best start prayin'. No man calls Jack Mills a swine and gets by with it."

"I have the Word," Draegan said with deadly

calm, producing a small worn Bible in his left hand, "and *this*." The pistol he gripped in his right hand drew a bead in the center of Jack Mills's forehead. The two men stopped, wary now, and Draegan looked to the militia captain, who was watching the scene with a look of expectancy. "Will you call off your slavering hounds, Quill, or risk losing them to a night of drink and excessive stupidity?"

"To Hell with him!" Jack Mills shouted. "He's got but one pistol, and he ain't gonna use it. I ain't never seen a parson yet what could handle a weapon."

He lunged at Draegan, who adjusted his aim a fraction and squeezed off a shot.

The big man clapped a huge hand to the right side of his head and set up a howl when it came away bloody. "Crazy sonovabitch shot off the top of my ear! Aw, Jesus, now my damned hat'll be lopsided! Goddammit, Tom, stop laughin' and help me find it afore I bleed to death! You infernal jack-ass!"

"Don't take on so, dammit," Tom Neelly replied, still highly entertained by his friend's predicament. "I'll help ye find it, and after Mildred sews it back on fer ye, we'll come back here, tar and feather the cooper, just fer the hell of it, and kill that blasted parson."

Tom Neelly was on his knees, searching the floor for Jack's ear, when Draegan drew the other loaded pistol from his belt and stepped up beside him. "Your friend Jack was mistaken. I've not one weapon, but two, and vocation aside, I don't like being threatened. So unless you want Jack, here, to be scouring the premises in search of the other side of your head, you had better go on home."

The room had gone still except for Jack's shuffling movements, and in the ensuing quiet, Draegan heard Tom Neelly swallow hard. "I *am* rather

tired of this, here, game at that," he said, starting
to rise, but Draegan's well-placed boot on his back-
side knocked him sprawling.

"No need to rise on my account, friend. After all,
you'll want to continue your search on your way
out."

Tom Neelly's face was livid, yet he said nothing
further, just crawled to the door and disappeared
into the night. Draegan turned to look for Jack
Mills, but he had seemingly decided that one ear
was better than none and taken himself on home
to Mildred, which left only Jacob, the cooper, and
Randall Quill, who was looking rather pale.

"Is something amiss, Captain?" Draegan politely
inquired. "You look as if you've seen a ghost."
With a low chuckle, he thrust the spent pistol
through his belt. Then, taking the cooper firmly by
the arm, he left Captain Randall Quill of the Esopus
Rangers gaping in his wake.

"Fallon. Fallon, are ye awake?" Willie's voice, accompanied by a soft, insistent tapping on the bedchamber door, dragged Fallon from her dreams.
"Fallon!"

"A moment, Willie," Fallon replied, her voice a
husky whisper. Shading her eyes against the bright
flood of spring sunlight pouring through the case-
ment window, she drew back the covers and slid
her arms into the sleeves of her flannel wrapper.

Willie's voice sounded again, petulant now.

Fallon freed the latch and the door inched open;
through the crack Willie's blond curls and wide
blue eyes appeared. "Mother sent me to check on
ye. When ye failed to rise at yer usual time, she got
worried that ye were ill."

"I was up rather late last night," Fallon said evasively. "I suppose that's why I overslept."

"Bad dreams?" Willie came into the room and perched on the end of the bed.

Terrible, haunting dreams of canvas shrouds, Draegan's sunken face and a death's-head grin . . . and Randall's endless echoing laughter.

Fallon crossed to the washstand and poured tepid water into the porcelain bowl. "Nothing worthy of mention. You seem lighter of heart this morning. Have you resolved your difficulties with Zepporah?"

Willie's glance met Fallon's in the glass, then just as quickly slid away. "Well, not exactly. But thanks to the reverend, I think we may have found a way around it."

"*Draegan?*" Fallon glanced sharply up, meeting Willie's gaze in the glass. "What has he to do with this?"

Willie reached into her apron pocket and produced a knotted white handkerchief, which she untied and held out to Fallon. "He sent me this, just yesterday."

Lying on the field of white linen were three gold coins and a scrap of paper, neatly folded. "That was very thoughtful of him," Fallon said.

"Not half so thoughtful as this." Extracting the paper, Willie opened it and read:

My dearest Wilhemina,

Enclosed are three guineas, one for the past, one for the present, and one for your glorious future with Thomas. Spend it on a bridal wreath and gown, or if you so choose, use it to procure a fast mount to see you both safely to the Congregational Church at Albany, where Pastor Jonathan Akers presides. Tell him that I sent you. Live long and live well, and above all be happy for what you have

*found with Thomas. It is more precious than you
will ever know.*

Willie refolded the note, replaced it in the kerchief and pressed the lot to her bosom, sniffing back her tears. "Oh, Fallon! Isn't it wonderfully romantic?"

"Yes," Fallon said with a frown, "wonderfully so." She'd thought Draegan's talk about Willie and Thomas and seizing the moment a subtle attempt at manipulation, a way to bring her willingly into his arms. Now she had cause to wonder.

Willie rattled happily on, jolting Fallon from her musings. "I sent word to Thomas directly, and he agrees that we need wait no longer. I'm to meet with him tomorrow night outside the garden gate, and we'll go to the rectory together."

Fallon glanced sharply up. "The rectory?"

Willie nodded, smiling wistfully. "Because of his thoughtfulness, Thomas and I decided that we'd have no other but Reverend Mattais to wed us. We deem it only fitting, after all he's said and done."

Fallon was stunned. She'd feared all along that the impetuous Willie might decide to run off with Thomas, against Zepporah's wishes, but never had it occurred to her that she would insist that Draegan perform the marriage. Draegan, who'd had but two scant years at Harvard College before his expulsion. Draegan, who in reality was not a minister at all, but a base fraud and a spy-catcher who doubtless had no inkling of the trouble he had caused by encouraging Willie.

And the trouble was now settled squarely in Fallon's lap.

She couldn't stand by and allow him to perform this farce of a marriage, the repercussions from which could very well be devastating! Yet short of betraying Draegan to Willie, or Willie to Zepporah, there seemed no way to stop it.

Staring into the glass, Fallon saw her own reflection, her paleness and the blue smudges that underscored her golden eyes. By contrast, Willie looked wonderfully happy—ecstatic, almost. Willie, her one true friend.

Torn between her loyalty to Willie and loyalty to Draegan and his cause, Fallon tried to tread carefully. "It's a wonderful thought, Willie, but not at all what he intended. Otherwise, he wouldn't have directed you to the church at Albany."

"But this is so much better!" Willie insisted. "Don't ye see? If we go to Albany, then ye can't be there with me. And Fallon," Willie said, clasping her hands tightly in her lap, "I do so want ye there when I speak my vows." She leaped from the bed and hurried over to stand behind Fallon, her confident blue gaze meeting Fallon's worried one in the looking glass. "Ye've been my friend all my life—why, almost my sister! It just wouldn't be right to marry Thomas without ye there to stand up for me." She placed a plump white hand on Fallon's shoulder and looked beseechingly into the glass. "Please, Fallon. Say ye'll be there for me tomorrow eve."

Fallon blinked back a sudden rush of sentimental tears. "I'm not at all sure that I approve, but how can I possibly refuse? Yes, Willie. I'll come stand up with you."

Later that night, two shadowy forms emerged from Vanderbloon's Wood. "It's him, I tell you! Major Youngblood, the man we hanged from that very limb last April."

"So now it's *we*, is it?" Lucien said sarcastically.

"You are every bit as guilty as I!" Randall shouted. "*You* were the one we were chasing, *you* killed Jim Sike, and *you* were the one who rightly should have been hanged that night. 'Twas you alone who planted the papers in Youngblood's belongings and then left him there unawares to suffer the consequences! If he's come back from the grave to wreak his vengeance, then he must know that you are just as guilty as I!"

Randall's shout was torn from his lips and whisked away down the hollow by the rising wind. A storm was brewing.

The sky was black, the stars hidden behind a great bank of clouds. Lucien had been watching the heavens while his partner in crime ranted and raved. Now he looked at him, a calculating look, which bore an equal measure of wry humor and disgust. "Lud, you do excel at histrionics. So much so that you should think of joining a thespian traveling troupe. It would give you free leave to practice your hysterics at will and would keep you away from Abundance."

"Histrionics!" Randall cried, still caught in the throes of a violent passion. "You can make light of it because you did not see what I saw or hear what I heard last night!"

"Yes. Yes, I know," Lucien said, his attention focused on his nails. "Hounds of Hell, or some such thing."

" 'Slavering hounds' is what he said," Randall corrected irritably. " 'Will you call off your slavering hounds,' just as he said it that night!"

"Yes, well . . . I can see why you're so overwrought," Lucien said dryly. "That's quite a piece of evidence you have there, a veritable mountain of indisputable facts with which to support your claim that Reverend Mattais is in reality Major Youngblood, come, as you so colorfully put it, 'back from the grave to wreak his vengeance.' "

Randall set his jaw. "I knew that you would not believe me."

They had come to a stop beneath the spreading boughs of the sentinel maple; at the foot of the carefully tended grave, Lucien leaned on his cane. "Now, now, do not be peevish with me. It is not that I place no credence in your claim; I should simply like to know if you have some other piece of evidence to support it, something more substantial."

"How do you mean, substantial? There is Mattais himself—or Youngblood—or whatever in Hell he is calling himself now!"

Lucien clucked his tongue. "Not enough. There must be more—proof positive that Mattais is who you say. Something that would shore up your shaky claim."

"What possible proof can there be?" Randall demanded. "The night we supped together at the manor, he knew me! And I thought I knew him—or at least a part of him—those eyes! I'll never forget those unearthly green eyes."

Lucien sighed and turned his face heavenward. "God grant me patience. I do not deal well with imbeciles." After a pause, he continued, "I rather thought it might be obvious, but I suppose I must point it out to you. *The grave*, Randall." He thumped the mound with the tip of his cane. "The grave is proof to substantiate your theory or to blow it to bits! Take that spade, there, and dig it up. If you find the poor, unfortunate major is still there, moldering away, then you can sleep again at night without a candle burning on your bedside table. If not—well, we shall deal with that eventuality, if and when it comes."

Randall just stood and stared at Lucien, looking unnaturally pale, until Lucien snatched up the short-handled spade and thrust it at the younger man. "Put your back into it, damn you! Time is wasting, and there is no telling when Mattais will return!"

Randall hesitated only a moment; then, casting a look of pure, unadulterated hatred at Lucien, he took up the spade and sank it deep into the hallowed earth.

Over the course of the next hour Randall labored and Randall cursed. Sweat ran in runnels down his face, and the veins at his temple and neck stood out.

Lucien leaned on his cane to watch his partner's progress, listening to the rising wind soughing in the boughs of the sentinel maple, but he did not offer to lend a hand. Quill, after all, had gotten them into this mess with his hellish temper, and Lucien was of no mind to extract him just yet. Let him suffer and worry and sweat awhile longer, he thought; the experience would do him good.

At nine minutes past the hour of midnight, the first flicker of lightning streaked across the sky, followed by a low rumble of thunder that nearly drowned out the hollow ring of the metal spade striking wood.

"I think I've hit—" Randall said. "Yes. It's definitely a coffin."

"Of course it's a coffin, nitwit. Strike it open and see what's inside."

Randall hesitated, glancing first at the plain wooden box encrusted with earth, and then at Lucien. "Perhaps you'd like to do the honors." He handed the spade to the older man, scrambling out of the grave and averting his face.

"Ever squeamish," Lucien muttered, climbing down into the wound in the earth. Using the metal spade, Lucien pried at the lid of the coffin until the nails creaked free, then shoved it aside to examine the contents. "You may turn and look, boy. The box is unoccupied."

A jagged streak of lightning cleaved the night sky, making Randall's round face look deathly pale. "I was right. Mattais *is* Youngblood. How can that be? It makes no sense. I hanged him myself! How can he not be dead?"

Lucien smiled. "You hanged him, yes. But are you certain he was done for, Randall?"

"Done for—"

"Dead. Was he dead?"

"I-I think so—y-yes. Yes, he must have been."

"But are you certain?"

When Randall did not reply, Lucien persisted. "Did you stay until he was cold? Did you put him in the ground yourself, or witness his interment?"

"I left just after the hanging," Randall reluctantly admitted. "Everyone was gone by then."

"Everyone?"

Randall nodded jerkily, still clearly unnerved. "Everyone. Private Deeter walked out before the deed was done, and the others left shortly thereafter."

Lucien glanced sharply up at Randall. "Jacob Deeter was there that night?"

"It was the last night he was with the Esopus Rangers. After that he drifted away, keeping to himself."

Lucien climbed out of the hole and brushed the dirt from his hands. "If everyone was gone, and Youngblood was dangling at the end of his rope, who cut him down and dug this grave?"

Randall's head came up, and his eyes narrowed. "Jacob Deeter. He said he came back some hours later to cut the man down and give him a decent burial in hopes of salving his conscience for the part he'd played in the 'evil deed.' "

" 'Evil deed,' " Lucien repeated softly. " 'Salving

his conscience.' There is the answer to your question, young sir. If Deeter's conscience was hurting him so hard, he might have lingered and watched, and, the moment you turned your back, scrambled to cut down the unfortunate major."

"That does not take away the fact that Youngblood was hanged! How could he have lived through such an ordeal?"

Lucien casually waved a hand in the air. "Oh, it is possible, if conditions are right. I saw a murderer hanged in Kingston once, when I was just a lad. The hangman was careless in placing the knot, and the condemned man took a terribly long time to die. It was slow strangulation, instead of a snap of the neck. It was quite untidy."

"Then I was right," Randall said, pacing nervously by the side of the open grave. "He has come back for retribution. Dear God, Lucien, what if he knows? What if Youngblood knows about the muskets and the men, and all the rest? He might have talked, told his superiors!"

Lucien took Randall firmly by the arms and gave him a hearty shake. "Save your theatrics, boy! This is no time for you to lose your spine. Think about what you are saying. If Youngblood had spoken of that night to his superiors, if they'd had the smallest shred of proof as to Sparrowhawk's identity, we would not be standing here now, would we? Of course not. Therefore we must assume that we are safe—for the moment. Yet, if we are to remain safe, something must be done."

"Yes. But what?"

Lucien turned slightly, pinning Randall with his chilly stare. "You must finish what you started here that night. It's as simple as that. And I think it only fitting that Jacob Deeter aid you in your task, don't you?"

*   *   *

Fallon Deane stood naked in a sun-drenched field of tall meadow grass and bright summer flowers, her coppery tresses loose and flowing . . . a shimmering curtain through which the coral tips of her full young breasts, the curve of a girlish hip, were barely visible.

Sweet, she was, beguiling. A veritable wood nymph designed to ensnare and torment, to tease and to deny—only him.

She was his penance for a life too fully lived, for the scores of petty indiscretions that had sullied his soul, shamed his family, blackened his reputation.

She was unreachable, the one woman he couldn't have, couldn't possess, couldn't hold.

The only one he wanted.

Standing at the edge of the field, with his loins on fire and his heart in his throat, Draegan called her name, begging her to come to him. But she would only smile her sweet, innocent smile and beckon him forward with a wave of her slim white hand.

Faced with the choice of dying of his desires or chancing the unsteady ground that lay between them, Draegan started forward, sinking deeper into the marshy ground with each step he took, feeling the chilly quicksand drag him down, while Fallon called his name. . . .

"Reverend Mattais, sir! For the love of God, please be there! Reverend Mattais!"

The dream image shattered into a thousand tiny fragments and fell away. His heart pounding against his ribs and his brow beaded with cold sweat, Draegan groaned, turning onto his back.

There were several seconds of silence, and then the feverish pounding resumed, accompanied by the cooper's querulous voice. "Reverend, sir! Reverend Mattais! Please, sir, you must come!"

"I *am* coming, dammit. I'm coming." Draegan

dragged himself off the bed and made his way to the door, lifting the latch and jerking the panel open. "What the devil is it? Oh, McCord, it's you. What brings you by in the middle of the night?"

"Jacob, sir! 'Tis Jacob. He came by Sike's this evening and was kind enough to see me home. He was just about to leave, when this big cat come out of nowhere and spooked his mount. Jacob fell, sir. He's in a real bad way, and he asked, would you come?"

"Where is he now?" Draegan asked.

"He's at my place, on the far side of Vanderbloon's Wood. I'll show you the way, reverend, sir. But hurry!"

"I'll get my coat and be right with you," Draegan said, turning away.

Taking one of the pistols from the great cupboard, he donned the black coat and followed the cooper into the night.

The rain had ceased earlier, and now an insidious fog crept through the hollows, blanketing the ground, muffling the rhythmic sound of the horses' hooves.

North for a quarter mile, they progressed at a snail's pace; then they turned east, along Kingston Road. A lightless track, it snaked its way through soaring stands of virgin timber, around boulders larger than a one-room cabin, up hill and down.

They approached a sharp bend in the road, and the cooper slowed his mount.

Draegan shot the older man a frowning glance. Damned if he didn't seem intent upon dragging his heels all the way home, an odd attitude for a man who'd been frantic for him to hurry just a few moments before. It was almost as if McCord had forgotten that Jacob lay in desperate need of assistance the moment they'd taken to the road, and instead had developed a keen interest in their surroundings. Mounted on a potbellied mule, McCord plodded along a few yards ahead of Draegan, his head turning first this way, then that, for all the world as if it were mounted on a swivel.

What, Draegan wondered, or whom did the fool expect to see in this blasted fog?

There was a sudden horrible sinking sensation in the pit of Draegan's stomach, too strong, too instinctive, too sickeningly familiar to be discounted. It was the same sensation he'd had looking down the muzzle of Lucy Greenhill's horse pistol, and again when Quill's man had reached into his belongings and come away with those infamous papers. An intuitive inner voice that screamed a warning it was already too late to heed.

In the time it takes to draw a breath, the night, so quiet until that moment, exploded with sound. A hoarse warning cry high up on the left bank— from a voice that sounded uncannily like Jacob's— tore through the stillness, followed by a vicious curse, a series of thumps, and the sound of something heavy striking the earth.

In that same instant, Draegan wheeled his mount and sank his spurs into the stallion's side. The stallion lunged forward, but the movement seemed slow and awkward.

Several figures armed with muskets raced down the bank to Draegan's right, with Jack Mills in the lead. Down the incline he barreled, and into the road, letting go a booming laugh as he grabbed the stallion's bridle.

Draegan reacted without thinking. Snatching one of the pistols from his belt, he aimed at Jack Mills's brawny chest and shot the big man dead. The stallion seemed to sense his master's urgency and thundered on, his hooves churning the mist so that it swirled up around them.

To the rear, Mills's companions reached their

fallen comrade and sent up a collective howl. There was a flash of fire and a resounding "boom," and a ball whined precariously close to Draegan's head. There was another shot, and something plucked at his sleeve.

Bending low over the stallion's neck, he spoke to the animal, urging it to greater speed. Safety lay in the sharp bend in the road a few yards ahead. If he could just clear the turn, he thought, his attackers would have no time for a second volley, and he could get safely away.

Within sight of his goal, Draegan plunged recklessly around the turn and saw the big-barreled roan standing broadside in the road. Randall Quill sat calmly astride the animal, pistol drawn and ready.

There was no time to slow down, no way to avoid Quill's big-barreled mount—to avoid catastrophe—so Draegan clenched his jaw and madly dashed straight ahead to embrace it. With nightmarish clarity, he saw Quill's stark white countenance, his nervous glance. The captain's finger tightened over the trigger as Draegan booted the white into a high forward lunge. Banshee's broad, muscled breast struck the smaller mount like a battering ram and knocked it aside, unseating its rider. At the same time the captain's pistol barked, and spat orange flame.

Draegan felt the catch in his left side, just below his ribs, and then the searing pain that followed. In the darkness to the rear Quill's virulent curses filled the still night air, mingling with the shouts of his men, the continuing sounds of pursuit.

Slipping a hand inside his coat, Draegan grimaced. It came away warm and slick with blood. He'd have to hole up—soon—see to his wound, and prepare his next step.

He'd have to stay astride long enough to lose

himself in Vanderbloon's Wood. The wood flanked
the rear of the church and rectory, it was nearly
impenetrable in places, and it offered concealment.

At that moment, with the night swirling madly
around him, it seemed his best and brightest hope.

Chapter 15

Good fortune seemed to smile upon Willie, for just as the following day was about to begin, Zepporah received an urgent message requesting that she help at the childbed of her cousin, Sarah Vaughn, in nearby Kingston. Willie dutifully accompanied her mother to the carriage, while Fallon looked on.

"Take care to be quiet as mice while I'm gone," Zepporah warned. She handed her bag up to Brewster, Lucien's servant, who would drive her to her destination. "Master Lucien has taken to his bed with a vicious headache, and must not be disturbed."

Willie smiled beneath Zepporah's affectionate pat on the cheek. "We'll be very quiet, Mother. Do you know how long you'll be gone?"

The housekeeper shook her head. "Babies are unpredictable little creatures. And they take their own good time about coming into the world. Sarah's time is near, but there's no way to tell when the babe will put in an appearance. It could be two days—or as long as a week—perhaps two!" She peered worriedly at each girl in turn. "Dear me, are you certain you can manage without me? I

261

could write a letter to Aunt Gertrude, and have her go in my stead—"

"Mother, you wouldn't do that to poor Cousin Sarah! You know she and Aunt Gertrude don't get along!"

"Yes, I suppose ye are right," Zepporah said, "but I do so hate leaving ye girls alone!"

"We aren't alone," Willie insisted. "We have each other. Isn't that so, Fallon?"

"And Uncle, and Brewster," Fallon added pointedly. "So we really aren't being left to our own devices at all."

"Always the voice of reason," Zepporah said, laying a work-worn hand along Fallon's cheek. "And the two of you are little girls no longer. In a few years, ye'll likely have husbands and babes of yer own!" Zepporah sniffed at the thought. "Where does the time go?"

She hugged them both. "Well, I'd best be on my way. There's enough supawn in the kitchen to last several days, and the larder is filled nigh to overflowing. Take care to stay indoors near dark. I don't want to hear ye've caught chill. And Fallon, let Brewster worry after yer uncle. He's dealt with Mister Lucien's spells for years, and knows what's best." She mounted the carriage step and took her seat beside Brewster, who cracked the whip above the horse's head and sent them rattling off down the drive.

Fallon and Willie stood side by side on the stoop, waving, until the carriage rounded a bend in the drive and Zepporah was gone from sight. Then Willie grabbed Fallon's hand and pulled her into the house. "If we hurry, we can be at the rectory within the hour!"

Fallon dug in her heels. "An hour! You said that you and Thomas planned to meet this evening."

"Yes! But with Mother away, there's no need to

wait! I can send him a message, and we can be wed right away, this very morning! Oh, Fallon, isn't it grand? We'll have time for the wedding and a wedding night as well! By this time tomorrow I'll be Mrs. Thomas Smith in truth, and it will be too late for arguments. Mother will have to accept him."

Fallon understood her friend's reasoning, but she was not as happy about this sudden turn of events as Willie. There was, after all, the illegality of the marriage to be considered, a problem to which she had found no ready solution. "I wish you didn't have your heart so set on this impromptu wedding. Think of your mother, Willie! Your wedding day, God willing, comes but once in your lifetime. She's bound to be angry and hurt that you didn't include her."

"I have thought of Mother, endlessly; I've pleaded and cajoled, and I've tried to reason with her. She refuses to listen, you know that. She wants things her own way, but it isn't her life, her future, that's been set aside to warm on the hob. It's my life, Fallon, and Thomas's, and with the war still draggin' on, we've no time to waste. I want a home of my own, and babies. What's so wrong with that?"

"Nothing," Fallon said, "nothing at all." Oddly enough she meant it. Not long before, her life's purpose had been the everyday tasks associated with running the estate. Books and accounts, taxes and rents paid in bushels of corn, oats, and wheat. Then Draegan had entered her life, and everything had changed.

These days, more often than not, she caught herself dreaming of a home and a husband, a marriage bed, and babies with hair like rich sable and eyes of uncanny pale green.

It was silly, of course, Fallon knew—a girlish fancy in which she chose to indulge while knowing full well it could never come true. Draegan Mattais was an adventuring rogue who took his pleasures where he found them, careless of the broken hearts and shattered lives he left along the way. He was hardly a marrying man.

Yet even though she recognized his shortcomings and clearly saw the danger he represented, she could not seem to convince her heart that it was wrong to care for him.

Willie, at least, had chosen wisely. Steady, reliable, devoted Thomas would shield and stand by her through good times and bad. And as Fallon followed Willie from the house a short time later, she thought that Draegan had been profoundly correct about one thing: the love that her friend had found with Thomas was indeed more precious than she could ever possibly know, and Fallon found she was strangely envious of Willie's good fortune.

The mist was still thick in the hollow when Fallon, Willie, and Thomas walked up to the rectory door. Fallon knocked. There was only silence. She rapped again, insistently, dreading the prospect of seeing Draegan again after their last night together, while at the same time yearning for a glimpse of his dark, handsome visage, aching to hear the soothing sound of his voice.

A moment passed, and the door creaked open the smallest fraction; Jacob Deeter's grizzled face appeared in the crack. He peered first at Fallon, then over her shoulder at Thomas and Willie. "Aye, what is it?" His manner was odd—wary, almost fearful—and Fallon had the strong impression that he would have liked very much to close the door in her face.

Frowning, she stiffened her spine. "Jacob, it's Fallon Deane. Would you please inform Reverend

Mattais that Willie and Thomas are here to see him?"

"And tell him it's urgent," Willie put in. Thomas whispered something that made Willie giggle and Jacob frown.

"Sorry to disappoint ye, Miss Deane, Miss Rhys, Master Smith. But the reverend ain't here. Called away, he was—early this mornin'. Aye, terrible early 'twas."

"Called away?" Fallon repeated. "Are you quite certain?"

"Aye, miss. It happened real sudden. Word come from Albany that his ma was ailin', and he decided to go."

As he talked, Jacob kept a firm grip on the door. His posture seemed unaccountably tense; he shifted his weight from foot to foot, as if impatient for an end to their exchange, and he refused to meet Fallon's gaze directly.

"He's gone to Albany, you say? To visit his mother?"

Jacob bobbed his head.

"Do open the door, Jacob. I should like a word with the reverend."

"Miss?" Jacob was visibly pained.

"His mother resides in Connecticut," she said stiltedly. "Now, please summon him or step aside."

Jacob swallowed hard and hung his head. "I'm afraid I can't do that, miss," he mumbled.

"Must I remind you that this church and rectory were built on lands belonging to my family?" Fallon softly asked. It was an underhanded tactic, one to which she disliked resorting, but she was convinced that something untoward was going on here, and equally determined to find out just what it was.

"No, miss," Jacob replied, "ye need not. That is a fact of which I am well aware."

"Good. Then I will politely ask you again to step aside so that I may enter. Something passing strange is going on here, and I intend to find out precisely what it is."

Jacob opened his mouth to speak, but the voice that answered was not his. It was too lazy, too cultured, too impudent, issuing from the deep shadows near the kitchen hearth. "A valiant effort, my friend, and while I laud you for your unflinching loyalty, I must also advise you to do as Mistress Deane bids. I have learned from experience that it isn't wise to stand in her way when she's determined to have her own head."

Jacob half turned, still blocking the entrance, and peered wordlessly into the shadowy recesses of the dimly lit room; then, slowly, reluctantly, he opened the door. "Sorry, miss," he said softly. "But 'tis not a good day to call. Not a good day at all." To Draegan he said, "I'll be close by, sir, if you need anything."

With a deferential nod, the caretaker brushed past Fallon and Willie and went out into the churchyard.

Fallon turned her suspicious gaze once again to Draegan. He was leaning against the parlor doorjamb, and even in the uncertain light, his face looked deathly pale. "What did he mean by that?" she asked.

Draegan shrugged, and Fallon thought she saw him wince. "You must not mind Jacob. He means well. Now, why don't you tell me what brings you here so bright and early, aside from the unquenchable desire to gaze once more upon my pretty face?"

At Willie's answering giggle, he straightened. "Who's that with you, Fallon? Why, it's Wilhemina, the blushing bride, and her Thomas. What brings you both out here? You can't have returned from Albany so soon. Ah, I see. You're on your way, and stopped by to say a fond farewell."

Willie came forward, standing before Draegan. "Not exactly, Reverend, sir. 'Twas the gift you sent. It touched me so! It was so kind, so generous, so wonderful of you to help us when no one else approved! Thomas and I talked it over, and we agreed that there was no reason to go all the way to Albany. We can start our lives, seal our love, right here in Abundance, if only you'll give us your blessing."

"Blessing?" Draegan said, glancing from Willie's upturned face to Fallon's clouded one. "I'm afraid I don't understand."

"We want ye to say the nuptials," Willie replied.

Draegan's look was one of incredulity. "You're joking, of course."

"Oh, no, sir! We've never been more serious!"

"I tried to tell her it would be impossible," Fallon said. "That they would need to go to Albany."

"Fallon is correct, of course," Draegan affirmed. "Marriage is a serious matter, not to be entered into lightly. And there is also the small matter of a license. I could not legally marry you without one."

Thomas crossed the room and took his place at Willie's side. "I have the license, sir. Everything is perfectly legal. All we require is for you to say the words over us. Willie is right"—and here he gazed down at Willie with a look of adulation—"your blessing would mean a great deal."

Draegan searched the faces of the young couple intently, and when he spoke again his voice had lost all traces of wry humor. "Are you certain this is what you want?"

Willie's face shone with a soft inner light. "Oh, yes! We're certain. We love each other, and all we want is to be together! Will ye do it? Will ye witness our vows here, right now?"

Draegan's mouth curved, but it was not precisely a smile. His pale green eyes bore a look of melancholy Fallon couldn't comprehend. "When you ask so prettily, how can I possibly refuse?" Pushing himself away from the doorjamb, he slowly turned and made his way into the chapel, with Fallon nearly treading on his heels.

"Are you mad?" she hissed when they reached the chapel. "You can't marry them!"

"Oh, but I can, just as soon as I find my prayer book. Now, where the devil have I left it?" He climbed the steps leading to the pulpit and rummaged through the small stack of books and papers stowed away beneath it. "Come, now, Fallon, don't look so damned disapproving. You heard her, the same as I. They've sworn their love for each other and want only to be together. Who the hell am I to deny them?"

"It isn't legal. It isn't right! Besides, you told them to go to the Congregationalist church in Albany! They were supposed to go to Albany!"

He turned on her, prayer book in hand, and the sunlight streaming through the windows struck full upon his stark white face, filling his eyes with pale green fire. "But they did not go to Albany, did they? They chose instead to come to me."

"Out of ignorance of your position!"

He chuckled, weakly, Fallon thought, and shook his head.

Fallon laid a hand upon his sleeve, much as she had the night he'd made love to her in the rectory kitchen, and begged him to see reason. "Draegan, please don't do this."

"What should I do? Send them away with no explanation? Tell them the truth? Or would you have me send them north to Albany, through war-torn lands, risking life and precious limb just to procure a bloody signature on a damned piece of paper—when all they want, Fallon, all they ask, is to be together?" He laughed, then gasped. "Oh, God, what *am* I thinking? You're Fallon of the iron will, the unswerving pragmatist."

"That is not fair!" Fallon said.

But Draegan wasn't listening. "You think that life will wait for you to be ready to live it, that your tomorrows are without end. What a young and naive little fool you are. Happiness doesn't wait, Fallon, and the future can be snatched from you in an instant. When it comes, you have to seize it, savor it, as Willie and Thomas are doing. Because if you wait, you may well miss the only opportunity you'll ever have . . ."

The impassioned speech had cost him. He leaned heavily against the pulpit, his breathing shallow and ragged, sweat streaming over his ashen brow.

"A pretty sentiment indeed, sir, but you overlook one important factor: this marriage won't be legal."

He shrugged. "When all of this is ended they can be wed again in secret. No one ever need know."

"*I* shall know," Fallon said, unwilling to let the subject go, though she was painfully aware she'd lost the fight. "And do sit down. You look perfectly ghastly. It would appear that all of your gadding about at night has caught up with you."

"A lovely compliment," he replied sarcastically. "One you may be sure I'll treasure. Now, be a good, cooperative lass for once and call the young lovers in."

Fallon did as he requested, against her better judgment. She did not approve of his methods, but some small romantic portion of her soul lauded his sentiment, his genuine caring for Thomas and Willie. And besides, she was sadly outnumbered.

And so she stood silently watching as Draegan bestowed his dubious blessing upon the young lovers, and she wiped away a tear as the pair indulged in a passionate kiss.

There was a round of handshakes and hugs, kisses and farewell wishes, and the newlyweds were gone. The chapel was once again brooding and silent. Jacob had entered and nervously edged forward, stopping a few paces from Draegan, who noticeably swayed on his feet. "Perhaps you'd better go home as well," he said to Fallon.

Fallon eyed him critically. "I thought I'd stay a little while and see you put to bed. It's clear you're coming down with something."

Draegan twitched his bloodless lips. "It's nothing, really. A passing twinge."

"From the looks of you, I'd judge it to be far more serious than a passing twinge. Here, let me help you." She came close and reached for his arm.

Draegan sought to avoid her, to push her away, yet he couldn't seem to summon the strength. The energy that had kept him upright until that moment bled quickly away, down his body and limbs, to pool in his boots. As if in a dream, he felt her fingers clutch his blood-soaked sleeve, saw her shocked expression, her dawning horror . . . heard her desperate cry for Jacob as he slowly slumped forward into her outstretched arms. . . .

Jacob eased Draegan's unconscious form onto the puncheon floor; Fallon knelt by his side. "There's brandy in the great cupboard, Jacob. Bring it, and some clean, dry linen, a towel, a shirt, whatever you can lay hands to quickly."

"Aye, miss. Right away."

Jacob went in search of the requested items, while Fallon worked to lay bare the wound. The coat Draegan wore was soaked with blood and sticky to the touch. Fallon laid the long tail back, eased the shirt from the waistband of his breeches, and removed the rude bandage that bound his lean middle, dreading what she might find.

"Thank God." She closed her eyes and fought to still her trembling. "Thank God, it is not mortal."

The ball had plowed through his left side in front, just below the ribs, tearing its way through muscle and vein, before exiting in back. The entry wound was large, the exit even larger; both still seeping blood.

Draegan had been fortunate, Fallon thought with a shudder; a similar wound in the lower right side would have killed him.

Jacob returned with a partially full bottle of brandy and two linen towels, which, at Fallon's direction, he tore into strips. "When and how did this happen?" she asked the caretaker, soaking a single cloth in liquor and carefully cleansing the wound and the area around it.

Jacob wrung his hat in his hands and sniffed. "This mornin', it was, an hour or two before dawn. They drew him into ambush, miss, and I fear I'm much to blame. I shouldn't 'ave fetched him down to Sike's, night before last, to aid that rascally cooper. If not for that, they wouldn't have known what they know, and none of this would've happened."

"Master McCord?" Fallon frowned up at the older man. "What has he to do with Draegan's being shot?"

"The tavern, miss. He was in his cups, and got a mite loose in the jaws. When I saw there was gonna be trouble, I come back here to fetch the reverend."

"Draegan went to Sike's Tavern?"

"Indeed, he did, miss. The last night you was here. He saved the cooper's scrawny arse—beggin' yer pardon, miss—then had a parting word or two with Cap'n Quill. I wasn't close enough to hear, but I saw the cap'n's face go white. Then, last night, some time after dark, Cap'n Quill and Jack Mills busted into my place and said I was to help them lure the reverend out. When I refused, they knocked me on the head, and the next thing I knowed I was lyin' in the bushes by Kingston Road.''

"I don't understand," Fallon said. "What reason would James McCord have to harm Draegan?"

"Love of his own scurvy skin," Jacob said. "The man's a Judas. Quill threatened to burn him out if he didn't carry the message to the rectory that I was at his place, and ailing. He gave up the reverend without so much as a whimper; lured him out there in the wilds, where Quill and his wolves were waitin'.''

"What became of McCord?" Fallon asked, placing thick pads of linen over the wound in back and then in the front, securing it with strips of bandage around Draegan's lean middle.

"He got clean away. I saw him run outta there just before I slipped back into the woods."

"And the others?"

"Jack Mills won't trouble us no more, or Timothy Neely, for that matter. Jack's dead, and Tim left town this morning."

"And Captain Quill?"

"He took a bad spill in the road, had to put down his mount, and I heard him cussin' something awful that he'd busted his arm. Too bad it wasn't his neck, I say."

Fallon knotted the bindings tightly around Draegan's waist and sat back to survey her handiwork. "Then he is still a threat."

Jacob nodded. "Very much so, miss. We'd best pray the reverend makes a fast recovery, 'cause he ain't gonna be safe here for long."

Fallon sat back on her heels and frowned down at Draegan. "He's lost blood, Jacob, and he's bound to be weak for a while. Barring a miracle, he'll be abed for at least a week—two, perhaps, if he takes fever."

"It's too long, miss. Quill will be here soon, and if he smells blood or weakness, we're in serious trouble."

"He needs time, a safe place to rest and regain his strength."

"Aye, miss. But where? This is the first place Quill is bound to look. My place is the second. There ain't no house in the village safe from Quill's fury, no place he won't think to look."

Oh, but there was a place, Fallon thought, the one place where Randall would never think to look, whose peace he would never dare to disturb. Her gaze slid from Draegan's countenance, so pale and ghastly, to Jacob's. "I have an idea," she said. "One that just might save him, if indeed we can manage to carry it off without further incident."

Jacob looked doubtful. "If it's what I'm thinkin', I can tell ye, he ain't gonna like it."

"I don't care what he likes or doesn't like," Fallon said matter-of-factly. "My only concern at the moment is saving his life. Besides, he's in no condition to think clearly or to make such an important decision—a decision upon which, I might remind you, his entire future, or lack thereof, rests! His life is in my hands now, and I must do what I deem best. We will move him before nightfall."

They allowed Draegan to rest on the floor where they had placed him for as long as they dared. Then, as the sun began its rapid descent behind the great black bulk of the Catskill Mountains, worry over Randall Quill took precedence over considerations of Draegan's strength, and Fallon and Jacob undertook the arduous task of moving him to the safe haven Fallon had chosen.

Draegan was taller than Jacob, but the older man possessed a wiry strength that belied his years, for which Fallon, at this moment, was unendingly grateful. Together she and the caretaker knelt beside him, Fallon on his injured left side, Jacob on the right, and by placing his arms over their shoulders, brought Draegan to his feet.

Dragged from his unconscious state, Draegan mouthed an unintelligible curse and bade them leave him be.

"You can't stay here at the rectory," Fallon said patiently. "Randall is still abroad, perhaps searching for you. If he should come and find you here . . ." There was no need for her to finish. They all understood the threat Randall represented to Draegan in his present vulnerable condition.

"Quill—aye—Quill. Owes me, damn him. He'll pay—handsomely."

He mumbled something else Fallon couldn't understand, then once again fell silent. She glanced worriedly up at him. Sweat ran down his ashen cheeks in runnels. His eyes were glazed with pain. Though awake, he seemed far from lucid. He made no protest as Fallon took up the lantern from the foremost pew, and they moved toward the gaping black maw that was the entrance to the catacombs.

The steep, winding stairs were hard to negotiate. Draegan sagged between them. His movements were uncharacteristically clumsy, awkward, and slow. Halfway to the bottom he swayed on his feet, and Fallon caught her breath.

"It's all right now," Jacob reassured her. "I've got him. A few more treads and the worst will be behind us."

But Fallon knew the caretaker believed that no

more than she. Several hundred yards lay between them and safety, yet at that moment, with Draegan a cumbersome, half-conscious burden between them, weak from loss of blood and wracked with pain, it might as well have been a hundred miles.

Defeat crowded close to Fallon, doubt and fear paved the way ahead, while cold dread brought up the rear.

Had she erred in moving him so soon? How could they possibly make it to the manor? What if the ordeal was too much, and his wound reopened, starting to bleed again? How much blood could he lose and still live? And far, far worse, what if Sparrowhawk discovered them? Or Randall?

Holding tightly to Draegan's arm with one hand, clutching the lantern in the other, Fallon shuddered. The possibilities were endless, and endlessly frightening, too horrible, too worrisome, to contemplate.

She had made the right decision, Fallon told herself—the only decision—one that she had known from the beginning was not without certain risks. It was a decision to which she was now wholly committed.

It was too late to turn back. There was nothing for it now but to see it through, to do everything within her power to bring Draegan safely to the manor. To achieve her mission, she had to thrust aside her doubt, and her dread, and help him take another step, and then another.

After a time she ceased to think at all beyond what must be done. They came upon the splintered crates, which not so long before had held the brown Bess muskets. The toe of Draegan's boot caught on the debris; he stumbled, cursing aloud, nearly dragging Fallon to her knees before a sweating Jacob righted them again. They continued on, past the crates, past the fork in the tunnel and the passageway to the cavern, until they reached the foot of the stairway. Draegan stood there, wavering between them. "Can't," he said. "No more. Just— can't."

Fallon held the lantern high. The flickering light fell upon his face, a ghostly cameo in the half-light and deep shadows. "You must try. It's just a moment more. Please, Draegan. You must try."

As he looked blearily down into her face, she felt him fill his lungs with air, exhale on a deep sigh, and his body went slack between them.

Jacob caught Draegan as he fell; bending down, he draped his limp form over one shoulder. "Lord, but he's a heavy one," he said. "Go on ahead, miss, and clear the way. I'll bring the reverend along."

Fallon led the way, up the stairs and into the library. The house was silent and dark. With Lucien in his third-floor chamber, Willie with her Thomas, and Zepporah away, there was no one to witness the progress of the odd trio along the shadowed halls to Fallon's bedchamber.

Fallon opened her chamber door for Jacob, then set aside the lantern while he placed Draegan on the bed. "Looks like the bandage held," the caretaker said. "Wound's seepin' a mite, but none so bad as I feared from all this jostlin' about." He straightened, turning to Fallon, the expression on his weathered countenance one of concern. "Are ye certain ye're up to this, miss? I expect I could put off goin' back to straighten things up a bit, if need be."

Fallon gave him a weary smile. "Thank you for the thought, Jacob, but there's really no need for you to stay. Besides, you're needed elsewhere. Someone must erase all traces of our passage from the rectory and catacombs. No one must be able to guess that we passed that way, or that Draegan is here. I'm depending on you, Jacob." She glanced at the still figure on the counterpane, and her throat tightened. "We both are."

"I won't let ye down, miss." Jacob took up the lantern but turned back at the door. "Send word by my place if ye need me. Otherwise—" He paused and cleared his throat. "Well. I trust he's in good hands." With a final bob of his head, Jacob Deeter exited, leaving Fallon alone with Draegan.

Through the lace curtains that graced the bed-chamber window came the lonely cry of a whip-poorwill calling to its mate. The last of the golden light reflected in the wavy glass panes was rapidly fading. Darkness was nigh, and except for the candle burning on the bedside table, Gilead Manor was silent and dark.

The darkness created a temporary solitude, for which Fallon was grateful. On the morrow she would gather her strength to deal with the hazards of her current undertaking. Tonight, at this moment, she could think only of the man lying so stark and still in the midst of her big feather bed.

Reaching out, Fallon pressed her hand to his cheek, then brushed back a lock of sable hair that had fallen forward onto his brow. "It pains me to see you this way, so vulnerable, unable to defend yourself against those who would seek to destroy you."

He groaned softly, deep in his throat, and stirred in his sleep. "Ssh," Fallon said. "Rest, now. I'll see to everything. Just rest."

She would see to all his needs. Everything she needed was close at hand, and she knew it would be much more convenient to care for him here at the manor than at the rectory. She placed bandages and an herbal infusion, salve and scissors next to the bed.

All that she required in order to begin was to undress him. Moving to the foot of the bed, she grasped the heel of his boots, one at a time, and pulled each one off, placing both neatly to one side. His stockings came next, and posed no difficulty, but when she came to his breeches, Fallon paused.

"It is work, nothing more," she assured herself. "A task that must be completed in order to assure his comfort, as well as his recovery." She frowned. "Fie, Fallon, the garments are soiled and blood-soaked. They must come off—immediately—without delay."

Still she stood, hesitating, biting her lip. "There is no one else to do it," she whispered, "and he obviously cannot manage on his own." She fought down a tide of embarrassment and was expressly glad he could not see. "Do not think of it, then; think of something else."

She searched the corners of her mind for something, anything, that would distract her long enough to see her through the task at hand. "Burdock. The burdock is especially hearty this year," she mumbled to herself. "I expect Zepporah will want me to dig some root for drying."

She took hold of his breeches. Her knuckles brushed skin that was warm and satiny smooth, and her face grew hot. "And the catnip is seeding nicely. *Vrouw* Schoonmaker asked for some seed last year—Mrs. Vandermeer's Priscilla got into her herb bed and shredded the new plantings last fall—naughty cat that she is."

A moment of fumbling, and she urged the buttons through their moorings. Fallon caught her breath; her blush grew painful. The garment had parted, revealing a belly that was taut and corded with muscle, skin that was tawny and smooth.

"Goodness," she breathed. "Lobelia—I must not forget to gather some lobelia, lest someone suffer a toothache."

She purposely averted her gaze; it errantly slid

back again to the parted garment, the wondrous male form half-revealed. Fallon squeezed her eyes shut. "Any difficult task is better done quickly," she said. "And you may take heart in the fact that after another moment, the worst will be through."

Screwing up her courage, she opened her eyes and grasped his trousers, urging them down, inch by torturous inch, over lean hips and sleeping manhood. In less than an instant, she'd whisked the offending garment away, and he lay naked, except for his shirt.

For a long moment, Fallon stood by the bedside, congratulating herself on a task well finished—while she drank in his image. She knew it was wicked of her to stare at him while he lay defenseless and unaware, yet the wanton in her would not allow her to look away.

Broad of shoulder and breast, lean of hip, he was beautiful, the sort of man women dreamed about, an angel come to earth.

Yet, as Fallon well knew, that image was deceptive. There was nothing angelic about Draegan, as the scar on his thigh and the hole in his side attested. And she would have been wise to remember that.

One last lingering look, an appreciative feminine sigh, and she carefully covered him, folding the quilts down at his waist before turning her attention to his shirt. The buttons that closed the garment from hem to throat were made of bone, small and closely set. Fallon nonetheless managed to free them, one by one, until his knotted neckcloth was the only thing remaining.

She started to loosen the knot; he groaned and twisted half away, clamping a rough hand over her wrist. "Fallon," he said, his voice slurred. "W-what are you doing?"

"I'm going to loosen your shirt, to make you more comfortable. Go back to sleep."

"No," he said. "No. Leave it. Leave it be—you must. I—I don't want you—to see."

"Don't be silly. You can't possibly rest in your shirt and neckcloth."

She reached for the neckcloth again, but he shook his head and thrust her hand away. "No. No! Darkness—only in darkness."

"It's all right," Fallon said, covering the hand that gripped her wrist with her free one. "You're safe now. I'm here, and no one will harm you."

"No. No—you don't understand. The light, dammit. Never the light. Too many questions—pity and pain. I—can't—face it. *Oh, God*, please. Not again. Never again . . ."

He quieted, and Fallon, thinking he had once again drifted off, loosened the knotted cloth that encircled his throat and began to unwrap it. The movement, however slight, brought him plunging out of his semiconscious state. Before she could stop him, he rolled to his side and cleared off the bedside table with a violent swipe of his hand.

The candlestick, the empty basin, cloths, and various paraphernalia went flying, plunging the room into sudden and total darkness. "Of all the perverse, half-cocked notions. Darkness indeed," Fallon muttered. On her hands and knees, she felt around for the scattered items, this time placing them far from his reach. "Very well, then, sir. You shall have it your way—at least until I can get some brandy into you." She found the decanter and splashed a liberal amount of the liquor into a tumbler. "The light is gone now, and you will be perfectly safe, unless, of course, you continue to behave in this boorish, uncivilized way."

His only reply was a groan, the sound a

wounded creature makes, low in its throat. "Safe. Not safe—no."

God help her, he was not lucid, and he remained blissfully unaware of the danger discovery could bring. She was aware that if he continued to ramble on unchecked, Lucien might hear, and leave his third-floor lair to investigate. It wouldn't bode well for either of them if Reverend Draegan Mattais were found in her bed. Her uncle would be furious she knew—angry enough, perhaps, to revoke Draegan's position, to toss him in gaol, or force them to wed. The possibilities were limitless.

Fallon realized that she had to quiet him, and at that point, brandy seemed her best option. "You are safe," she said, hoping to penetrate the thick fog in his mind. "Come, I've brought you some brandy, to numb the pain and help you sleep."

His hand closed over hers. Fallon brought the glass to his lips and urged him to drink. When he'd drained the glass, she set it aside, pushing him back into the pillows. "So tired," he said.

"Yes," Fallon said softly. "You've lost a lot of blood. But you'll be well again soon." He hadn't relinquished her hand, and still held it loosely in his. "It's safe to let go, my love," she whispered. "Safe to sleep. Your secrets are safe with me."

"Safe . . ." he murmured. He sighed, and his breathing slowed, falling into the regular rhythm of a deep, untroubled sleep.

Fallon eased her hand from his loosened grasp and slipped off the bed. Then, with the aid of the tinderbox she kept in the wardrobe, she rekindled the candle's flame. Warm and mellow light blossomed in the room, dispelling the shadows, if not the unease his agitation had wrought.

Only in darkness, he'd said. *Never the light. Too many questions. Pity and pain. I can't face it.*

What questions? Why pity or pain? What

couldn't he face? And why would this magnificent man shun the light?

With a doubtful shake of her auburn head, Fallon carefully unwound the trailing ends of the neck-cloth. "Madness," she said to herself. "Sheer madness, this talk. The mutterings of a fevered mind." The trailing ends of the neckcloth slid away from his throat, and Fallon went very still.

A wide band of scar tissue covered his throat, the likes of which Fallon had never seen. It was an ugly livid red, thick and uneven, as though the flesh had been wrenched and torn and then allowed to heal.

She slipped her fingers under the heavy silk of his hair at the nape of his neck, and a frown creased her brow. The ring of scar tissue was continuous, as though something very rough and abrasive had encircled his throat, like a hempen rope—almost as though he'd been hanged.

But that was impossible.

Hanged men did not live, and Dreagan Mattais was very much alive. She lay her fingertips to the side of his throat, gently. He stirred weakly and murmured her name. The flesh of the scar felt like thick, rumpled velvet; the pulse beneath was steady and strong.

Unbidden, an image formed in her mind, but it was too horrible to consider, too nightmarish to contemplate. And so she pushed it away, desperately seeking something else on which to focus her thoughts.

The rectory, the first night they'd been together, the night of her would-be seduction on the parlor divan. She remembered quite clearly the way that he'd made her feel, how desperately she'd wanted to feel his skin on hers, how she'd reached for his neckcloth and he'd abruptly ended the encounter. And that last night, before he'd unbuttoned his shirt, he'd deliberately snuffed the candle, throwing the room into darkness. When she'd pressed her lips to his throat, he'd held his breath, as if waiting. . . .

Waiting for what? For her to notice the scar's existence, to recoil? Surely he knew that she wasn't so shallow!

There was surely more to it than that. There was surely a great deal more that Draegan Mattais was keeping from her, and she had every intention of finding out precisely what else he was hiding.

After changing her gown and splashing tepid water on her face, she sat down in the chair by the bedside to wait, a long list of questions swirling in her head. Was it possible that Draegan had been hanged? And if so, how had he survived? More importantly, who could have been cruel enough, villainous enough, to have done such a thing?

There were so many questions. Yet Fallon found a certain comfort in knowing that at last the truth would come out—every last morsel of it, no matter how ugly—for this time she would accept nothing less.

Chapter 16

Draegan's ramblings continued intermittently throughout the night, disjointed and often confusing, drawing Fallon down torturous paths, deeper and deeper into the vast wasteland of his past. Dutifully, she followed where he led, mopping his fevered brow, seeking to soothe him when he grew restless in the company of the voluptuous beauties he'd methodically wooed and betrayed and he called out Fallon's name. . . .

During those first hours, in the blackest part of night, the man she now discovered was Major Draegan Mattais Youngblood poured out the secrets he'd previously withheld from her. Fallon—once so avid to learn his secrets—tried not to listen, but it quickly proved an impossible task. The things he said were at times difficult to hear, yet she didn't leave his bedside for a moment or falter in her task.

Rebel hero or heartless roué, saint or sinner—the fact remained that Draegan needed her. Weeks earlier she would have spurned him for the truths she learned that night; but their relationship had gone too far for that. She had invested more in him than simple hopes and girlhood dreams.

She had invested her heart, and having done so, she could not now withdraw it; she could only hope that he wouldn't cast it carelessly aside, as he had done to all the others who'd gone before her.

The sky outside the bedchamber window gradually lightened. Dawn was not far away. Worn from his ramblings, Draegan at last lay quiet and still.

Fallon pressed the back of her hand to his temple and sighed in relief. The fever that had gripped him throughout the night was abating. His battle was won. From that moment on he would grow stronger, more in control. But Fallon's fight, the fight for truth from this complex man, had only begun.

It was nearly noon when Draegan finally emerged from the tangled morass of his dreams and opened his eyes. His surroundings were unfamiliar. Soft green moire covered the walls beyond the curtained bed, and Irish lace fluttered at the open window. The fine linen sheets covering the soft feather mattress on which he lay felt wondrous against his naked skin. He studied the bed for a moment as his feeling of disorientation intensified. It was not the narrow cot he occupied at the rectory, but a tester bed, large enough for two.

Soft humming drifted through the parted curtains at the foot of the bed, a feminine voice, a siren's song, dulcet and sweet. Instinctively, he sought the source of the sound, pushing himself up in the bed, stifling a curse as pain shot through his left side.

The humming ceased. There was the soft tread of footsteps, the swish of silk skirts; then a feminine hand pushed back the bed curtain and Fallon's bright face appeared. "You're awake," she said, sounding surprised. "How are you feeling?"

Draegan frowned, settling back against the pillows. He was naked in the bed, and Fallon was smiling down at him. Surely this wasn't real, he thought. He couldn't be lying there, his secret exposed and the room bright with the midday sun, not after all the considerable trouble he'd gone to, to keep it from her.

Fate could not possibly have been so cruel.

But it was real, terribly, horribly real, and he was cornered and vulnerable. "How am I feeling?" he asked with rising indignation, his hand at his throat. "Naked and betrayed, that's how I'm feeling."

"Jacob said that you wouldn't be pleased with this arrangement--" Fallon began calmly.

That quiet calm incensed him. "Jacob," he said flatly. "Blasted coward. At the first sign of adversity he succumbs, and leaves me to the wolves."

"Wolves?" She elevated one finely drawn brow as she peered at him. "You are raving, sir. There are no wolves here. Your fever must have returned."

She would have felt his brow, but Draegan deftly caught her hand and pushed it aside. "That is a matter of opinion."

"You are bent on being difficult," she said with a tight smile. "I can see you are feeling more yourself. Would you like some broth?"

Draegan's face flushed dark at her patronizing tone. "You may shove your damned broth, madam. I'm not an invalid, and I won't be treated like one." He struggled up, gritting his teeth against the pain his movements brought on, intent upon extracting himself from this dread situation.

Fallon would not allow it. She placed her hands on his shoulders and forced him down onto the pillows. "Lie back and be still before you break open that wound and start bleeding again!"

The feel of her hands on his bare skin took some of the rancor from him. He'd never stopped wanting her. The deep-seated hunger to possess her, to take her and make her his own, had never ceased. Yet he couldn't let go of the bitter regret, the hurt that had so long been a part of him. "Where is this place?"

"Gilead Manor."

He closed his eyes and let go a groan. "This cannot be happening. It must be a nightmare—a horrid dream brought on by frustration. As a dream, it shall pass." He lay quietly a long moment, waiting, then slowly opened his eyes once again to the same large bed and brocaded bed curtains, the same flood of bright light, and Fallon, standing by the bed, the soul of patience. "What possessed you to bring me here?"

"It is the one place I could think of where you would be safe from Randall's fury. He would never think to search for you here, and even if he suspected, he would never dare intrude upon the peace of this house."

Her logic about Randall was flawless, but she was ignorant of one important factor. Gilead Manor was Sparrowhawk's base of operations, his refuge. And she had unwittingly brought him into his enemy's stronghold.

She seemed to sense his next question. "We brought you through the passageway, Jacob and I. It was a very difficult undertaking."

"Jacob again," he said sourly. "It seems I owe him a considerable debt. Tell me, Fallon, was it Jacob who gave you leave to put me in this bed and relieve me of my dignity?"

Fallon met his smoldering glance with a look of pure defiance. "Your dignity, Draegan Mattais, is hardly my first concern. I have been far too worried about you losing your life to consider the bumps and bruises sustained by your manly pride."

"This has to do with much more than simple pride."

"Indeed?" she inquired, perching on the side of the bed. "Go on, sir. Explain. I'm listening."

"Ever curious, aren't you?" he replied, but when she didn't retaliate in kind, he softened the smallest bit. "I have dreaded this day, and worked very hard to avoid it."

"You've gone to great lengths to keep your secret," she said. "Those nights in the rectory when we—" She broke off, lowering her gaze, and a faint, telling blush touched her cheeks. "Why?"

He looked sharply up at her. "That much, I would think, should be obvious. I loathe this scar, and everything it represents. It shames me, Fallon. I did not want you, of all people, to see—and now the choice has been taken from me."

"I did not mean to pry—I did not intentionally examine your person—" She broke off, blushing to the roots of her hair. "What I mean to say is—"

"What you mean to say is that it was waiting there under my clothing, and in the process of stripping me naked as a newborn babe, you could hardly overlook it." He would not have thought it possible, but her color deepened. Draegan felt a fleeting twinge of guilt, fleeting, because he derived a perverse pleasure from lying in *her* feather bed, watching her stammer and blush—a purely feminine reaction to his heartless baiting, and utterly charming. His reaction to her, on the other hand, was undeniably male, despite the nagging throb in his side.

As he watched, she laced her fingers together before her, seeking control. "Your clothing was bloodstained and soiled, and Jacob, trustworthy soul that he is, is not a good nurse. Had I ignored my duty and left you there at the rectory, you would likely have succumbed to an infection by now, or worse."

Draegan shifted uneasily in bed, painfully aware of how deeply indebted he was to Fallon, yet not quite able to curb his tongue. "And if I weren't such an ungrateful wretch, I would thank you for efforts on my behalf."

She said nothing. She merely sat, waiting for him to apologize for his rudeness, for his ingratitude, waiting for the explanation he knew was now unavoidable, because he could deny her nothing.

It was hard to countenance, Draegan thought, and even harder to admit that after a lifetime of scapegrace behavior and scandal he'd fallen hopelessly, endlessly in love with this guileless slip of feminine logic and practicality. He hadn't the slightest idea of how or when it had happened— or, worse, what to do next. He only knew that she alone could purge him of his bitterness and anger, fill the aching emptiness where his vitals once had been.

"You have nothing to fear from me," she said softly. "You can set aside your shadows, Draegan, and step into the light."

He passed a hand over his face. "Tell me what it is you want from me."

"Something only you can give. The truth, Draegan. It's as simple as that."

"There is nothing simple about it," he said. "Nothing pretty about my past, Fallon."

"We all have regrets," she assured him. "Things that we would do differently if it were possible."

"Your regrets in no way compare to mine. You are an innocent; you have not used men as I have used women, bedding them for sport, for the information they provided me, betraying their trust with no regard whatsoever to their feelings. I have done all of that, and much, much more. In point of fact, I rather made a career of seduction, short-lived though it was. Kitchen maids in Tory households, wives of Tory and British officers, lonely, vulnerable women susceptible to a bold glance and a devilish smile.

"I devised the game, and for a time, I played it very well. The Tory faction in New York City knew of my rebel leanings, yet I let it slip in certain influential company that I was disgruntled with the lack of appreciation my superiors displayed toward my obvious military talents and was rethinking my loyalties."

"And this worked to your advantage?"

He nodded. "My uncertain political stance and my position in the community as heir to Grandfather's holdings were enough to assure my acceptance. The rest came easily. Too easily, perhaps, for by the time I met Lucy Greenhill at a New York soiree, the excitement had worn thin and I'd grown rather bored with it all, negligent and indiscreet."

"Lucy Greenhill," Fallon put in, "the woman who shot you." Draegan arched a black brow at her and watched as she shrugged. "You talk in your sleep."

"Do I indeed?" he said wryly. "I shall try to remember that. Lucy came along at the height of my arrogance. She was nearly thirty, but still handsome of face and figure. She was also the wife of Sir Percy Greenhill, a major general serving under Howe. Sir Percy was forty years Lucy's senior, a cold English fish, and Lucy was starved for affection, a fact that I should not have so blithely discounted."

Fallon was watching him closely, an earnest expression on her small piquant face. "Were you in love with Mrs. Greenhill?"

"In love with her?" Fallon had taken him quite by surprise with that one. He tried to answer honestly, yet talking about his past indiscretions came unbelievably hard. "I suppose I was fond of her, in my own careless fashion, but no, I did not love her. I daresay I didn't grow a heart until I came to this shady mountain hollow." He sighed, and trailed the tips of his fingers over the back of her hand, a wordless plea for clemency. "Are you certain you wish to hear this?"

"Indeed. Go on. I'm listening."

"Yes, well. As I said, I never imagined that Lucy had taken the affair so seriously until Christmas Eve of '76, when she sought me out with the news that she had been widowed, and found me otherwise occupied."

"You were with another woman? How horrible for her!"

At her exclamation, Draegan grimaced. "I would not be so quick to rush to Lucy's defense. She had a hideous temper, and she exacted a heavy toll for a minor dalliance. Thanks to Lucy, I'll walk with a limp for the rest of my days, and doubtless she's forgotten all about the entire episode by now. I'm sure she's gone back to England and married some drooling old fool in his dotage. She does not deserve your sympathy."

"I think I shall reserve the right to disagree," Fallon said. "Any woman who has fallen victim to your lethal charm deserves a measure of sympathy. How did you come by the scar?"

"My, what a bloodthirsty little wretch you are, anxious for every detail, no matter how horrid."

She lifted her chin, an endearing trait uniquely hers. "I saved you from Randall and removed you from Jacob's doubtful care. Surely an explanation is a small price to pay."

"That depends on which side of the telling you're on. Where I happen to sit, the price you demand seems exorbitant."

"Cease your complaining and finish your tale," Fallon said. "It's nearly one, and you haven't even had breakfast."

He sighed, resigned to the fact that he was a virtual prisoner and had little choice but to continue. "Word of the sordid affair got around very quickly. Soldiers in winter encampment seek out the most mundane diversions—anything to relieve their incessant boredom, however temporarily. When I returned to Valley Forge, I was greeted with a great show of enthusiasm and not a few sniggers. My commander in chief, however, wasn't the least bit amused by my exploits. By the end of the day, he'd sent me packing, back to Schuyler's command in Albany.

"I was angry, filled with bitterness toward Lucy and my former commander's high ideals. At the time, I felt it was the lowest point in my life. But I was wrong. I was two days' ride from Albany when foul weather struck. I'd been pushing hard to reach my destination, and hadn't shaved in nearly a month. Gaunt and weary, in a uniform that had seen better days, I looked the worst sort of vagabond, yet even a vagabond needs shelter from a howling icy wind. I found it in a most unlikely place. An abandoned stone chapel, situated off the way."

She inclined her head slightly to look at him, lips parted. "Aye, Fallon," he replied softly, knowing her thoughts. "The very same. It offered shelter and a sort of peacefulness that beckoned. There, in a high-backed wooden pew, I fell asleep. I woke several hours later to a ring of strangers standing around me. With them was a young militia captain who questioned me, asking me who I was and how I'd come to be there. The captain admitted that they had been in pursuit of Sparrowhawk, to whom they'd lost a man, and had chased him to the chapel where I sat sleeping. I vowed that I'd seen no one enter, that I'd been there the evening through, but no man among them was willing to listen. Quill lifted a cloak from the back of the pew on which I sat, but it was not the tattered woolen garment I had worn into the chapel. It was a gentleman's cloak, still dotted with sleet."

He paused and drew a deep breath, releasing it slowly. His hand, which a moment earlier had toyed with Fallon's, curled into a fist, the knuckles showing white against the pale green coverlet. With a sigh, Fallon gathered her courage, closing her own small hand over that iron fist, an offer of wordless compassion, the only thing she could give. "The rest happened so quickly," he said. "Quill gave the order and one of his men searched my things, producing a fistful of papers that had belonged to Sparrowhawk. Everyone by now was closed against my claims of ignorance and innocence. In the space of a heartbeat I was convicted of spying for the British and was summarily condemned."

He paused again, and a shudder ran through his lean frame. "You need not tell me the rest," she said.

But Draegan continued his tale as if he hadn't heard. His gaze was fixed on some point in the distance, and Fallon knew he was looking into the past. "They bound my hands behind my back and forced me out into a night that was miserably cold. It was still sleeting, and the stump that served as a hasty gallows was slippery and wet. I remember cursing Quill as I stood there with the storm wind howling around me, the hempen noose around my throat like the chill, damp embrace of the grave. It is the last thing I recall, except for the blinding agony of being wrenched apart, skin from muscle and sinew from bone."

The tears that had gathered in Fallon's eyes slipped over her lower lashes and coursed slowly down her cheeks. Through that shimmering veil she saw him cover his eyes with one hand. "For the love of Christ," he said, his hoarse whisper filled with emotion. "Don't pity me. It is the one thing I could not withstand from you."

Fallon shook her head, needing him to understand. "Not pity. Empathy for your desperate plight. Sorrow that you have continued to suffer alone . . ."

He reached out and smoothed away her tears with gentle fingers. "It was too difficult to speak of, too raw a wound. In hiding the scar, I kept unwanted questions at bay. I could not bear for you to know—could not risk having you recoil from me. And then there was the small matter of Randall Quill to be considered. I couldn't be sure of your feelings for him, your loyalties."

"Randall." Fallon sniffed, wiping the moisture from her cheeks with the tips of her fingers. "He's the one part of this puzzle I can't seem to understand. If he's a Tory in truth, in league with the British, then why would he want to hang Sparrowhawk, a British operative?"

"I can only guess," Draegan replied, taking her hand in his and slowly drawing her down. She lay half atop him, her cheek pressed against his naked breast, her body close to his uninjured side. "But my theories on the subject of Randall Quill can keep awhile longer. Just now I have other, more pressing concerns."

Fallon lifted her head, and her face was very close to his. She could see the slight smudge of blue beneath his beloved green eyes, the coarse black stubble that shadowed his cheeks, jaw, and chin. "But if he should discover your true identity—"

"I fear he already has." He kissed the point of

her chin, the turn of her jaw, then took her soft, fragrant earlobe in his teeth. "After the incident on Kingston Road, Jacob discovered that someone had desecrated Major Draegan Mattais Youngblood's grave at the foot of the sentinel maple. The grave *meant for* me. Finding it empty was all the proof Quill needed." He spoke with a deadly calm. Fallon sniffed again and would have buried her face against the hard, muscled wall of his chest, except that he cupped her chin in his hand, forcing her to meet his clear, bright gaze. "I must deal with him soon. You know that, don't you? And this time, the outcome will be different."

Fallon nodded gravely. What had begun more than a year before in the small stone church not far from Gilead Manor would have to be played out, she realized, though she found herself dreading the outcome. Randall was treacherous, and since he was in league with Sparrowhawk, he was capable of anything. "I wish it were otherwise—not for Randall's sake, but for your own. Twice, now, he's nearly killed you."

"Faith, lady," he said with a semblance of his old knowing smile, "is that caring I see in your bright, tigress eyes?"

Fallon would have risen then, would have turned away in an effort to hide her true feelings, yet Draegan held her fast. He was not as weak as she had supposed. "You know I care—" she began.

He slipped his hand under her arm and dragged her up against him. Fallon felt the heat of him through the sheet and the coverlet, felt the hard evidence of his desire hot against her hip. "Care," he said softly, threading his fingers through the soft strands of hair at her temple and watching her so intently with those penetrating pale green eyes. "Do you care, as any decent soul would, for a fellow human being in dire circumstances? Or do you perhaps feel something more, something deeper, more difficult to resist—something that sends sleep to the devil and renders the flesh mere tinder to the fires of passion?"

Fallon wished to shake her head, to deny she felt what he was describing. Yet all she could do was lie there, her heart beating madly in her breast, and hang on his every word, his every breath. "Tell me you feel it, Fallon. Tell me you feel what I feel."

"I don't want to feel it," she answered miserably. "I don't want to care for you. There have been so many others before me, women of experience, who've suffered heartache and worse at your hands. Lucy Greenhill, Lettice, and the legions of others . . ."

"Lettice?" He frowned. "Would that my loosened tongue had choked me in my delirium. It would have been kinder by far."

"You will not attempt to deny that there have been numerous others?"

"There have been numerous others. Tavern maids and wealthy young widows, Tory wives and a scullery wench or two, but I swear to you on my life, Fallon, there has never been anyone like you. Not a single maiden among them, and none that I've given my heart to."

Fallon's heart was in her throat. "Sir, what are you saying?"

"I'm saying that as incredible as it may sound, as hard as it is to accept, I love you. I'm saying that I need you. That I'll expire here in your bed and make an impossible situation even more difficult if you don't soon give me hope that there is the smallest chance for the two of us." He raised his body slightly, meeting her lips in a kiss that clearly conveyed that he meant every word. Still she said nothing. "Fallon, please. If you can't give me back my life, then I beg you to put me down quickly."

She answered him wordlessly, coming quickly

into his arms. "As incredible as it may seem," she whispered against his carnal mouth, "I have fallen in love with you. But Draegan . . . ?"

"Hm?"

"Do you recall Lucy's pistol?"

He smiled, his green eyes glinting from under lowered lashes. "Without fail, every time it rains."

"Take it to heart. *I* would not miss."

He chuckled and lifted the coverlet. "Lie with me," he said, patting the soft feather mattress. "Be my lover in truth. I swear to you, you'll not regret it."

Fallon's face pinkened. He was naked, keenly aroused, and completely bared to her gaze. She knew that she shouldn't have looked but she couldn't look away. "Here? Now? Oh, Draegan, I couldn't! It's midday! And there's your wound to consider. You haven't the strength for what you have in mind."

"But I'm feeling much better," he countered with his secretive smile. "Think of it, Fallon. The two of us, here in your soft, scented, comfortable bed, sunlight streaming through the lace curtains gilding our skin. What could be more perfect? And I vow I'll be flat on my back. I won't move a muscle. Well," he said wryly, "on second thought, maybe one or two."

What he was suggesting was scandalous, despite all that had happened there that day. There was, after all, no marriage vow between them, no guarantee of what would come later. His future was uncertain at best. If he got her with child and lost the final contest with Randall and Sparrowhawk, she would be ruined.

But if she denied him, turning aside for the sake of propriety their one chance at happiness, and lost him . . .

It could happen, she knew.

Once he had left the sanctity of the manor walls, he would again enter his world of secrets and shadows, danger and death. And she might never gaze into his beloved green eyes, hear his laughter, feel his wondrous touch again.

The fear of losing him was enough to seal Fallon's fate. She would take what he offered; indeed, she would take all that he wished to give, and she would revel in it. Just this once, she vowed to be impetuous, to savor each moment they had together, as if it indeed were their last.

With trembling fingers, she unhooked her bodice and slipped it over her shoulders and down, listening as she did so to his soft exclamation, to his deep, appreciative male sigh.

The blush that had tinted her cheeks earlier deepened. She averted her gaze but kept on. The garment parted, and she flicked it away, reaching for the lacings that held her petticoat in place. In a moment, the lacings were loosened. Fallon stood up, and the tawny silk pooled around her ankles, leaving only her stockings and thin lawn chemise.

Now she hesitated, catching her full lower lip in her teeth. Draegan only smiled at her reluctance and lifted the hem, slipping a hand beneath. "All, Fallon," he said seductively. "Leave everything there on the floor but your glorious innocence, and come to me."

At his gentle urging, Fallon removed the last remaining shred of her modesty and stood before him blushing and completely unadorned. "God, look at you," he murmured. "You are exquisite, pure temptation . . . every creamy inch."

Taking her hand, he drew her down beside him until she gingerly sat on the edge of the bed. "I have never—" she said. "I don't know quite where to begin."

He nuzzled the palm of her hand, took her smallest finger into his mouth and teased the whole with his tongue and his teeth. Fallon watched his lashes lower, sooty crescents against his cheeks. He breathed deeply, a sigh of contentment, and pressed her hand to his chest. He guided it down over the smooth tawny expanse of his chest and stomach, across the wrappings at his waist, to his belly and the proud swell of his manhood.

The sheath that enclosed his maleness was softer than satin, and with Draegan to guide her, Fallon eased aside the velvet foreskin to reveal the wonder within. Tentatively, gently, she touched him, marveling at the sensation of miraculous pulsating life in her small hand. "It is . . . beautiful," she said softly. "Not at all what I imagined." She closed her hand around the turgid shaft and felt his answering throb. "This does not pain you? Your wound—"

"Wound? What wound? He gave a shallow sigh. "Fallon? Have I told you yet that I love you?"

"Yes," she said with a coy little smile. "But if you like, you may tell me again. I doubt I will tire of hearing it anytime soon."

She was seated by his side on the mattress, the length of her thigh pressed against his thigh and hip. Slowly, he reached out and tested the weight of her breast in one hand, teasing the nipple to hardness with his finger and thumb. "Come closer, won't you? Being forced to lie here with so much distance remaining between us is torment. I need to feel you in my arms. I crave your sultry kiss."

Fallon leaned forward, kissing him, parting his lips with her lips, teasing his tongue with her tongue, just as he had taught her. Then she trailed her kisses down his cheek, his jaw, to the strong column of his throat, and listened to his heartfelt groan. Nibbling her way along the length of his collarbone, she paused to tease his nipples to hardness with her tongue and her teeth.

He tried to rise, but she placed her hands on his shoulders and pushed him back into the pillows. "Wound be damned," he said. "I grow desperate."

She slanted him a look from her glowing amber eyes but said nothing, choosing instead to trail the tip of her tongue along the thin strip of sable hair knifing down the center of his flat belly. When she reached his maleness, she paused and, lowering her lashes, bent to kiss the heart-shaped tip. She heard his breath catch in his throat, and she parted her lips, kissing him lightly, teasingly, before drawing him slowly in.

The hand that a moment before had been on an intimate quest now urged her wordlessly up and onto the mattress beside him, into his sinful, all-knowing embrace. Parting her thighs, he worshiped her flesh, even as she worshiped his.

Shared kisses, shockingly hot, unbearably intimate . . . evoking sensations that were half-remembered yet keenly anticipated, wildly thrilling, delicious . . . These feelings were all the sweeter to experience since she was certain that Draegan, her dark and dangerous lover, experienced them too.

Fallon felt his tongue pass the folds that protected her womanhood, felt it delve deep, touching, caressing the passion-born ache that unfurled so deep in her belly. She heard a breath swiftly drawn, a sigh, and then he was urging her to release him, drawing her up and up, until she sat astride his lean hips.

"Come to me, Fallon. Come to me now, love . . . rise above me. Give me your heart, your trust, your sweetness, your all."

Her heart thundering in her breast, wanting desperately to please him, Fallon rose above him. Still moist from his sensuous kisses, the soft folds of her woman's flesh slowly yielded before the insistent pressure of his male ardor, momentarily opening to him, then settling once again around him, gripping him tightly.

At that moment, Fallon paused, suddenly aware of the barrier of her maidenhead. A feeling of intense and slightly painful pressure centered in her belly, taking momentary precedence over the pleasurable ache. She grimaced and would have withdrawn, but Draegan took hold of her shoulders, preventing her retreat from the discomfort.

"A moment of pain for a lifetime of pleasure," he whispered. "One quick thrust is all that's needed, and it will all be over. You'll be mine in truth." He touched her flushed cheek with gentle fingers. "Though I must warn you: once it's done, there won't be room for second thoughts or cold regret. I will never let you go. Do you understand what I am saying, Fallon?"

He released her shoulders; she nodded gravely. Her reply was a shaky whisper as she drew herself up. "This most precious gift I have to give, I give to you."

An upward thrust, swiftly executed, as he had so wisely suggested, and her maidenhead was no more. The pain was instantaneous but swiftly fleeting. The gravity of what she'd done left her shaken and weak, unresisting as he gathered her against him.

"You are brave to entrust your future to a rogue like me," Draegan said. "But I pledge to you, I'll try my utmost not to bring you undue heartache."

"Not brave," Fallon replied softly against the scar at his throat. "Not brave at all. I am afraid, so terribly afraid, of losing you."

"Don't speak the words," he said. "Don't let the world intrude. We're here together now, bound by a love that is more powerful than anything or any-

one out there. Let's make the most of it, shall we?"
He stirred inside her, insistent, strong.

Fallon felt it keenly, felt his life force fill her, and
wordlessly, she moved against him. The ache, forgotten in a moment of solemnity and pain, was re-
born in that instant. It grew rapidly, filling her with
a need, a desire, so intense that it blotted out all
else. The world as Fallon knew it, the uncertainty
of their future, swiftly retreated, moving farther
and farther away, until nothing existed outside
those bedchamber walls—indeed nothing at all except Draegan and the unholy passion he kindled
within her.

The passion burned now, a huge conflagration,
beyond all control, beyond all imagining. The old
Fallon was quickly consumed by the white-hot in-
tensity; her innocence and naïveté turned to fine
ash and fell away. Out of those ashes, phoenixlike,
a new Fallon rose, a woman newly awakened to
the wonder of the ways of man and woman, to
aching, endless love and unbearable intimacy.

Slow thrusts and slower withdrawals. The flames
raged high, roaring in her ears, licking, caressing,
her naked woman's flesh. The heat intensified, her
breathing grew increasingly ragged, the pressure
built and built, and Fallon became desperate. She
gave a mindless whimper, low in her throat, a
wordless plea. . . .

Her dark lover heard, and slid his wondrous
hands down the length of her spine to her dimpled
derriere, cupping the soft curves, urging her closer;
until she held every inch of him tightly inside as
he tilted her hips.

She felt rapture beyond all recounting, an explosion of physical delight. Fallon gasped as it swept
over her, engulfing her beleaguered senses, dragging her down into a swirling dark mist.

She cried out softly, triumphantly, and Draegan

dragged her down into his arms, surrendering to the shattering ecstasy, filling her virginal tightness with his hot flood of seed.

Long after the initial glow had faded, he lay holding her lithe form against him. Worn from their lovemaking, Fallon softly slept, her bright head pillowed on his chest.

She was bound to him now, by love and by carnal deed, by the divulging of secrets long kept. He swore he would do all in his power to strengthen that bond in the little time left to them. He would pray to whatever god was listening that it would be enough to sustain them through the difficult times that lay ahead.

The future looked shadowy and dark. And Draegan knew that the same sharing of ugly truths that had brought her trembling into his arms could very well tear them apart.

Chapter 17

D raegan finished eating the last of the pork pie Fallon had brought for his dinner. He set the plate on the bedside table and lay back against the soft feather pillows. "Delicious, filling, yet I find I've a sudden uncontrollable craving for something sweet." He smiled a slow and somewhat lecherous smile, watching with satisfaction the blush suffusing her cheeks. "Tell me, dear lady, did you by chance bring dessert?"

She had perched on the foot of the bed as he dined, but now she rose and made a great show of tidying the chamber, which, for the past three wondrous days and nights, they'd been sharing.

"Fallon?" Draegan prompted, when she did not answer.

She glanced his way. "Yes, I brought it, though I can't imagine what lascivious thoughts you are entertaining in that deviant mind of yours." She fished in the deep pocket of the apron she had donned while preparing his dinner and brought forth a slim volume bound in crimson leather.

Draegan's smile grew even more wicked. He patted the coverlet with one sun-browned hand. "Come, love, read to me."

She stared at him, incredulous. "Aunt Edith's French novel?" She dropped the book on the bed next to Draegan. "Oh, Draegan, I couldn't! Very well, then, if you truly wish me to read, I'll go and find Voltaire and be back in a moment."

"Voltaire will put me to sleep," Draegan said, "and I've something else entirely in mind." He wagged the spine at her. "*The Wicked Comtesse.* What a wonderfully titillating title. Aren't you the least bit intrigued?"

"A romance? Never!" She glanced away, then back again. "Well, maybe just a little."

Smiling darkly, he opened the cover and leafed through the pages. Finding the passage he wanted, he started to read. His tone was soft, the prose seductive. From the corner of his eye he saw Fallon edge forward, saw her budding interest, the gentle rose that bloomed high on her cheeks. He closed the book, marking the page with his finger. "But you don't wish to hear more. It's only a romance novel—we'll just slip this one back on the shelves, and Voltaire it is."

Fallon smoothed the counterpane, fluffing Draegan's pillows. "Perhaps another page or two—just to humor you."

"Are you certain?" Draegan questioned. "I would not wish to compromise your principles."

She sat down on the edge of the mattress.

Draegan smiled. "Are you certain?"

"I have a little time," Fallon admitted. "I spoke with Brewster just this morning, and Uncle is feeling better but still keeping to his rooms. Zepporah sent word that she won't be home until late afternoon. I could linger, if you like, an hour . . . maybe two. . . ."

Draegan lay the novel face down on the counterpane and, taking her hand in his, drew her up beside him. "First, let's take off that apron. You are a hand in the kitchen, my love, but I willingly confess, it isn't your culinary talents I'm interested in. In fact, the moment we're wed I'll hire someone to see to the more mundane tasks of managing a household. You'll be much too busy seeing to your husband's ravenous sexual appetites to care what goes on in the kitchen."

"Did you say 'wed'?" She looked pleasantly surprised.

"Aye. *Wed*. Married. Bound to one another by a sacred pledge and a legal license issued by the governor."

"Draegan Mattais Youngblood, are you asking me to marry you?"

Smiling, he again lifted the novel. Fallon listened in rapt attention as Draegan read on, describing in lurid detail the desperate, fiery passion that raged between the fictional lovers. Caught up in the story of a doomed and desperate love, enthralled by the blatant note of seduction in his voice, she slowly sank into his arms and watched with feigned disappointment as he put the novel aside. "You aren't finished?" she said, gazing into the passion-bright depths of his eyes.

"Finished? My sweet, untutored innocent. We've barely begun." He shifted on the pillows, rising slowly above her, pressing her back.

"But the desperate young lovers," Fallon said teasingly. "How will I learn how it ends?"

"I'll be happy to show you," he whispered against her parted lips. With studied care, he unhooked her gown and whisked the garment away. At last she lay completely bare to his hungry gaze.

Fallon tried to rise, to press him back into his heretofore prone position, but this time he wouldn't allow it.

"Your side," she said anxiously, but he stifled her words with a passionate kiss.

"My side is well enough," he murmured against her cheek. "Open to me, Fallon. Welcome me in."

At his urging, she parted her thighs, sighing as his weight pressed her down into the soft, encompassing mattress. How blissfully sweet to lie beneath him like this, Fallon thought, reveling in the feel of his arms enfolding her—so tightly!—in the heady seduction that was his kiss. As he bade her, she took him to her, wrapping him in her embrace, welcoming him in, meeting each of his powerful thrusts with her hips poised high. She ached, wanting to weep at his slow withdrawal, until he filled her again and again and again and the shuddering climax claimed her, at which time the world beyond the big feather bed crumbled and fell clean away.

Exhausted from their passionate play, Fallon slept soundly. Curled on her side, her cheeks still touched with gentle rose and her bright tresses tumbled, she was too beautiful to look upon—a woman too innocent and too trusting, too good, surely, for a rake and born deceiver such as Draegan to hold for long.

Yet try to hold her he would.

He wanted her forever, a lifetime of basking in her innocence, thousands of days in her sweet company and nights in her arms, time in which to convince her how deeply he cared. And who could say that, if he were exceedingly lucky and was granted the time with her he so desperately craved, some of her inherent goodness might not rub off?

It was a pretty dream, and Draegan clung to it as he rose from the bed and took up his clothing. Freshly laundered and mended by Fallon's own hand, his clothes lay folded on a chair by the window. Careful not to wake her, Draegan put on his stockings and breeches. Then, boots in hand, he crept noiselessly from the room.

The house was quiet, the second-floor hallway deserted. Noiselessly, Draegan crossed to the stairwell and started to climb, his movements carefully calculated to accommodate muscles stiff from inactivity.

The time he'd spent with Fallon had been wonderful, but he'd been idle too long. He had to return to the rectory and resume his investigation.

On silent feet, Draegan ascended the final flight of stairs. At the third-floor landing he paused to listen.

There was dead silence. Not a wisp of sound, not a breath, not the smallest movement met his ears. Brewster, who served both the house and grounds as required by the master, was nowhere to be seen. The long hallway, flanked by an open balustrade on the right and two doors on the left, was empty.

Draegan moved forward, pausing in the shadows near the first door. Fallon had indicated that Lucien had sought refuge in his third-floor chamber when he had succumbed to one of his infamous headaches days before, yet Draegan had cause to wonder. Lucien's headaches seemed to come with alarming regularity, striking without warning and lasting for days, days in which the invalid saw no one, received no one, communicated with no one but the loyal Brewster.

But Draegan was suspicious.

If Lucien were as ill as Fallon seemed to believe, then why was no physician summoned? And why this unnerving, unbroken silence? Stepping close, he put an ear to the door; then, slowly, carefully, he turned the handle and eased the panel open.

A bedchamber, richly appointed and momentarily unoccupied, lay beyond. Draegan moved down the hall to the second door, listened, and then eased the panel open.

The second room was in great disarray. Sunlight filled with dust motes streamed through the leaded windowpanes, illuminating the hodgepodge of papers, books, artifacts, and curiosities that covered every surface of every table and chair, not to mention the great, massive desk that dominated the room.

Lucien Deane's lair was an eccentric's dream, and every housekeeper's nightmare, a treasure trove of clutter. Draegan was intrigued. If appearances were any indication, then Lucien Deane rarely discarded anything, and Draegan could only wonder what he might find of interest amid the disorder.

Leaving the panel slightly ajar, Draegan entered the room. Listening for the slightest sound that might signal someone's approach, he set about sifting through the mess.

There were half-finished drafts of letters addressed to Joshua Trumbolt, various treatises on scientific discoveries, theories, and carefully documented facts. A twenty-minute search yielded nothing of value. Disappointed, Draegan was just about to leave, when his eye lit upon an oilskin packet tucked between an untidy stack of books and the leg of a nearby chair. Inside was a thick missive sealed with wax and addressed to Lord Lovewell Artemis Stone, at Fort Niagara.

Draegan stared at the packet he held. In his hands was the evidence that would connect Lucien Deane to Sparrowhawk, a goal toward which he'd tirelessly worked for months, and dreamed of for even longer.

At long last, his day of reckoning was at hand.

He should have been wild with elation at his victory. Yet all he could think about, all that concerned him, was the tumbled beauty slumbering peacefully in the second-floor bedchamber, the woman who'd sacrificed all for him, who'd given so generously of herself—the very same woman whose loved one he was about to destroy.

Later that same afternoon, Lucien crossed the large portico and rapped on the solid oaken door of the stone farmhouse with the head of his cane. When no one answered immediately, he waited a moment and rapped again.

A few seconds passed, and the door was jerked open. "What the devil is it?" Randall demanded; then, recognizing his visitor, he softened his tone. "Sir, I did not expect you."

" 'Tis obvious, dear boy," Lucien replied, eyeing Randall's dishabille with a tight-lipped smile. "Tell me, do you always lie abed till afternoon, or is this a celebratory bout of slothfulness? Well, no matter. I am sure you will manage to pull yourself together, now that I am here. I just returned, and am most anxious to hear all the details."

"Randall, lad, who is it?" a quavering voice demanded from the shadowy depths of the parlor.

"It's nothing to concern you, Mother," Randall called impatiently over one shoulder. "Go on about your business."

"If it's them wretched friends of yourn, you send their worthless rebel arses packing!"

Lucien chuckled dryly. "I begin to see how you come by some of your more endearing traits. Reassure the old dear, won't you, then meet me by the hedgerow. We've a great deal to discuss."

As Lucien turned away, he caught a glimpse of a diminutive gray-haired prune in a drab gown straining on her toes to catch sight of her uninvited guest.

Glad to be away from the farmhouse and

Madam Quill's malicious curiosity, he ambled toward the high hedgerow, where his mount cropped grass and where he might wait undisturbed for Randall.

His wait was not a long one. Randall came quickly over the grass, the tail of his nightshirt now tucked into his breeks, his left arm tied up in a sling. "Quarrelsome old bat," Randall muttered. "I should have ordered her dunked in the millpond years ago."

Lucien clucked his tongue. "Such venom for the dame who once suckled you at her breast. But alas, now that that breast is withered, you would see her seated on a ducking stool and doused in the millpond as punishment for her sharp tongue." A rattling laugh. "Faith, dear boy, there's hope for you yet!"

"Sir," Randall said stiffly, "do not bait me. I am in no mood for it."

Lucien leaned on his cane. "That much I can see. The question that plagues me is why. You should be elated, my friend. The threat Youngblood represented is alleviated, is it not? My plans are set. And all is right with the world—except for your arm, of course. I can see he put up a struggle before you took him down, but no matter. You're a stout young fellow, hale and hearty still, and I'm sure you'll be better in no time. Now, give me the details, will you? How did the bastard die? And where does his moldering body lie? Did you plant him in his intended grave, as poetic justice would indicate, or leave him to the wolves?"

Randall looked discomfited. He licked his lips, and could not meet Lucien's gaze directly. Lucien felt a stir of unease deep in his vitals. "Come, now, Randall, there's no need to be modest. Tell me, how did you pull it off? Did he talk? Did he indicate who sent him here, if anyone?"

"He didn't talk," Randall admitted, "and the threat he represents is more alive than ever."

"How do you mean, 'more alive than ever'?" Lucien asked. "Damn you, sir. Explain yourself!"

Randall shook his head, paced several feet, then turned and came back. "He isn't moldering in the grave, Lucien, nor is he bait for the wolves. He's alive, and he's out there somewhere ... waiting, may God damn his soul to hell, always waiting!"

Lucien seized Randall by the breast of his nightshirt and shook him hard. "Leave off your foolish mutterings and tell me what happened! Why did you not succeed?"

"I don't know," Randall replied. "Everything was carefully planned. By all rights, he should have been dead. The others were waiting in the wood by the edge of the road when he came by with the cooper, and I had ridden east to block the road. He was nearing the place of concealment when he wheeled his mount and spurred it toward me. It was the damnedest thing, as though he sensed something—almost as if he *knew*."

"Oh for pity's sake! You aren't going to start that again!"

Randall shook his head, and his look was like that of a small boy who's had a fright in the dark and is forced to face the unknown again. "You weren't there. You didn't see him, Lucien. He charged straightaway for me, though I leveled my pistol and fired. His face was white and set like stone, his eyes burning unearthly bright—"

"Superstitious blather," Lucien pronounced, "and you, sir, are an imbecile! I can't imagine why you let him get to you. He is as human as you or I, and every bit as vulnerable to chance, with one small exception—he has cunning, boy! He has a keen sense of survival, and the devil's own luck to carry him through."

Randall seemed reluctant to let go of his wild imaginings, despite Lucien's logic. "If that is so, then why didn't he fall? I didn't miss my mark. There was blood in the road, and blood at the rectory, yet not a sign of him or his mount anyplace, and I've searched everywhere."

"Blood, yes. Because phantoms, haunts, avenging angels do not bleed. Did you think to check the catacombs?"

"I found nothing."

"What about Jacob Deeter's cabin in Vanderbloon's Wood?"

"Deeter has not been there for days, and there was no sign that Youngblood had ever been there at all. I freely admit, I'm rather unnerved by this whole episode."

"Well, buck up, man, and stiffen your spine. There's work to be done! If indeed Youngblood has been wounded, then he can't have gotten far. He's holed up in a safe place somewhere, licking his wounds. But he won't stay there long. He'll come out of hiding the moment he's able to sit that white menace he rides, and I expect he'll come looking for you. If you give a tinker's damn about your worthless hide, you'll find him and finish this before he finds you."

Randall looked shaken and ill. Lucien took his uninjured arm in an unyielding grip. "Somehow you must manage to end his life, and with it this insanity. And this time," Lucien said in a near whisper, "you will succeed. It is your last chance to prove yourself, and if you blunder again, I swear to you, I will personally put an end to your incompetency!"

In the second-floor bedchamber at Gilead Manor, Fallon watched as Draegan rose from the comfort of the feather bed and dragged on stockings, dark breeches, and tall black boots. An hour before, he had kissed her awake and, amid blissful sighs and passionately whispered endearments, made love to her yet again.

Fallon's woman's flesh was swollen and tender, her spirit oh, so very sated and content. She wanted nothing more at that moment than to lure him back to their cozy nest so she could dream in his arms. Instead, she watched as he buttoned his linen shirt and tied his neckcloth.

He was leaving the manor, returning to the rectory. And though Fallon knew it was inevitable, had known all along that this moment would come, she was not all pleased. Draegan was well aware of her feelings.

But his strength had returned, and with it his hardheadedness. Her feelings, her fears for his safety, seemed to make little impression upon him. He had a ready reply to each one of her protests, and to Fallon's fury, each one made perfect sense. "You shouldn't even be thinking of leaving so soon. Your wound is far from healed. You could break it open, start bleeding again, and there's no one at the rectory to look after you."

"It's better this way, for both of us. Willie has already returned; Zepporah will very soon. You risked your reputation bringing me here, and though I am endlessly grateful, I will not press our luck any further than need be. If I were to be found here, it would only cause difficulty, and I fear Zepporah's wrath more than Randall Quill's and Sparrowhawk's combined." He sat on the edge of the bed and pulled her between his knees. "Now, come kiss me again and tell me that you'll be here waiting when I return for you tomorrow."

"At the very least, let me come with you," Fallon countered. "I can leave a note for Willie, and help you prepare for the morrow."

"There is nothing you can do."

"Draegan, please—"

"I want you to stay here." He kissed her, hard. "I want you safe. One more day, and then nothing will come between us ever again."

They went downstairs together. When they reached the library, Fallon closed and latched the door and came into his arms one last time. "Take care where Randall is concerned," she warned. "There is no telling what he will do."

"He's not my main concern," Draegan told her. " 'Tis you. I want you in my life, Fallon, for now and always." He took her face in his hands; his pale eyes seemed to burn brightly in his deeply tanned face. "Promise me that when all of this is through you'll marry me. Promise me that nothing will ever come between us again."

She nodded, close to tears. But that didn't seem to satisfy him. "Swear you will!"

"I swear it to you, by all that's holy. I won't desert you ever!"

The clamor of voices raised in greeting, the sound of hurrying footsteps, the crunch of hooves on the crushed shell drive, intruded upon their leave-taking. Draegan kissed Fallon one last time and, releasing her, stepped into the shadowed recess of the passageway and was gone.

Sniffing back her tears, Fallon unlatched the library door and went into the hallway. At the same instant, Zepporah entered, followed closely by Willie.

Willie hugged her mother's neck, then stood back, beaming. "It's wonderful to have you back, Mother, isn't it, Fallon?"

"Yes, wonderful," Fallon said.

"Thank ye, dears. I've missed ye both terribly. Why, I suppose I might as well admit it, I even missed the master! My, it's good to be home again!

Now, tell me, what's happened while I was away?"

"Happened?" Willie said as quickly as she could manage. "Why, nothing to speak of, really. Reverend Mattais wed Thomas and me a few days ago, but we can talk about that later. The trip must have taken its toll upon ye, Mother. Ye're looking rather tired. By the by, how is Cousin Sarah?"

"Recovering nicely, I think. She's nursing a strapping lad, and won't be out of childbed for a few days more, but all went very well." Willie took Zepporah's arm and whisked her away down the hall toward her chamber. Suddenly, Zepporah halted in her tracks, frowning at her daughter. "What was that ye said a moment ago about the reverend?"

"The reverend?" Willie sent a pleading glance Fallon's way, but Fallon only smiled. "Oh, yes, the reverend. Perhaps, after all, ye'd like to lie down, Mother."

Zepporah placed her fists upon her ample hips and bent a hard stare upon her daughter. "Wilhemina Rhys!"

Willie swallowed. "Smith," she said in a small voice. "Wilhemina Smith. Thomas and I are wed."

Fallon held her breath in anticipation of the housekeeper's explosion, but none was forthcoming. "Married?" Zepporah said in a quiet voice.

Willie nodded her saffron-colored head. "Yes, ma'am."

"Without my consent or approval? Without my presence?"

Willie gave another nod, looking abashed.

"I see," Zepporah said coldly. "Well, miss. It seems you've gone to great pains to make yer bed. Now ye'll have to lie in it." With a last, cold glance at her recalcitrant daughter and another sent Fallon's way, Zepporah stalked back up the hall to the kitchen.

Chapter 18

⟲ ◦◦◦ ⟳

The house was in turmoil from Willie's admission. Zepporah knocked pans and plates about in the kitchen, creating a terrible din. Lucien came downstairs briefly to inquire after the source of the noise, but, not wanting to involve himself in a sticky familial dispute, he made himself scarce once again. Willie sulked about the house like a wistful shadow, alternating between anger at her mother for being so unreasonable and tearful remorse for the havoc her impetuous actions had wreaked.

Fallon had tried once to mediate, but, having received little more than an indignant sniff and a resentful stare from Zepporah, did not try again. The marriage and her mother's approval, or lack of it, were Willie's problems, not hers. And Willie must be the one to deal with them. Yet Fallon found that she could not help but empathize with her friend, who had wanted nothing more from life than the love of Thomas Smith.

The price one paid for love, however, was sometimes very dear.

Seated now at her desk in the library, quill in hand, Fallon stared into space, seeing Willie's tear-

stained face as she'd perched on Fallon's bed a
week earlier. "Ye don't understand," Willie had
said. "When ye're this desperate in love, each minute ye're apart seems ten thousand years!"

Fallon sighed and put down the quill. At the
time she had thought Willie naive, her proclamation little more than theatrics.

But oh, how wrong she had been.

She herself had been naive, not Willie, and her
friend's proclamation had been much more than
simple theatrics; it had carried the profound ring
of truth. To love someone and to be separated from
him, even for a moment, was bittersweet torment.

Rising from her chair, she wandered to the windows, and stood staring out over the sunlit
grounds. Several hours had passed since Draegan
had taken his leave from Gilead Manor, and she
already missed him terribly.

She pressed her brow to the cool glass of the
leaded windows, her lids drifting dreamily down.
Where was he at this moment? she wondered.
What was he doing? Was he sparing her a moment's thought as he prepared to meet Randall the
next day? Would he be angry if she broke her vow
to remain at the manor and went to him, or would
he be secretly glad to see her? Would he welcome
her into his strong embrace and seek to reassure
her?

Fallon opened her eyes and sighed. A heavy
stand of woods separated the church from the
manor. In winter, when the trees were stark and
leafless, she could just make out the church steeple
from this very window. Now she could see nothing
but an endless sea of verdantgreen.

In her mind she walked every step of the way.
It wasn't far—little more than a pleasant stroll
she'd made hundreds of times on her way to the
village, both alone and with Willie. She could be

there in no time, she thought, and back before twilight. No one at the manor would even miss her, and surely no harm could come from her dropping by the rectory to tell Draegan one last time how very much she loved him. Surely in the face of her genuine sentiment, whatever anger he might feel could not linger long.

Her mind set, Fallon took up her wide-brimmed straw hat, her cotton gloves, and, on a whim, the romance novel she and Draegan had been reading together. Then she hurried from the room.

The afternoon was uncomfortably warm for late spring, the air thick with a blue-white haze that softened the harsh outline of the distant hills and rendered the simple walk to the small stone chapel more of an exertion than Fallon had anticipated. By the time she arrived, she was winded, and wanted nothing more than to sit in the comparative cool of the rectory, basking in Draegan's presence for just a little while, if indeed he would allow it.

She rapped lightly on the door and pushed the panel inward, eager to escape the relentless heat of the sun. "Draegan?"

She paused in the open doorway. The kitchen, Fallon saw, once her eyes had adjusted to the dim light, was deserted. But the sound of voices issuing from the sanctuary betrayed Draegan's presence. Drawn by the sound of his voice, she crossed to the door leading to the sanctuary, where Jacob's words brought her up short. "It's nearly done, then. Ye've got the proof ye've needed all along to implicate the great man. What happens now?"

"After I've seen to Quill, I'll take both him and Sparrowhawk north, to Schuyler at Albany. There will be a trial, after which, I'm sure, the general will derive great pleasure in stretching their necks. Let's pray, for both their sakes, that Schuyler's man does a more thorough job than the captain did. I want this ended as quickly and cleanly as possible, with no undue harm to Fallon. It will be difficult enough for her after . . .''

Standing in the doorway of the sanctuary, Fallon had been about to call out, to announce her presence, when she heard her name spoken. Her words stuck in her throat. Draegan's voice was cold and remorseless, so unlike the man with whom she had fallen so completely in love. Despite the warmth of the day, she felt suddenly, inexplicably cold.

"Poor little lass," Jacob said as she listened. "She lost her parents when she was just a tad; she ought not lose another loved one in so cruel a fashion." A slight pause, and then, "What'll become of her, Reverend?"

"She'll want to go north, to be with her uncle. And perhaps, after all, that's what's best for all concerned. I have family in Albany, and the name Youngblood is not without influence. Once we are wed, I will do all that I can to shield her. But I won't lift a finger to help Lucien Deane."

At the mention of her uncle's name, the novel she was clutching escaped Fallon's nerveless grasp and clattered to the floor. The gaze she raised to Draegan was filled with horror. Oddly, she felt the world retreat. Nothing about that scene—the sudden sickening quiet, the look of regret on her lover's face—seemed real. She shook her head to clear it, and heard herself say, "No. No, not Uncle Lucien. You can't think that he would be connected to Sparrowhawk."

"You weren't to find out this way," Draegan said.

Fallon heard the regret in his voice. It was like salt in a freshly inflicted wound. She wanted a denial from him, an apology. She wanted him to recant his words, to declare that he'd been mistaken, but no denial was forthcoming. Stricken, she retaliated, her own tone venomous. "No? How, then, was I to discover that you've been plotting the destruction of my family? When?"

He reached out to her, palms up, beseechingly. "Fallon, please, you must listen."

She shook her head again, this time in disbelief, and began to back away. "Listen," she said indignantly. "Listen to what, sir? More of your evasions, your half-truths? More of your lies?"

"I never lied to you."

"You kept the truth from me!"

"To protect you!" His shout echoed in the ensuing silence of the sanctuary and was slow to die away. Draegan stood rigidly, clenching and unclenching one hand as he sought control. "You can deny it all you wish," he replied tightly. "It doesn't change a damn thing. Your uncle is up to his eyeballs in intrigue and murder, and has been for months."

"You have no proof of that," Fallon said. "This is madness. Your anger and bitterness have consumed you, and I will not hear another word!" She turned and stalked across the length of the parlor, intending to leave, but Draegan would not let her go. Before she reached the kitchen, he caught her arm and held her fast.

Pointedly, she stared at the elegant fingers biting into her tender flesh. "Let go of me, sir," she said softly, distinctly.

"So that you can return to the manor and warn Lucien that I plan to take him? I can't do that, Fallon. I won't. I've worked too long and too hard to let him slip through my grasp."

"You cannot keep me here against my will."

It was a moment before he answered, and when at last he replied, his voice was terrible in its softness. "I can and I shall. You have given me no choice."

While they stood toe to toe, glaring at each other, Jacob ducked through the parlor doorway and hastily made his exit. "Reverend, sir, I'll be outside if ye should need anything. Miss Fallon. Good day."

"Coward," she said.

"Don't fault Jacob for his unswerving loyalty," Draegan told her. "We share a common goal—a goal that you shared as well, not so long ago." He reached out and traced the line of her jaw with the fingers of his free hand, frowning as she flinched away from his touch. "It's clear, however, that your loyalties are strictly familial, and preclude the combined causes of justice and liberty. I cannot imagine why I'm surprised. They do say, after all, that 'blood is thicker than water.' "

Fallon swallowed the lump in her throat. She could no longer see the Draegan she knew—a man so dear to her heart, so passionate and caring, her lover, her newly betrothed. To think of what she'd lost would only inflict more suffering upon a heart that was already near to bursting.

Anger was her salvation, a lifeline to which she would cling until the hurt lessened, until the bright dream of their future had faded and died away beneath the weight of his treachery. Anger; yes, anger would save her from drowning in a sea of frantic confusion and stark misery. "You came to the Catskills a stranger," she said, "alone and friendless, and we welcomed you in. We invited you into our home. I stood by your side each Sabbath morning, smiling while you made fools of my neighbors and friends. Yet in the end, it would appear, the greatest fool of all was I. I somehow managed to convince myself that you were acting nobly, for the benefit of those unfortunates like Greetje and Jan

Krieger who had fallen prey to Sparrowhawk."

She laughed shakily. "How naive I was! Fooled by the same handsome face and devilish smile to which all of the others before me succumbed, and, God help me, with the same end result."

"It was not like that, Fallon, I—"

"You used me!" she said. "To get to my uncle, to get revenge for some imagined wrong you feel he committed against you, long past."

"An imagined wrong, was it?" With a flick of his deft fingers he tore open his neckcloth, baring the livid scar to her gaze. "This pretty neckpiece I wear is hardly imagined, lady. Indeed, it's all too real. And there are other scars from that night I bear, scars you cannot see! Do you think for a moment that I could forgive and forget in a year, or ten, or a thousand, the man who did this to me?"

He laughed harshly and pushed her down onto the divan, then stood scowling at her. "Yes, God-dammit, I wanted revenge against Sparrowhawk. And, truth be known, I want it still. That's why I leaped at the opportunity to venture to a tiny Cat-skill hamlet. That's why I donned these cleric's clothes, when nothing could have been more ill-suited to my nature. That's why I stood at that pul-pit each Sabbath morning, fighting back the bile of my hypocrisy. All of that I did, and much, much more, but I was not the first to implicate your uncle as Sparrowhawk. That blame, my love, you may lay at the gout-ridden feet of General Philip Schuy-ler and a captured Tory spy named John Phelps."

She frowned up at Draegan, her small face ab-normally pale. "I don't understand. If this Phelps knows my uncle, then how is it I have never heard of him? And what has General Schuyler to do with this?"

"A few days before Schuyler put the proposal to me, two men were caught trying to infiltrate his camp. One of them escaped. The other, John Phelps, hastened to tell everything he knew, in hopes of getting off handily. Phelps was the first to bring up the name of Lucien Deane in connection with Sparrowhawk. He claimed to have had dealings with Lucien. Schuyler listened avidly. And I must admit, Phelps told a convincing tale. But it wasn't enough to satisfy the general. He wanted proof."

"And so they sent for you," she said.

"Schuyler, thank God, is more open-minded and slightly less pious than Washington. He is also a friend to my father and Uncle Jon, which in no small way worked to my advantage. He called me to his headquarters late one evening, and Uncle Jon was there. Together they laid the plan out before me, neither one aware that I had a previous, dark history here in Abundance—indeed, in the very church where I would be expected to preach. I could not believe my good fortune at being offered an assignment that would lead me to Sparrowhawk and allow me to gain my revenge legally. Needless to say, I accepted, and the preparations began in earnest. Schuyler, it seemed, had thought of everything. He supplied my clothing, and Uncle Jon provided my instruction.

"It was all too perfect," he went on, smiling grimly down at Fallon. "And I was totally prepared to find the proof I needed to put an end to Sparrowhawk, or so I thought, until I arrived in Abundance and found that Schuyler had neglected to inform me about one very important thing—a fire-haired young bookworm with a gamin's face and frank amber eyes—my enemy's niece. You can imagine my chagrin when I was informed that I would be working directly, not with your uncle, but with you."

"How very inconvenient for you."

It was not said unkindly. Draegan took heart. She was softening, not a great deal, but by slow degrees. Enough, perhaps, to listen. "Damned inconvenient," he reiterated, "since I couldn't seem to keep you from my thoughts. And then Captain Quill came along to complicate matters, as if they weren't complicated enough."

"You were going to kill Uncle Lucien, weren't you? That's why you accepted the assignment and came to Abundance."

There it was, the worst of it, out in the open and lying between them. Draegan's first instinct was to evade her pointed question, to bury it as deeply and as quickly as he could. But she was looking at him, watching him with her frank tigress eyes, so wide, so lovely, so unrelenting, and he knew that nothing less than the absolute truth would do. "I had every intention of doing just that when I first came here," he said softly, "but things do seem to have a way of changing."

She lowered her dark lashes, masking the pain in her eyes. "Would that you would change your way of thinking, and look elsewhere for Sparrowhawk."

"Would you have me pick and choose my truths, Fallon? Do you want me to ignore the facts before me because they fail to fit my hope of a future with you? Would you have me turn my back on all of the innocents who stand to lose their homes, their lives, their children, to Sparrowhawk's machinations—"

"You know I would never ask that!" she shot back. "But think of what it is you are saying. Why, Uncle Lucien's physical limitations alone should be enough to convince you!"

"If indeed they are true limitations."

She stiffened. "You have seen him for yourself, sir. He has difficulty walking. To sit on a horse would be an impossibility, let alone to undertake what you are suggesting."

"Perhaps," he said. "And yet perhaps he is not as frail as he seems. Maybe the guise of invalid scholar has worked perfectly to his advantage, so perfectly that those closest to him, his own loved ones, don't realize his capabilities."

"He only rarely leaves the grounds of the estate!"

"But you don't know his every move. Think of it, Fallon. Think of the headaches he suffers, headaches that last for days at a time. He spends long periods locked in his rooms, with the express wish that he not be disturbed. And who among you tends to his needs?"

"Brewster."

"Brewster," he echoed. "And where do Brewster's loyalties lie?"

"Why, with Uncle, of course—"

"Is Brewster loyal enough that he would strive to keep your uncle's secrets?"

"I don't know—yes, I suppose that he would. Yet it still proves nothing!"

"It proves that it is possible for Lucien to leave the house and grounds and be absent for days at a time without anyone being aware of it—you, Zepporah, or Willie. But he would need to slip out unnoticed, in dark of night, after the house was sleeping, or by some other available means."

"The catacombs—"

"He was nine years old when the connecting tunnels were constructed. He must have known of their existence."

She sat, silent and unwilling to respond. But Draegan could see that he had managed to plant the seed of doubt in her mind, and as cruel as it seemed, he hastened to nourish it. "The night of the hanging, Sparrowhawk entered this very

church and planted on me the papers that sealed
my fate, before he disappeared. For months his disappearance plagued me. How, I wondered, had he
managed it? How had he vanished into thin air,
with Quill so hot on his heels? There couldn't have
been more than a moment between the deed and
Quill's entrance, for the sleet that dotted the cloak
had yet to melt. And it was a gentleman's cloak.
The answer lay locked away inside these hallowed
walls. It wasn't until I discovered the passageway
that I unlocked a portion of the mystery and could
give absolute credence to John Phelps's claim and
Schuyler's suspicions."

"Credence, perhaps, but you still have no proof."

It was time to play his final gambit. Producing
the packet of papers, he placed it in her hands.
"Here is your proof."

She raised her gaze to his, a frown of suspicion
creasing her brow, and waited. "This is Uncle's
seal. How did you come by it?"

He crossed his arms before his chest, steeling
himself for his final admission. "Yesterday, while
you lay sleeping, I went to your uncle's rooms.
Brewster had returned to the stable; the rooms, his
study and chamber, were empty, and this was lying in the open."

She held the packet in her hands, hesitating.

"Go on," he said. "Open it."

Still she sat, motionless.

Draegan took the packet from her slack hands
and emptied the contents onto her lap. "These are
letters of intent, crucial information as to the
strengths and weaknesses of the settlements both
north and south of here. All of them are penned in
your uncle's hand—information he could not have
asked you to transcribe. And they are addressed to
Lord Lovewell Artemis Stone, who shares a joint
command at Niagara. All of the pieces fit. The

church and catacombs, the headaches, the frequent missives to Joshua Trumbolt, a known Tory, missives carried by Randall Quill. Tell me, Fallon, do you still doubt my sanity?"

She lowered her gaze to her lap and the evidence he had gathered. "How can this be possible?"

"Careful planning, a brilliant mind, a deception that has been built brick upon brick. Lucien is thorough, I will give him that. He thought of everything, including the hurt the truth would bring if it ever came to light. I have little doubt that you are the reason he went to such great lengths to conceal his activities beneath this cleverly contrived deception."

Looking down at her, Draegan felt something catch in his chest. Her darkly golden eyes shimmered with unshed tears, but she did not turn to him for the solace he would gladly have given. Instead, she held herself apart—carefully, chillingly distant.

He wanted desperately to hold her, to extinguish the hurt he saw in her eyes, yet he knew he did not dare. Yesterday he had been her lover; today he was her enemy. The shock from the blow dealt her was too fresh, the wound of what she would surely view as his betrayal too raw, too new.

Given time, she might view his part in the drama differently. But now now, not at this point. For the moment, all he could do was try to protect her, to keep her apart from Lucien and Randall and away from the coming conflict.

Unaware of the direction of Draegan's thoughts, Fallon stared at her hands, folded in her lap. How very odd that she was able to appear outwardly calm, even for a moment, when her thoughts were in such violent turmoil.

A gathering of facts. Cold logic. Level-headed reasoning. It all made a terrible sort of sense. And in her hands lay a packet of the most damning sort of evidence, addressed to a British lord and officer at Fort Niagara. It was definitive proof that Lucien was in truth Sparrowhawk.

Draegan, her spy-catcher, her dark, errant lover, the man who would blow her world to bits very soon, was nothing if not thorough, in everything he did.

"Uncle as Sparrowhawk," she said softly, "who could possibly have credited it?" She gave a shaky little laugh that ended in a strangled sob. Through welling tears she saw Draegan reach out to her, saw his deeply troubled look, and put out a hand to ward him off. "What will happen now? What will happen to Uncle?"

"I must take him north, to Albany."

"To trial?"

"Yes."

"They will hang him, won't they?" He didn't reply. *"Won't they?*

"Yes." His voice was soft, yet it cut like the keenest of blades.

"Not so long ago you stood in the pulpit and spoke of the wages of sin. If what you say is true, then Uncle Lucien has done a great wrong, one for which he will pay with his life." She shook her head as her tears began to flow. "But there is a part of me—the little girl who once played on the floor near his feet while he busied himself with one experiment, one project or another—who does not wish to believe it. He has been so unfailingly kind to me, more a parent than even Father was. He answered my questions and never made light of my concerns. As a child I would go into the garden in search of curiosities, odd-shaped stones and bits of plants and flowers, insects and twigs, all of which found their way into his study. At day's end I would sit on his lap and listen while the mysteries of my world were painstakingly unfolded—always with such patience."

Wordlessly, Draegan knelt before the divan and drew her to him, holding her tightly as she wept her heart out. "Fallon, love," he said in a taut, aching voice, "you rend my heart." He held her until her sobs ceased, until she grew quiet in his arms, and still he did not release her. "There is nothing I can do to help him. You know that, don't you?"

She nodded, struggling to gather the tattered remnants of her pride about her slim shoulders. Her face was mottled with red, her lids puffy from the tears she had shed, but her voice when she addressed Draegan was once again steady and strong. "You have the facts, the proof, the theories, but do you have the reason? Can you tell me why a man like my uncle, a man who has been unfailingly caring and good his entire life, would take part in this macabre masquerade?"

"Your uncle alone knows the reason," Draegan said.

She slowly stood, smoothing her skirts with her hands. "Then I must go to him. I must know why."

Draegan took her by the shoulders and urged her to sit. "It isn't safe to let him know what you know."

"Uncle would never harm me," Fallon insisted.

But Draegan would not be swayed. "The risk is too great, and I doubt you'd be able to resist pouring your heart out to him, if in fact you went back to the manor. Until this is over, you must remain here with Jacob. It's the only way I can be assured of your safety." Releasing her, he looked to the older man, who had reentered the sanctuary and taken up a post near the door. "Don't let her out of your sight."

"Draegan, wait," Fallon cried, but it was too late. Draegan was already gone.

*   *   *

The hours that followed seemed without end. Minutes ticked slowly by; the angle of sunlight slanting through the parlor windowpanes gradually shifted, deepening into the mellow gold of evening, while Fallon continued her restless pacing, from the hearth to the window and back again.

Jacob watched, always vigilant, lest she disobey his master's edicts.

The evening wore on; darkness fell.

Jacob brought her food, but Fallon couldn't eat. Her mind was in turmoil. She needed answers— answers Lucien alone could provide, and she needed them immediately. If forced to wait, she knew she would only grow more agitated, more furious with her uncle, when she needed desperately to understand. She would grow more furious with Draegan's wretched insistence that Jacob keep her there, a virtual prisoner.

The whole situation was intolerable. There was still a great deal she did not know. How and why had all this come about? What twist of fate had brought them all to this terrible pass?

Lucien would tell her everything, she was certain. Lucien would explain the inexplicable, just as he always had done. Once she had confronted him and he had realized that the inevitable had happened, he would rectify his mistakes and surrender. Once he'd realized there was no escape from justice, that his secret was out in the open, he would make a clean breast of everything.

Once she understood his reasoning, she would be able to help him. It was the only course left open to them.

Fallon paused in her pacing to stare out the window at the night. "Where do you suppose he is now?" she asked.

Jacob seemed relieved that she had broken her

moody silence. "I expect the reverend's lookin' for the cap'n, miss. But there ain't no need to fret. He'll be back here by and by. He always comes through in a pinch."

"I wish I had your confidence," Fallon said.

"Not confidence, miss. Faith. The good Lord snatched him back from the jaws of death that night in the churchyard. I witnessed it myself, and have pondered it much ever since."

"And what conclusions have you drawn, Jacob?" Fallon wasn't sure what made her question the caretaker—was it simple curiosity or a genuine need to know?

"Only that the Almighty must'ave had a good reason to give him back his life. Until he fulfills his purpose, he'll bide with us still."

"And I will wait and wonder," she said. "But I suppose there is no help for it." She turned her face back to the night. "Is there food left in the kitchen?"

"Yes, miss. There's ham, fresh boiled eggs, and bread and cheese. If ye'll come and sit, I'll be more'n happy to fix ye a plate."

"That sounds wonderful, Jacob. But I'd like a few moments of privacy first, if that's all right." She glanced meaningfully at the small alcove that was the bedchamber, and when Jacob still looked blank, she elaborated. "I'd like to use the chamber pot. Despite what Draegan said about your not leaving me out of your sight, he surely wouldn't be so cruel as to object to you granting me a few moments of privacy."

Jacob's face went scarlet. "Oh, no, miss! I mean, aye, certainly! Oh, dear me. I'll wait just outside the kitchen door. You be sure to call out when you're through." He turned and made a hasty exit, his battered hat crushed in his hands and his head bowed.

Fallon took up the candle burning on the nearby table and hurried into the sanctuary. The ruse had worked. A moment or two was all she required.

Chapter 19

⟨ ⟩

Guided by the flickering light of the candle's flame, Fallon descended the curving stone steps and moved as quickly as she dared along the narrow underground corridor.

By now the dank smell, the rumble and groan of the earth and the trickle of stone were all familiar, and did not strike the same chord of fear in her breast as they had the first time she'd ventured there alone.

Indeed, the things she had always feared—the darkness, rats and bats, and the looming unknown—seemed paltry at that moment. They were the bugbears of childhood, all of which paled in comparison to the weighty concerns she now had to face.

Draegan's revelations had blown her world to bits, yet oddly enough, in the midst of the dust and the rubble that had once been her life, a single spark of hope continued to burn brightly. It was the hope that somehow a mistake had been made, that some logical explanation would be found that would clear Lucien's name and restore their shattered lives; and though the chance was exceedingly slim, Fallon was reluctant to let it go.

Lifting the candle high, she tried to peer into the stygian darkness. The crates that held the brown Bess muskets were just ahead. Muskets smuggled into the Catskills by Lucien.

She shook her head. It was still too incredible to be believed.

Ten paces ahead, bits and pieces of splintered wood littered the floor. The muskets were gone, the crates now destroyed. Fallon picked her way cautiously through the debris and continued on. She passed the last overhead beam and was nearing the wedge-shaped stone, when the sound of movement and the distant murmur of voices drifted in from the adjoining cavern.

Fallon blew out the candle's flame, pressing close to the wall.

"You said there have been complications." It was the voice of a British gentleman, decidedly lazy, bored, almost; a voice she didn't recognize.

Fallon pressed closer to listen, but her heart raced at the sound of the answering voice.

"A minor inconvenience. Nothing to merit your notice, my lord. A certain Draegan Youngblood has been sniffing around our operation. Fine-looking young fellow, but devilishly hard to kill. Like a cat with nine lives, the uncooperative bastard keeps coming back."

"I trust the matter has been taken care of."

"Indeed, my lord. By now Quill will have done for the major quite nicely. This time he's to bring me his lifeless body as proof that the task has been properly seen to, or forfeit his own in the bargain."

There was a general laughter, but Lucien didn't join in. When the laughter quieted, the Englishman spoke again. "Schuyler, that gout-ridden old he-goat. I haven't seen him in years. Are you certain this Youngblood has had no communication with him concerning your activities?"

Lucien chuckled again, dryly. "As certain as I can be. Youngblood has had little contact with anyone, aside from the sodden old caretaker who lives near the church, and my niece, Fallon. Deeter isn't bright enough to fathom what's been happening here, and I have gone to great lengths to assure that Fallon is unaware of it. I should like very much to keep it that way."

"You may do as you wish, of course, but if she were my niece, I'd tell her the truth. It will save you a deal of explaining when she discovers you're for Niagara."

"I have already thought of everything," Lucien replied.

In that instant, the last bit of hope Fallon had harbored flickered and died. She put a hand to her mouth in an attempt to smother the sob that came welling up and out of her throat but was not completely successful.

"What the devil was that?" the Englishman demanded.

"I'm sure it's nothing," Lucien hastened to reassure him. "The settling of the roof above the beams, or the scurrying of a rodent. These catacombs are old, and rife with the creaks and groans that inevitably come with the advancing years."

The answer did not seem to satisfy Lucien's companion. "Joseph, you and Wears-A-Hat make certain that we haven't been overheard."

Fallon didn't stay to hear more. She turned and fled. She had to find her way back to the church. She had to warn Draegan. He had escaped death twice at Randall's hands. If he was fortunate enough to triumph again and return to the church, only to find her gone, this was the first place he would look.

Torchlight flared to the rear. Her breath sobbing in her throat, Fallon gathered her skirts in her hands and ran. But before she reached the crates, a hand from behind seized her elbow and jerked her around hard.

She cried out in frustration and rage, a wordless plea for freedom.

Her captor grasped her other arm and shook her, hard. He was an Indian, slightly taller than Fallon and stockily built. Sharp features and fierce black eyes peered from beneath the brim of a battered black tricorn edged in tarnished silver lace. Ingeniously, he'd cut a hole in the crown, and from the ragged hole, a scalp-lock and a decorative silver brooch protruded. "Stone says you come," he said, giving her arm a subtle squeeze. "Joseph, take her other arm so she don't make to run again."

"Please, let me go. I must get back, I must!"

Lucien, who had come to stand in the entrance to the cavern, watched impassively as the two Indians brought her forward.

"How could you?" Fallon cried angrily. "How could you help them?"

"Come, now, Fallon," Lucien said. "Don't make a scene. In case you haven't noticed, we have guests."

Lucien took her from Joseph and Wears-A-Hat and steered her into the cavern. "My dear, may I present Lord Lovewell Artemis Stone, Earl of Blakeney Downs, Surrey. My lord, this is my niece, Miss Fallon Margaret Deane."

Stone was a tall, spare man in his middle forties, with keen blue eyes and a long hooked nose. His clothing was dark and nondescript, his brown hair thinning, and except for the circumstances of their meeting, Fallon might have mistaken him for any American country gentleman. "Charmed, dear lady," he said, out of habit reaching for her hand, which Fallon pointedly withheld.

"You will understand if I fail to return your sentiment," Fallon acidly replied. "It is not every day that I encounter an officer in His Majesty's service so near to home." She turned her icy stare on Lucien. "Or in the company of my uncle."

Stone chuckled. "Thought of everything, did you, old man? It seems, after all, that you will need to explain. She is not as amenable as you seemed to think she would be." He nodded deferentially at Fallon and crisply turned his back upon them, strolling to the far side of the cave, where he struck up a discourse with Wears-A-Hat.

"Plotting and instigating murder," Fallon accused. "Using these catacombs to smuggle muskets and house the enemy beneath our very noses while they seek to destroy the lives of honest, hardworking folk!"

Lucien heaved a ponderous sigh. "I can see that you are disappointed in me."

"Disappointed? I am shocked and appalled and bereaved—for the Lucien Deane I thought I knew, my beloved uncle, that model of fairness and forethought after whom I patterned my life, is dead."

"A bit overstated, now, don't you think?"

"Pray, sir, do not patronize me!" Fallon snapped. "I am not a child, and in the light of all you have done, I will not stand for it!"

"No," came Lucien's soft reply. "No, my dear, you are a child no longer. You have grown into an exquisite young woman, one who deserves something more than to be tucked away in these mountains with an ailing uncle and a hardheaded Dutchwoman and her daughter for company. You deserve the world, Fallon, as did your dear mother, Sabina. Have I told you how very much you resemble her?"

"Let us leave Mother out of this."

He gave her a dark look, full of hidden meaning. "I should like to oblige, but I am afraid that Sabina is an intricate part of this quaint little puzzle. I was in love with her once, you see, long, long ago, and for a time it seemed that she returned my affections."

"You and Mother?"

Lucien gave her a crooked smile. "Do you find that so incredible, my dear?" He laughed, low and humorlessly. "Yes, I suppose that you do. Well, 'tis true enough. My entire world revolved around Sabina, whose sparkling presence made all things seem possible. What spirit she had! She could brighten the darkest room, the darkest life, just by entering it. . . . I was about to ask for her hand, when your father announced their engagement."

He gave another sigh, genuine, this time, and continued. "I do believe that was the day that my heart began to wither. I settled on your Aunt Edith shortly thereafter, a gentle ghost of a woman, who, not unlike me, paled in comparison to her shining sibling. It seemed the only course left to me, and we made a fine match, she and I, both ill-suited to society, cerebral, reserved. I even came to care for her, after a fashion, during the short time I knew her."

"Aunt Edith's death was tragic, and I am sure you were lonely in your grief, but it cannot excuse what you have done, Uncle."

Lucien went on, seeming not to have heard. "The loss of my bride and my son seemed unreal to me. She had touched my life so briefly and had so quickly departed it. It was almost as if she had never been. . . . " He paused and shook his head. "And then there was Osgood, the fortunate son, the one upon whom the gods always seemed to smile. Osgood had everything—looks, wealth, a lovely bride so full of life . . . and you."

"And you resented him for his good fortune?"

Fallon prompted, uncertain just where this conversation was leading.

"I resented him deeply, though he was never aware of it. I was the eldest son, and as such the yoke of the inheritance fell onto my sloping shoulders. The weight, at times, was crushing. When Father died, I took control of the estate, and along with the rents and taxes, repairs and endless responsibilities, I cared for your father. His debts became my debts, his failures my failures. He played at life, while I worked endlessly. When his shipping interests failed, he came to live beneath my roof. And when Sabina died, you were left to me. I daresay it was the only good turn my brother ever did me, even though it was done selfishly. You see, you looked so like her that he could barely abide the sight of you. You forced him to remember how much he still missed Sabina. That's why he stayed away so much of the time."

"Why are you telling me this, Uncle?" Fallon asked. "If you are trying to hurt me by dredging up the past, then you are succeeding."

"Hurt you? My dear, I would never seek to hurt you. Not purposely. No. You asked me to explain; I'm but trying to comply. Indulgent, yes, that's me, to the bitter end." He laughed low again, his peculiar, rusty laugh. "Being the good and dutiful brother never got me anywhere. Your father played at life, and he won. I worked without ceasing, and all I got for my pains was a kick in the teeth. At every turn, it never failed. Even after his death.

"And then in '73 I met Stone, and he offered me the recognition I had longed for, a chance to make a name for myself in the work I so loved, a chance to leave the shadows of my past in this wretched mountain hollow far behind me. And you, Fallon, I imagined how you would shine in London! Everything was arranged, but in the space of an instant my dreams of success were crushed, along with my wretched spine. For a time after, I still had hopes that once I recovered—" He broke off and shook his head.

"And then this blasted war came on, and it seemed that all was lost. At my lowest point, Stone contacted me, this time with a proposal of a different sort, and because I was desperate, I accepted." He chuckled darkly. "Somehow I expected it to be yet another dismal failure. I was pleasantly surprised. This little game of wits and intrigue was one at which I excelled, and my success— my infamy— was heady indeed."

"You think this a game?" Fallon was appalled. "There are lives at stake—women's and children's! After all that you have lost—Aunt Edith, Mother, Father—how can you treat life, any life, so cavalierly?"

"My dear Fallon, it was war. And those poor unfortunates caught in its path are casualties of war, nothing more."

"What about George Antwhistle? Was he a casualty of war also?"

Lucien's smile turned sly. "It would appear that you are intent upon dragging all of my skeletons out into the light."

"He was a man of God, Uncle, who to the best of my knowledge never hurt anyone!"

"That's a matter of opinion," Lucien said harshly. "He came poking his ecclesiastical nose into places it didn't belong! He threatened the whole operation, my last chance at success! And as a result, he got precisely what he deserved."

"Which brings us to Draegan," Fallon said softly. "When you found him asleep in the church that night a year ago and planted those papers in his belongings—then left him to face the noose that you yourself had earned—did he get what he deserved?"

"The whole unfortunate incident was an accident of fate, pure happenstance. The major was in the wrong place at the proper time, and I had to escape, don't you see? Randall and his dogs were hot on my trail. Youngblood served a purpose, and at first I looked upon him as a gift from God, a peace offering for the Hell He had made of my life. I did not mean for him to die—not back then.

"If not for Randall's insane temper, the major would have been questioned and perhaps held for a time before he was released. But Youngblood provoked the lad's temper, and in a fit of rage he decided to hang him. Not because he was suspect, mind you, but strictly out of spite. Randall knew full well when he laid hands on that cloak and found my lathered mount that I'd been to the chapel. He knew whom he'd been chasing. It was information he would employ later to blackmail me."

"So that's how he became a part of this," Fallon said.

"Oh, yes. He thirsts for glory too. It's the one thing we have in common. It might all have come off smoothly, too, had it not been for our persistent friend the major. Randall thought he'd seen the last of him when he left him swinging in the storm wind. And indeed I must concur that any decent, obliging fellow would have succumbed, and put an end to the whole sordid affair. But not Youngblood. No, he *would* prove uncooperative to the last. I should have taken better aim when I fired upon him weeks ago, but I believed him to be the Reverend Mattais late upon the road, and killing two of God's disciples would have been pushing the bounds just a bit, don't you think?"

Fallon felt suddenly ill. How could he have persisted in this madness without her knowing? How could she not have seen? "What I think," she said, "is that the fall you suffered affected you more deeply than we know."

"Ah, yes, madness. I rather thought that would be forthcoming, but your conclusion, my dear child, is incorrect. I have never been more lucid, for in aiding Stone on behalf of King George, I have secured our future. A glorious future in London, far away from this place and all of its less-than-pleasant memories. Stone will see to everything—a London house, my patronage, and a husband for you—some right and proper English country gentleman who can give you all the things in life you so richly deserve."

"It's your dream, not mine," Fallon said. "And it's a dream that's built upon a foundation of lies and deceit, upon the blood and bones of innocents. I cannot share it with you, feeling as I do. And I could never live in England, don't you see? What I want is here."

Lucien wrinkled his nose in distaste. "Merciful God, not again! It's Youngblood, isn't it? That pestilent young bastard has used you to get to me, and he's stolen your heart in the bargain."

"He did not need to steal it, Uncle. I gave it to him gladly." Fallon sniffed back tears. "He is my life, my heart, and in conspiring against him, you have conspired against me."

"You were bound to take this hard, that much I can see. But I know no way around it. By now, Randall will have properly seen to Major Youngblood, and this time there can be no going back. It's over, Fallon, all of it—our life here in the Catskills, your infatuation with this man. It's time to start anew."

"No!" Her shout drew the frowning attention of Stone and his two companions, but Fallon was beyond caring. "It's not over! It will never be over! Randall failed twice, and he will fail again. Draegan will best him, and when he does, he'll come for me."

"He is dead, Fallon!" Lucien said mercilessly. "Bait for the wolves and the carrion crow. And you and I are going to Niagara with Lord Stone."

It was nearing ten o'clock on that same moonless evening when Draegan walked his white stallion through the village of Abundance and drew rein outside Sike's Tavern. The village itself was silent and dark. Most citizens, weary after the long day's labors, had long since sought their beds. But the lights still burned bright at Sike's, and the occasional burst of raucous laughter drifted out into the street.

The man Draegan sought did not take part in the revelry; he was slumped at a corner table, his back to the wall, staring morosely into the dregs of his whiskey. But as Draegan's shadow crept across the table, Quill raised red-rimmed eyes and swallowed hard. "Satan's liege in the guise of a religious," he said, his voice slightly slurred. "No mortal man can survive the noose, no matter what Lucien says. And then last week—my shot was true—I saw the blood—" He broke off and shook his head. "Who are you, really?"

Draegan's answering smile was chilling. "Vengeance is my name, and I've come to claim you. Will you come with me peaceably, or must I spill your blood on Samuel's puncheon floor?"

Randall seemed to be waging some inward struggle. "Come with you now? To Hell, sir?"

Draegan chuckled low. "Hell comes later, Captain. First we must needs go to Albany." Reaching inside his coat, he drew forth a pistol, which he trained upon Randall. "You've had too much to drink," he said silkily. "Your mind is playing tricks upon you. Why not come along with me? I'll find you a nice, safe place where you can sleep it off. By the time you awaken, I'll have taken care of Lucien, and we can begin our trek to Albany."

"Lucien," Randall said. "Goddamn his eyes. It was his doing. All of it."

"Not all," Draegan countered. Softly, he drew the hammer of the pistol into full cock, its click underscoring his words. "That first night, it was your choice, your decision alone, to end my life."

"An honest mistake," Randall said, his face growing red with fury and drink. "The papers, the cloak, and our man lying dead in the road—dear God, man! I thought that you were Sparrowhawk! How was I to know you were telling the truth? How was I to know that it had been Lucien all along?"

"I seem to recall telling you that I was innocent," Draegan said. "But you were in no mood to listen."

"By the time I found out that Lucien had left the lathered horse and sent yours off into the night, it was too late to go back. The worst was done. I had no choice, don't you see? You were not his only victim. I had no choice except to join him, in the hopes that I could begin again. He said that we would go to London—that he and I and Fallon would start anew."

Draegan reached out and seized Quill's deerskin coat in an iron fist, hauling him half across the table and pressing the muzzle of the pistol to the hollow beneath his ear. "You could have turned him in," he snarled.

"They would have hanged me!" Randall cried, his face crumpling. "Lucien would have told them I'd killed you. And Lucien had gotten me into this mess. He owed me something, dammit! He owed me!"

"It was not all Lucien," Draegan ground out. "Who cried for the rope? Who stood in the teeth of that howling gale and kicked my legs from under me, without the benefit of a hearing?"

Randall began to snivel, and Draegan leaned down into his face, snarling. "You cannot imagine how I have dreamed of this moment, Captain. How I've savored the thought of putting a ball through your brain, of hearing you whine for your worthless life before I took it from you, just as you took mine from me!"

"Kill me, then!" Quill sputtered. "But for God's sake, do it quickly!"

For a long moment Draegan leaned over Quill, the cold steel of the pistol pressed to his quivering flesh, while those watching held their breath. The tension reached a soaring peak. Draegan's finger tightened on the trigger. He was fully prepared to send the ball into Randall's brain and send Randall to the devil. Then, into the black fury that swirled all around him, came the voice of caution. "Not this way, Reverend, sir. If ye take his life like this, he'll haunt ye the rest o' yer natural days."

His mouth taut, his eyes burning, Draegan looked up at Jacob "Let it go," Jacob said. "It's plagued ye long enough. 'Tis a fitting end, don't ye think, to give the hangman his due?"

"Why are you here?" Draegan said, easing the hammer back into place. "Why aren't you with Fallon?"

"Gone, sir," Jacob said hesitantly. "That's why I've come. She asked to use the chamber pot, and when I turned my back, she slipped away."

"Did you check the passageway?"

"Aye, sir. First thing. And after that, the manor. Nobody's seen her, and Master Deane's gone too."

Randall laughed, giddy with whiskey and the knowledge that the crisis had passed. "You see now, Youngblood? Lucien. It's always Lucien."

Draegan hauled Quill up, a fist at his throat. "What do you know about this?"

"I know that he's left me to pay for his crimes and he's stolen Fallon from you. If he has his way, and likely he will, you'll never see her again."

"Where has he gone?" His voice was soft, but the threat was clear. "Where has he taken her?"

"That's the beauty of it," Randall said, dissolving into peals of drunken laughter. "He's taken her to London."

Draegan turned the pistol in his hand and brought the butt down hard on Randall's head. Then he thrust the fallen man away and stood. "Samuel, is there a room here where you can secure the captain until my return?"

"Aye, sir," Samuel said. "There's a root cellar in back, with a hasp and lock."

"Then get him from my sight," Draegan said. "And post a guard. If he's not here waiting for me upon my return, there will be hell to pay. Do you take my meaning?"

Samuel gave a vigorous nod. "Aye, sir. Don't trouble yourself about it. I'll watch him myself, if need be."

Draegan made for the door, but Jacob called him back.

"What happens now, sir?" the caretaker questioned anxiously.

"Now I find them," Draegan said quietly. "If I must dog his every step to Hell, I'll find Lucien Deane. I swear by all that's sacred, he will not keep Fallon from me."

Chapter 20

During the hours that followed, the small party rode steadily toward the northwest beneath a brooding midnight sky. There was no moon or stars to light their way, nothing but the unerring, houndlike instincts of Joseph and the indomitable Wears-A-Hat, who brought up the rear and fore of the small column, to guide them.

The going was difficult, the ground increasingly uneven and strewn with rocks and broken branches. For what seemed the hundredth time Lucien's hunter faltered, causing Fallon to waver on her precarious perch. Lucien, riding before her, instinctively reached out a helping hand, yet as his fingers brushed Fallon's sleeve, she righted herself and jerked away.

Lucien sighed in disgust. "You are being childish, clinging to your anger. What's done is done, and can't be rectified. It's time to let it go."

She cut him with a look, the same way he had cut her with his betrayal. "Pray, sir, what did you expect from me? Not approval, surely!"

"Fallon, you are young and naive. In time you will come to view things differently—"

"I am not so young that I can't discern right from

wrong, good from—" She could not bring herself to finish the harsh assessment. Lucien, however, harbored no such qualms.

"—from evil," he said in silken tones.

"Yes." Emphatically.

Lucien looked at her, a long and measuring look. "So that's how you view me, as evil. A veritable monster, in your eyes. Tell me, won't you, for I am most interested to know: is this your opinion, or is it more of Youngblood's insidious poison?"

"My opinion has nothing to do with Draegan's influence, and everything to do with your callous disregard for everyone around you, your schemes and machinations. You played your devil's game, Uncle, and you won. But your ambition has blinded you to one painful truth: you cannot have your success as Sparrowhawk, do all the evil you have done, and still have my respect." She drew a deep breath and tried to still the trembling brought on by her anger. When she continued, her voice was deadly calm. "You can force me to accompany you to Niagara, but I vow, I will never set foot on English soil. I will find some way to escape you."

She did not say what she was thinking, that she would find a way to return to Draegan. It would only have prompted more scorn from Lucien, further assertions that Draegan was lost to her. Fallon could not abide to hear the words again, could not allow herself to believe for an instant that the only man she would ever love had fallen victim to her uncle's and to Randall's treachery, that she would never see his beloved face or gaze into his pale green eyes again.

Sensing that she had withdrawn again behind her icy shell, Lucien turned away. Fallon couldn't help noticing that he seemed to bend just a bit, and it was all that she could do to keep from trying to make amends.

He was her uncle, her flesh and blood; and though she deplored what he'd become, hated the man who was Sparrowhawk, she somehow couldn't let go of the notion that somewhere deep down inside that twisted shell, something of the man he'd once been existed still.

She was destined to remain torn between love for Draegan and loyalty to her uncle.

Lucien did not try to speak with her again, for which Fallon was grateful. When they reached the narrow cleft between Hunter and Plateau mountains known as Stony Clove, the Englishman dismounted to confer with his men. Lucien made to do likewise, glancing at Fallon. "It seems this is going to be a lengthy discussion. If you'd like, I'll help you down, so that you can move about."

"That won't be necessary," Fallon said. "I can manage on my own." She alighted without difficulty, walking a little distance and back again, stretching her cramped muscles. All the while her interest remained keenly fixed upon Stone and the others.

They kept their voices low, barely above a murmur, but Fallon could see the Mohawks were upset, and from Wears-A-Hat's sharp gestures, she gathered it had something to do with the vale. Moving closer, she seated herself on a fallen log and bent to examine a small flowering shrub nearby, pretending disinterest in the low-voiced discourse taking place.

"You can surely see," Stone said to the two guides, "that foul weather is imminent. We must stop somewhere and seek shelter."

"There is a stopping place two leagues hence," Wears-A-Hat said stolidly. "We stop there."

"Two leagues won't do," Stone argued. "We'll find shelter in the valley just ahead, and we'll carry

on after daybreak, despite your misgivings. Is that
clearly understood?"

Wears-A-Hat and Joseph exchanged black looks
but said nothing, at which point Lucien entered the
discussion. "What the devil's going on here? Why
have we stopped in the open?"

"Bad spirits dwell in this place," Wears-A-Hat
said solemnly. "Bad things happen to those who
disturb them."

"Superstitious nonsense," Stone fairly spat.
Turning to Lucien, he said, "They insist the valley
just ahead of us is haunted, and flatly refuse to seek
shelter there. Wears-A-Hat wishes to carry on two
more leagues to the far side of the valley, but if we
venture so far, we risk a drenching."

"I fear you are right," Lucien said, stroking his
chin as he studied the lowering black sky. "There's
rain in the air; besides, I am not sure Fallon can
endure the additional miles. The emotional up-
heaval of our abrupt departure has obviously taken
its toll upon her; she needs to rest and recoup her
spirits before we press on. You are the commander.
Can't you simply convince them?"

"There is nothing simple about dealing with sav-
ages," Stone informed Lucien. "They will not go
against their beliefs. I'm afraid we have reached an
impasse."

As Fallon watched, the first rain drops fell,
driven by the wind to splatter on the ground near
Lucien's booted foot. The uncertain weather
seemed to fuel his impatience. He glanced at her,
but Fallon kept her expression purposely impassive. "A compromise, then. Surely we can reach a
compromise."

Stone frowned heavily. "What manner of compromise?"

"A modest one. Let them make their camp right
here, on this side of the valley walls. We can pro-

ceed, find the shelter we seek within, and rendezvous with them when we break camp later in the
morning. In that way, they will provide us protection as sentries without invoking the wrath of their
imagined evils, and we maintain a semblance of
comfort."

"It seems reasonable," Stone affirmed, but there
was still a thread of skepticism lurking in his voice
when he turned to Wears-A-Hat. "Are you agree-
able to the terms Master Deane suggests?"

Wears-A-Hat nodded gravely; then, with a lingering look at the sheer rock walls looming blackly
against the predawn sky, he turned away, toward
Joseph.

Stone started forward, walking his mount toward the narrow defile; Lucien took up the reins,
beckoning to Fallon. Knowing she had little choice,
Fallon rose from her seat on the log and followed
her captors into the cleft.

The valley was rumored to be the Devil's favorite
haunt, and Fallon understood well the origins of
the Catskill legends. Towering mountains rose
straight and steep for over four thousand feet on
either side of a track too narrow in places for the
three to walk comfortably abreast. With its blasted
trees grotesquely bent from the tearing winds, and
the crumbling precipice upon which huge boulders
precariously sat, Stony Clove did indeed appear a
byway to Hell.

Fallon glanced at the sheer rock walls, and the
fine hairs on her arms and the nape of her neck
stood erect. The night air, which a moment before
had been soft and balmy, now held an unearthly
chill. She couldn't help but wonder if perhaps, just
perhaps, Wears-A-Hat had been right—that bad
spirits did inhabit the cleft between the twin mountains, and by disturbing the unearthly stillness of

the valley, they were risking much more than they could possibly know.

They made camp near Stygian Lake, where Lucien and Stone cut boughs from the balsam fir and fashioned a rude shelter to protect themselves from the elements. Fallon kept her distance while they labored, wandering to the shore of the lake, where she stood, a brooding, silent windswept figure, gazing back across the rippling dark waters to the mouth of the valley, toward home.

She knew that Willie and Zepporah would be worried sick by now, and she wished for some way to let them know that she was well and thinking of them. And then there was Draegan. Was he out there somewhere, searching? How would he find her? When?

Tears stung her eyes, but she blinked them back, striving hard not to dwell on her current circumstances. She chose instead to cling stubbornly to the small shred of hope left to her. Stony Clove was just twenty miles from Abundance, close enough for her to find her way home, she thought, if she could but manage to slip away.

Stone finished the shelter and stood, dusting off his hands. "Blasted wind," he said to Lucien. "We shall be lucky indeed if its infernal howling doesn't whisper to our sentries that they would be wise to take themselves off and leave us." At Lucien's questioning look, Stone chuckled, a dry, unpleasant sound. "They are very much like children, these Mohawks, in need of constant supervision and direction, which, regretfully, I must provide. And, to that tiresome end, I must beg your leave. Mistress." He bowed to Fallon, who stood stiffly watching. Then, with a nod to Lucien, he smartly turned and melted into the shadows.

A few more scattered droplets fell, striking Fallon's rigid shoulders. She turned her face up to the lowering sky. The black of night was turning gradually to deep gray gloom. Dawn was perhaps another hour away.

The scrape of a dragging step sounded behind her. Fallon started, half-turning to glare at Lucien.

Weariness showed in his every lineament. "You need not speak. I only ask that you come in out of the weather. It's deuced cold in this valley, and I fear you might take ill." He licked his lips, seeming to falter. "Please, Fallon. I—"

He would have gone on, except for an odd sound that issued from a little distance along the lakeshore. An odd, gurgling moan, half-human, it chilled Fallon far more than the preternatural cold of the defile.

"Stone?" Lucien called into the darkness. "My lord? Was that you?"

Stone did not answer. Indeed, the only sound above the soughing wind was the gentle lapping of the lake against the shore, waters that had been calm a moment before, except for the noiseless ripple of the wind across the black surface.

With a muttered imprecation, Lucien snatched up a burning brand from the fire and held it aloft. The golden light shone brightly, reflecting off the black surface of the water, illuminating the still form of Lord Lovewell Artemis Stone, floating face down in the stagnant lake.

Lucien moved closer to the water and grasped the Englishman's boot, pulling him into the shallows. As Fallon watched, one hand hovering at her bloodless lips, he turned the man over.

Fallon averted her gaze. She could not look at the Englishman; she could not look at Lucien for fear that he would read her thoughts.

Draegan had come.

He'd said he'd never let her go, and he had been

true to his word. He'd come for Lucien and to claim her. He was out there in the shadows, waiting.

The realization filled her with a wild elation, a trembling, soul-numbing fear.

"He's dead," Lucien said tonelessly, rising. "Strangled with a rawhide thong." He crossed to Fallon and took her arm.

Fallon tried to pry his fingers from her arm, but his hold was too desperate, too sure.

"This is no time for stubbornness. Whoever did this is still out there, lurking. We must go. Now!"

"There is no use running, Uncle. He won't let me go, and I won't leave him again."

As Fallon's words died away a somber figure, garbed in unrelieved black, emerged from the shadows. His shining sable locks were loose and tousled by the wind, and his green eyes burned in his pale countenance with an intense, unearthly light. In his right hand, he held his ever-present pistol, trained on Lucien's heart. Its mate was thrust through his belt.

"Youngblood!" Lucien hissed. "Damn your pestilent soul!"

"You were expecting Captain Quill, perhaps?" Draegan said with a humorless curve of his hard mouth. "I'm here to convey to you the captain's regrets. He's been detained, and won't be joining you after all."

"Therein lies my only folly," Lucien sneered. "I should have killed you myself, instead of entrusting the task to that incompetent young imbecile."

"Yes," Draegan agreed, "I suppose you should have made better work of it, even though it would have meant soiling your hands, a concept I have little doubt you find abhorrent."

Lucien uttered a rasping chuckle. "You know me

that well, do you? Then you must also know I won't allow myself to be taken."

Draegan cocked the piece he held, but the double click of the hammer being drawn back was all but lost in the howling of the wind. "This time you have no choice. Stone is dead, and the sentries you posted thought better of disturbing the spirits that inhabit this place and took themselves off nearly an hour ago. There's no one left to aid you. Nowhere for you to turn. It's done, Lucien—finished. Let Fallon go and give yourself over to me. If you let our struggle end peacefully, you have my word that I'll do all I can on your behalf when we reach Albany. For Fallon's sake, if not your own."

"And if I don't?"

The dark face above the pistol sights hardened almost imperceptibly. "Then, regrettably, I shall be forced to kill you."

Fallon moistened her lips. "Listen to him, Uncle, please. What Draegan suggests is the right thing, the honorable thing, for you to do. You cannot hope to win against him, and I cannot bear the thought of your being hurt at his hands!"

"Stay out of this, my dear. This is between the major and me. It has nothing at all to do with you." Lucien tried to push Fallon behind him, but she broke free and ran into Draegan's arms.

His free arm encircled her shoulders, and for a moment he held her tightly to him. Pressing her cheek against his shirtfront, she closed her eyes and heaved a ragged sigh. "He said you were—that Randall—" Her voice broke on the last syllable. "I was so afraid that I would never see you again."

"I'm here now to make things right," he said. "But you must trust in me. Can you do that, Fallon?"

She nodded, beyond words, while Lucien scoffed. "My, how very touching. If I didn't know better, I might think that caring facade of yours is genuine. But I do know better, Youngblood. I am not as naive as my niece, or as easily convinced, and I can see straight through to your black heart. Not unlike me, you are passing good at erecting false facades, at making others believe you are something you are not. And you have employed your talents at chicanery relentlessly where Fallon is concerned, worming your ruthless way into her affections with the sole purpose of undermining her loyalty toward me. It would seem that you have succeeded admirably, and it will take a good deal longer for her to get over your demise than I had at first imagined."

On the last word, Lucien swiftly flung the burning brand he still held. At the same instant, Draegan pushed Fallon aside and squeezed off a shot.

The rest happened quickly. The brand bounced and rolled, flinging live sparks onto the hem of Fallon's skirts. Fallon gasped as the embers burst into tiny flames, and frantically slapped at her skirts with her hands, but she could not extinguish all of them, and the flames spread swiftly, filling her with mindless panic.

Desperate now, she bolted, heading toward the dark waters of the lake, toward her sole salvation. Her breath was sobbing in her throat, her chest was on fire, and then hard hands seized her, flung her to earth, and Draegan smothered the flames with his coat.

Pulling her up, he gathered her in against him, holding her tightly, stroking her hair to soothe her. "It's all right. You're safe now."

Fallon fought to control the quaking of her limbs. "Where is Uncle?"

"He slipped away," Draegan said. "And I think it best we do the same."

"But Uncle—"

"I'll see to him the moment I'm assured of your safety."

Draegan turned away, but Fallon was slower. She had seen something, a blur of movement from the corner of her eye. Pausing, she turned her head toward the blue and saw Lucien coming swiftly out of the darkness, a stout cudgel raised high above his head. Fallon opened her mouth to cry out a warning, but it was already too late, too late to do more than to watch in horror as the staff came arcing down toward Draegan's head. "Uncle . . . no!"

At her cry, Draegan half-turned, and the cudgel caught him a wicked blow on the temple. He fell to his knees, stunned, and shook his head.

Lucien swung the staff down again, hard, and Fallon screamed, lunging for Draegan as he fell forward from the blow, cradling his head in her lap. His face was ashen. Blood trickled from a gash at his temple, wetting her hands, staining her pale skirts.

Lucien moved in for the killing stroke. "Come away from him, Fallon. Come away, now, and let me finish it."

Fallon was wild with grief and anger. Tears streamed down her cheeks, scalding her chilled skin, blinding her. "No! No! I won't let you hurt him ever again! I love him, Uncle! I need him! And I won't let you take him from me!"

She touched the still white face of her lover with fingers that shook uncontrollably, feeling for the pulse at his throat. It was there, steady and strong, as strong as her love for him. "Go away," she said, with desperation in her voice. "Go to Niagara, or London, and start anew. I am giving you a second chance, and all I ask in return is that you leave us!"

Lucien shook his head, and the gesture seemed almost sad. "I can't do that, child, don't you see?

If I let Youngblood live, he will dog me the rest of my days. It must end here. I must kill him. It is the only way. Now, be a good and dutiful girl and move away from him."

As Lucien raised the cudgel high, Fallon's fingers closed around the worn walnut grip of the pistol in Draegan's belt, and she dragged it forth.

"You will not kill me, Fallon. You are a gentle soul, so very much like Sabina. You haven't the heart to harm any living creature."

With shaking hands, Fallon raised the piece and leveled it at her uncle's chest. "Uncle Lucien, please!" she cried. "If you ever cared for me at all, if you ever loved me, you will not make me choose!"

She pulled the hammer back. Over the barrel she saw the man who had raised her, the gentle, caring man who had indulged her whims and satisfied her childish curiosity, swing the heavy staff with all his might, and Fallon squeezed the trigger.

The weapon bucked and roared, belching fire and acrid smoke. The loud report mingled with Fallon's full-hearted wail to echo eerily down the narrow cleft as she saw her uncle fall.

The sound of her soul-wrenching anguish dragged at Draegan, drawing him slowly from the soft, all-encompassing darkness into which he had retreated, toward the breaking dawn and Fallon.

The sight of her, when he opened his eyes, tore at his heart.

Her sweet face was ravaged by her tears, and in her eyes, her beloved amber eyes, there was a wretchedness and pain unlike any he had ever beheld.

At a little distance lay Lucien Deane, a cudgel held loosely in his grasp, a spreading crimson bloom upon the pale breast of his linen shirt. His eyes were closed as if in sleep, and Draegan had no doubt about what had happened here, no doubt about the depth of Fallon's sacrifice.

She had risked her own heart to save his life, and there was no way to thank her, no way to ease her pain. He could only love her and pray to a merciful God that time would indeed heal this most grievous of wounds.

"Fallon," he whispered around the painful lump in his throat. "My sweet Fallon. I love you so." His own eyes were moist as he took her hand and urged her gently down, holding her while she wept out her broken heart.

After what seemed an eternity, her tears ceased to flow, and she grew quiet in his arms. "Madness took my uncle from me," she said miserably. "I could not allow it to claim you as well. I love you too much to let you go."

With reverent fingers, Draegan raised her chin and gazed into her tear-reddened eyes. "My love," he whispered. "My one and only love. My life was so barren without you, so empty and dull. Now it is rich and brimming with promise. I beg of you, humbly, don't ever leave me . . . never, ever, let me go."

Chapter 21

Albany, New York
September 27, 1778

The great stone church was filled to overflowing this afternoon in late September. Friends and neighbors, colleagues and family, and not a few grieving young women, hankies in hand, had turned out in force to witness the nuptials of Albany's most eligible bachelor and the young lady who had captured his heart. At that very moment, Draegan Youngblood was busily wearing the nap off the Turkey carpet in Jonathan Akers's parlor.

He paced to the hearth, to the window, and back again, much to the amusement of Lysander, Christian, and Payne Youngblood. "What the devil could be taking so long in there?" Draegan demanded. He dragged out his timepiece, checking it against the mantel clock, then snapped it closed again. "We're to begin in five minutes, and there's still no word from Ardis when Fallon will be coming down."

Lysander and Christian exchanged wry looks; Payne laughed outright.

Draegan's irritated glance swept over the trio.

"This isn't the least bit funny," he said. "Have you given a thought to the fact that she's been closeted with Mother for most of the afternoon? You know, as well as I, Mother's views on men and marriage! Why, there's no telling what nonsense she's put into Fallon's head."

"Draegan's right, lads. You know how Mother is when she gets her back up, and with her and Dad sharing the same house for two weeks running—" Lysander broke off and shook his dark head, while Payne took up the tune.

"I heard her say just this morning that she'd had enough of Dad's 'outlandishly old-fashioned male arrogance' and couldn't wait to get back to Gran's in New London. Draeg'll be lucky if she doesn't pack Fallon up and take her along."

Draegan turned to Christian, a look of dawning horror on his face. "You don't suppose she's changed her mind."

"Don't let them upset you, Draegan," Christian said, putting a comforting arm around his older brother's shoulders while giving a broad wink to the others behind his back. "You know how disloyal they are. If you show first blood, it'll only get worse."

"You always were Mother's favorite," Draegan said to Christian. "Would you go up and see what's happened? Perhaps you could manage a word with Fallon on my behalf. Tell her I'm dying out here—no! Oh, God, don't tell her that!"

Christian clapped Draegan's shoulder. "Trust me, big brother; I know what to tell her. And if it'll put your mind at ease, I'll be more than happy to brave Mother's wrath."

Draegan nodded. "Aye, it will help, greatly. Thanks, Chris."

Christian left Draegan to the doubtful company of Lysander and Payne and made his way up the

stairs to the bedchamber where Elloise Youngblood, their sister Ardis, Aunt Lydia Akers, and the
bride-to-be had been closeted for the past hour and
a half. When at last he reached the bedchamber, he
tapped lightly for entrance.

Inside the chamber, Fallon glanced at her
mother-in-law-to-be, who gave her new daughter's
hand a reassuring pat. "Don't worry, dear. I'll see
to it. You shouldn't be rushed on your wedding
day."

Fallon bit her lip and said nothing. Like her second son, Elloise Youngblood was a strong-willed
woman, and it was easy to see why she and Draegan ofttimes did not get along.

Thinking of Draegan caused Fallon's stomach to
flutter nervously. She'd seen so little of him in the
two months since they arrived in Albany, and always in the presence of company.

Jonathan Akers and his wife, Lydia, had graciously opened their hearts and home to her upon
her arrival. They had shielded her from the unwelcome details of Randall Quill's trial in early
July—in which Draegan had played a significant
part—and subsequent hanging, and they had
proven vigilant chaperons in those rare moments
when Draegan found time away from his duties
and came to call.

Fallon had quietly chafed under the new restric-
tions. Being aware that Draegan's uncle and aunt
were acting in her best interests did not make their
constant attentions any easier to bear. And then
there was Elloise, who, upon receiving the news
that her errant son was soon to be wed, had come
straightaway to Albany with Draegan's brother
Christian and sister Ardis, bringing a trunk full of
cream-colored satin and old ivory lace.

Upon her arrival one month before, the preparations had begun in earnest. Endless fittings with

dressmakers had ensued, as well as strident family discussions in which Draegan and Fallon had had little say. From the moment the sable-haired termagant had set her small slippered foot in her brother's parlor Fallon hadn't known a moment's peace.

Near the end of August, Draegan's brothers Lysander and Payne had arrived from the Mohawk Valley, bearing the news that Claire, the eldest Youngblood daughter, was in childbed in New London; Anna, younger than Claire by just a year and Clayton's twin, was with her. Edmund Youngblood, a fine-looking fair-haired man in his middle fifties who sat on the New York State Assembly and who had fathered this riotous brood, was also often around.

It made for a lively atmosphere, filled with distractions. Sixteen-year-old Ardis charmed Fallon with her incessant talk, his brothers took turns trying to steal her away from Draegan, Edmund expounded on the war, and Jon and Lydia looked on with indulgent smiles as Elloise took charge of them all.

There had been barely a moment for her to think in the midst of this constant tumult, and there had been no time at all to steep herself in self-pity, to dwell on the ugliness of her ordeal just past, for which she was endlessly grateful.

The Youngbloods had made her adjustment a little easier, filling the empty hours when duty called Draegan away, but now, at last, she was happy to be moving on.

Elloise opened the door a crack. "Yes, what is it?"

"It's Chris, Mother. Open the door."

"Has your brother sent you here? For if he has, then you may tell him that patience is a virtue, and crucial to a new marriage. Indeed, tell him to ponder it at length, and Fallon will be down in a little while."

"Don't you think he has suffered enough?" Christian's voice came clearly through the crack. "This isn't fair, and if you don't desist, I shall be forced to betray you to Father."

Elloise's fine dark brows drew down. "You wouldn't dare."

"I won't if you listen to reason and cease this interfering. Draegan is fairly wild with nerves. I've never seen him this way."

"I am not interfering," Elloise said. "I'm trying to help. It won't hurt him to wait a few more minutes. Indeed it may lend him a greater appreciation for Fallon, and prevent him from neglecting their marriage in the same callous fashion in which your father has neglected ours!"

"If Draegan discovers that you are purposely withholding his bride, he'll come up here and throttle you."

Elloise would have retorted, had Fallon not chosen that moment to enter the fray. "Chris," she said. "Tell Draegan that I love him endlessly, and to go to the sanctuary and wait there for me. I shall be down directly."

Christian flashed her a grateful smile through the crack and was instantly gone.

Fallon turned back to the looking glass into which she'd been anxiously peering before the battle lines had formed, assuring herself that every ribbon, each scrap of lace, was precisely in place.

The gown was exquisite, the stuff of dreams. Shimmering satin clung to the curve of her shoulders and plunged in a wide V in front, exposing a daring amount of creamy flesh. The sleeves were tight-fitting, as was the bodice, and adorned with a generous fall of Mechlin lace at the elbow. The full skirt held out with the aid of side panniers, trailed behind.

When Fallon turned from the glass, the three women—the hub of her new family—were waiting together. She hugged each in turn. "Lydia," she said, "thank you for everything." She moved on, kissing Ardis's blushing cheek. "Ardis, what a dear you are. I always wanted a sister. And now I have three!"

Which brought her to Elloise, who dabbed at her pale green eyes with a crisp linen handkerchief. "I know that he's very dear to you," Fallon said softly, "and I vow I will do my absolute best to keep him from further mischief."

"Dear Fallon," Elloise said, smiling. "You are precisely what he has always needed, and I can only wish you both the happiness Edmund and I shared, the twelve times that we were together." She gave Fallon a warm embrace and then released her. "My dear, welcome to the family."

Fallon turned and swept from the room. Edmund was waiting at the foot of the stairs. He offered his arm, and she took it; then, together, they walked to the chapel, where friends near and dear patiently waited.

Vrouw Schoonmaker beamed from the second-to-last pew; Killian, holding his cold pipe in his hand, smiled beside her. In the same pew were Greetje Krieger, little Alida . . . and Jan, whom Draegan, after a great deal of negotiating had managed to bring home from Niagara. In the next pew sat Willie and Thomas, quietly married a second time, in June, by Pastor Jon Akers, this time legally and with Zepporah's hearty blessing. Willie's eyes were shining, and Zepporah, who sat on Thomas's left, openly wept.

They were all there, friends and loved ones who had touched her life, all but one. Fallon couldn't help but think in that moment that wherever he was, Lucien was looking on too, and perhaps, just perhaps, because she had made the only choice she could have made, he understood.

"Are you ready, my dear?" Edmund asked.

They were almost there. A few feet away, Draegan stood, resplendent in the blue and scarlet of his uniform coat and his snow-white breeches, his dark face filled with love and longing.

Fallon nodded, beyond speech. Edmund kissed her cheek and stepped back, taking his seat by Elloise's side.

The church grew silent.

Those gathered bowed their heads in prayer as Jon Akers asked God's blessing on their union, but Fallon knew that God had smiled upon them from the first.

Their love had surpassed a trial by fire and had risen from the ashes. Their happy ending had been predestined. Her dark angel, without a doubt a gift from God, was hers to love throughout eternity.

Avon Romances—
the best in exceptional authors
and unforgettable novels!

MONTANA ANGEL   **Kathleen Harrington**
                              77059-8/ $4.50 US/ $5.50 Can

EMBRACE THE WILD DAWN   **Selina MacPherson**
                              77251-5/ $4.50 US/ $5.50 Can

MIDNIGHT RAIN   **Elizabeth Turner**
                              77371-6/ $4.50 US/ $5.50 Can

SWEET SPANISH BRIDE   **Donna Whitfield**
                              77626-X/ $4.50 US/ $5.50 Can

THE SAVAGE   **Nicole Jordan**
                              77280-9/ $4.50 US/ $5.50 Can

NIGHT SONG   **Beverly Jenkins**
                              77658-8/ $4.50 US/ $5.50 Can

MY LADY PIRATE   **Danelle Harmon**
                              77228-0/ $4.50 US/ $5.50 Can

THE HEART AND THE HEATHER   **Nancy Richards-Akers**
                              77519-0/ $4.50 US/ $5.50 Can

DEVIL'S ANGEL   **Marlene Suson**
                              77613-8/ $4.50 US/ $5.50 Can

WILD FLOWER   **Donna Stephens**
                              77577-8/ $4.50 US/ $5.50 Can

Avon Romantic Treasures

Unforgettable, enthralling love stories,
sparkling with passion and adventure
from Romance's bestselling authors

America Loves Lindsey!

The Timeless Romances
of #1 Bestselling Author

KEEPER OF THE HEART	77493-3/$5.99 US/$6.99 Can
THE MAGIC OF YOU	75629-3/$5.99 US/$6.99 Can
ANGEL	75628-5/$5.99 US/$6.99 Can
PRISONER OF MY DESIRE	75627-7/$5.99 US/$6.99 Can
ONCE A PRINCESS	75625-0/$5.99 US/$6.99 Can
WARRIOR'S WOMAN	75301-4/$5.99 US/$6.99 Can
MAN OF MY DREAMS	75626-9/$5.99 US/$6.99 Can
SURRENDER MY LOVE	76256-0/$6.50 US/$7.50 Can
YOU BELONG TO ME	76258-7/$6.50 US/$7.50 Can

Coming Soon
UNTIL FOREVER
76259-5/$6.50 US/$8.50 Can